The Secrets of Castle Ravenswild

A DARK ROMANCE

MISTY STEWART

Cold Deck Press
www.colddeckpress.com

Published by Cold Deck Press

ISBN 978-0-6450962-5-5

Contact Misty Stewart for all enquiries: misty@mistywriter.com

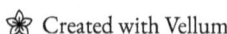 Created with Vellum

Content Warning

This book is a polyamorous romance. All sexual acts between the three central characters involve explicitly given consent at all times.

However, the work also includes:

- Consensual power exchange arrangements within relationships
- Slavery and non-consensual power imbalances within relationships
- Spankings and beltings given as punishment
- References to historical prison sexual assault
- Off page sexual assault (not between the main characters)
- References to historical abuse, verbal and physical (in prison, in childhood)
- Dubious consent (not between main characters) in a sexualised context
- The threat of sexual assault used as a means of control
- Attempted sexual assault on the page (not between main characters) - brief, quickly stopped
- References to self-harm and disordered eating

This is a love story about trauma overcome and healing found in each other, where optimism and hope win out. In order to make that victory definitive and significant, the initial trauma of the characters is equally as significant.

For KM
Thanks for the guidance

CHAPTER 1
Salryanna

S he sat alone in her throne room listening to the sounds of the coming war. Not merely coming; it was already here. Right outside, an unexpected strike, a coordinated assault on the castle they had no hope of withstanding, wham, bam, done. A crash. An explosion. An incoming force of arms.

Her eyes closed. She winced with each battle cry, breathed through every crashing door and breaking of glass, even as they came closer and it was clear the invaders were into the main hall. Not long and they would find her now. It was better that it was quick. It would mean less casualties on both sides. Less death. It wasn't like this castle was truly defended once you made it past the protections of its reputation, and its natural geography, set into the mountain above the valley. And her magic. They'd blown through any magical barrier without pause, which suggested a strong sorcery on the side of the invaders.

She'd sent everyone else away as soon as it became clear what was happening and ordered her soldiers, ceremonial as they were and not even genuinely familiar with the castle, to fight only in self-defence. Run, she'd told them. Resistance was not possible now and she'd not have more blood on her hands than absolutely necessary.

There was too much of that as it was.

Another crash. She breathed out, a shaky gasp, and tried to prepare herself.

Her closest advisor flung open the throne room doors without any of their usual ceremony, rushing in, panic across their face. Tall, androgynous, middle-aged and kind, she always tried to listen to their advice, but knew already what they would say. They pushed the doors closed, barring them hard as she watched from her uncomfortable golden throne at the other end of the hall. She didn't say it would do no good to barricade the doors, it wouldn't stop any invading army long and especially not this one.

As soon as the doors were locked, the newcomer ran up the plush carpet runner along the middle of the hall. It was a measure of their panic they didn't even stop to bow as they reached her.

'Your Majesty,' they said. 'Please, you can't be here, you must—'

'I'm not running,' she cut them off. 'Not from this. The valley is under my protection. If I run now, every person in it, every family, every child, will be lost. Even those damned invading soldiers. I won't have others suffer for my mistakes, Francis.'

Francis shook their head. Not only her closest advisor, they were Governor of the valley and perhaps the only person she'd been able to consider a friend these last five years. Not close, exactly, but closer than she'd allowed any others, and they knew the truth of her position like no other did.

'Then let me get you away from here. You can regroup, return with force enough to retake the valley,' they said. 'We have lost the day, Your Majesty. The armies of the Light have the upper hand. But we can escape, hide, then return to regain ground. If we go now.'

She let Francis say their piece before shaking her head. There were escape routes from the throne room and places she could hide, of course there were. She'd mapped them all out back when she'd first been granted power in this place, the throne, this castle.

Then she'd destroyed all the maps. Betrayal had given her this position. Her betrayal of another and now she would bear the consequences. She knew very well who led the armies now coming for her.

'If I run, others will pay the price,' she said. 'You know that, Francis.

I cannot leave this castle. I will not leave innocent people exposed and vulnerable.'

Francis clutched their hands together. 'Please, Salryanna! *He* is leading their armies. You know he won't be merciful, not with you.'

Her eyes closed momentarily. No, *he* was not going to be merciful. But she hardly deserved for him to be. She'd broken too many promises to him, five years ago, when he'd trusted her and came out the worse for it. She would find out the cost of that soon, no doubt.

Instead of saying as much, she sat straighter and moved her hands in front of her, murmuring a soft mantra. Hoping to summon up...well, anything, really. She was used to power at her fingertips, a magic that was hers to control.

Now there was nothing. No gestures, words, or reserves of power would conjure up a single leaf, vision, or protection. She'd been trying and failing all morning to summon any power at all.

She wondered if the demon she'd sold herself to had also abandoned her. Perhaps; that creature revelled in blood and pain, and this would lead to great amounts of both. More likely the sorcerers of the invading army had planned well in advance and ensured she was blocked from using her power before they even came near.

It was like becoming suddenly deaf or blind. Whole senses taken away. Yet it would be taking significant energy to maintain such a dampening on magic across the castle. So he must have brought powerful magicians indeed.

He would bring the Light. And she, who belonged to the demon, would suffer for it.

'I'm without power,' she said, trying to be as open with Francis as she could. 'I won't be able to protect you. You need to get out. Get down to the valley. Look after the people. I'll do what I can from here.'

'Salryanna, no! They will parade you a prisoner, so all will see their victory, then they will execute you. You have to come with me. Hide. Evade capture.'

'They won't kill me. He won't kill me.'

She believed that with every bone in her body. He wouldn't kill her, but only because he would want her to suffer and death would make that too quick.

A crash sounded near. Out in the hall. A thumping followed on the big doors to the room.

She stood, turning to the back corner of the room and the small door hidden behind the tapestry there. Pushing Francis towards it.

'Go, Francis.'

They pulled back. 'If you're staying, so am I. That General needs to know the truth and you won't tell it to him.'

'How would doing so change anything? Go. *Go*. You can't help me if you're captured too.'

Which was the only argument to hold traction. They swore, hesitating, looking towards the hidden door and the only possible escape.

'I will find a way to reach you,' Francis promised. 'Keep faith, my Queen. I will find a way to help.'

'Run, Francis.'

And they did. At last. Just in time, for she only just made it back to the dais with her throne when the doors were finally flung open, despite the locks and bars upon them.

A golden army, a troop of men, stormed into the long hall. Swords and sweat and the white-yellow uniforms of the Light spreading out through her throne room. She tried not to react to the Light's iconography now surrounding her. It was hardly as if the demon she served was any better than their god.

She stood tall before the throne, head held high, but not because she felt proud. Wiping clammy palms against the rich fabrics of her red and black dress; the colours unofficially associated with the demon. She might have felt better if she'd worn weapons on each hip, but she didn't even have a dagger hidden in the folds of her skirts. What good would it have done? She no more knew how to wield a weapon than these soldiers understood what they were storming into now.

None of that mattered. She was not planning to resist.

As the men filtered through the room, in their middle, striding a path between them and all falling out of their way to make room for him, came their leader.

He marched in as if he owned the place, as if he had every right to it. Dark hair swept back, strong and tall, absolutely furious. Insignia of the

Light on his shoulder, the uniform of the General, ultimate leader of the Light's armies on the ground.

His eyes landed on her from the first. Walking to where she stood in front of her throne. There was hurt written across his face. Perhaps not as raw as five years earlier, when she had so badly betrayed him, landing her power and position by doing so. Yet it was clear her betrayals and lies had not been forgotten, and certainly not forgiven.

So be it. She hadn't forgiven herself, either.

He came to stand in front of her, face-to-face for the first time in five long, lonely, heartbreaking years. She wondered desperately what she could say.

'Callum,' was all she managed, in a strangled, hoarse tone.

He looked at her a moment longer. Then he turned his back.

'Arrest the witch and get her the fuck out of my sight,' he ordered his men. 'We've got work to do.'

It was his men who bound her hands, then dragged her away. He didn't even bother to see to it personally.

She laughs as she lies back on the forest floor. Not caring for the dirt or twigs or leaves, simply content to enjoy the warmth of the day, gazing up at the sunlight speckled through the high canopy above. Beside her, he has propped himself up on one elbow and is stealing kisses when she lets him. They are innocent kisses, their passions are spent, for this moment at least. They'd return soon enough, no doubt. They always did.

'I love it here,' she says, almost a confession. She never tells anyone else the things she tells him. Only here, only with him, does she feel safe enough to be honest. 'This place, where I can see the sunlight and the trees.'

'You spend way too much time in that awful old castle,' he says. 'That's your problem. You need to get out more.'

He's joking; he knows she's not allowed to leave the castle at all. Sneaking out here to meet with him is going against all the rules of her order—an order that is diametrically opposed to everything the army he serves stands for. He is a private, conscripted by the Light, because aren't they always conscripted? She is a novice in the dark castle and so far as she can tell the entire point of novices is to obey orders, and it chafes. It isn't the life she would choose, had she ever been given a choice. But it is the life she has, so she makes the best of it.

She turns to him with a serious expression.

'Yes,' she says, simply, then lifts one hand, makes a complicated motion in the air. Out of nowhere, a small white flower is conjured, appearing within her fingers. A daisy. It's a common flower, a weed almost, but it is pretty and it reminds her of him. Flowers which bloom and stretch towards the sunlight.

She hands it to him, suddenly shy, and he takes it, contemplating its leaves.

'She loves me, she loves me not,' he says, with a hint of his wicked grin, though perhaps some vulnerability too. He only shows her that out here, in the forest, with the warmth of the sunlight through the trees on their faces, but she knows it's there inside him. That he is sometimes just as scared and overwhelmed as she is.

He doesn't move to pull any petals off as he says it.

'She loves you,' she says, with a smile, and he leans down to kiss her again...

...the freezing darkness was broken only when the flap in the bottom of the dungeon door pushed open to allow a strip of light and a plate of some muck shoved through. Gruel, or porridge, or the like. She crouched in the back corner of the cell, which was so tiny she couldn't lie straight. If she stretched out a leg she could kick over the plate. She wrapped her arms about her knees instead, as if that might help conserve some body heat, shivering even so. They'd thrown wet and fetid muck all over her, soiling her dress, before pushing her into the cell to freeze.

The dungeons of the Witch Queen retained a frightening reputation, but they used to be worse. There'd once been sloping cells which they could fill to the knees with freezing water, so the inmate didn't dare risk falling asleep, not even after days and days of staying awake, lest they drown. Other cells open to the high sun with no shade in the blistering heat, for an inmate to be stripped of all clothes and their skin to burn day after day. So many tortures possible before an interrogator bothered to pick up a pair of pliers.

She'd shut it all down not long after she took over. Not that she didn't make some moves to maintain the frightening reputation of the place, which could be useful, but the worst of the dungeons she'd had filled in, and the others she'd just never used. She would've liked to have claimed it was because she was better than those who had come before her, that she was more moral, or fair, or just. Really, it had just been her guilt driving that move. Guilt and her memories.

When I am in charge... She remembered that, joking with him in the forest. The two of them so damn young, and so equally at the bottom of their respective orders, that ever being in charge of anything seemed a ridiculous impossibility. He was cannon fodder, conscripted to die in one of the Light's many brutal wars. She was a novice to use up and slave for those more powerful in her order.

When I am in charge, I will free all the prisoners, she had declared back then, so imperiously. *On both sides, because obviously I'll be ruling all.*

I'd fill in some of those castle dungeons if I were you, he'd answered with a chuckle. *Never keep a dungeon as a supreme ruler that you wouldn't survive being thrown in yourself, I reckon.*

They'd laughed at that. At the very idea either of them could ever be in charge of anything.

She pulled her knees closer in and wished she had other memories to turn to, but they were the only ones she had where she'd felt warm and safe and, despite it all, loved. Perhaps there might've been other memories of when she was very small, with her family, but that'd all been taken away. She'd been so little when given to the castle and there were only vague and blurry glimpses of her past before it left in her head, images she barely understood.

So she turned to her memories of him to keep her warm, no matter it would only hurt more in the long run. When he'd confronted her in the throne room, nursing his pain and anger, she'd seen a hatred in his eyes that threatened to make these warmer memories a lie. No matter. She clung to them still. They were all she had now.

Some indeterminate hours later—time didn't pass in the tiny black cell like it did elsewhere, at least not when you were stuck in it—another plate was shoved through the crack in the door. She no more leaned over to eat from it than she had from the other. It was possible the food was poisoned, but that wasn't what stopped her; she might've eaten it if she'd known for certain it was. It was probably spat in, but if she'd truly been hungry that wouldn't have stopped her either. She simply couldn't find the will to eat. She barely had the will to move.

She closed her eyes and wondered if maybe he wouldn't come for her at all. Maybe he'd just leave her to rot in this cell, forgotten by the world. No light, no warmth, no sound beyond the scrape of the plate occasionally pushed through the flap in the door. A person would quickly go mad down here, but maybe that would be a relief. Delusion was probably nicer than reality right now.

It was a fantasy. The plates they pushed in were metal. Maybe cheap, but there'd be a finite supply; they'd be back to collect those at some point. She couldn't starve herself forever.

So she sat. And waited. Maybe she slept at times. Maybe she didn't. The darkness and the cold were all she knew.

And then...the door opened.

She blinked against the light, turning her head away. Large, male bodies crowded the doorway. One reached down to grab her arm and drag her up, his grip bruising. He and his companions pulled her from the cell and shoved her out into the corridor beyond. She stumbled, only just managing to stop herself falling.

When she finally saw them in the light, dim though it still was, she didn't recognise the men, but she did recognise the uniforms. Soldiers of the Light. They would have secured the whole castle, maybe the valley. Her heart twisted. Would the valley and all those who lived there, in the shadow of this castle, be safe? He wouldn't have harmed the people just to lash out at her, would he?

The boy she'd known, that conscripted private, would never. But he was a General now. He was a ruler himself. And the people of this valley were vassals of his enemy, her own dark lord.

She took a long breath, despite the air in the corridor being no better than the thick stench in her cell. She had to keep thinking straight. So long as she was in this castle, the people of this valley would be protected. Nothing else mattered, including what was done to her.

Three men had come to fetch her. She couldn't tell their rank, she didn't understand the insignias of their uniforms. They were all large, muscled, ferocious. Bigger and stronger than her. While she had none of her magic to protect herself with.

'You've an appointment to meet, witch.'

They bound her wrists behind her, so tight it hurt, cutting into her skin. She didn't resist. She wasn't going to win against them, there was no hope for that, so all she could do now was endure and survive. She went with them when they marched her forward, up out of the dungeons, into the lower basements of the castle. The kitchens and the servants' spaces, empty for five years. Now, the place bustled and not only with soldiers. There were others, cooks, new servants, people to organise meals, feed the castle, see to the needs of the invading army.

And long before they reached the great hall, she heard the people gathered. Murmurs, movement, voices. She understood, then, what was to happen now. This would be as public as he could make it.

As they entered the great hall, it took everything she had to find courage enough to keep putting one foot in front of the other. The entire space was filled. Soldiers in their white and yellow uniforms, villagers from the valley spread throughout the hall. Balconies full of watching faces. There were so many. Such crowds. The soldiers all wore weapons, long swords at the ready, though nobody was resisting. All understood who was in charge, the castle had been taken by the Light. And its Queen would be conquered publicly.

Maybe this was personal, after all.

Right down the far end of the cleared central aisle was the dais upon which sat the throne. Claimed in the name of the Light, *his* gods, like they were any better than her own.

'Stars and earth, give me strength,' she murmured, unable to help herself when they pulled her towards it.

A weighted first connected with the side of her head. 'No magic, witch.'

As if she had any to draw upon. She fought to keep her focus, despite the wallop to her head, but could do nothing to stop them dragging her forward. To the throne upon which *he* now sat.

The hard, unyielding resentment in his eyes brought iced terror to her gut. It was that throne, the one he sat upon now, and the power it represented, for which she had betrayed him those years ago. She'd had reasons for the choices she'd made, ones he might even understand if he could ever bring himself to listen to her, but what did her reasons matter when it had all been such a terrible mistake?

She'd chosen poorly. He'd paid the price for it. There was no coming back from that.

Now he was here, assembling the biggest crowd possible to witness her capitulation to him. She clenched her teeth down hard. Pride be damned. Her humiliations were going to get a lot worse before this was done. All she could do was endure and hope to somehow survive.

They dragged her to him, then pushed her to her knees. The cold steel of a sword pressed into the back of her neck to remind her not to move, so she didn't. She kept her eyes on the stone of the floor and tried not to shake as she knelt in defeat.

The hall, despite being filled with so many, was silent.

He stood from the throne. Walking down the steps with a resounding echo of each footfall, until she could see his boots in her vision. Army regulation, if quality leather. Different from the falling apart cardboard pretence they gave privates back when he'd been one. He was the General of the Light now, of course his uniform was better quality. Had he improved the equipment and uniforms provided to his lower ranks as well, since he had taken supreme command? Did he enjoy being a General? He'd always hated being little more than cannon-fodder when he'd been a private, but had enjoyed the camaraderie of the military.

Did he—

His hand reached down and grabbed her dungeon-matted hair at the back of her head. She squealed pain as he jerked her head up and he bent to meet her eyes.

I love it here...

You need to get out more...

She loves me, she loves me not...

She loves you.

His eyes were neither kind nor forgiving. Not an ounce of feeling in them. That, more than anything, broke her heart, because the boy she'd known had been full of feeling. A young man of passions and emotion and care for the world. Even if he couldn't feel it for her anymore, even if he hated her for what she'd done, she didn't want to think of him so closed up and shut off from all that feeling inside of him.

She could barely see the boy she'd known in the face of the man who towered above her now.

I love it here. This place where I can see the sunlight and the trees.
This place where I can be with you.

'Salryanna. You're mine now,' he said, a low, dark tone of threat.

Then he threw her back down and walked around her, leaving her panting, hard, on the stone.

CHAPTER 2
Salryanna

'Your Witch Queen has been defeated! The army of the Light is in charge. I rule here now!'

He spoke at volume, for all the crowd to hear. While she knelt on the stones, her hands still bound so tight her fingers were tingling and her shoulders aching. It was going to get worse, for she knew what this was: the public demonstration of conquest. Victory over the defeated displayed for all to see.

Her defeat, his victory. Francis had warned her she'd be paraded as prisoner. They'd also warned her she'd be executed, but he couldn't do that, not yet. She was the only person in existence who could tell him the secrets of this castle and until he had those he hadn't truly taken this place, not with any permanence. Her dark lord was still very much in residence; his gods were not.

Which only meant this was not going to be quick.

'All those who pledge allegiance to the Light will be unharmed! You will be welcomed!' he called to the assembled crowds. 'But be warned, any who remain loyal to the demon lord of the Witch Queen will be put to death.'

No. She closed her eyes, forced her lips together so as not to utter a sound. It would not help to protest. She could only hope that the boy she'd known was not so far lost within the cruel General standing beside her and that maybe, just maybe, he wouldn't be the sort to put innocents to their death for no reason.

He'd been full of honour, once. A goodness. She clung onto the hope that he retained at least some of that now and would allow her people to live and prosper, even if he didn't grant her the same.

'As for your Witch Queen...'

She shuddered at the ominous tone in his voice. He moved away from her, but she didn't look up, it was all she could do to concentrate on her breathing and not think about all the people watching.

Sounds, movement. Stomping feet. Then soldiers surrounded her, grabbing her by the arms and hauling her straight, if still on her knees. She bit the inside of her own cheek to keep from making any sound; tasted blood, as another grabbed her hair, so full of muck from the dungeons she wondered he could bare to touch it. He held her head still and high.

'The witch is now no more than my slave,' he told the watching crowd, then gestured to his men. 'Do it. Put it on her.'

A cool metal went around her neck and she clenched her teeth so as to not whimper at the low, cold burn of it. She recognised what it was immediately. Whatever spell his sorcerers had cast to neutralise her powers throughout the castle couldn't last long; to maintain that over such a large place would take immeasurable power. They wouldn't sustain it.

Only this metal they placed around her neck now, this collar, was seeped in the same neutralising effect. It killed her instinctive, magical senses, severing her from the world beyond which she could see and hear and touch. An alienating sense of isolation and fear made her gasp as she was cut off from any magic at all, with hard finality.

They sealed the golden metal collar around her neck with a thick lock, then they handed him the key.

The affront of it was almost as bad as the dampening sense of having no magic at all. The humiliation of having it done so publicly. They hauled her up once it was finished and turned her around, displaying her with that weighted collar to the crowd.

His soldiers cheered. The rest of the crowd were silent. She couldn't look at any of them, not wanting to meet any eyes. It seemed she did have some pride left after all and it was torn asunder now.

When he turned, with such fury glared her way, she could not hold his gaze. Her eyes dropped to the floor.

He walked past her to the throne and threw himself down on it.

'Show her around, boys. Make sure they all see what's become of their oh-so-powerful Witch Queen.'

Laughter. His soldiers full of cheer and victory, taking her by the arms and hauling her forward. Down the central aisle, manhandling her without care or gentleness, pushing her one to the other so she stumbled, before pulling her up and shoving her between them again.

She landed in the arms of one with a dark beard and nasty eyes, who sneered as she bit back a cry, then pulled her to him and ran his tongue up the side of her face.

'Uh...'

She yanked away on instinct, not ready for that, stomach turning with the wet and slimy feel. It only caused more laughter from her captors, and the next, emboldened by his fellow, shoved his hand down her blouse to grab her breast.

'Oh stars, no,' she said, struggling to get any sound into her voice. Not that it would help even if she had screamed it out aloud. She knew what this was: making sure everyone could see she was truly vanquished. It was a strategy, a political manoeuvre. Her intellectual self could appreciate the importance of it, even as the panic began to take hold.

He had to ensure everyone knew his victory over her was total, or else his hold on the castle would be weakened. That meant he had to diminish her in every possible way. Enslaved, publicly, with heavy collar locked around her throat. Everyone knew what happened to slaves. The valley had no slavery, not anymore, because she wouldn't allow it, but these were soldiers of the Light. They had no such reticence.

Slaves existed to be enjoyed by others. The soldiers yanked at her dress and she could hear the tear in the fabric, even as they forced her down to the floor. She tried to kick out her legs, but there were too many, too strong, and her arms were still bound. She had no magic and no strength. She couldn't even pray. Not that the demon was ever one to pray to and she would never supplicate to their gods.

Stars and earth, but there were at least half a dozen surrounding her, and would they all take turns? Was that what they would do? Rape her repeatedly in front of everyone?

In front of him?

As they got her to the cold stone floor, one pulled her head upwards, so she could see him. Sitting on her throne as if he had every right to be there. His eyes on her as they shoved her down and yanked her legs apart. She felt one of them right there between them, pushing up her skirts, and gritted her teeth, trying very hard not to cry.

She could understand the political need to illustrate victory. She could even understand a personal desire to lash out in revenge, to hurt her as she had once so badly hurt him. But the coldness in his eyes didn't even suggest that. He looked simply like this meant nothing to him at all.

That was the moment her head dropped and she just gave up.

'Enough.'

The command from the throne was hard, loud, and certain of the obedience that would follow. The men about her stopped instantly, and though they did not let her up, they did look to their leader for further instruction.

She couldn't raise her head. There seemed nothing left in her body that would give her the strength to do even that. But she heard him stand, heard his boots come towards her.

'Take her out of here,' he ordered.

They dragged her up and out one of the side doors beyond the throne, rather than down the main aisle. She didn't hear what else he said after that. She didn't hear anything.

She expected them to take her back to the dungeons. She even might have welcomed it. At least there she could hide in the dark.

Instead, they took her up one of the many large staircases in the castle, then along a wide landing to a suite of rooms which hadn't been used in a long time, at least not during her tenure here. There were many unused rooms in the castle since she'd taken over. She'd never welcomed others to stay within these walls and sent everyone away the instant she had the power to do so, telling them she preferred solitude. She was the Witch Queen, so who were they to question it? There were some who had to come by necessity, a couple of serving women who cooked and cleaned and who would arrive of a morning once or twice a week, then go again well before dusk. Francis, her governor, and occasionally other advisers on matters relating to the Valley, but she mostly left that kind of governing to them. Otherwise, she'd not populated the many towers and corridors and rooms. She'd left them all to the dust.

Now, the place was being opened up. New servants wearing the colours of the Light bustled about, and soldiers, and people she couldn't place in the scheme of things, perhaps civilians, or camp followers of the army. The suite they dragged her to had been aired out and made ready for use with a full sense of luxury. She didn't doubt who had adopted it.

This was the biggest suite in the castle, built for the Queen. It was far grander than the small set of rooms she'd used at the top of one of the spires. These rooms were central and massive and decked out for a supreme ruler to take what was their due, so it was no surprise he had chosen them for his own.

The men shoved her inside without compassion or care. She stumbled, almost falling to the thick rugs of the huge sitting room the main doors opened onto. There was a lounge suite around a fireplace to one side, a meals table on the other, doors to the sides leading to the rest of the suite. An arched doorway to the left led into a private study. A large double-doorway to the right opened onto a magnificent bedroom complete with dressing room and separate entrance to what was the real drawcard, a bathing room complete with warm mineral-springs fed pool. The mountain range hosted an extensive network of underground mineral springs which came up in a series of rock pools speckled throughout the valley. The castle was built into the mountain and this suite of rooms had been created around the filtered pool of constantly refreshing water.

It was magic, or so she had always assumed. She knew this suite as well as she knew any in the castle, every inch of it, and yet despite the grandeur and luxury here, she missed her own small set of rooms. Up high in a spire where she could see the ravens the castle was named for flying in the distance. Where she could look out her window to the forest.

Along the back of the sitting room was a wall of glass, a series of long windows and doors opening out onto the balcony. The view here looked down over the valley itself. Perhaps he preferred that, the chance to survey all that he had conquered. Perhaps it was as meaningless to him as it was to her. She'd been offered these rooms once, expected to take them herself upon becoming Queen. She'd seen too quickly the trap that they were. The pretence of luxury when the castle was not a home to her, it was a prison.

One of the men yanked her arm back and the pain flared from the ties cutting into her wrists. Her fingers were numb, shoulders aching from the stress position. It was the least of her physical concerns right now. Four men had marched her in here, all of them had swords, and none of them looked kind.

Did she really need four professional soldiers to guard her in defeat? All those weapons? All that muscle? Hadn't they realised by now that she was none so imposing, she was small and insubstantial? Or did they still think she had some access to her magic?

The collar weighed about her neck. It was a blunt instrument. She couldn't feel any sense of anything beyond the physical and immediate, not even what had been the constant undercurrent sensation from the last five years of the demon she was bound to. In other circumstances, that might have come as a relief, except she knew it changed nothing except to make her blind to his presence. Something more dangerous than not.

Perhaps these men, armed soldiers who glared at her like she was a genuine threat, were simply terrified of her reputation. The Witch Queen of Castle Ravenswild, devotee of the demon, her dark lord, demon lover even, and wielder of the darkest magics for her having sold herself so. It was a useful reputation, in many ways. It kept people away. Sometimes she even wished it had anything of truth to it.

Now that reputation would haunt her. The men who pulled her to a stop in the middle of the room looked at her as if she was some demon-loving creature who'd long sold out her humanity. And an enemy denied humanity could be harmed in the worst ways. They laughed, jeering as they knocked her sideways. She stumbled, off balance. One caught her and knocked her back again. She closed her eyes and tried not to wish for anything. She simply had to endure.

One man grabbed her dress at the front and tore it down. She clenched her teeth hard to bite back the frightened cry, anything to stop herself from begging them to stop. Such would only spur them on. She knew this sort. Her fear and pain was what they wanted, even more than her body, and while she might not be able to stop them abusing the latter, she could at least refuse to give them the former.

They would not have the satisfaction of her emotions. Her interior life was her own and nobody else's, no matter what collar was around her neck. No matter what they did to her body, they would never have *her*.

The men surrounding her didn't seem to care for such nuances. Their sinister cheer only increased as another tore her dress further, revealing her corset beneath, which was tugged and pulled until her breasts were exposed too. One man grabbed them and she screwed her eyes shut, fought not to scream. *Endure, Sal. Endure.*

It didn't make it any easier.

'I said enough!'

The men immediately stopped at the furious command from the doorway, stepping back smartly in attention and saluting. Leaving her standing unsteady in the middle, hands still bound, dress hanging off her in shreds, body exposed beneath. She stared at the carpet, not at him.

The General stalked into the room.

'Public demonstration of victory is one thing, but I will not tolerate such behaviour in my own damned rooms!' he snarled with real fury.

His men swayed where they stood and did not move, did not speak. Their salutes frozen in place.

'There is much work to do. Go see to it. Go,' he commanded. 'Leave the slave to me.'

They all smartly chorused *yes, sir!* Then promptly marched from the room. Possibly they went with relief, given the anger in their General's voice. Her head was spinning from being knocked around and the only thing she was sure of was that his anger was not about being protective of her.

She wondered, vaguely, when he'd developed such skewed principles: declaring rape as valid for political purposes was still horrific, even if he didn't countenance it in other settings. It did not align to the boy she remembered, who'd been gentle and empathetic and kind.

Clearly he was no longer the boy she remembered.

Once, she might have called him out on the contradiction in his morals. Right now, she didn't say a thing. She was quite sure he'd throw her back to his men if the mood took him.

He approached her, pulling a knife from his belt. She stepped back in a sudden fear, but he only took her arm, spinning her around. He was not gentle, moving her with some roughness, but it was not like being manhandled by his men, there was no darker intent. All he did was cut the bindings at her wrists.

Feeling rushed back into her fingers. Her arms began to tingle as she was able to move them again.

He turned away without once even looking at her face.

'There's food on the balcony. Go eat,' he said, and it sounded just as much an order as when he'd spoken to his men. She risked peering up, because he hadn't bothered to even glance at her and it felt safe enough. Unfortunately, she did so at the same time he looked back over his shoulder and she caught his eyes by accident.

He looked down the length of her with clear disapproval. Unimpressed.

'And take off those rags. They stink of the dungeons.'

She swallowed. She stank of the dungeons, not merely the clothes she wore. Her long hair, her one source of vanity, was matted and filthy. Her body unwashed. But she doubted she could ask for the chance to refresh herself any time soon.

'What would you have me wear in their place?' she asked softly.

He shrugged. 'You're a slave. You have nothing, you can wear nothing.'

His tone was so dismissive and uncaring that she didn't get the sense he intended the same kind of sexual violence his men had been so keen to commit. The refusal to allow her clothes was a humiliation, not a sexual titillation. No doubt it wouldn't be the last of the humiliations she would experience either, but what was such to her anyway? It was nothing. It meant nothing.

Endure.

Still, she stood hesitating, rubbing her hands to speed up the returning feeling. He took off his uniform coat with a careless ease, throwing it over the back of a chair in the sitting space, his sword belt with it. The weapon itself he took more care with, storing it in a cabinet by the wall.

He obviously didn't see her as any kind of threat. He was right about that, too. She didn't know how to use a sword and even if she had, what use would physically fighting him be? Even if she had the strength to overpower him, where would she run? Possibly she could hide somewhere in the castle, she knew it better than anyone, there were places. Only what would that solve?

She didn't want to run. She didn't want to be here like this, but she didn't want to run from him either. This was not how she'd wanted to meet him again, indeed it was the worst possible way they could have come back together. And yet she had still spent every day of the last five years desperately wondering how he was, where he was, what he was doing. Missing him with every fibre of her being, day in and day out.

She'd known he would be angry. She'd prepared herself for his enmity. He was the General of the Light coming to invade the valley and take her castle by force; she had not imagined it would be a pleasant reunion. Yet she was not prepared for the glowering fury in his eyes. She was not ready for the intensity of his rage or the sharper edge in it she began to suspect was genuine hatred.

Had she done that? Caused him so much pain he could not only refuse to forgive her, but could hate her with such force?

'Did you not hear me?' he snarled with such implicit threat that she began to undress immediately. After all, what did it matter? Her clothes hung off her in rags anyway, hardly covering a thing, and her pride had been shredded out in that hall.

She was slave now. So be it.

She stripped, her whole body numb. Letting her ruined clothes drop where she stood, because she had no idea what else he wanted done with them, and right now she wasn't sure she could move without instruction. Defeat washed over her as she stood, naked but for the collar and a myriad of bruises his men had inflicted upon her. She still stank, it wasn't just her clothes. She was about to ask if he'd like her to wash, but he was already opening the doors to the balcony.

'Eat,' he repeated, and gestured with a pointed look to the table outside, laid with food. Two servants in the colours of the Light bowed silently to the General, before slipping away to a hidden corner door at the edge of the balcony. Servant's corridor. The castle was littered with them.

She wasn't hungry and didn't think she could keep down any food, but he wasn't giving her a choice about it. So she followed him outside, fresh air on her skin. She breathed deep of it. The dungeons had been fetid. Even the air of the hall had been close and thick from the crowds congregated within. It was a relief to breathe back the spring breeze, feel the warmth of the sun on her skin.

'Sit,' he commanded. She did as he bid and sat at the table, staring at the food, waiting for something to appeal. It was a selection of fruits, sweet breads, cold meats; luncheon fare. Imported from out of the valley; his supply lines must be strong. She supposed he had torn through any resistance before mounting his attack on the castle. She wondered where his strategic nous had come from.

He sat across the table from her, pulling some breads and meats onto a plate for himself. At a dark look from him, she tentatively took some sweet bread onto a plate, but didn't raise it to her mouth. He did eat, but when he noticed she wasn't, he gestured for her to do so with frustrated impatience.

'You've been in the dungeons for three days and I know you ate nothing there,' he said, and she wondered how he knew. Did his guards report back her untouched plates? 'You're all skin and bones as it is. Put something in your stomach, for god's sake.'

She tore off a small piece of bread and put it in her mouth to appease him. It tasted like ash on her tongue, felt like she was trying to eat stone. It took effort to swallow that mouthful and she didn't take another after it.

'Do you know why I'm here?' he said.

She pressed her lips together, shaking her head. Staring down at the food on her plate for which she could not drum up an appetite, rather than meeting his eyes.

He let the silence sit, eyes held on her, until she felt almost compelled to break it.

'I might surmise,' she said, softly. 'It would be a presumption. Your gods do not like mine.'

'You don't follow a god. You bound yourself to a demon,' he snapped. 'One who's spread destruction and evil throughout many lands. The trail of blood leading to this valley is well recorded.'

A hundred and fifty years ago. Since then, the Witch Queens had been in place and the demon confined to this valley. Still, she didn't say that, because she knew very well that the demon could and would destroy as many lives as possible given the opportunity. She would not defend that entity. There were reasons she could not leave the castle, one being that if she did, the demon would leave with her and wreak havoc far and wide.

None of it mitigated the destruction his own forces of Light imposed on the lands they conquered. His gods, or at least their representatives in the world, were empire builders, insisting all others submit to their will. Hers at least didn't expect others to happily acquiesce at pain of death if chosen otherwise.

Once, he would have understood that. Now, she wasn't about to get into a philosophical debate with him.

'I am here to uncover the secrets of this castle,' he said, entirely up front. 'The secrets of your demon. I will unravel his hold on this valley and this world, and return him to the hellish plane from whence he came.'

She closed her eyes, but said nothing. She doubted it would help to suggest that if he banished the demon, then nothing would stand in the way of his gods and their representatives on the ground taking over everything. Those were his forces, after all.

He sat back slowly and crossed his arms. She could feel his eyes hard on her.

'The secret is in this castle,' he said. 'You know where I can find the demon, how I can confront the creature and destroy him. It is the secret you are sworn to protect. I am here to uncover it.'

'I understand.'

'Do you?'

She looked up, at last a kind of emotion deep down sparking the reaction. She could take humiliations and endure abuse, but she would not stand for being assumed some kind of naive fool.

'I understand you wish to destroy the demon,' she said. 'And that you will destroy me in doing so.'

'If I have to, yes. So don't doubt it,' he said without hesitation, so calmly it rocked her. He would squash her without a second thought if he needed to.

She looked back to her plate. Sitting stiff in her seat, staring at the food in front of her, not taking a morsel, because how could she eat? How could she take anything in? Maybe Francis had got away. If they had, and could get her a signal, maybe she could still make this work. It wouldn't matter if Callum destroyed her, or hated her, or sold her off on the slave markets to a life of brutality and pain. She already lived such a life. This wasn't about her. It hadn't been about her for a long time.

'What's the matter, Sal?' His tone was bitter. It spoke of pain underneath. 'Think you'd get a fond reunion after all this time?'

She found herself blinking back sudden tears. Ridiculous. After all she'd faced these last five years, after all she'd done and caused to be done, the sacrifices made and horrific choices before her, it was only now the tears threatened? Not when facing rape, not when forced into a collar and enslaved, not when thrown to the dungeons.

It was her name on his lips that did it. The dismissive mention of a reunion she'd never stopped imagining, every moment of every day, for the last five years.

'I didn't expect to be forgiven,' she said, suddenly. 'I know I don't deserve it. So I did expect your anger, for that I do deserve. And your hatred, all of it. Only, I...'

She let her words drop. She wasn't even sure how to say it.

'What?' he challenged in a dark voice.

'I never expected your cruelty,' she said, so soft it was almost a whisper. 'I'd hoped I might get the chance to say sorry, even if I couldn't expect you to forgive me.'

His chair pushed back from the table with a hard, slow screech. There was so much simmering fury in him. He stepped away, as if he were going to walk off and leave her sitting there. Only he turned back at the last moment and slammed a hand down, hard, on the table in front of her.

She jumped at the sudden aggression, her whole body pushing back. He leaned over until he was right in her face.

'I lost everything because of you,' he said. 'I came running that day because I thought you needed me. Because I would've died for you. Only for you to throw it in my face. You turned your back and left me for the wolves.'

He straightened, giving her some breathing space, though he glared down at her still.

'When I was caught, I copped a public flogging that put me out for six weeks,' he said. 'And when I survived that, against all expectations, I was sentenced to a year in the salt mines for the betrayal.'

She gasped, unable to help herself. 'The salt mines?'

'Yes. Most don't survive six months out there. No one survives a year. But it turned out the making of me.' He crossed his arms, looking furiously down. 'I led the rebellion of the miners. I got us all out. Then I marched on the Light's command and negotiated my own position.' He pointed back inside. 'Those soldiers, they're loyal to me. Not to my god, not to the Light. To me. I trust none but them. And no, you will not be getting your fucking chance to apologise, because it is way too late. You don't get to say sorry just so you can feel some kind of absolution. I'm never allowing you that.'

'Callum, I didn't know, I couldn't have, I—'

He turned his back, waving a dismissive hand. 'Eat something, then go wash. You stink of the dungeons.'

He stalked away, leaving her sitting in front of all that food, thinking only the salt mines. That slow death sentence of the worst kind of cruelty, each day an agony worse than the one before it, over weeks and months, until the body gave up. How long had he suffered there, before he'd found a way to fight back? How bad had it really been?

The tears blurred her vision despite herself.

'I'm sorry,' she whispered anyway. 'I'm so sorry.'

CHAPTER 3

Salryanna

S he remained sitting at the table out on the balcony for as long as
it took to stop crying, then for a little further time again, enough
for him to think she'd tried to eat something. She didn't, she
couldn't take a single bite, but she pulled apart the bread on her plate
and added half a strawberry, so it looked like she'd had something.

When her emotional armour was back in place, and her pretence at
eating would be enough to satisfy a casual glance, because she doubted
he'd give it anything more than that, she got up. He'd told her to wash
and that was one command she could follow without reservation. She
really did stink.

He wasn't in the sitting room. For a moment she thought he'd gone
from his rooms entirely, until she heard movement in the study. Her
destroyed dress was still where she'd dropped it, so she picked it up and
took it with her into the bathroom. It couldn't be saved and he didn't
want her wearing it anyway, so she dumped it down the garbage chute
off the main bathroom, a long drop down to the rubbish pits far below.

She would not resist his orders, she would be his slave, if that's what
he wanted. Obedient and as compliant as he liked, because she had no
other choice now and she still felt so numb it was hard to care about
such things. When she did let herself care, when she allowed a crack of

emotion through, like when he'd told her about the salt mines and what he must have suffered, it became too much and she couldn't bear it. She had to shut it off. It seemed to work for him, after all.

The mineral-springs fed pool took up the back third of the huge bathroom. Continually refreshed water filtered through from the warm natural springs below, available for bathing at any time. She'd always assumed it was magic, though when the last Witch Queen had used these rooms, one of the servants had told the novices that it wasn't sorcery so much as cunning artifice. Pipes built into the castle to capture the water and bring it flowing to this interior pool, other pipes to take it away again so it was refreshed and didn't become stagnant and dirty. She still thought it was magic, or as good as.

Walking into the bathroom now, she rather wished she could go back to those days and ask that servant how it worked. She would've liked to know such things. It was luxurious to slip into the warmth of the water, the grand pool built for Queens. Almost too hot, but she liked that sensation. Once in, she scrubbed and scrubbed, until her skin was red raw and stinging.

Her hair was a lost cause. It almost brought her further tears, as ridiculous as that was given all else. The long raven locks of her hair had always been the one thing, perhaps the only thing, about herself that she'd genuinely liked. She'd always kept it long and when loose it hung to her hips, though she'd braided it most of the time. They'd pulled the braids down in the dungeons, yanking her hair out of its ties, then thrown muck all over her before leaving her to freeze in the dark. Now the length of her hair was so matted she couldn't even unbind the few braids that were left to wash them properly, and the hair she could release remained sticky and slimey, even after thorough washing.

So be it. She stepped out of the wonderful bath and down the room to the long counter with the polished mirror travelling its length. Not acknowledging her own reflection, because she didn't want to contemplate that collar around her neck or the finger-shaped bruises on her breasts. Or the fact that he was right. She was all skin and bones.

She looked about her for something sharp. He hadn't bothered to hide his sword from her, nor did he seem to be guarding her particularly closely, so she assumed he wasn't caring about other potential weapons being in her reach. Maybe he thought he'd easily counter it if she did try for a blade; he was a professional soldier and she was undoubtedly no match for him physically.

She didn't intend to fight him, just as she didn't intend to resist.

Spread out on the bench was a shaving kit. Cloth rolled open, brush, straight-edge razor, soaps, comb. The sight gave her pause and for a few seconds she could not even step towards it. It felt almost an intimate thing. To think of the General, Callum, shaving, a private moment, not one where he put on a public face. It was hard for her to picture it. She could no longer imagine what he must look like behind the furious facade he put up.

She made herself move to the kit and found, along with a sharp-edged razor, a pair of small scissors. They'd do.

She had to look in the mirror then, heart dropping as she did. She looked awful. Not only her matted hair, but the bags under her eyes, the misery in them. All skin and bones. It'd been a long time since she'd worried about her appearance, there'd been so little reason to care. Now it was like seeing herself for the first time in years. She did not look good.

Focus. What she looked like didn't matter. Hair. Without further hesitation, and without letting herself think, she pulled all of her matted long hair into a low tail, tied loose at the neck. Then she used the scissors to cut through the lot.

The weight dropped from her head in cascading locks. Hair falling to the floor around her. She cut right through the single tail, then let what remained free, so it hung about her face. It sat about chin height, all the same length, mostly. The scissors cleaned up any stray bits that looked out of place.

Frowning at her reflection, she couldn't decide if it were awful or just strange to see herself without long hair. Ultimately, she decided it was okay. Different. Not bad. It was only hair. What use was vanity for her now?

She put the shed locks into the garbage chute, chasing her clothes, went back to the bath and washed the hair that was left. It was so much easier, and lighter, and almost freeing, really. She spent quite a time in the bath, half-expecting him to come yell at her throughout, but he never did. Eventually, she got out and looked in the mirror again. Still awful, but the hair was an improvement.

She had no makeup here, and could only use his comb, which she hoped he was okay with. When she was done, she put everything back exactly as she'd found it, carefully aligning his things on the bench so as to imply she'd not touched anything. Just as she'd artfully arranged her plate outside to make it look like she'd eaten. A different kind of magic.

When she turned, he was standing in the doorway watching her. Leaning against the doorframe with his arms crossed and his expression narrow. She jerked straight, with a sudden flush for not knowing how long he'd been standing there.

'You cut your hair,' he said.

A bolt of nerves tied up her stomach, for his tone was grim. Not the same hurt fury she'd heard from him before, though. This was mildly disapproving, perhaps a little surprised, but no more.

'It was matted. I tried to wash it. But after the dungeons I couldn't, I mean, it was impossible,' she said, stumbling her words and hating herself for it. 'Cutting it off was the only option.'

'Hmmm.'

He stalked forward and it took all her willpower to hold her ground, not shy away. When he took her by the arm, she almost squealed with shock, rather than genuine fright. He'd kept a physical distance between them this whole time, only coming near her when he needed to cut the bonds around her wrists, then backing right off again afterwards.

She wasn't ready for the physical contact, nor the way he firmly turned her around and pushed her downwards, to lean over the bench. She found herself bent over it before she even knew what was happening.

Then he gave her half a dozen hard wallops across her backside with his open hand.

Her gasp was audible. It hurt, stinging badly, but it was the shock which took her breath away. Her eyes wide and cheeks flushed red when he let her up again. She straightened slowly, with a confused frown.

'You're my slave now,' he told her. 'You might have sold your soul to the demon, but this body belongs to me.' He gestured to her, up and down with hand. 'You'll not do anything to it without my explicit permission. Understand?'

She gaped, still feeling the warmth on her buttocks. Only slowly getting her head around what had just actually happened. He had *spanked* her.

She had no idea what to say, but he was clearly waiting for some kind of acknowledgement.

'I understand,' she finally managed, with a dry mouth.

'You're lucky I like it,' he said, then turned to walk past her towards the pool. 'Short hair suits you.'

Thankfully that last was thrown over his shoulder, so he wasn't looking at her when he said it, because she could feel herself go bright red in the cheeks and wasn't sure if it was from the spanking or the offhand compliment on her hair. The whole thing left her standing awkward, shifting her weight foot to foot, and feeling way more exposed than at any other point so far.

He was by the bath, fiddling with the cufflinks on his shirt. A formal kind of uniform for parading victory, including her very public enslavement. After a moment's frustrated trying, he gave up on the cufflink with a terse cluck of his tongue and held out his arm towards her.

She hesitated, not immediately understanding the unspoken order. When he raised his eyebrows at the delay, clear warning in his expression, she jumped forward.

'Sorry,' she muttered, still playing catch up. Slave. Right. 'Sorry.'

She took his wrist and undid the cufflink for him, then the next, and put both carefully on the bench. He didn't move or voice any other command, but the expectation was obvious, so she undid the buttons and ties of his shirt next, undressing him in silence. It was a service one might typically expect of a slave and, though she'd outlawed slavery in the valley the instant she'd come to power, she still knew how it worked.

It was a good thing he'd told her about the flogging he'd experienced before the salt mines. She wasn't sure she could've kept her silence on sight of his scars if she hadn't been warned. Even still it was hard not to gasp at the severity of scar tissue across his back, stark against the otherwise warmer tones of his skin. The flogging must've been very bad. He said he'd been put down for six weeks, which was a long time and suggested muscle damage, or maybe there'd been infection of some kind.

To recover after a flogging like that would not have been expected. Then to the salt mines after. It was an execution by any other name; they'd been trying to kill him.

This was the result of her choices, her decisions. Her lies and betrayal of him. He'd disobeyed his superiors solely to save her, risking everything for her sake, and she'd turned her back on him, let him be captured. To face the consequences of simply daring to care for her. Nobody had ever cared for her except him and this was what he suffered for doing so.

She fought not to call attention to the suffering written across his body, though he must know all she was seeing as she undressed him. As she returned from putting his shirt aside, struggling to keep the emotion off her face, he lifted a hand to her chin. Turned her head to one side, then back the other way.

Examining her new haircut.

'It's very different,' he said, as if it were some clinical inspection. 'You always had such long hair.'

She let him manoeuvre her as he will. As he'd said, her body now belonged to him, he could do with it what he liked.

'It will grow again, if you prefer it long,' she said.

His eyes clouded and he let go of her chin. 'We'll see,' he said, with such severe neutrality she wondered what his plans for her were. Growing her hair would take time and perhaps he did not intend to spend such a length here. His aim was to divine the castle's secrets and find the demon. That meant her secrets, for she was the Witch Queen, that was her role, to protect what she knew. To not let anyone share the knowledge she had been given, friend or foe.

That was who she was. It was the entire point of her existence since her binding. Before even that, for wasn't that why she'd been given to the order as a child? To prepare her for a life bound to the demon?

He knew that. Which meant he must have some plans for trying to draw information out of her, for he'd know she'd never willingly give it up. Interrogation, maybe? She didn't doubt he was capable of it, even to torturous degrees. Even to her. Once she wouldn't have thought so, but now she'd seen enough to not hope for mercy.

One way or another, he didn't plan for this situation to continue long term.

After a curt gesture to continue, she undid his belt, then his boots, kneeling to slip them off his feet. His pants too. She kept her eyes to herself and was very careful where she put her hands. It wasn't that she hadn't seen him naked before. On the contrary, it was very hard not to think of the last time, out in the forest before everything went awful. A warm day like this one, spring sun speckled through the canopy above, the two of them kissing, touching, revelling in what little time they could be together.

Planning to run away. So full of plans, they'd been. So determined to find a happy future together, no matter the odds stacked against them.

They'd been so naive.

She couldn't help but notice he was fairly hard as she stripped him of his pants, even though she tried not to look. Would he require sexual services of her? Was that what this was? It wasn't unusual for slaves. She wasn't concerned about her physical capability of performing such duties, but emotionally how would she manage? Sex with this man, only not like it was before, now as his slave. Surely it would break her heart all over again.

She shook that thought out of her head. What did that matter? He would order and she would fulfil those orders and, broken heart or not, she would endure. She had survived the last five years, she could deal with this too.

In the end, he only turned to step down into the bath.

'Attend me, slave,' he ordered. The anger of earlier had dissipated, but the cold distance in his tone was cutting.

She followed slowly, stepping carefully into the water. The bath was long, rectangular, with steps along the sides to sit upon, and deep enough to rise to the waist even for him, who was significantly taller than her.

He waded across to the far side, but when he turned, he jolted unexpectedly, with a hiss of genuine pain.

'Are you o—' she began, before cutting her own question off. It was not her place to ask.

He waved away her unspoken concern. 'My back,' he said, dismissively. 'I've been inside and inactive for too many days. The scars stiffen up. It'll pass.'

Oh. Just one more thing she was responsible for. Chronic pain caused by his one-time efforts at rescuing her.

'I'm sor—' she began on instinct. This time, he was the one to cut her off.

'Don't you dare,' he said, snarl back in his voice. 'I've told you, you don't get to apologise. You're going to live with your guilt.'

Her shoulders drooped and she stared at her hands, as if there were blood on them still. Like she wouldn't be living with this guilt for the rest of her existence, whether he let her apologise or not. She could've thrown herself to her knees and begged him to forgive her, and he could even have said that he did, that she could have all the absolution it was within him to provide, and it would make no difference. For this, she would never forgive herself.

But it would be of no use saying any of that.

'Tell me if I'm overstepping, but I trained as a healer,' she said, still looking at her hands. 'Sometimes, massage can help with scar tissue. I could...I mean, only if you wanted...'

Her useless words dragged off. She risked a glance up to find his eyes on her, cold as ever, if also turning rather cynical. For the longest time there was only silence and she regretted speaking to the very marrow of her bones.

Until he huffed a breath.

'Go on, then,' he said, like he'd waged some internal battle and somehow lost. 'Might as well try.'

It made her wonder just how bad his back could get. He was a warrior, a soldier, his physicality was at the core of his life, his ability to move as he needed to. These injuries had not held him back, he was the most successful General in the history of all their lands. Yet having seen those scars up close, and hearing too the resignation in his tone now, she knew they must cause him ongoing discomfort, if not outright pain. He didn't show it, for the most part. But he'd given her a glimpse just now.

She sat behind him on the steps, half out of the water, and with tentative hands reached to his shoulders. Touching him for the first time in five years. The scar tissue across his back was bad indeed. Had he received any aid for his wounds at the time? Probably not. They hadn't been trying to heal him.

Yet he hadn't been killed, despite all they'd done. He'd survived, healed, and thrived. He must be proud of that. She was proud of him for that, for all the lessons he must've taken from it he was now using against her. She'd always admired the strength of him, the drive and passions he was full of. He'd had such optimism and hope when they were young. She'd always been the more cynical one, but he thought he could change the world. And he could. He did.

Perhaps he hadn't realised that he would also be changed, in his efforts to change the world around him.

Her hands moved softly over the mess of scar tissue, smoothing across his shoulders and back. Slowly, allowing her touch to firm. Not much at first, it would take time to understand where the worst of the stiffening was and the points of pain. Her training came back to her as she worked, the one part of her novice years she'd actually enjoyed, lessons in healing and in growing things. Flowers. Daisies, even.

He hissed momentarily; she'd accidentally pressed too hard on a pain point. She pulled her hands off him instantly, heart thumping with the mistake.

'Sor—'

'Keep going,' he cut her off. 'And stop damn well saying sorry.'

She put her hands back on his skin, massaging his shoulders and along his back carefully. Learning the tighter points, pressing firmer once she was more sure of herself, to work at the knots in the muscles and the rough scar tissue where it was worst.

'The scars must hurt at times,' she said, unable to help herself.

'I've got used to it. Pain is like that,' he returned, so darkly she had to bite her tongue to stop herself apologising again.

'Yes,' she said instead, because pain was like that. You got used to its presence after a while. It became a part of you, until you couldn't tell who you were anymore without it. Until pain was all you were.

Not all pain was physical.

'You will remain in my rooms for the time being,' he said and she had to shake herself to focus. 'I don't intend to lock the doors or set a guard, but you would be well advised to obey my command not to wander. Inside my rooms, you will be physically safe. Step outside them and my men will view you as fair game. You will have no protection. I will not call them off next time.'

Her lips tightened. 'I see. These rooms may be larger, but they are just as much my prison as the dungeon cell was.'

'You have no freedoms now. Best you understand that.' He rolled his shoulders under her hands. This time he didn't grimace or twinge in pain; maybe the massage was doing him some good. 'You will obey and you will serve and I will not hesitate to turn to corporal punishment if I deem it warranted to teach you a lesson, either.'

She thought of the spanking earlier. That should not have brought heat to the pit of her stomach, but she found it very much did and had to catch her breath in confusion at her own response.

To cover, she clucked her tongue softly.

'I will not disobey you. I fully understand my situation,' she said. 'You do not need to threaten me with sexual violence to ensure my compliance. Is that how the Light always operates? Through use of public rape as a weapon?'

He stretched his arms, experimenting with movement in his shoulders. His range did look freer now and she was glad of that.

He glanced back. 'How else do you think they kept us in line in the salt mines?'

Oh. Oh no. Her jaw snapped shut, her indignation at being threatened suddenly evaporating in the face of his direct experience. He moved across the pool from her, not dropping his gaze. While her whole being drooped with understanding.

'Oh Callum, I'm so sorry—'

'One more attempt at apology from you and I will flog you myself. You'll know how it feels then.'

She pressed her lips closed and absurdly felt like apologising for trying to apologise too much.

'Maybe I should tell you all the fine detail,' he said, some of the cruelty back in his tone. 'Perhaps that's the interrogation path I should adopt with you. Tell you all about the rapes, the starvation, the beatings. What salt does to the lungs when you breathe it in day and night, how it feels under your fingernails, in your eyes, down your throat. That would wear you down faster than any other technique I might employ, I'm beginning to think.'

She couldn't blink the tears away, mute with the misery of it. She was afraid to open her mouth lest she say sorry again. He didn't want her empathy, he'd made that quite clear. He most especially didn't want her sympathy. What he wanted were her secrets and he was quite prepared to use her emotional trauma, and his own, against her to achieve it.

She wiped hard at her eyes.

'Are you so surprised?' she said. 'That I might feel awful to know what I'm responsible for? That you suffered so much because of me? I didn't do what I did from a lack of care for you.'

His expression closed up.

'Save me the song and dance about how hard it was for you to hurt me. Believe it or not, I can deal with a little heartbreak,' he said. 'This isn't actually about us. I have a job to do here. My only care is to discover the secrets of this castle, the secrets you protect. How to reach the demon and how to destroy him. That is all.'

'I can't give you what you want,' she said, not hiding her despair.

'I never expected you to do so willingly. You made your choices five years ago, when you chose the demon's power over any affection you might've felt for me,' he said. 'I will get your secrets from you. I will do whatever it takes to break you down in order to get them. If that means twisting your guilt until you're a quivering psychological mess, at least that'll leave less blood on the carpet. But if that doesn't work, I'm perfectly capable of doing it the old-fashioned bloodied way too.'

Her whole body shuddered with the threat of it. Shivering with panic. If he'd strapped her down to a chair in the dungeons and brought out a whole host of metal torture implements, she'd have coped with that far better than this.

Maybe she should just tell him the truth. If he was prepared to detail out his suffering in order to hurt her, maybe she should do the same back.

Only it wouldn't be the same. She'd made her own knowing choices all the way along and she wore the responsibility for their consequences. He'd had no choice, and no responsibility, for any of it.

'I cannot tell you what you want to know,' she said. 'Even if I wanted to. It doesn't matter what you do to me, or how fierce the tortures you put me to.'

'Don't try to tell me you don't know. The Witch Queen exists to protect the demon.'

'It's not that. It's only...' She swallowed, mouth dry. 'It's part of the binding. What I went through when given to the demon, when becoming the Witch Queen. The binding stops me from revealing the demon or how to reach him on this plane. I can't tell you such secrets, the binding won't allow it. That is my burden to bear.'

He was silent, watching her with narrowed eyes. Perhaps trying to decide if she were telling the truth or lying to protect her own skin.

'Your burden to bare?' He sounded cynical.

'More than you could know.'

'Hmmm. My magicians warned me such was probably the case,' he said. 'I have not come unprepared. Even now the Light's best sorcerers are preparing methods of breaching the binding upon you.'

Her chest tightened. 'The binding is impossible to break.' Which was perhaps not entirely true, but it was close enough.

'We might not need to break it entirely. Simply breach it enough to force you to speak what is forbidden,' he said. 'That's what my magicians believe. They know what they're doing.' He gestured to the metal collar around her neck. 'They've managed to keep you quite subdued, Witch Queen.'

Her entire body went still. His magicians were powerful, she knew that already. Were they powerful enough to skewer the binding? They could never break it entirely, but could they crack it open enough to get the information they wanted? Make her tell them the truth about the castle's secrets? Where and how to find the demon?

Her heart thumped with the fear of it. She fought that down. It would take them time even if they could do it and they probably couldn't. None were stronger than the demon, that was why the Light marshalled so many forces. Her dark lord's power was greater than any, especially here in the castle.

But...what if he could? What if Callum could do it?

What if he could beat the demon, after all?

Never in her life had she considered it a possibility. Now, a sneaking wonder wove its way under her skin. *What if...*

Before she could say anything at all, a noise came from the other room. A door opening.

A call: 'General?' Official, loud.

Callum turned to step out of the bath to go see to his business. While she remained shaking in the water, slowly coming to understand that all her assumptions about the few protections she still had, protections this castle had afforded her for five years now and which she'd been relying upon to defeat even Callum and his armies, might just be useless after all.

CHAPTER 4

Salryanna

'Towel,' he commanded as he stepped out of the bath. She had to wade out, find a towel from the stack in the corner and bring it to him, while she was still dripping herself.

At least he didn't have her dry him. Perhaps he was in a rush to see his man waiting outside, for he waved towards his clothes and she fetched them for him, pants first, slipped over his hips. She tried not to notice the way his abdominal muscles were so well defined as he moved, like his arms, like his thighs. He was a soldier, a fighter. Fit, despite the physical trauma he'd suffered.

Unlike her, who was scrawny and underweight. *All skin and bones.* Once, back when he last knew her, she'd been plump and rounded. Full of curves. She hadn't ever thought herself vain, except maybe when it came to her hair and she'd already cut that off. Now she stood dripping onto the mosaic tiles of the bathroom floor, very conscious of her own physicality and how it could not compare to his.

He threw the towel at her when he was done.

'Dry yourself, then come with me,' he ordered. Maybe he saw the look on her face, eyes widening and a horror settling in, for the corner of his lip turned up. 'What's the matter, slave? Too proud to show yourself unclothed around my men?'

'It's more fear than pride,' she said. She'd always been honest, at least about some things, and she was still covered in bruises from when his men had manhandled her earlier.

'I told you that you'd be physically safe in my rooms,' he said, then smirked. 'Well, from others, if not from me.'

He was enjoying this. Her anguish and fear. Her vulnerability. The cruelty was back, the gleam in his eye that hadn't been there when they were younger. So it had been learned since. Somewhere in the intervening years, he'd become hardened, lost the softness he'd once had. From what he'd told her he'd gone through, she could hardly be surprised. Experiences like that changed a man, surely.

Yet she didn't doubt he meant it when he said she'd be protected from his soldiers. She knew there'd be threats to come, but for now she was safe.

'Yes, of course,' she made herself say. 'I'm sorry.'

'You're always sorry,' he said, with a barely suppressed roll of the eyes. 'But to show I'm not an entirely unmerciful man, you can wear my shirt, if you like.'

Her eyes swivelled sideways to the folded garment she had yet to hand him and she wondered, vaguely, if that might not be worse. Following him out of the bathroom clad only in his dress uniform shirt, which would barely cover to her hips, would mark her as his property even more than if she'd appeared naked.

Still, it was something, and she tentatively reached for it, slipping it over her shoulders. It stuck to her back and arms where she was still wet.

'Thank you,' she said as she did up the buttons.

He reached out and put a finger on the third button from the top, not letting her do up any higher. It left his shirt gaping down, showing a great deal of her cleavage. She wanted to plead with him to let her do up another button, but his smile was telling.

'I like this look on you,' he said. 'My slave, in my shirt, doing my bidding. That's what you are now. And that's what I would have the world see you as. Understand?'

She couldn't meet his eyes, possibly because of the warmth rising on her cheeks. The provocation in his tone when he said such things, *I like this look on you*. It was different to the cold cruelty which came when he spoke of his purpose for being here, or the suffering for which she was to blame. There was almost a challenge to this.

She tried to rise to it. 'Yes, sir.' And failed, yet again. She'd meant the honorific to sound sassy, to say it with a bit of sarcasm. It only came out sounding resigned.

At least it looked like it pleased him.

He led the way out and she followed, because she had been ordered to. Nerves wracking her stomach, not merely for being forced back into the company of his men, who terrified her still. The humiliation was purposeful and she understood it, but it was more than that. It was, simply, all the people. Strangers, crowds. She'd been given to this order as a very young child and had almost no memories of life before it. She'd grown up a novice in this castle and known maybe only a dozen other novices in the early days, far fewer by the time she had grown, and those who ran her order. The old Queen, her attendants, and servants. Novices were not encouraged to play or socialise. They existed to work and that had been their lives. Work and exhaustion and devotion to the demon.

It had been a lonely life. A cold childhood without family or the warmth of affection. Later, after she'd become the Witch Queen, grown into the greatest power there was and finding out the hard way exactly what novices were kept for, she had banished the rest. Set all others free, cut the castle staff down to a skeleton few who never stayed more than few hours, and kept everyone else out of the castle entirely.

She lived her life alone. Just her and this big old empty castle.

Only now he'd filled it with people and it terrified her in ways she wasn't ready for.

In the sitting room waited a tall, blonde man with the looks of an angel. He was beautiful, in an innocent kind of way. The fact he wore a uniform, was an officer of the Light and one of Callum's army, told her he wasn't actually innocent at all, but he had the kind of face that the greatest painters would want to memorialise on canvas.

He smiled when Callum appeared and it brought a flash of warmth to the room. Callum sauntered in wearing nothing more than his pants, while she followed in only his shirt and the collar. It was an obvious and deliberate entrance. Callum knew well how manage appearances and present a particular image to suit his political aims.

The soldier saluted, but only after he smiled.

'General,' he said, with warmth.

Callum returned the salute in a perfunctory manner, but also, she was rather stunned to see, with a smile of his own.

'At ease, Rorks. You have the reports?'

The man immediately relaxed, producing a folder from under one arm, thick with papers. He brought it to the table at the back of the room, spreading out documents upon it and pointing to them as Callum joined him to see.

'We're going through the place now. It's like a goddamned maze, I tell you,' Rorks said. He sounded familiar and comfortable with his General. 'I'm confident we've found and dismantled all physical protections. Frankly, there weren't that many. No guards to speak of. Or even servants. God knows how the place ran.'

She kept back by the wall, pressing her lips together. She could have told them there were no servants, but it wouldn't matter and why draw attention to way she'd lived her life here? It would change nothing.

'Don't get too complacent, Captain,' Callum warned. 'This place belongs to the demon. I'm told there'll be a room, probably disguised, hidden with magic, that is the centre of its power. Like an alter room or a worship room. We need to find it.'

'There's still some locked spaces, the men are breaking through where the locks are physical,' Rorks said, and pointed to what seemed to be a map on the table. 'But here, and here, and here, those areas are magically secured. I've got the magicians working on them now. They're strong protections, so it'll take time.'

'We have some breathing space now we've physically secured our hold,' Callum said. 'This is good work, Rorks. Keep on with it. Well done.'

The smile that spread across the Captain's face could have lit up dungeons. There was no mistaking the hero worship in the way the blonde man looked to his General. Callum clearly knew how to engender loyalty in his closest advisors, but wasn't his entire army known for that? For their loyalty to their General, over and above all other things?

'Yes, General.'

Callum straightened, giving him a nod. 'You keep at the locked spaces, I'll work on the Witch here. We'll break through.'

For the first time, Rorks glanced directly at her. She swallowed a breath, in the spotlight, never something she was comfortable with. This man wasn't one of the frightening ones, when it came to Callum's men. He hadn't been one of the soldiers who'd manhandled her yesterday and she saw only open curiosity in his expression now, with the slightest troubled frown, which suggested even a little empathy.

Not that she doubted he could be a threat to her, if Callum ordered it. They all were. Even Callum himself.

Especially Callum.

I'll work on the Witch.

'How are the men? How's morale?' Callum asked, as Rorks rolled up the map.

'Full of victory and cheer,' he said. 'The hardest part is stopping them celebrating when there's still too much work to do.'

'Don't hold the reins too tight,' Callum advised. 'They've been marching long, they've worked hard. Give them some celebration. Just stagger it. We need at least some men sober for duty, after all.'

They shared a laugh. There was such an easy familiarity between them. Smiles and warmth. That, more than anything, kept her back by the edge of the room. Standing by the glass doors leading to the balcony, where the remnants of the lunch remained on the table. There seemed such genuine regard between the men, affection even, and there had always been so little of that in the castle.

'I'm onto it, Boss,' he said. 'I learned from you and you're the best leader a man could hope for.'

Callum clapped him on the shoulder. 'And celebrate yourself, okay? No over-working, Rorks. You deserve a break too.'

Rorks caught his arm. 'Come celebrate with me, Boss. The men would appreciate it. So would I.'

Callum smiled. A bright, sincere smile of genuine feeling. Where had the cold, cruel General who commanded her enslavement, who threatened her with rape, gone? This look in him now reminded her of the younger man she'd known five years ago, the one she'd fallen so deeply in love with.

She looked away. He'd been right, back in the bathroom. This wasn't about him, or her, or their traumas, however entwined such were. He was here to do a job. And she had no choice but to stand in his way.

As she forced her gaze off the men and beyond the room, out to the balcony, servants appeared from the tiny half-hidden passageway used to allow them access to the suite without bothering the ruling inhabitant. Two of them, in the Light's livery, beginning to clear the luncheon things away.

She frowned. There was a familiarity to the movement of one, a tall servant muttering to the other. The shorter one took several plates and disappeared through the concealed servant's door, leaving the other to finish clearing the table.

Once alone, the remaining servant looked around and she caught a glimpse of a face.

Francis!

Her heart thumped, even as their eyes met and she could see theirs widen, nod. Callum was laughing with Rorks and not paying attention to her, so she slipped out onto the balcony. She was careful to remain within his line of sight, she didn't want to draw his suspicion by disappearing, even momentarily. Hopefully he wouldn't care she was just stepping outside. She even picked up some sliced apple from a plate yet to be cleared away, then looked out over the balustrade to the valley stretching beyond, as if that's all she was out here to do. Admire the view.

Francis continued cleaning the table without looking up at her. Nor did she look at them.

'Francis, what are you doing here?' she whispered.

'I needed to reach you. Has he hurt you, Your Majesty? Are you alright?'

To their credit, Francis sounded genuinely worried. But there was no time for such pleasantries, not even to assure Francis she was fine. Especially when she wasn't sure that she was.

'My research, Francis. You must get to it,' she said, in as low a voice as she could manage. 'He thinks he can breach my binding to the demon. I don't know if he can, but we cannot risk it. We need to proceed on the research right away.'

Though she was not looking directly at them, she was aware of how stiff Francis went.

'It's not ready. We're not ready,' they tried. 'Doing that might—'

'We have no choice. Please, Francis, you're the only one I can trust. I can't leave here. I must remain and keep him occupied, distracted. With his eyes on me, you can prepare a new vessel.'

'My lady, it could destroy you.'

'He'll destroy me either way. Isn't that the role I was destined to play all along?'

The upset in Francis's voice was palpable. 'What about the other novices? The ones you sent away?'

She risked throwing them a hard glance, full of a fury of her own. 'I will not subject another to this. I haven't worked hard for five years only to give up now.' She turned her head back to the valley, expression tight. 'Get the research together. That is an order, do you understand?'

Francis was silent. Her expression turned darker than anything Callum could put on at the delay.

'I said, do you understand, Francis?' she snapped, for all it was under her breath.

'Yes, my lady,' they whispered, sharply, then focussed back on the plates.

Just in time as steps were heard at the doors to the balcony, and she recognised the weight of them. *Him*. Callum. Coming to stand in the doorway behind her.

Francis finished clearing off the table and disappeared to the servants' door. She took a breath and turned. He'd dressed. New shirt on, more casual. Boots too. His eyes on her were suspicious, but she didn't think he'd heard anything of her whispered conversation with Francis.

For a moment, they just looked at each other. How had they come to this? Having hurt each other so badly, when all either of them had ever wanted to do was to protect the other. She'd loved him so fiercely for so long. Now she stood in his shirt, collared and enslaved, and she wished she could say she had stopped loving him because of it, but she couldn't. Because she hadn't.

'I have business to see to,' he said, tone firm. 'Stay in my rooms, do not step beyond them. You know what will happen if you do.'

'I know. I won't.'

He didn't move, head cocked as he considered her. Like he was trying to decipher something. Like he was trying to figure her out.

'Earlier, you said you expected my anger, but not my cruelty,' he said, rather suddenly. 'That's only because you didn't know it in me before. I learned cruelty in the salt mines. I learned to be ruthless there.'

She looked down to her hands, her nails filed short and unpainted. The cuffs of his shirt rolled up because the sleeves were too long for her. His warnings about his own capacity to hurt her were starting to get repetitious.

'You will be ruthless with me. I do understand,' she said. 'You have a job to do.'

And you will destroy me to do it. She didn't say that last bit. She only thought it.

'I'll tell you what I expected,' he said and she looked up again. 'I expected your fear. An invading army, a general who holds a personal grudge, your public enslavement as orchestrated by myself. It is only right for you to be afraid of me.' He paused. 'So yes, I expected fear. What I did not expect was your...compliance.'

'Compliance?' She straightened. 'You mean you expected me to fight more? With what? How? You hold all the power here.'

'Perhaps that is the wrong word. I think I expected more...' He frowned to himself. 'Fury from you. Hatred maybe. Or at the very least, resentment. I didn't expect you to so willingly accede. I thought I would have to break you.'

She sighed. Was that all he was worried about? She let her shoulders drop, an old weight across them.

'Only now you've discovered I'm already broken,' she said, too tired to do this any longer. 'Don't worry, as you try to get this castle's secrets, you'll get the fight you're looking for from me. I won't have a choice.'

'Believe it or not, I'd actually prefer this not to be a fight. If it doesn't have to be.'

For some reason, that made her blink fast to contain a sudden threat of tears. Why? Because he was speaking to her without the hurt and pain driving him? Because the cruelty wasn't there, for the first time since he turned up to take her throne?

Because he was almost making her an offer—we could do this another way. We could find a different way forward, one where we aren't on opposite sides. Maybe.

Only that choice had been made five years ago. She'd been the one to make it.

'I'm bound to a demon. You serve the Light. What other way can it be?' she said quietly, then turned away to gaze out over the valley.

In the same moment, his friend Rorks called out to him, and he moved, calling back, and she listened as he walked away from her. As the door closed and she was finally, truly, alone.

CHAPTER 5

Callum

Callum slipped back through the doors to his rooms long after midnight, half-expecting her not to be there. Only she was, curled up asleep on the couch in the main sitting area, still in his fucking dress uniform shirt and that golden collar.

She hadn't even tried to find other clothes. If it'd been him, he'd have been raiding the drawers in the bedroom at a bare minimum, finding something else to wear. He'd probably have looked for a weapon, too, and found a way out, no matter what threats had been made. He'd faced down those same threats himself back in the salt mines and they'd not been idly made there. It'd taken him three tries before mounting a successful rebellion. What they'd done to him after the first two attempts was unspeakable, yet it only made him more determined to succeed.

Nothing he'd told her had been a lie. Even if he had been deliberately brutal about the way he'd said it.

He stood for a moment by the doors, just watching her sleep. His head buzzed with the liquor he probably shouldn't have drunk so much of. This was still a critical time, they were shoring up their hold on the place, there was too much to do. He couldn't afford to be complacent. But Rorks knew the pressures he'd been under and how little he let himself relax. How everything, just everything, was always a plan, a path forward, the next step, the new goal, and there was never a moment to simply rest. These last five years had been about survival. Once he'd managed to secure the basics of that, which had been hard enough, it'd become about finding ways to ensure its continuation. That was all. Nothing else. Relaxation was not an option.

So he'd had a bit to drink on his Captain's urging. Big deal. Rorks would look after things for now.

Salryanna looked young when she slept. Like the girl he'd fallen in love with all those years ago, more open in her expressions and responses and words. Unlike now, when she was constantly guarded, like she was afraid of giving anything away to anybody. Her newly cut hair fell across her face, so damn short. It'd been such a shock when he'd come into the bathroom to find she'd cut it away. Her hair had never seen a pair of scissors in her life, he knew that, he remembered from five years ago. It'd been the only physical aspect of herself she'd ever liked, her one vanity she used to say. She'd laugh about it back then, though underneath the laughter were scars she didn't like to reveal, so maybe she'd always been guarded to an extent. Her childhood had not been an easy one, growing up a novice in this damn castle. Thinking well of herself had been beaten out of her young.

Her hair had meant so much to her. Now she'd hacked it off without a second's hesitation. He hadn't even been in the room. As if it were nothing. As if it had never meant anything.

Yet it had meant everything to her. And she'd cut it away.

He'd also meant everything to her once, but she'd still made the decisions to cut him away too.

Why didn't she fight back? Why didn't she turn on him with resentment, with hate, with resistance? After what he'd done to her, all he was responsible for putting her through. He'd have fought every step of the way, if he'd been in her place. He'd done so back in the mines, when so much had been done to him, and there there'd been no-one around to call *enough*. Everything was a fight in the mines and he'd made sure he was strong enough to win it. He'd had to for survival.

She didn't fight. She never fought. He wasn't sure what to do with that.

There were things she was keeping from him, more than the castle secrets she was sworn to protect. His experiences these last five years had changed him, shaped him differently, for good or ill. Yet she had changed too. She was like a ghost of herself. Well, he had stormed in with an army, taken her prisoner and made her a slave in the most humiliating fashion he could devise. But the girl he'd known five years ago would've made it clear exactly what she thought of that, and of him for doing it, even if she'd had no choice but to comply. Salryanna now wasn't even doing that much. It was like she was so full up with her guilt it didn't matter what punishment he came up with or how he lashed out at her; she'd already dealt worse to herself.

All the while, she kept hidden inside what she really felt. What she experienced and thought. Perhaps they were a bit the same like that.

He could wake her. Torment her some more. That was the plan, wasn't it? To be so cruel to her, to wring her out emotionally, so that he didn't need to progress to actual physical interrogation to discover her secrets. In the end, even he was a coward, it seemed. He wasn't sure he could send her to the interrogators to face their tortures and techniques. If he could find another way, even if she hated him for it, surely that was better? It would let her move on afterwards and live a life beyond this, beyond him. In his own way, he was still trying to set her free. He didn't want to see her destroyed.

Yet it was scary how easy it was to torment her. Something about the woman brought it out in him. She'd called him cruel and he knew it was true. It was a part of him now. And it was so easy to turn that on her, because she'd hurt him so badly. Because he did blame her for that.

Then here she was, curled up asleep on the couch, collapsed from exhaustion. While he stood wobbling on his feet and trying to make sense out of his drunken brain. She hadn't even gone to find the bed, though maybe that was out of fear of what would happen if he found her in it. Perhaps he should call her to it. Rorks had asked him if he would. She was enslaved to him now and it was only what was expected of slaves. His cock stirred as he remembered her in the bathroom, her wide eyes shocked after he'd spanked her, and the lord knew what had possessed him to do that, but it had got him pretty damn hard. How she'd not resisted. She'd practically melted under his hand, accepted the punishment, promised not to do such again. Her cheeks had been pretty flushed after it too.

It'd taken all his willpower not to fuck her in the bath. Only the worry that if he had it would expose too many of his own weaknesses stopped him. They weren't playing games with each other here. He had a job to do, and she was in the way of it, and they were not on the same side.

They were not on the same side.

She'd hurt him too badly the last time. He wasn't going to offer himself up to be torn apart by her all over again.

He clung onto it. The pain of the past. The betrayal she'd committed. Calling for his help, then turning her back on him when he'd come running. It'd almost killed him, literally. Her willingness to make him her sacrifice in her quest for the demon's favour.

The Witch Queen. The face of evil. The enemy of the Light.

It helped. It snapped him out of this stupid, liquor-induced, melancholic reflection. He wasn't dealing with an innocent here. This was a woman who had deliberately sacrificed him in order to become the Witch Queen and bond with her damn demon, an entity more powerful than any and responsible for bringing despair across the lands. She protected the creature he was sworn to destroy.

She was right. What other way could it be, except to come down to a fight?

He didn't lose fights. Not anymore.

He headed through to the bedroom. Yet he couldn't help but pause as he passed the couch and pull the throw-rug from across its back to lay over her. She would at least have some warmth, then, even as she slept out here alone.

CHAPTER 6
Salryanna

The nightmares came, just as they always did. Sometime before morning, screams in her throat, limbs thrashing to ward off the pain of it, the fear. The searing of skin, the burning, the agonies her body had tasted already, enough to know what awaited her when this flesh was finally exhausted and she was carried by the demon in spirit at last.

Usually, twisting in her bed, her legs would tangle in blankets and she'd awake drenched in sweat and sobbing, until she could get her mind clear enough to acknowledge it was just a nightmare. Only now she was not in a bed fit for a Queen, or in any bed at all. She was curled up on a couch with hardly any room to move and the instant she began tossing about, she fell off with a solid thud.

'Sal!'

The call came as she hit the floor, waking her sure enough. It still took those first few moments to come back to herself. Sobbing and curling herself into a ball, trying to crawl away and hide.

'Salryanna? What the hell?'

There were hands on her, but they were gentle. Someone crouched beside her on the floor in the dim lantern-light. She shied away, but the soft touch was a comfort and his voice was familiar and her mind began to clear. To know herself. To know it was a nightmare. To know she was not there, in that place with the demon. She was here.

She remembered.

Oh. She wasn't sure if that was worse.

Her eyes opened and she forced her expression to unclench, realising she was on the floor in the sitting room, having falling from the couch, her legs still twisted in the throw rug from the back of it. She must have pulled it down over herself sometime during the night.

Callum knelt beside her, his hands on her shoulders to help her sit up. It was still dark outside, the only lighting a couple of lanterns around the edges of the room, creating shadows. Not even morning yet.

She risked glancing at his face, then wished she hadn't. He didn't look angry, for all his sleep had obviously been disturbed by her nocturnal fear. He did look like he'd want an explanation. Only what could she say to explain?

'I'm sorry,' she said, forgetting she wasn't meant to apologise. 'A nightmare, that's all. It's nothing. I'm sorry I disturbed you.'

'If that was a nightmare, it was not nothing,' he said and somehow still sounded gentle. 'Come on, sit up. Shake it off. It's over now.'

He helped her sit straight, the simple practicality of his tone taking her off guard. So she let him assist, leaning on his arm as she made it back to the couch. Why was he helping? She was too afraid to ask. If his anger wasn't targeted on her right now, that could only be a good thing.

Once she was sitting on the furniture again, the dregs of the nightmare falling away, he stood straight. Not yet dawn and he looked half-asleep himself, wearing some kind of loose pyjama pants but no top, his hair a mess.

'You good?' he asked.

'Yes, thank you. I'm s—'

'Yeah, I know, you're sorry. Forget it. There's a lot you maybe should be sorry for, Sal, but not even I'm going to blame you for a nightmare.' He rubbed his face, exhausted. 'Look, it's not even dawn. I'm going back to bed to sleep off a bit more of this hangover. Wake me when breakfast arrives, will you?'

'Oh. Yes. Of course. Goodnight.' She paused. 'Thank you.'

He waved acknowledgement of that with a weary hand, then went back through to the bedroom. She watched him go, eyes on his back and the scars which defined it, unable to take her gaze off him the entire way.

She couldn't go back to sleep, she was too afraid to try. Dawn wasn't so far off anyway. Once she was sure he'd gone back to bed and she could hear him softly snoring in the other room, she got up to tiptoe across the suite to the bathroom. Entering from the second door straight from the sitting room and keeping as silent as possible so as not to wake him.

The warmth of the mineral springs pool was incredibly luxurious. Maybe she should've made more use of this suite when she'd been Queen. She didn't care about the grand size of the rooms, but this constantly refreshed natural bath was a delight she hadn't expected. Not that she let herself spend too long in it, he was just in the next room sleeping, so she washed and got out again quickly. Drying herself before putting his shirt back on, because she had nothing else to wear.

Her fingers hesitated at the top buttons. He'd made a point yesterday of only letting her do it up so far and though it left her feeling more exposed, she made her hands drop, not doing them all the way up. It wasn't like the shirt really covered her properly anyway.

She caught sight of herself in the mirror, almost accidentally. Her short hair managing to catch her by surprise. For a moment, she stood looking at herself. Was he right—did short hair suit her? It was so different to how she'd always looked, she couldn't tell. There were bruises across her skin from the men who'd manhandled her and, when she finally got up the courage to check, bruises across her buttocks as well. From him. When he'd spanked her for cutting her hair without his permission.

The memory brought a warmth to her cheeks all over again, so she banished the thought fast. The last thing she could afford was to indulge any kind of infatuation or attraction to the man; it was hard enough to ward that off, particularly when he kept walking around without his shirt on. Not even the scars on his back detracted from the sheer physicality of him; on the contrary, they only seemed to reinforce his strength. A reminder of how much he'd survived and was still standing strong.

Best not think along those lines. She busied herself hanging up her towel so it might dry. Then another which had been left damp on the floor, and which he'd probably used when coming in last night. She didn't have to clear up after him, he hadn't commanded it and the Light clearly brought their own servants along, already installed in the castle. But she liked things to be neat and she was supposed to be his slave; if she wasn't going to fight it, she might as well lean into it.

There were things she would have to fight. That's what he didn't understand when he expressed his confusion about why she didn't resist him more. The real fight was yet to come and she had learned the necessity of picking her battles carefully, these last five years.

She didn't like the fight. Maybe he didn't understand that either. It wasn't that she couldn't, but she was exhausted by it already, the constant need to be on the defensive, ready and alert, facing into some battle or another. For him, it was all physical. Rebellion in the salt mines, floggings, armies.

Her battles had never been as physical, yet they were as real and as constant, and left her weary with the inevitability of them.

It was actually nice to just let it go for a little while. To not fight just yet. Even if that couldn't last.

She slipped out of the bathroom and back into the sitting room to find dawn shifting across the valley, lighting the room from the long windows along the back wall and doors out to the balcony. Breakfast probably wasn't that far away, but she had little to do in the meantime. She fixed the throw rug on the couch and made sure the cushions were righted, so it didn't look quite so much like someone had spent a restless night sleeping there. Then she looked about her. Yesterday, after he'd gone, she'd lain down on the couch and hadn't got up again. She'd been aware of servants bringing dinner, but she didn't get up, didn't touch it, and then they'd taken it away. So much food wasted. She should ask about that, there were families in the valley who could use the help putting meals on their tables. A question for another day. Last night she'd slept, that was all. She'd not even heard him come in.

There were four rooms to the suite, but she'd only been in three of them. She turned to the other arched doorway, on the opposite side to the bedroom and bathroom. The study.

Almost unable to help herself, and feeling a little like she was trespassing, she tip-toed into it. It was a long room, if cosier and a little smaller than the others, with a fireplace that would be nice in winter, a large desk, bookshelves lining the walls. He'd moved some things in here already, books, papers.

The file his friend, Rorks, had brought him yesterday. It lay in the middle of the desk and she flicked it open to find maps of the castle; internal layouts across different floors, with handwritten notes marking additions, adjustments, changes. They were trying to map the place, which was something of a feat if they could achieve it. This castle didn't lend itself to such a thing, there were entire wings hidden by magical means, secret basements, concealed doors. Still, they were doing their best to pin it down on a page.

She sighed and let the folder drop. Maybe they would succeed. Find the alter of the demon, confront him in his place of power and destroy him after all. Maybe Callum could do that. He had the determination and drive and courage for it.

Maybe, if she really thought he had any chance of success, she might even have confessed her own secrets to him. Such as she would not be unhappy if the demon was defeated. If she thought it at all possible, she would do her best to help.

And he wondered why she did not fight him?

It was an impossible thing. She knew that. He would learn it. And she shouldn't be in here. There was nothing worth examining. The books he'd brought were all treatises on tactical strategy, military thinking. Once, she remembered him liking poetry; now, he kept only works of the most practical, pointed. His papers were administrative. Concerned with the governance of the valley, which admittedly he was putting more effort into than she ever did.

Only one thing, behind the books and papers, caught her eye. A small, leather-bound notebook at the back of his desk. A personal journal.

She glanced quickly to the door, then unwound the leather strap around it, opening the pages within. They were filled with inked text in his small, cramped handwriting. Sometimes there were sketches, drawings. Most of it was practical; considerations on how to take the castle, strategies for the assault on its defences. That would've dated from well before he got here, for she'd kept no real defences and he'd practically been able to walk in and take over as he liked. That must have surprised him, seeing as he'd apparently put quite some thought into how to take control and had clearly expected a lot more resistance than he'd actually got.

Some of the journal was more personal. On one page he'd sketched a tree, for seemingly no reason. On another, some men around a campfire, in uniform, laughing. Snatches of scenes from his life. There were even a couple of quick sketches of what she thought must have been the salt mines; dark, gloomy images that conveyed a sense of despair and horror. Those were on later pages, as if the memories of the place would not leave him and remained to haunt him so.

Part of her wanted to read this journal in fine detail. Another part wanted to drop it like it was red-hot iron and run. Just looking at it now was crossing a very obvious line, but she couldn't help turning a few more pages anyway.

Something was struck between a couple of the pages towards the back and as she flicked through, the book opened to it. She frowned. There were two thin sheets of tissue pressed between the pages and something kept between them, so she put the book on the desk and carefully lifted one sheet to see.

'Oh.'

Her hand rose to her mouth to stifle any sound. Between the pages he kept a dried, pressed flower. Carefully preserved. A daisy. Just as she had conjured that last day they'd shared in the forest, before it all went wrong. The last happy day of her existence. That which she'd created, just for him.

He'd kept it.

She stared at it for the longest while. Then, with shaking hands, she put the tissue back, carefully, and closed the journal, winding the leather strap around it tight. Then she placed it where she had found it and left the room, fast.

~

Servants brought breakfast to the balcony. Appearing from out of the concealed corridor, laying it out with quiet efficiency, then disappearing again. She tried to see if one of them was Francis but recognised neither face, so she didn't go near them.

The morning was crisp when she stepped out to investigate, waiting until the servants had gone before she did. They'd left warm and cold options. Toasted bread with churned butter spread. Fruits and yoghurts. Far more than would be needed for two people, even if they both ate to their fill, and even if she was someone who ate big meals, which she never had been. He'd eaten heartily yesterday, so he did enjoy his food. She bit her lip, contemplating the possibilities. What might he like from the table now?

He'd said when she'd awoken him with her nightmare that he was hungover and he'd certainly looked as if he'd needed more sleep. Coffee was probably a good bet, then. She poured a mug from the pot steaming in the centre of the table, along with a cup of water. Then she took both back inside, to the bedroom.

He was still sleeping, sprawled across the bed in the most haphazard way, half out of the blankets and on his stomach, so she could see the scars on his back. The position would stretch them out, so maybe it helped with the stiffness of them. Very quietly, she placed the drinks on the table beside the bed, stepping back once she'd done so. The bed was large, the room dim-lit, curtains pulled across the closed glass doors out to the balcony.

Retreating to a safe distance by the door. He'd said to wake him when breakfast arrived, but maybe if she just—

'Thanks.'

She stifled a gasp at his muffled voice, turning to find him stirring in bed. He grimaced as he did; maybe his back was stiff.

'Um. I brought coffee,' she said, with a nervous gesture to the beside table. 'In case you drink it. I don't know if you do. And water. You said you were hungover, that means dehydrated, so it might help.'

Inwardly, she cursed her own stammering nerves and just how obvious they were when she spoke.

'Perfect,' was all he mumbled, one arm thrown over his face.

'Breakfast is on the balcony. You said to wake you when it arrived. I could...' She paused, swallowed, and tried again. 'If you tell me what you like, I could bring you something. Or. Yes. Um.'

He lifted his arm just enough to peer at her through tired eyes, then rubbed at his face and slowly pushed himself upwards, leaning against the headboard. She forced herself to stop stammering, for surely silence was better than the fool she was making of herself right now. She didn't know what to do, what he wanted. This was going to be hard enough without actively angering him further.

Once sitting up, he twisted to reach for the coffee on the bedside table. Only the bed was massive and he had to turn quite a bit, and something must have pained him, for he stopped, grimacing.

'Fuck,' he muttered.

She stepped forward quickly, fetching the coffee for him and handing it across so he didn't have to twist further to reach it.

'Is it your scars?' she said.

'For once, no. Just the hangover,' he said, taking a sip of coffee and sitting back against the headboard with his eyes half-closed. 'I don't usually drink. Rorks tempted me to more than I'm used to.'

'You are celebrating victory.'

Which got his eyes open again and looking directly at her. 'I'll celebrate when I've destroyed your demon.'

She stepped back again almost on instinct, looking down to her hands. Did he know how many had tried to do that over the years? How many had failed? Did he know the price of such failure? Probably he did, but he would think himself the one to succeed where others had failed. He had led rebellion in the salt mines after all.

She shouldn't be surprised that merely claiming the castle, and her along with it, wasn't enough victory for him to celebrate. The General of the Light would need something far grander than that.

'My scars are better this morning than usual,' he said, into her silence. 'That massage yesterday must have helped. I shall have you do it more often.' He paused, watching her. 'Slave.'

Her cheeks flushed, she could feel it, couldn't help it. His tone wasn't even pointed, it was amused, challenging perhaps, but not the cold anger of yesterday. He was prodding and poking at her to see where he'd get a reaction. It didn't help she was extremely conscious of the way he now sat, lounging back in bed, naked from the waist up, only in thin pyjama pants and the blankets pulled messily across him.

Feeling more flustered than she should be, she made to smooth down her skirts. Only she wasn't wearing any. Just his shirt from yesterday, so she smoothed down that, and pushed her hair behind her ear, only there was barely anything left of that, too.

'Would you like me to fetch you breakfast?' she tried, because at least that was something to do, and it would get her out of there.

'Hmmm.' He sipped his coffee. 'You're being awfully obsequious this morning, aren't you?'

She frowned. 'I'm simply trying to do what you want of me. You said yesterday you don't want to fight. I am your slave, am I not?'

'Until a handful of days ago you were a Queen.' He rubbed at his face again and upended his coffee mug. 'I'm the one who deposed you. So excuse my suspicions as to your motives.'

She threw her hands up in momentary, uncharacteristic, frustration. She was so tired, exhaustion eating at her bones. Disrupted sleep was standard for her, indeed she hardly knew what it was to sleep full nights, but she usually managed her own time, didn't feel so exposed and vulnerable. Her guilt was a constant, but it had become a background companion over the years, unlike the last few days when it had arisen stark once more, and yesterday when he had thrown it in her face.

Her limbs felt heavy and her head fuzzy. Maybe she should eat something herself, instead of worrying about his breakfast so much. Only the thought of food turned her stomach. Hunger was the last thing on her mind.

'I'm trying, okay?' she said. 'That's all. That's all it is. A peace offering, giving you what you want. Because yesterday was so awful and I can't face another day like that.'

'Huh. Really.' He didn't sound convinced.

'I know, I really know, that I deserve it,' she said, running a hand over her own face. 'Your anger. Your hatred. Don't you think I know it? All I'm trying to do is keep as much peace as possible, so that maybe we can all live through this somehow.' She closed her eyes, hands dropping useless by her sides. 'Because I'm not sure we all will, but I don't know how to fix that. I don't know how to fix anything.'

He let her speak, despite her incoherence. This outburst that came from nowhere and which she didn't even understand herself.

His face was serious at last. 'There are some things you can't fix.'

'I know. I'm just tired.' She sighed. 'So you win, okay? You win and I'll do what you say, because I don't know what else to do now. I'm exhausted from all the fighting.'

She must have sounded so dreadfully confused and on edge. She must have sounded half-mad.

He didn't say anything for the longest time. Until at last he gave her a slow nod.

'Toast and fruit,' he said. 'That's what I like for breakfast. Toast and fruit and a lot of coffee. So fetch me some. Slave.'

A sense of relief dropped through her. She could do that. It was something within her control to manage.

She went to see to it straight away.

CHAPTER 7

Callum

He picked at the fruit on the plate before him, the second he'd sent her for already, because hangovers always left him hungry. Drinking last night had been a foolish move. He couldn't fault Rorks for wanting him to have a couple of hours enjoyment, of course. Rorks knew his history, they'd been close for a long time. Meeting in the salt mines right at the start, when he could still barely walk from the damage done to his back. They'd looked out for each other, rebelled together, fought together. Rorks knew what this mission meant to him on a personal level, as well as professional. Hence the offer of whiskey and companionship last night.

It didn't make the hangover any easier.

The water she'd brought him helped. Coffee and water set beside his bed. The thoughtfulness of the gesture had thrown him. It wasn't how he would react in her place.

Because yesterday was so awful and I don't know I can face another day like that again.

Yes, yesterday had been awful, but today was likely to be as bad. Indeed, the next few days were all going to be as awful as the first for her and he had no choice but to make it so. Perhaps he'd come into this expecting a battle, only to be blindsided by finding a Witch Queen already so fragile a slight breeze might knock her over. But he couldn't go easy on her, this plan wasn't actually about her. It was about her demon and that was his only aim here.

Destroy the demon.

He took a sip of the water, frowning as he put the glass back on the table beside the bed. The water she'd thought he might need and so had quietly put in place.

'You've eaten something yourself?' he asked, handing her back his second emptied plate.

She took it with a nod and a vague gesture, mumbling something that sounded like, 'before.'

Like a mouse, she was. Movements small and contained

'Hmmm. Have some coffee. You didn't sleep particularly well last night.'

Her head shot up, eyes wide as she stared at him. Standing there in his damn shirt and the golden collar, which set off the hazel flecks in her eyes. He was glad for the blankets covering the lower half of him. There was something about the way she looked, the way she moved, that got him hard, but now was not the time to start indulging. He had to maintain some level of self-control.

'It was a nightmare,' she said, as if she weren't sure what else to say.

'I know. But today, I'm afraid, is likely to be every bit as awful as yesterday, so you might want the coffee first.'

Her eyes dropped. 'Oh. I see.'

She slipped out of the room like it was an escape. He used the opportunity to get up and head into the bath, already confident that she'd follow once she'd disposed of the breakfast things, because he'd set that expectation yesterday. And for reasons beyond his understanding, she was genuinely trying to do what he wanted.

So he allowed her, when she reappeared, to slip into the bath with him, and when she asked, with such tentative uncertainty if he'd like it, he gave the assent to her massaging his back again too. It'd really helped yesterday. He hadn't felt as free of stiffness for a long time. It wasn't merely that he enjoyed the feeling of her hands warm on his back, firm on the knotted muscle, and bloody hell, he had to maintain self-control, but he was only human too.

Rorks had pointed that out last night. When it was just the two of them and half a bottle of whiskey left. *Have you had her yet? Called her to your bed?*

He'd shook his head. *Not going to. That isn't what this is about.*

Not what this was about. Which didn't stop the flush of warmth her touch on his skin brought, her hands against him, her body at his back. More than that, it was the service rendered, the way she so willingly offered herself up. It threatened to undo him in ways he hadn't expected.

God, he'd known it wouldn't be easy coming back to face Salryanna again, but he'd thought he'd been prepared for what he was walking into. Only she was everything he'd not been expecting.

'I will have you accompany me today. I need to meet with my officers, then I'll be granting audience to petitioners,' he said, gruff, if leaning into the massage because he was unable not to. 'Your people from the valley. I will have you there with me for that.'

Her hands stilled momentarily, a fluttering sensation he suspected betrayed a shake. Not that his officers were the same men who'd pawed her yesterday in front of the hundreds assembled in the hall, but she wasn't to know that. Of course she was afraid. He'd threatened that should she step outside these rooms his men would be free to have their way with her.

He'd lied to her about that, of course. His men were under strict orders never to rape anyone, especially her, no matter if she did wander the halls of this castle. She was unable to leave the building regardless, the magicians had tied her to the castle by way of that collar, so he wasn't worried about her escaping. All his men would do if they saw her was capture her and drag her back here for him to deal with, nothing more.

They'd not touch her. The scenes yesterday had been deliberately orchestrated to inspire fear, and yes, he had weaponised the threat of sexual violence, for he knew its power. But he'd survived rape himself. He'd been forced to witness others suffer it in the salt mines. He might make use of the same threats because he knew how well they worked, but he would never allow his men to actually commit such an act.

He would be the only one to touch Salryanna and he was not

allowing himself that. Not even as her hands resumed their firm touch on his back and his body warmed with it.

'Did you hear me?' he said sharply, demanding a response.

'Yes. Yes, sir.'

Oh fuck, that woman. His men called him *sir* all day long, he was their General, he was used to goddamned ranks and formalities. Yet somehow when she did it, it melted his insides. She didn't have to, he hadn't asked that of her. She offered it up just the same.

He took refuge in gruffness, turning his voice harder. 'I'd advise you to stay with me, because you know what happens if you don't.'

There was a moment's hesitation before she spoke. 'You won't leave me alone out there, will you?'

Something about her tone caught him off-guard. He straightened, turning to take hold of her arm and pull her around, so he could see her. He needed to see her face. Read her expression. Only doing that was impossible, he'd been trying since he arrived here, and she was opaque.

He wasn't gentle when yanking her around to face him, his grip hard on her arms, but she didn't fight his hold. She never fought him, no matter what he did to her.

'Are you worried my men will take you? I've already told you when you're with me you're safe,' he said, trying to figure out this new mood in her. He'd expected another protestation, *I know, I understand, I'm trying aren't I?* Instead, she sounded...

Afraid. Afraid that he'd leave her alone and unprotected.

'No. Well, yes, I'm terrified of that, you've made it clear the threat is only too real.' She stood hunched in and awkward. 'But that's not what—'

She stopped, cutting her own words off.

Despite himself, he was curious. She never reacted like he thought she was going to. Now she was almost shaking, arms wrapped about herself. The bruises left on her skin yesterday were stark.

'What?' he prompted.

'People,' she said.

He frowned. 'I told you yesterday that you're my slave and I will have the world see you as such.' He crossed his arms, glaring down at her. 'I intend to display you publicly, to make sure there is no doubt in anyone's mind of exactly who is the new ruler here.'

'It's not that.' She waved a messy hand. 'I don't like that, of course I don't. The humiliation of it is awful.' A flush rose up her cheeks as if to emphasise her point. 'But that's the point, right? Humiliation. Display of victory and of defeat, to consolidate your control. I do understand why you insist upon such things.' She hesitated. 'I only meant there were so many people in the castle yesterday. Crowds and noise and I'm not used to it. This place has been empty for a long time.'

'You've been ruling from here for five years now,' he said. 'You grew up in this castle. There were others around then, from you used to tell me. You used to complain about the novices you had to share space with.'

Her shoulders drooped. It was almost a giving in. Like her head was full of secrets and thoughts and moods and he wasn't privy to any of them, even when she offered herself up to do everything he asked and follow any order he gave. He still couldn't find a way to order her to be open with him. To tell him what she was thinking or feeling.

This woman used obedience like a fucking defensive armour.

'I sent them all away when I became Queen,' she said. 'I sent everyone away. This place is cursed. I would not force others to be here if they don't have to be.'

This place is cursed.

Did she mean that? She was the demon's Queen. Which also meant the demon's lover, or so the legends went. Privately, he doubted that. It didn't exactly pair with what he'd seen of her so far and not once had she actively defended the demon or the castle. She'd told him she would uphold her vows to the place, and if he wanted to destroy the demon he'd have to destroy her to do it, but she hadn't fought for her beliefs.

That's what had been missing. That's what he'd been looking for in her all along, yet hadn't seen. A belief in something that she might fight for. A faith, or a vow, or a position she would battle to maintain, or defend, or at least hate him for taking from her.

Something that meant anything to her. So far, there'd been nothing. Not even her own physical self.

'Why did you send them away?' he asked.

'A couple of servants would come in of a morning, leave before dark. My advisors would come weekly to meet with me,' she said. 'The castle wasn't closed off. People could come and go. Deliveries. I just...' She shrugged. 'Mostly it was just me here. It was best that way.'

She said it like it was a secret. Huddled in and reluctant. It wasn't one of the big critical secrets of the castle. It wasn't where the demon's physical power lay, or where to find him, or how to defeat him. This was just a little fact she didn't want to say, but he'd asked it, so she would answer. She was so full of these surprising little turns, he didn't think he'd ever get to the bottom of them all.

The salt mines had been crowded. They'd been locked into cells with no room to lie down and when they were unlocked to go work in the mines, there were bodies around them at all times. Later, when he was leading his men on the Capital, forming his army and facing down the upper echelons of the Light to force them to accede to his position, there'd always been others at his side. Constantly

He'd never been alone. He couldn't imagine five years isolated in a castle like this.

'Why?' he said. 'Why was it best that way? It wasn't like that when we were young. When you were a novice.'

'Those who ruled before me had other views,' she said. 'I changed things when I became Queen.'

This conversation was going in circles. Why did talking with her always do that? He couldn't even order her to explain it to him in simple terms, because she'd give him some round-about explanation that didn't actually tell him anything.

He took hold of her by the arms, pulled her right in front of him in the water. 'Tell me why.'

She stared back with those wide eyes, and he was aware suddenly of how close they were. Each of them naked and her expression almost innocent. Except Salryanna was no innocent and the Witch Queen of Ravenswild could not be trusted.

'The demon is death,' she said. 'The demon is destruction. All powerful destruction and I sent everyone away because to be too close to that power is to tempt that power, and it's hard enough for me to keep it controlled as it is.'

She looked away. Shaking in his hands. Pressing her lips together as if stopping herself saying anything more, though what she said still made no sense.

'Sal?' he pushed. 'Explain it to me. What does that mean?'

Her eyes closed. He frowned to see a tear seep from the corner of one of them.

'If you're going to do this, General, if you're determined to find a way to destroy the demon, then do it fast,' she said. 'Because if you start this, it must be finished. The consequences for everyone in this castle, maybe the whole valley, will be catastrophic if you don't see it through.'

'Of course I'll see it through. That's why I'm here.'

She bit her lip and tried to nod and didn't appear convinced. Turning away as soon as he let his fingers release their grip on her. Running from him again, yet another escape. But nothing he could think to ask would help enlighten him any further and he wasn't sure how to make her explain. He still didn't know if what she'd said was meant as a threat, a warning, or a challenge.

Or maybe, despite it all, she even meant it as a plea.

CHAPTER 8
Salryanna

H e led her on a chain. Which was as good an indication as any that he meant it when he told her today would be every bit as awful as yesterday. The humiliations weren't going to stop, obviously, though this seemed a particularly petty one.

He even smiled when he'd attached the chain to her collar prior to leaving his rooms. The gleam in his eye wasn't born of the same cruel anger of yesterday, there was entertainment to it now. He was enjoying this.

'So you won't stray,' he said, with clear amusement.

She frowned at him, trying to ignore the flush heating her skin at his tone, at the very act of being held on a chain. This wasn't a game, no matter his amusement. Not that she was afraid. She didn't fear Callum in this mood. Despite the five years and her betrayals and his suffering, along with her own, she still knew this man. She knew him to his core.

'You have me on the end of a chain,' she said, careful to keep any challenge out of her voice. 'You must know it's not necessary to keep me in place. I will not run from you. I promised to obey.'

'Yes, but that is not the reason I have you on a chain,' he replied. 'Something you must know yourself.'

She sighed. 'Yes,' she said. And then, to show she understood the point of public displays and demonstrations of control, she added, 'sir.'

His lip twitched, almost a smile. 'Good girl.'

Which flared a scorching heat on her cheeks and a rush of something strangling in her throat. She looked away fast, uselessly trying to hide her confused flush, fiddling with her rolled up sleeves. He'd dressed her in another of his shirts again, he seemed to like the look of her in them. Or maybe he just wanted to give the world another sign of his ownership. No matter, it was better than being publicly naked, as some slaves were kept in the Capital.

This shirt was cut slightly longer than the other, which gave her a bit more cloth over her hips, reaching down to her mid-thighs. He was far taller than her, so his shirt hung loose. She wasn't sure if he'd deliberately chosen it for that reason, or if his choice was entirely arbitrary. That it had been his choice was inevitable.

She left the top two buttons undone without needing to be asked. He'd said he liked the look of her like that and there was something warm to the idea that he dressed her like this not merely as a demonstration of victory, to secure political aims, but because he personally enjoyed it. Something almost comforting in knowing he didn't despise everything about her now, was maybe even a little attracted to her still, despite his anger and cruelty.

Not that she was prepared to admit any of that out loud, most especially not to him.

The Throne Room. That was where he would receive petitioners. Her people, the conquered, who would now come to meet their new ruler. She'd never received petitioners as Queen. She'd always delegated the requests of others to Francis and other advisors, leaving all operational ruling to them. While she'd hidden away, not seeing anyone at all if she didn't have to.

Callum was a different type of ruler than she was. She understood his need to be public about it; a castle held by military might would be overthrown again as soon as a stronger force arrived. A castle held because your authority was viewed as legitimate and accepted by the people, unquestioned by all, was not so easily taken from you. He was a leader of rebellion, the man who'd forced the Light Command to meet him on his own terms, then struck whatever deals he had with them, coming out of it as their strongest, brightest, highest General in command. He knew how this worked.

So did she, for all she was not as accomplished or experienced in such matters. She'd lived in this castle all her life and never rebelled against anyone, not even when she'd wished desperately to be able to do so. But she understood his aims in displaying her as his property; the right of conquest was accepted in the Valley, just as it was in the Capital. It helped to legitimise his position in the minds of those he now assumed rule over.

Never had the castle contained so many people, not even back when she was young. There were livered servants, tradesmen in work clothes, and of course soldiers in uniform everywhere, who'd all snap to attention and salute as Callum passed, her following behind on the chain. The more people she saw, the closer she kept to him, fighting an increasing urge to cling onto him. She was almost relieved when they reached the Throne Room to find it mostly empty, except for two of his soldiers waiting.

One was Rorks, the Captain and his friend she recognised, who'd looked kindly on her the previous day. The other was darker-haired, with hard eyes and a stubble, and he did not look kindly on her, but leered in a way that made her skin crawl.

Both saluted when Callum entered. He returned the gesture in a perfunctory manner as he met them by the bottom step of the dais leading up to the throne.

'How many are you prepared to see today, Boss?' Rorks said. 'There's hundreds out there, by my reckoning. I've got someone registering and prioritising claims, most appear to be nothing.'

The darker one's eyes roamed over her. 'Reckon they're just here to gawk at your new slave, General,' he said and she couldn't help but pull even closer towards Callum. She might not have access to her magic, but every warning instinct in her body shot to high alert around him.

'To be expected. Also, the point of this little melodrama,' Callum said, with a sigh. Then he moved up the steps to the throne and threw himself back on it with a decided lack of care, tugging her along with him as he did.

She stumbled up the steps after him, aiming to stand behind the oversized, uncomfortable chair. She'd never liked this throne and had almost never used it, but she'd also never held an audience for the general populace. When meeting with advisors and councillors, she'd used one of the small rooms near the front of the castle where they could easily get to and then be gone again, taking any issues of governance with them.

The throne served a purpose, one he would use this morning.

'Down,' he ordered, along with a tug on the chain. She immediately complied, a flush rising up her cheeks at the way he spoke, a feeling not entirely unpleasant. She sat by his feet, tucking her legs under her and finding a position in which she could arrange his shirt to cover her thighs and not display more of her flesh than she was comfortable with.

His hand went down on her shoulder as she sat, a warmth. She decided to take it as a sign of approval and relaxed a little under the weight of it.

'Partition off any serious claims,' he said to Rorks. 'Record them and decide who is best to deal with each, then assign as required. Escalate to me if needed, but only if needed; if everything is sent right up the chain it'll create a bottleneck. We need to give these people and their concerns proper attention. We want to gain their trust, show them we will look after them.'

'You got it, Boss.'

She glanced up to find Callum's face serious. Knowledgeable in ways she didn't remember him being four or five years ago. He sounded like he knew what he was doing and that his intentions were genuinely good. A flood of relief hit upon realising he wanted to ensure the people of the valley were looked after. She could endure this, she could live with the humiliations and the public displays, now that she knew her people would not be targeted. That they'd actually be listened to.

He must have felt her stare, because he glanced down with eyebrows raised. She quickly looked away, though was glad when he didn't remove his hand from her shoulder.

'This morning, however, is different,' he said to his men. 'This morning is about witnesses.'

'How do you want to play this, sir?' Rorks asked.

'Select the more frivolous claims, ones quickly dealt with, and send them in one by one,' he said. 'They'll be the ones making up excuses to come see what's happening in the castle. To check if it's true what they've heard about the deposing of the witch.'

Eyes turned to her. She felt them, but didn't look up to meet them.

'There's certainly plenty out there,' Rorks said, pulling the attention off her again, for which she could only be grateful.

'Good. Those will be the people more likely to gossip and talk and spread the word, and that's what we need right now,' Callum replied. 'We deal with as many as we possibly can this morning, it's all about the numbers. Got me?'

'Absolutely, General.'

She leaned against the corner of the throne and focussed her gaze on the pretty mosaic patterned tiles across the floor. It was ancient, supposedly full of demonic wards, at least according to local legend. If anyone had ever bothered to ask her, she'd have told them that no, it was just pretty patterns on the floor. Callum must have thought the same, or else he'd have had his men dig it up.

The people of the valley were good people. Perhaps they'd lived in the shadow of the demon's control, but that didn't make them disposable, or even enemies of the Light. She'd done what she could for them, in her own way, and mostly what she'd been able to do was keep the demon at bay. It had taken all her energy and effort. As a result, the Valley hadn't had a real leader in a long time.

Maybe Callum could be that leader for them. Maybe that was one good thing she could hope for out of all this.

If he survived finding the demon. If they all did.

Rorks took up position to the right of the throne. She risked glancing back over her shoulder, not expecting him to be paying attention to her, but instead accidentally caught his eyes upon her. She froze to meet his gaze and he seemed equally surprised by the moment. Then he gave her the slightest of smiles. Hesitant. She was so unsure what to do she looked down again and leaned closer to Callum's leg.

The other, the stubbled man who'd sneered at her, gave orders to men outside the doors, before looking back at his General.

'Okay,' Callum said, with resigned breath. He clearly wasn't any more enthusiastic about this than she was. 'Let's get this done. Let them in, Seth.'

Seth opened the doors and in they came. One petition at a time. Old men, young women, families with children. Each with some reason or excuse to come petitioning their new King. If he was styling himself as a King. Callum hadn't referred to himself as such and the petitioners were instructed to refer to him as General. It was possibly an error on his part. These people understood monarchy and absolute rule, even if she hadn't been as hands-on about it as her predecessors. They weren't so used to military hierarchy or rank.

Still, he gave them the trappings of a King, and that they could comprehend. He sat upon the throne, met with petitioners to hear their claims, ruled on each and decided as needed. For all these were only the trivial claims sent through, he listened to each attentively and treated them all seriously. He didn't dismiss a single claimant as beneath his notice or not worthy of his time.

He had them. She realised it early, after the third one in. Each one walked through the doors with open curiosity, suspicion or just looking for gossip, with their made-up frivolous petitions as an excuse, and he didn't even dismiss that. He saw that as a human response, a perfectly valid reason for coming here. He gave them respect as human beings.

In turn, every single one went away with a growing respect for him. He listened to them and they listened to him once he had.

She watched it as an outsider, observing this way he presented leadership. The way he acted on it. Somewhere in the last five years the boy she'd fallen in love with had not only grown into a strong, authoritative man, he'd become a genuine leader. A good one.

It made it easier. Sitting at his feet dressed only in his shirt and that golden collar around her neck, attached to a chain he held, there to be seen. At first she kept her eyes on the floor. She hadn't wanted to see the faces of the people who came through. But she started glancing up after the first couple, as his leadership began to shine through. The floor was uninspiring, for all its pretty mosaics, and while the humiliation of her position still burned, boredom dulled the worst of that.

She wondered vaguely how his men stood it. Rorks remained in position at his shoulder, a literal right-hand-man, for the positioning was made obvious. Even Seth, down by the doors, was an obvious guard. Neither faltered the entire time. Whereas she felt exhausted as petitioner after petitioner kept coming.

They must have been going for well over three hours before a young family were shown through. They had tried to dress well, but were clearly dirt poor. A young man and woman, with a little girl of maybe three or four holding their hands between them. The child was thin, listless.

All three bowed respectfully.

Rorks, who had been reading out each claim, hesitated at the paper provided to him for this family.

'My apologies, General,' he said, in the first break from process since this had begun. 'I believe this family would be better to appear in the separate session, with those claims that may take longer to resolve, as escalated to you.'

The serious claims. She glanced up; their registration system had slipped. This family weren't here with some frivolous matter.

'No matter,' Callum said, calmly. 'I'll hear it now.'

'Sir, if I may suggest—' Rorks began carefully, but Callum raised a hand to forestall him.

'Thank you, Captain. I said I will hear them out now.'

Callum's voice was sharp. Rorks stepped back with a bow. 'Of course, General.'

She shifted closer to Callum's legs, made unsure by Rorks's uncertainty. The eyes of the little girl were on her, wide and without judgement, but the parents only looked to the General on the throne. Unlike everyone else who'd come through the doors this morning, the two adults didn't even glance her way. She'd been the centre of every covert look and outright stare for three hours, and she had played her part, knowing the purpose of all this. She'd sat by his feet, obedient, defeated, captured, enslaved. She hadn't even minded after a while, because it was fascinating hearing how good he was with the people, listening as he displayed leadership, even more than he displayed her.

But Callum had been right. Those with frivolous claims had been coming only to see her; to see if it were true that the demon's Witch Queen had indeed been so thoroughly brought down. This family, however, had a serious claim and they were not here to stare or hunt for gossip. They looked...distressed.

Callum waved them forward. The husband and wife glanced at each other. It was the woman who spoke.

'My lord, General, if you please...' she began, hesitantly. Then she reached over for her daughter's hand and tugged her forward, pushing her ahead. 'My daughter, she was born almost six years ago. She was marked at the time to be a novice here in the castle.'

Salryanna's breath caught. She straightened, looking up, but nobody was paying attention to her.

'Only the old Queen died and the new—' Here the woman did look to Salryanna, with an expression of pain. 'The new refused to take more novices. She banished those already here.'

Oh no. Oh the stars. She sat very straight now, every muscle stiff with tension.

A hand fell upon her shoulder. Callum's touch, doing no more than resting there. He didn't pull her back or squeeze or give warning. Just reminding her, maybe, of where she was, who she was with.

Strangely it helped, to feel his hand. To know he'd recognised this as something of significance to her, even if he couldn't have any idea what it meant.

'I'm aware the Witch sent away the novices,' he said. 'It was five years ago, I believe.'

The woman took several breaths. Trying to find courage. Her husband openly wiped at his eyes; tears.

'Our daughter was marked, then not accepted. Rejected. It...' The woman hesitated, took a breath, tried again. 'Such marked our family. We were...isolated. Ostracised. We have no money, no work, no home. So we hoped... that is, now that you are here and have taken over from the Witch Queen, that maybe you intended to return the novices to the castle? Maybe you might...'

She faltered. Her husband stepped up. 'We know she's older than the usual. She's almost six. But she was marked out at birth. She could do something here. Even if it's just cleaning or scrubbing or laundry or the like?'

Salryanna almost couldn't breathe. Her whole body was wound up like a spring ready to snap. No. This girl had been marked? She couldn't be in the castle, she had to be as far away from it as possible. They had to get her away.

Only what did they mean, the family had been ostracised? Had they no work at all? The girl hadn't been rejected. That wasn't what it had been about. Novices had not been taken, that was all. For good reason. Important reasons. She'd done it to save them.

She'd been trying to save this girl and the others like her. This was not...

The hand on her shoulder squeezed, just a little. It brought her back out of her swirling, desperate thoughts and into the immediate physical moment. Gasping for breath. She could feel the girl's mark, so close. They had to get her out of here.

Hold on, Sal. Just hold on...

She couldn't help it, she leaned into Callum's leg, cowering back and holding onto his calf for want of anything else to cling onto.

'You mean you are here to give up your daughter into my care?'

Callum said it very carefully, as if he wanted no misunderstandings. He did not react to her hands gripping his leg, fingers digging in tight. He also didn't remove his hand from her shoulder.

'Yes, General,' the woman whispered.

There was silence. Salryanna felt the tears in her eyes, desperately trying to blink them back. She couldn't stop the shivering. This girl, this child, had been marked. Her parents didn't even know what that meant. But the hand on her shoulder was firm, holding her into him. She leaned into it, her head against his thigh. She needed something real, something human, to keep her grounded. To stop the whirring in her head and the panic rising in her chest.

'What has struck you into such poverty?' Callum asked. 'I was under the impression the Valley was prosperous.'

The man hesitated, sharing a glance with his wife. 'I was a woodcutter. Only the woods around here were cursed and it's forbidden to cut the trees. Once...once it became known our girl got rejected from the castle, I couldn't get no other work,' he said. 'And my wife, she's a seamstress, only her hands, they've gone crippled. None would find her other work neither.'

She heard him take a terse breath above her. Could feel the tension in his own muscles at that.

'I do not intend to take your child from you,' he said, very firmly, in a voice of clear and certain timbre. 'A child of that age should never be separated from their parents and should not be put to work.'

The couple all but fell apart at that. The woman openly crying, the man shaking his head, looking like he might even throw himself to his knees to beg.

But Callum wasn't done.

'The problem isn't that this castle no longer takes novices,' he said. 'It is that your poverty has been allowed to go unrelieved, and your isolation from your community has harmed your entire family. That cannot remain so. You will find community here.'

The woodcutter looked up with sucked in breath. His wife swayed, with a stunned look. Callum waited only until it was clear they had processed that, before continuing.

'You say you worked with wood and tools?' he said to the man, who nodded, mute with surprise. 'Then if you are willing to join my ranks as a builder, you will have a job here, you will be able to provide for your family. Your wife's hands will receive medical attention and care. If she has other skills not impacted by such a disability, then she too will be given work, for suitable payment, to provide for your family.'

He stood up. Holding the chain attached to her collar, towering tall above her. She stared up at him, even as she clutched her arms about herself. Such anger in his voice, a fury at an unjust world, underlain by his determination to make things right.

This was the Callum she knew. The man she'd fallen in love with.

'You will be given work. Nobody should ever need to give away their children!' He declared it with such force. 'You will be supported to raise your child yourselves. And that same goes for anyone in this valley in the same situation.'

The couple looked stunned. The woman pulled her daughter back to her, holding the little girl close. And the man really did come forward and go straight to his knees before Callum.

'Thank you,' was all the man was able to say. 'Thank you.'

Callum nodded. 'Stand. Take your family back out to the waiting room and in a very short moment one of my men will be with you, to sort things out.'

The man staggered up, wiping his face and backing away with bows and more thanks and gratitude. The woman taking the girl, doing the same.

Salryanna barely heard the orders he gave. She pulled her legs close in tight and clung to them to hold off the panic. Desperately waiting for that little girl to be taken away again. Removed from the castle, she needed to be out of the castle. It was a struggle to keep the swirling emotion in, to keep hold of herself. She swayed where she sat.

She watched the family leave and managed to get through to the point where the doors closed firmly behind them.

And then she burst into tears.

She tried to be quiet about it, but the sobs escaped her, bitten off from behind her clenched teeth in every effort not to make a sound and failing even at that. She was the only echo in the mostly empty throne room now, and for a moment that was all there was. Just her sobs and shaking, while the three men all stared at her, perhaps surprised. She hadn't even cried like this when they'd been threatening to rape her in front of a crowd, after all.

Callum moved to act. As decisively as he had with everything else that morning.

He turned to Rorks. 'Captain, please go see to that family. Ensure they have something to eat, then see about ensuring work for them and a place to live.'

Rorks saluted. 'Yes, General.'

'Seth, go tell those waiting that I will receive no more petitioners this morning,' he said. 'What I require is that all petitions be recorded, along with where to contact each petitioner. Then send them home with the assurance that we will go through every single petition and deal with them all in a timely manner.'

Seth also saluted. 'Yes, General.'

Salryanna could feel their eyes on her. She tried to hold in the desperate sobs, but the tears wouldn't stop, nor would her shaking.

'Go, now. Both of you,' Callum ordered, in a hard voice. 'Leave us.'

They did. Two sets of smartly marching footsteps over the pretty, ancient mosaic tiles which had seen centuries of pain and trauma. For as long as the demon had existed in this place, there had been suffering. She was just the latest round of it.

He waited until the men had left and they were alone. Then he came down the dais steps and sat beside her upon them.

She tried to calm herself, get her head together. Why had he come to sit beside her? Why hadn't he yelled at her for an explanation, or laughed at her for her hysteria and foolishness? He didn't touch her or reach out. All he did was sit quietly next to her. He didn't even say anything, or try to make her say anything. He let her cry until the worst of it seemed expelled and her sobs subsided.

'You want to tell me what that was?' he said, only then. His voice was very calm and strictly neutral. It was like a balm, a soothing kind of sound.

She tried to wipe her eyes. 'It's not important. I promise. It won't impact your mission here.'

'I've seen a lot of things from you in the last few days, Sal, from begging me to let you apologise, to staring at me with outright terror,' he said. 'But not once have I seen you cry, no matter what I've put you through. Not like that. So tell me what all that was about.'

'I don't know that I can.'

'Is that due to some demon binding or magic?'

She wished she could tell him yes, because he might not ask further then. Only she didn't want to lie to him. She'd hurt this man too much in the past to lie to him outright now.

'No,' she said. 'It's just... It doesn't matter. So long as whatever home you find that family, please make sure the child is far from the castle. She can't be near the castle.'

He nodded slowly, considering that. 'Then tell me why.'

She sighed, miserably. 'Please don't ask.'

'Sal, this isn't the old days, where you get to make cryptic statements and I don't push for more detail,' he said, still in that exceedingly neutral voice. 'You're my slave now. I put a collar around your neck before a fuck tonne of witnesses. So you will answer me in full, or else explain the reason you cannot do so. And if you choose the latter, you better hope it's a good enough excuse for me to accept, or else I will do something about it that you will not enjoy.'

He said it calmly, no anger. Just stating a fact. Somehow, that made it easier. To know that she had no choice, he had asked it, commanded it, and she was to obey, and that's what they were now. Master and slave. She could resist that, of course. If she chose. Fight it, and fight him, refuse to capitulate. Make him force her to do his bidding, and while he'd undoubtedly win any such fight because his was the power here, at least she would have stood up for herself and not just caved in the instant he claimed victory.

Only she hadn't resisted him because it was almost a relief to let go. Let someone else lead, make decisions, deal with all the horrors of this place. It was a coward's response, she knew that. She was running away from her responsibilities and hiding behind him. But right now, she chose to let that happen.

If he wanted to be the big leader with all the responsibilities, and relegate her to mere slave without any at all, then she wasn't entirely upset about that. It was a respite from, well, everything else.

'The little girl, she was marked,' she said, quietly. 'Do you know what that means?'

'No.'

'The demon had marked her as his own.' She looked at her hands, twisting her fingers together. 'It was a ritual, all novices went through it. She was probably lucky she was baby when they did it to her and so wouldn't remember.'

'You went through it, then?'

'Mmmm.'

She didn't want to dwell on that. She hadn't been so young, certainly not a baby; she'd actually been a similar age to that girl now.

Five, maybe. Six. Old enough to remember. Old enough to know what she'd lost in the family who'd given her up to the castle.

Old enough to recall the searing, burning agonies of it.

'It's like a brand. A spiritual brand,' she said. 'And it hurts the same as any physical branding, maybe worse. The mark can't be seen visibly, not after it's healed. But it is felt. Always. It...allows the demon to...'

She faltered, not sure how to explain. Not wanting to. Tears back in her eyes and her breath shuddering. Damn it, she needed to keep herself together, it wasn't like this was anything new to her, she should be far more capable of talking about it. She cursed herself for not being so. What must he think?

That little girl would've been in the last group to be marked, just before the old Queen died. Before she was bound herself, with such finality, to the demon. There'd been a lot of novices when she was younger, but they became fewer and fewer as she got older. There'd only been three left when the old Queen died. None, by the time they crowned her.

That baby had been meant to be hers. A novice for her as the new Queen. But if that child had been but a baby when marked, she would never have made it to adulthood in the castle.

'What does it allow the demon to do, Sal?'

His voice was almost kind. She didn't know how to resist that.

'To feed,' she whispered, then felt him stiffen beside her.

'What?'

'The demon draws...energy, life-force, sustenance, from us. He is sustained by it,' she said. Not looking at him. She couldn't bare to look at him while she said this. 'There were maybe two dozen novices when I first came here. By the time of my binding, only three of us remained.' She swallowed, her mouth too dry. 'The weaker ones go first. So if that child had been but a baby when marked, when offered up to this castle, she would...she would not have...'

She dragged back a breath, struggling to say the words.

'She would what?' he prompted, if with new caution in his tone now, as if he knew he wasn't going to like hearing this.

'She would not have been one of the strong ones,' she whispered.

'She would've been drained and destroyed long before her tenth birthday, after years of the worst suffering.'

She felt him turn rather than saw it. Look to her with horror in his eyes. She didn't blame him, but she didn't want to see it either. The understanding of what she was, and what her order was formed to do, and the suffering within it, that she was part of. He'd arrived here thinking to break her, but she was already broken, long ago. She was a damaged thing, unworthy of the company or respect of others. She knew that. It was one reason she'd always kept hidden away.

'That's...' He stopped and took a sharp breath. 'Sal, was that happening to you too? When you were a novice?'

She put her head in her hands. 'It's okay. I was one of the strong ones,' she said. 'We'd watch as our friends became ill, as they suffered and were finally lost to the pain of it. One after the other, burning slow from the inside out. The rest of us never knowing if we'd be next.'

'You never told me,' he said, sounding almost breathless. 'You never said anything.'

'What was there to say? Nobody ever told us what it was. They don't actually explain any of it to the novices, we never knew what was happening to us,' she said. 'It was only when I became Queen that I found out. There were three of us left when the old Queen died, and I was the only one...the only one strong enough...and oh stars, but they went through both the others first, you know. They didn't survive it, they burned, they screamed so loud, so long...and I was all there was left. But I...'

She had to stop. Dragging back a long breath, dropping her hands in defeat and looking to him at last.

'I survived. I was strong,' she said and heard the bitterness in her own voice. 'I became the Witch Queen and was celebrated for it. After watching my fellow novices, my friends, twist and scream and burn from the inside out, suffering all the agonies and torments of the demon, I was celebrated as strong enough. I was the saviour of the castle and the valley.'

She looked back down at her hands, to where, as a very small girl, a mark had once been made. The inside wrist of her left arm, a burning, dreadful mark that could never be removed, not once placed.

Branded.

'I don't want to be strong anymore,' she said softly. 'I don't want to always be the strong one, watching while others burn. Not anymore.'

He said nothing. Instead, he put his arm around her shoulder and he pulled her into him and he held her, just held her, warm and maybe even, momentarily, safe in his embrace. They stayed that way for the longest time in silence.

CHAPTER 9
Salryanna

Rorks reappeared, at which point Callum dropped his arm from around her and stood up, putting distance between them again. He didn't pick up the chain, leaving it on the ground, so she remained sitting where she was. She'd long stopped crying, but hadn't wanted to move out of the comfort of his embrace, especially as she had no idea when or if she'd ever receive it again. It wasn't like she deserved it. She'd hurt him, like she always hurt people. That's what came with being the demon's creature.

It had been a long time since anyone had held her like that. Since the last time she'd seen him in the forest.

Seth followed behind Rorks and she curled further into herself on sight of him. She didn't mind the tall, angelic looking Captain, who was clearly a close friend of Callum and who'd only ever seemed to look at her with empathy, if tinged with obvious curiosity. But Seth set her warning senses off. There was something nasty in his eyes when he sneered at her, so she stared at the floor and tried to ignore him.

Callum went to Rorks, also ignoring Seth.

'We need a better process,' he declared as he met Rorks in the middle of the big, echoing hall. 'That might have suited our purposes to spread word, but I'm not spending half my days listening to petitioners complain about their neighbour's goats.'

Rorks bit back a smile. 'You didn't enjoy hearing about their goats, then?'

'I'll delegate that task to you next time, if you think it's so funny, Captain,' he returned. 'And what the fuck happened with that last one? That family should never have been made to wait hours to have such a serious claim heard.'

'Sorry, General. It slipped into the wrong pile, administrative error,' Rorks said, with a wince. 'I'm looking after that family personally. All other serious cases have been delegated someone to manage each of their situations directly, to cut the bureaucracy down. We'll see they're looked after.'

Callum gave that a sharp nod.

'Good. Make sure they have somewhere to live that's not inside the castle,' he said. 'We also need to identify if there are any other young women or girls who were marked as novices here, prior to the last five years. If any are found, they need to be looked after, and kept away from the castle. It's dangerous for them to be near this place.'

'Okay, Boss.' Rorks only briefly glanced at Sal, but didn't let his eyes linger. 'Is there a way to tell?'

'I'll work that out and let you know,' Callum said, not even looking her way.

She would tell him, of course. When he asked, as he would. She wouldn't hesitate now that she knew he would look after them, the girls who had been marked to be her novices, fuel for the demon. The ones she'd sent away. She'd tell him how to find them, so he could ensure they were no longer in danger. But she wouldn't tell him what he'd want to know after that, which was what it meant that demon had no novices to feed upon and only the Witch Queen in the castle left for him to reach.

She still had some pride left, some self-respect, didn't she? It wouldn't help his cause to know it, anyway.

'How long until our magicians think they can break the binding?' Callum asked Rorks.

She sat straighter, uneasy at the reminder. He'd told her what his plans were, he wasn't going straight for the demon, he wanted her secrets first. The ones that would tell him how to confront the demon where it could be trapped, how to defeat it. It would do him no good to interrogate or torture her into giving away those secrets while there was a still a binding upon her stopping the very words in her mouth; she couldn't give them up even if she wanted to.

Instead, he'd set his sorcerers against her. They were strong, she knew that from the collar cutting off her access to all magic. It was no small thing, given how powerful she was herself, fuelled by the demon at her back. She wasn't entirely certain how it worked as yet, probably blocking the magical flow, or isolating her from it; she'd work it out when she stopped to think on it properly, she just hadn't had the energy or the care to do so thus far.

Maybe she should have. What if his sorcerers were strong enough to breach her binding?

What if he learned the truth? What then?

She looked down at her hands, her wrists. There was no sign of the marking on the underside, yet she could always feel it there, the burn of it. She'd lived with the sensation almost all her life. Callum was here for a purpose and she couldn't forget that. A mission that sat even above his personal hurt and anger at her. He was here to destroy the demon and free the valley.

If he managed to get so far as to learn how to do that, she wouldn't stand in his way. She might even hand him the tools he needed. But he wasn't going to get that far, was he? The whole valley would be doomed before he could reach that point.

She needed to speak to Francis. To know if they got to her research, if she might be able to figure a way out of here for all of them.

'It'll be at least another day,' Rorks said, breaching her sudden panic, so she snapped back to this moment. 'But they're close.'

'As soon as we can. We need to move on this fast,' Callum said. 'What about the remaining towers we haven't yet accessed? Have we found a way in?'

'Those physically locked, yes. Most of those magically protected now too,' Rorks said. 'There's only one tower left now that we can't get into. The magicians have struggled with it.'

'Leave it. Get them all working on how to break the bindings on the

Witch. She knows the secrets of this castle and we need her to give them to us,' he said. 'What of the maps?'

'Do you have a minute to see? I've got them through here.'

Rorks gestured to an alcove off the back of the throne room and Callum nodded, following him to the back corner.

Her heart thumped as he slipped momentarily out of sight. He was just going to the nook attached to the back of the throne room, she knew it, it wasn't far. But she couldn't help the increasing rate of her heart, the tension in her limbs, when he disappeared and left her alone out here.

Not alone. With the guardsman. Seth.

That did not make her feel any better.

She kept her eyes on the mosaic tiles, clutching her knees into her. For several seconds there was silence only broken by his heavy breath and the rush of rising panic in her ears. It went on for long enough that she began to think maybe it would be alright and she was wrong to feel so uneasy and scared.

Only then he stepped towards her. One step, two.

She stood up on his third. The chain attached to her collar clanked and she picked it up so as not to tangle her feet in it, but she wasn't fast enough. As soon as she moved, Seth moved quicker.

He lunged forward, grabbing the chain. Then, with a hint of victory in his eyes, he yanked it towards him.

She stumbled, stifling a cry through her teeth and fighting to find her balance. When she managed it, she found herself forced right up close to him. She tried to turn her head away; she could smell the scent of meat on his breath and the unwashed hair on his head.

When she pulled away, he held the chain tighter.

'Got nowhere to go now, witch,' he said. Then he leaned forward and ran his tongue down her cheek.

'Ugh,' she uttered, yanking herself back. The collar held tight.

'Don't know why you're complaining, you're the demon's bitch,' he snarled. 'Reckon you take it every which way on a daily basis.'

He stuck his free hand under Callum's shirt.

She squealed, jumping back and raising her own arm, hitting him hard across the face. His head flicked sideways and he cursed, spitting blood; she'd split his lip. But that was the extent of the damage she'd managed to inflict and now he was truly pissed off.

'Fucking witch,' he hissed, then grabbed her by the arms and span her around with force, throwing her into the throne. She hit it, off-balance and unable to defend herself as he grabbed her left arm and yanked it up behind her back, while holding the chain, so her head was forced upwards.

The collar pressed so hard against her throat she struggled to breathe. Scrabbling at it with her free hand while he wrenched her other even higher and she uttered a strangled cry at the sudden shooting pain. She couldn't even fight him. He pushed her over the arm of the throne, so her head went downwards but her hips were still high, her buttocks bare and vulnerable.

'Get off me,' she said, a harsh, breathless attempt at defiance, but she couldn't get any real sound into her voice. She couldn't even scream. Instead, she felt him right there behind her, fiddling with his pants, while her arm bloomed agony and the collar pulled too hard on her throat.

'Get off me—'

Before she could finish trying to speak, there sounded thumping boots and a cry full of fury.

'Seth!'

Callum's voice, seething with rage. Her arm was released, the chain let go, so she sagged against the throne, sliding back to the ground beside it. Dragging in breath and shaking.

She heard the scuffle before she had the ability to turn her head to see. Callum throwing Seth halfway across the room. Following it up by raising his own hand and bringing a flying backhand down against the man, with far greater force to the blow than she'd been able to manage.

Seth staggered, tripping over his own feet and landing on the floor.

Callum towered above him, fury incarnate.

'Nobody does that in my army!' he snarled, and for a moment it looked like he might take the violence further. Only he turned, throwing a dismissive hand Seth's way. 'Rorks, get him out of here before I lose my self-control. Put him in the stocks until I decide what to do with him.'

Rorks looked horrified at the scene, pulling himself up straight as Callum delivered the orders. His shoulders back and chin raising high.

'Yes, sir,' he said, firmly, then reached down and grabbed Seth by the shirt, pulling him up.

Seth wasn't impressed, throwing Rorks a dark look and swatting him away. But he didn't stay to argue the point and didn't resist the dismissal.

At the door, Rorks commanded soldiers in the hall beyond and handed Seth over to them. Only after the man had been taken away did Rorks close the doors and turn back to them.

His eyes flashed momentarily to where she cowered by the throne, a troubled look on his face, but he focussed on his General forthwith.

'I'm so sorry, sir,' he said. 'I thought he knew better. He was a good man in the war.'

Callum's lips were set in a furious line.

'I don't care how good he was in the war, he's no longer an officer in my army,' he said. 'Rorks, we cannot afford any loose cannons now. The only ones we allow into our inner circle we have to know, trust. So only those from the mines. Got me?' He shook his head, jaw a hard ball. 'No one from the salt mines would've tried that.'

'Yes, sir. General...' He hesitated, distress showing through. 'Callum. I'm really sorry. I know I recommended him to you.'

But Callum waved that away. 'It wasn't your fault. I approved his promotion, didn't I?'

Rorks still looked uncertain, but did nod. Callum looked down at her, his own expression as troubled as his Captain's. He held out his hand towards her and for a moment she wasn't sure what he meant by the gesture. It took her a second to realise he was offering to help her up.

Tentatively, she took his hand and let him assist her to standing.

'Are you alright?' he said.

She made herself nod, though her arm was throbbing badly. 'Yes, sir. He didn't get far.'

'He had a split lip. Did you do that?'

She risked raising her eyes, then immediately dropped them. 'I hit him. I'm sorry if I shouldn't have. It was instinct. I—'

'You're allowed to fight. You were protecting yourself.'

Not that she'd managed it. She was so used to having magic at her fingertips, nothing could touch her when she did. Nobody would have dared hit the Witch Queen for fear of what she might do with the demon's magic at her call.

Now she was left vulnerable. But that was the point of his putting the collar on her.

This time, when she met his eyes, she didn't immediately look away.

'I won't fight you,' she said.

'I know.'

He said that so simply, and with such assurance, that it broke some of the tension in her body, brought a sense of relief.

Then he looked back at Rorks. 'I'm going to take luncheon in my rooms. Are you okay to finish up here, Rorks?'

Which the Captain was, of course, because even she could see by now that Rorks would do anything Callum asked of him. The man gazed at his General with adoration in his eyes. And, she suspected, Callum would do the same for Rorks. There was a comradeship between them that wasn't impacted by rank or hierarchy. They were friends. Close friends.

That warmed her to see. That among everything else, the pain and fear and the traumas of their past, he could have developed a positive and strong relationship with another human being, who genuinely deserved his regard.

When Callum turned back to her, she lifted the end of the chain, still attached to her collar, and held it out to him. Almost like an offering.

I won't fight you.

I know.

He took it in hand, then led her out of the hall.

Luncheon was already laid out on the balcony table when they returned to his rooms. He shut the door behind them and unclipped the chain, putting it away in a drawer, and for a moment they just stood there, looking at each other.

'You need to start telling me things,' he said at last.

She startled. That wasn't what she'd expected him to go with.

'Such as?' I cannot tell you how to reach the demon. My vows are binding.'

'I'm aware of that. My magicians are working to break the binding,' he said, as if it were that simple. As if he even understood what that meant. 'I'm talking about that girl's marking, what it means. I can't keep the people in this valley safe if you don't tell me what I need to know.' He paused, narrowing his eyes as he looked at her. 'And all else aside, I do believe you want to keep the people safe.'

She looked away with a piqued shrug. 'Yes. I do.' As if that was a kind of admission.

Beyond the sitting room, through the glass doors to the balcony, the day was one of glorious sunshine and warmth. Even inside here the suite was pretty with the sun shining through the huge windows. But she couldn't feel it. She could only feel cold.

'Then tell me what I need to know,' he said, with some frustration. Not anger, at least; she knew what his anger looked like and this wasn't it. 'I get that you won't share what you know of your damned demon and yourself. We're not allies, there is no trust between us. But when it comes to the people of this valley, I had thought we were at least some way aligned.'

'We are. I want them safe too,' she said. 'Callum, I'll answer your questions where I can. But I don't know what to tell you. I wasn't prepared for that family's arrival. I couldn't have foreseen they'd bring a marked child into the castle. I didn't think it a possibility.'

'Yet the risk must always have been there.' The man was unyielding. No wonder he had survived the salt mines. 'So what other risks do I need to know about?'

She bit off a retort. The impulse to say, *you took this place from me by force, now you want me to help you rule it?* He was right, she did want to keep the people safe, it was for that reason she'd sent away the novices.

'This whole castle is a threat, General,' she said, stiffly. 'Everyone you bring here is at risk, not only the marked. They are simply more vulnerable than most. But all are in danger and the longer you are here, the greater the danger becomes.' She met his eyes directly. 'There were reasons I sent everyone away.'

He crossed his arms. 'Everyone except yourself.'

'Yes.' Her shoulders dropped, a weight descending. 'I am the Witch Queen. This is my place. I belong to the demon.'

His jaw clenched. A fury flashed through his eyes. 'Not anymore. You belong to me now, slave.'

She wished, right then, that he could make that true simply by asserting it. She had never been free, not before and not now. So if he could force his way in here with military might, if he could make what he wanted true simply through declaration of it and the fierce strength of his willpower, then wouldn't that be better?

Only it didn't work like that. It didn't matter how much he wanted to cry it out to the skies, or how often he displayed her collared and sitting by his feet. She still belonged to the demon.

She gave him a nod anyway. 'Yes, sir,' she said, simply, as if that could make it any more true than his angry declarations.

He exhaled exasperation through his teeth. 'I have work to see to. Fetch me some lunch and bring it to my study.'

He stalked through to the other room without even a second glance at her. She wondered if he realised it was an escape, that he was running from this conversation. That was something she usually did. Perhaps he could see the truth of it, after all: it'd take more to claim her away from the demon than merely putting a magical collar around her neck.

Fetch some lunch. It was activity to get lost in and she was glad for it. An order to fulfil that she didn't have to think about. She headed to the balcony where the food had been laid out, took a plate and selected pastries and sweet breads to put upon it. Some fruit; he liked fruit. Some meats as well, he'd eaten such yesterday. Looking for the things she knew he liked, having paid attention to his previous meals.

'My Queen?'

Her shoulders stiffened at the whisper, her head twisting. There, to the side of the balcony, one of the servants.

Francis.

'Oh my friend,' she breathed, then stepped quickly over to them, gripping their hands. 'Tell me you've got the research? Tell me you found it.'

She spoke in whispers. Callum was just inside and she couldn't risk him overhearing.

Francis didn't look happy. 'It's in your rooms. But it's untested, my lady. We don't know what the consequences might—'

'We're not going to have a choice. His magicians will attempt to break the binding tomorrow.'

'Oh stars, the fools.' Their expression tore. 'Please, my lady, are you taking care of yourself? Are you eating? Please tell me you're eating.'

'You need to go, Francis. He's just inside,' she said. 'Keep an open ear, because things could happen fast. But go now.'

'Remember you won't help anyone by hurting yourself,' they said. 'You need to eat, my Queen. You need to take care of yourself.'

Her teeth clenched. 'Go Francis! That's an order!'

Francis sucked back a breath, bowed their head, and slipped off the balcony to the servant's exit in the corner.

She gave herself a moment to take in a few long breaths, glancing back inside, but the sitting room was still empty and the other glass doors leading to the bedroom on one side and his study on the other were firmly closed, with curtains drawn across them.

She let her heartbeat slow before returning to the table and the plate she'd begun preparing for Callum. She finished gathering food for it, then turned to take it back to him.

CHAPTER 10
Salryanna

He sat at his desk, papers in front of him. A quill pen in one hand, dipping it in the inkwell and inscribing words upon the sheets.

She paused in the doorway, plate of food in hand, watching him work. A few seconds where he was focused elsewhere and she couldn't help but stop and look. The line of his jaw, his face in profile, hair pushed back behind his ear. He looked older than the young man she'd first fallen so in love with. He'd been all but a boy then, full of care, sweetness, love.

Now he was a man hardened by suffering. He had grown into his position, battled his way to the top, no matter the traumas thrown his way. The flogging, the salt mines. He may have threatened her with rape, but he'd actually suffered it. That wasn't even the worst of it, from what she could tell of the little pieces he'd revealed. Glimpses into the horrors of his experience.

He'd grown stronger in spite of all they'd done to him. All she'd caused to be done to him. While she...

Well. She'd suffered too, of course. But she hadn't grown stronger, she'd been worn down by it, torn apart by it. She had none of the strength of him. What even was her suffering except by proxy, anyway?

She witnessed the pain of others, unable to help them. She watched as others burned, screamed and hurt. Always it was others. Who was she to even complain about her pain when she wasn't the one who'd had the flesh ripped off her in strips, or been held down and raped as punishment for insubordination, or been flogged to an inch of her life, or been burned from the inside out, a slow torturous candle.

It was never her who these things were actually done to. Her suffering was nothing compared to theirs, to *his*, and yet she was the one torn apart by it. She couldn't even bear witness to other's pain without crumbling.

He lifted the quill to dip it again in the ink. The movement broke her reverie and she stepped into the room, placing the tray of food quietly on the desk to his side, before stepping back to retreat.

He didn't look up from his work. 'Have you eaten?'

'Yes, General.'

'Hmmm. When?'

She frowned, not understanding that question. He was still writing something. Papers, they looked official. On the far side of his desk, in the corner and out the way, was the leather-bound journal she'd stolen a look at that morning. The one in which he kept a pressed and dried flower; a daisy a girl had once given him in a forest, before she so severely broke his heart.

'What do you mean?'

'I mean, when did you eat? You were out there barely a few minutes fetching my plate. You didn't have time to eat your own meal.'

'Oh.' Her chest loosened, though she realised her mistake in that same instant. In her habitual reaction to assure him she'd eaten, she hadn't thought that he might actually notice the conflicting detail. 'Um, I just grabbed something small while I was fetching yours. I ate a lot at breakfast and am not so hungry.'

He put down the pen. Slow movements, careful, considered. Something turned in her stomach; a warning, an instinct that something was not quite right.

He looked at her directly.

'You had coffee at breakfast,' he said. 'Nothing more. Even the coffee was only because I insisted.'

'I'm sure I had—'

'I saw that much with my own eyes. Do not lie to me again.'

His tone was grim. She caught her breath at it, realising too late that she'd been trapped into this. He hadn't asked if she'd eaten without purpose; it was a deliberate move to see how she answered. Because he noticed more than she'd assumed he had.

She shifted her weight, foot to foot.

'I was not that hungry,' she said again, a lame excuse.

His eyes narrowed. 'Not hungry now. Not hungry at breakfast. What about last night? Did you eat from the meal I know was brought here, because I ordered it to be so?'

Oh stars, was he really going to push this? It was all of four meals in his presence. Not even that, considering last night he hadn't even been here. Of course she hadn't eaten dinner last night; the food had come, and the food had been taken away again untouched. Which he seemed to know; he wasn't asking because didn't know the answers.

'I...' She didn't know what to say, if it wasn't to be a lie.

'You weren't hungry then either, is it?' His tone turned dark, an anger in it and she wasn't sure why. Why would he care? How did it matter to him?

She looked away, shrugging, perhaps betraying a little petulance, despite her intentions only to acquiesce.

Which got him standing, tall and fierce.

'Three days I had you in those dungeons and you didn't eat a single mouthful,' he said. 'I put that down to the state of the food there, but in the time since I have put the highest quality meals in front of you and still you have not eaten a thing. And you tell me it's because you're not hungry?'

She held her hands up in a gesture of confusion, of not knowing what he wanted to hear. So she hadn't been eating. What did it matter?

'I just...I didn't feel like it,' she said. 'That's all. It's not any big deal.'

'Four days!' he cried out, and she gasped at the fury in his voice. 'You don't eat for four days and you tell me that's not a big deal?'

She stared at the anger of him, the strength of him. She didn't know where it came from. She didn't know what drove it. Why? Why did he care?

'Yes,' she said, simply. 'It doesn't matter. Does it?'

He looked at her like he could hardly believe what he'd heard. 'Doesn't matter? Four days, Sal! If you really believed it didn't matter, why lie to me about it?'

She looked down to her hands. Her left was still throbbing from the attack in the throne room. The pain was quite intense really, when she let herself think about it. She supposed if she told him that her wrist was hurt by Seth, he would have it checked, perhaps even ensure some healer or another saw to it.

But that's why she hadn't told him about it. The pain of it throbbed through her. Just like the pain of hunger did. That was the point.

Pain.

Others didn't understand, though. She knew that through experience. Callum clearly wouldn't. Except the difference now was she'd never had to answer to anybody else before.

'People always make such a fuss,' she said, not quite hiding her bitterness. 'It's not like I starve. It's not like I'm dying here. I get around to eating eventually. Just it's...easier to not get into the discussion.'

His jaw stiffened. He didn't like that. She still didn't get why, it wasn't like this was even important. He was here on a mission and had better things to worry about than her eating habits, surely. What did he care if she starved herself or sort to hurt?

'Enough,' he said and she took an involuntary step back at the force of his tone. 'From this point on, all your meals will be supervised. You will eat, so help me. You are forbidden to skip meals.'

'I...I don't—'

'Do you understand me, slave?'

His extra emphasis on the last word took the breath out of her. Things had changed, she did have to answer to another now, and it wasn't the demon, who revelled in pain and encouraged her seeking it out. If she'd hurt herself in the past, it was only with that creature's approval.

Now she had to answer to Callum, who seemed genuinely aggrieved that she wasn't eating. And she still wasn't sure why.

Her eyes went wide. 'Yes, sir,' she managed.

He unbuckled his belt. She frowned as he slipped it from out of the loops of his pants. It was thick, black leather, with a heavy silver buckle. He held that buckle, then wrapped it a couple of times around his fist, before stepping back and gesturing to the desk.

'Over here,' he commanded.

'General?' she ventured, not moving. Her heart thumped.

'You lied to me. I will see you punished for that.'

Her chest constricted to the point where she couldn't breathe. 'But... but...' She tried to grasp breath. 'Callum, please, it was only food. It's not important.'

'It was a lie. A deliberate concealment because you knew I wouldn't approve.'

'I understand. I really do. I won't lie to you again. It was a mistake. Seriously. You don't have to—'

'Get over here now!'

It rocked her, the force of him, the commanding sound of him. He was unyielding. Her feet moved almost of her own accord, because she wasn't sure what else she should do. He had ordered it and she had promised to obey and something in her was compelled, when he spoke like that. When he took such control.

It brought a heat to her cheeks, and to her insides, and a shaky but insistent need *not* to resist. To give in to him entirely.

When she was standing in front of him, she hesitated. She wasn't sure what he wanted now.

'Hands on the desk,' he said and with a dry mouth she moved to do as he said.

She must have moved too slow, because as she put her hands on the wood, he put a hand between her shoulder blades and pushed her down. She bent right over, until her elbows were on the desk as well as her hands, which left her buttocks in the air. Bare, because his shirt rode up.

She thought of that belt in his hands and she knew what would be next. She just wasn't sure she could get her head around the fact it really was happening.

It was like the spanking. And it brought the same heat and tangled need to the insides of her. The sense of vulnerability combined with a surety that she was safe in his hands. It wasn't that she wanted this exactly, but the sense of his authority, the unyielding force of him that she could give in to, rely upon? That was a craving she couldn't deny.

'With any other slave, I'd have you flogged for dishonesty,' he said from somewhere above her and she clenched her eyes shut with a shudder. 'But frankly, I don't know if you'd survive a flogging. There's almost nothing to you. Clearly it's been a long time since you've eaten properly at all.'

She squeezed her eyes shut harder. 'It doesn't matter,' she said, a soft whisper.

'It damn well does!' he roared. She flinched. 'Goddamn it, Salryanna, you've been neglecting your own welfare for too damn long. Well not on my watch. I'm not letting it happen any longer.'

And somehow, for some reason she couldn't quite understand, she felt tears squeeze out from between her closed eyelids. The idea that she shouldn't neglect her own needs, that someone cared enough to notice and then got angry because she hurt herself, it was so unusual and so unexpected. Nobody before had ever noticed and she'd never expected anybody to.

It tore at her insides. 'I'm sorry.'

'I don't accept your apology.' He was so hard about it. A solid wall she could depend on never breaking. 'I'm going to give you a proper belting now, Sal. You will stay still to receive it, or else I'll tie you down and double the number of strikes. Understand?'

She nodded, eyes still shut. 'Yes, sir.'

He stepped back and she heard his movement. She tried to prepare herself. But the first strike, when it came whirring down and connected with a slap across her buttocks, shocked a cry out of her despite all her intention to take this quietly.

Oh the stars. Oh the earth. The intense sting of it shook her brain in her head and rattled her bones. Then, before she could even process the first strike, the second came over the top of it.

A cry escaped through her tight-closed lips.

This was pain. Not like the pain she caused herself, the pangs of hunger or the exhaustion of starvation and the fatigue of pushing through. It wasn't even like the throbbing pain of her wrist, an injury she chose to ignore. All that was her choice.

This was his. His choice, his command. The power of it had her swimming inside a flood of sensation. Pain, need, shame, worry. It took her out of her own head until all she could focus on was the physicality of it. Until there was none of the rest of it, those incessant self-recriminations that were her constant companions, becoming swamped and then lost to the immediate sensations in the moment. There was only the feel of his belt to her skin and nothing else.

Blessedly so. She fell into it almost with relief.

Over and again the leather snapped against her skin and though initially she tried to contain her cries, by the fourth it wasn't possible, and by the fifth or the sixth she'd stopped even trying. She quickly lost count, the strikes merging and blurring. Only the sting, beyond which she couldn't think, so her memories and the horrors of them, the sense she deserved all she suffered because of how much suffering she was responsible for in the world, it all fell away. In this moment, someone else was in control. Someone she could depend upon, whose strength she could rely upon, and whose judgement right now was better than her own.

Someone she could trust. It washed over her. It brought a flood of need and relief, knowing she didn't have to stand in judgement on herself and forever find herself guilty. Instead, she could hand herself over to him and he didn't think she was entirely irredeemable. He didn't think she should be neglected or staved. He saw something of worth in her.

It was more than she'd felt for herself in a long, long time.

The belting seemed to go on forever, until her entire world was physical and her mind was somewhere else.

And then it stopped.

She couldn't move, not at first. It took her some moments to bring herself back to her body, to acknowledge the desk under her elbows and hands, the awkward position she was in, the stinging of her skin.

The softness of his hand now cool against the radiating heat of her buttocks.

'I'm sorry,' she whispered.

'I know,' he said quietly. Almost gentle, now. 'I know.'

CHAPTER 11
Callum

He helped her stand, conscious of his own breathing and the need to control it. He was an experienced military leader, he knew how to approach discipline in his ranks. He'd even had slaves before, if briefly; the Light Command had assigned them to him as indicator of his high status, once he'd forced the bastards to negotiate. He only kept the couple so long as was necessary for the political look of the thing, to make a point, and then had quietly asked Rorks to find them a comfortable situation far enough away to be safe.

The point was, he knew very well how to discipline those under his command and he was no stranger to administering corporal punishment. It was a tool and one he did not shy away from using.

But this was different.

This was Sal, that was the problem. This was personal. His past and hers all wrapped up together, both their traumas and suffering stemming from that one moment when she'd left him. He no longer believed she'd done that uncaring for him. Whatever the reasons she'd made her choices, it hadn't been because she freely chose power and the demon over him. She hadn't wanted to hurt him. That didn't change the fact she'd still chosen and her choices had consequences.

She was so thin, so insubstantial. So different to what he'd expected to find when he'd led his armies here. There was almost nothing to her, as if she were being eaten away from the inside. It'd angered him badly to finally figure out she was doing some of that to herself.

He couldn't understand why. He cursed himself for not realising sooner. Why hadn't he seen she wasn't eating? Why the fuck wasn't she?

It was the way she'd told him it didn't matter, that's what cut him worst. The honest confusion in her face as she tried to figure out why anyone might care what was happening to her. As if nobody ever did otherwise. As if her own welfare had no matter or worth at all.

It might have even broken him, seeing that in her. If she hadn't already broken him more than five years before.

She gripped hold of his arms as she stood, no longer shaking, but unsteady on her feet. Not running from him, then. Not shying away full of fear, despite the violence he'd just administered on her body. Instead, she clung closer to him, hung onto him, like only he could steady her.

It brought him a heady rush. The power she gave him when she so meekly obeyed, complying with his every command. He couldn't deny how hard he was from delivering her that belting, either.

He pushed that aside. The fact he found himself aroused at having taken his belt to her was not relevant to anything right now. He was well aware of his own tendencies to power and command in the bedroom. Just ask Rorks, who happily waxed lyrical on the subject at any given opportunity, because that man enjoyed the opposite kind of role and they did fit together neatly like that. But they hadn't fucked around in a long time and Rorks had a myriad of different partners all over the place these days; he needed to freely enjoy himself as much as possible after the salt mines had come so close to destroying him. Callum loved to see him do so, encouraged it of him.

Yet he himself had reacted differently to their hard-won freedom. He hadn't bothered with other partners once he and Rorks stopped messing around in bed. He'd paid for it a few times, after achieving his command and the wealth it brought. A nice and easy transactional arrangement with no strings attached, some different girl or boy each time, so there was never any risk of ongoing attachment forming.

Never any emotional entanglement. He didn't have time. He didn't have the space in his life. He had a mission to complete.

Now Sal brought it all back out in him. The desperate need to have her where he could control her. To wield that power with a belting or spanking, simply because he could. Because maybe that way he might even protect her too, if she let him.

Maybe.

He put a hand to her cheek, wiping away the tears there.

'You won't skip meals again,' he said, keeping his tone calm, even gentle.

She shook her head. 'No, sir.'

'Good girl,' he said and watched her cheeks flush, heard her breath catch at the praise. Which was interesting.

She almost swayed where she stood. Still in the thrall of the sensations from the belt, not quite yet back to herself. Rorks had used to be that way too, after they'd done something particularly intense.

He cupped her face and made her look up at him. 'Now you're going to sit here where I can see you and you will eat some lunch. While I supervise to make sure you do.'

He reached for the plate of food she had brought in earlier.

Her eyes widened. 'Oh, no, please. That was your lunch. Let me go fetch something other. I will show you, if you need, I will eat, but I—'

She looked so distressed at the thought of taking food meant for him, even though it was only the same food out there, that he raised a hand to quieten her.

'We will both go out to the balcony and eat,' he said. 'And then I want an explanation for why.'

Her shoulders dropped at that. She wouldn't want to dissect her motivations for avoiding meals. He wasn't even sure she could explain it. But they needed to have a conversation about such things, and a proper one, at that.

She took the plate she'd put together for him back to the balcony, ensuring he was seen to, before she sat herself across from him. He accepted the service because she seemed to need to perform it, she took solace in it. She did seem calmer now, at least. She was also favouring her left arm. Trying not to show it, but it pained her still. Hurt in Seth's assault, undoubtedly. He didn't call her out on it right away, but he would need to keep an eye on that. She probably wouldn't, after all.

When she sat, it was gingerly, with some discomfort. He made her eat, but let her choose what. She took fruit mostly and the tiniest sliver of sweet bread. It wasn't much, but she'd not eaten for four days and he knew better than to force her to eat too much too soon. In the salt mines, they'd been regularly starved and there was never enough food. To force large meals into someone who'd been fasting for so long was a mistake. The body couldn't take it all at once; he knew from experience.

So he let her take just a little, so long as she ate it, and at dinner tonight he'd see she had more.

Had it really only been twenty-four hours since he'd first had her at his table? The fury he'd felt then, the tumult of emotion and hurt all directed at her, wanting her to suffer for all the pain she'd caused him, seemed a distant thing now. Perhaps because she was clearly already suffering. He was beginning to think there wasn't much he could do to her that was worse than what she did to herself.

'Did you ever truly plan to run away with me? Or was that always a lie?' he asked suddenly, surprising himself.

Her head shot up, eyes wide. 'Callum...'

'You won't be punished for your answer, whatever it may be. I just want the truth.'

'Of course I wanted to run away with you. If you believe nothing else, at least believe that.' She pushed a piece of apple around her plate. 'It was the only thing I wanted. But I was a novice of Ravenswild, I was promised to the demon. I don't get what I want.'

He took a shaky breath. Yesterday, he wouldn't have believed it. He'd have dismissed her words as an easy lie, another attempt to lure him in to betray him.

Now, he wasn't so certain. Now he wanted to believe her.

'Then...why?'

This wasn't the question he meant to ask her. He'd been planning to push on reasons she hurt herself, didn't eat, neglected her own welfare. This wasn't the *why* he had planned.

But it was the *why* he was desperate to hear answered.

'Do you really think I had a choice?'

'Yes. When we were in the forest that day, that last day, you could have come with me then. I asked you to come with me then. We could have just gone. Together.'

Her eyes were glassy, perhaps a threat of more tears. If so, she managed to hold them in.

'If I had gone, so many others would have died in my place,' she said softly. 'All the sacrifices who weren't strong enough. I saw them with my own eyes, how they burned. How many more would burn if I had turned my back on the role I'd always been destined to fulfil? The position I was brought up for?' Her eyes closed, she gulped a breath. 'I am so sorry.'

'I told you not to apologise to me. I accept it wasn't easy, I know it seemed an impossible choice,' he said, and he kept his voice calm, but firm. 'It is still the choice you made.'

'I know.'

'I won't give you absolution. You may not have wanted to hurt me, but you still did.'

A flinch across her face. 'I know.'

He exhaled a long breath. Trying to let the old pain go. Trying to find something like forgiveness within himself. It wasn't easy. There'd been so much suffering in the last five years. He couldn't help but think she might not have wanted that, but it had still been her fault.

Which was unfair. He knew it. She didn't actually deserve to bear that blame. That was becoming increasingly apparent.

'I am not here for revenge,' he said. 'That's not my purpose.'

Her eyes opened and she nodded, blinking to clear them. 'You are here to destroy the demon.'

'Yes. Whatever that takes.' He remembered her saying, *and you will destroy me to do it.* He didn't say that now, but he couldn't help remembering those words. 'Tomorrow, my magicians should be ready to attempt breaking the binding that is upon you. If they manage it, you should be free to tell me the secrets of this castle.'

She shuddered, looking very small and hunched in. She didn't say anything to that and for the moment he didn't push. He didn't want to ask if she would freely tell him once she was able to. He didn't want to know if she would resist then, to protect her demon, and her Queenship, and her own power, because it wasn't only the binding, it was her vows and she would fight to keep them.

He would have to ask. He would have to find out eventually.

'There is another way. A safer way,' she said. 'If you...if you go now, leave, no-one will be further hurt. All you need to do is close up the castle, seal it up, and that will end it. Have your magicians enforce the seals as strongly as they can. You can still claim this valley for the Light, you can fulfil your mission and rule as King, or whatever you like. You might not have destroyed the demon, but you will have contained him.'

He sat back, staring at her. Not quite understanding. It took him too long to figure it out, listening to her offering him this possibility, this new way forward. When understanding did come, it was rancid, foul on his tongue, bitter in the back of his throat.

'I'll make you a deal, Sal,' he said, because he had to be certain. 'I'll take that advice, I'll seal up this castle so no-one may ever again get in, and I will take everyone, and leave it behind.' He paused, and she looked up with wide eyes, maybe even a flash of hope. 'So long as you come with me.'

The hope died fast on her face. And he knew his rancid under-standing had been real.

'I can't,' she whispered. 'I can't leave here.'

'So what you're really saying is that you think I should seal up this castle *with you inside*,' he snapped, almost a snarl. The fury was back. 'Trapping you alone in this place forever? Leave you to that demon.'

'I belong to the demon.'

'You belong to me!'

His hand on the table curled into a fist. His frustration, anger, it boiled inside, but not at her. Somehow, in the last twenty-four hours, he'd turned his fury onto other targets.

The demon. This god forsaken place.

She sat looking at her plate, seeming so lost.

'I don't want anyone else to get hurt,' she said, desperately. 'Please, Callum. I don't want *you* to get hurt.'

'I've been hurt. I survived.' He clenched his jaw. 'You're my slave now Sal and I'm not giving you up to any fucking demon.'

She swayed where she sat, finally looking up at him.

'You say you didn't come here for revenge,' she said. 'You also didn't come here to save me. This is not about you or I or our personal traumas. This is about you defeating the demon, protecting the world from him.' She pulled back a breath. 'Sealing the castle is the only way.'

'I'm not sacrificing you to that creature.'

'I was sacrificed to that creature long ago. I made my choices, I consented for that to happen. You said that much yourself.'

He crossed his arms and glared across the table at her. 'And now I'm the one who gets to choose. It is no longer up to you.'

She expelled a sharp breath. He couldn't tell if it were worry or relief. But she did nod. Looking down at her plate, at the food still upon it.

He let the silence sit a moment, to make sure she understood she had nowhere to go with this ridiculous discussion and that he would brook no argument on the matter. It was not her choice any longer. It was his and he was not giving her up to some demon. He was not sealing her in this castle forever and walking away.

When she seemed to have accepted his last word on it, he gestured to her plate.

'Eat your lunch, slave.'

'Yes, sir,' she said, and put a morsel in her mouth.

They didn't say much more for the remainder of the meal. But she did eat everything on her plate.

He wasn't prepared to take her back into the castle after lunch. The morning had been tumultuous. Tomorrow was likely to get worse, as the magicians began on the job he'd brought them here to do. He didn't know what that would entail, but breaking a binding like the one the demon held on her couldn't be easy, or painless.

An afternoon's respite was about all he could offer. A few hours of quiet, out of the way of others, while he worked in his study writing reports back to the Light's command, and she curled up on the chair in the corner, supposedly making a list of those who had been marked and sent away five years earlier. Anyone who would be at particular risk in the castle and who he should ensure was kept away.

By the time a knock came at the door in the main room, she'd nodded off to sleep, and he didn't wake her. She hadn't slept well, what with that nightmare last night, and he'd put her through a lot already. He found it exhausting. She would even more so, and that wasn't even counting her breaking a four day fast, or the belting he'd given her over it.

She looked almost peaceful, sleeping in the armchair in his study. Still in his shirt, in the collar. Peaceful and...vulnerable. While she was making a list of those most at risk of being in this castle, he was beginning to think her name should be right up top of it.

'Boss, you here?'

Rorks. He got up from the desk to go to meet him in the other room, so as not to wake Salryanna. Through into the sitting room, really fucking glad to see his friend and old comrade and confidante there.

Rorks saluted, but Callum waved the gesture away. 'You off the clock?' he asked, heading for the drinks cabinet across the sitting room, glancing across with a question in his eye.

The other man grinned. 'I work for you. I'm never off the clock.' Then he shrugged 'But I am officially off duty, if that's what you're asking, and would absolutely say yes to one of those.'

Callum was already pouring a couple of whiskeys. He didn't want to drink again, not too much, not like Rorks had tempted him into last night and which, admittedly, he'd sorely needed. But one wouldn't hurt.

He handed across one of the drinks. 'Come out to the balcony where we can talk.'

He was conscious of Salryanna asleep in his study. If she woke, heard voices, she likely wouldn't come out to see; she'd stay hidden away, because that seemed to be her default coping mechanism of choice. Hide away from the world, cut everyone off. He'd practically had her living in his shadow these last twenty-four hours, but he still couldn't say what was going on behind those sombre eyes much of the time.

She would listen at the door, though. The woman might be damaged and she might be fragile, but she was not stupid and she was a survivor. He didn't plan on saying anything to Rorks that might be a problem if she overheard, but he also preferred to be someplace where he'd have warning if she were listening in.

The balcony would do. It was a lovely day out there anyway.

Rorks didn't hesitate to sit back with ease. They were soldiers, yes, and respected rank, yes, but they were also friends and former lovers and they'd fought in the salt mines together. Rorks had been the first Callum had asked to follow his lead in the rebellion, just as it'd been Rorks who'd got him through the first weeks in the mine, when his back wasn't yet healed and he'd hardly coped with the physical labour. Later, months later, it'd been because of Rorks that he'd finally rebelled. After Rorks had been dragged out for a public punishment, with Callum held down and forced to watch because they'd made the error of being too friendly, too close, and thus could be used against one another. Rorks had been punished as a means to hurt Callum and in that moment, Callum had sworn no more. *No more.*

This castle was a long way from the salt mines. They'd both come a long way. They were the ones in control here, he was the one metering out punishments where he deemed it necessary. Yet this castle still seemed more threatening than anything they'd faced to date.

'Where is she?' Rorks asked, without preamble, because he knew Callum too well.

'Asleep on a chair in the study,' he said. 'Sleeping off a belting.'

Rorks's eyebrows went up. 'What'd she do to deserve one?'

Callum looked out over the balustrade, across the valley. The views were really something from here. He'd been surprised to find these were *not* the rooms of the Witch Queen, for they were the most lavish and well-presented suite of rooms in the castle. But she had not used them. She'd shut them up, they'd been covered in layers of dust when his men had first got in.

They still hadn't found her rooms. The private spaces of the Witch. There was still so much he didn't know and it gnawed at him that he needed to. He was playing blind and she wouldn't tell him what he needed to open his eyes.

'Perhaps she did nothing at all,' he said airily. 'Perhaps I simply felt like putting her in her place.'

Rorks wasn't convinced. 'Bullshit. You've too finely attuned a sense of justice.' He paused. 'And I know what that woman means to you.'

Callum sighed and took a sip of his whiskey.

'She wasn't eating. Four days, including the dungeons. And she lied outright to me about it, to hide the fact. That's what she did to deserve a belting.'

His friend exhaled a long breath. 'Four days? Fuck.'

His grimace wasn't put on; Rorks had experienced the starvation of the salt mines along with Callum. They both knew what it was like from personal experience. Neither had any desire to return to it.

'Tell me, Rorks, how do I punish a woman who is already punishing herself?' he said. 'When the worst I can put her through can't even compare to what she habitually does to herself?'

Rorks let his shoulders drop. Swirling the whiskey around his glass. 'It's not what we were expecting when we first planned to storm this place, is it?'

'I was expecting a fight, that's what I was expecting,' he said, almost rueful. Looking down at his hands. Soldier's hands. Fighter's hands. 'I was prepared for a fight, I know how to deal with those.' He shook his head. 'I wasn't expecting her to simply let me in the door and hand over all control. And yet...'

He paused long enough that Rorks even prompted him. 'Yet?'

He looked up to meet his friend's eyes.

'And yet, she hasn't capitulated,' he said. 'She hasn't given a damn thing away. She hasn't given a single vow up. We're no closer now to defeating the demon than we were before we got here.' His fingers clenched into fists on the table. 'She won't fight me, she fucking obeys every word I say. But she's not giving in either.'

And he didn't know what to do with that. It was its own kind of rebellion, weaponised obedience. To a soldier like him, a fighter, a resister, it left him almost powerless as to how to deal with it.

He wouldn't have said this to anyone else, of course. It spoke to his own doubts and uncertainties, and he didn't let those show to just anybody. But Rorks was different. Rorks understood the kind of power dynamics that lay between people sometimes, and the ways such could impact situations. He'd always confided in Rorks.

The Captain sloshed his whiskey a bit more, clearly thinking on things. 'The magicians, tomorrow. Are you sure you still want to do it this way?'

He wanted to say *no*. He wasn't sure. To forcibly break a binding of this nature, if they could even do it, was sure to have consequences. He didn't know what those might be, only that she would be the one at the centre of them. Considering she was demon-bound, he didn't imagine they'd be pleasant.

Even then he wasn't sure she'd willingly tell him what he wanted— needed—to know. She might side with her demon even still.

'We don't have a choice,' he said, trying to remember that he wasn't here for revenge, and he wasn't here to save her either. This wasn't about him or her or their personal traumas, just like she'd said.

Trying not to remember the option she'd put in front of him. *Seal the castle and walk away.* The horror of what she'd really been suggesting—to seal her up with it—still sat seedy in the pit of his stomach.

He wasn't sure going the path of the magicians was going to be any better.

'Callum...' Rorks hesitated. 'If it works tomorrow, if we can break the binding, do you think she'll cooperate?' He looked momentarily into his glass. 'We were expecting a fight. She hasn't given you one. Maybe, if she is free too, she will actively help.' He paused again. Or was it another hesitation? 'Maybe you could even work together.'

'That's an awful lot of maybes there, my friend.' Callum heard the cynicism in his own voice. 'I don't know what's driving her. It's not power, it's not control. It's not status or public recognition. She doesn't care for any of those things. She doesn't even seem to care for her own welfare.' He clenched his jaw, frustration in his bones. 'But something is driving her and I don't think it'll allow her to willingly work with me. I'm think I'm going to have to force her. I can't just figure out why.'

Rorks's expression was sombre. He knew what Salryanna meant to him. He knew what that would mean.

'If you need me to take the lead on that, you know I will,' Rorks said. 'You don't have to be the one interrogating her or forcing her to anything. I will do all that is necessary, but only what is necessary, and no more.'

'Rorks, it's my responsibility. And this was my idea.' He dragged in a long breath, running hands through his hair.

'You also were expecting to find a hateful demon-bound Witch Queen who betrayed you and was happy about it,' his friend said. 'Who you could continue to blame for all the shit you've been through. Only she's not that, is she?'

'No. No, she is not.'

'You didn't expect to find a woman you might still care for.'

He couldn't deny it. For more than five years now he had blamed Salryanna for every moment of suffering he experienced. She'd broken his heart and left him to the merciless Light. His suffering had been extreme, and he could hate her through it, because she was far away and gone from him and he'd needed something to cling onto. He'd needed someone to blame.

But she wasn't the figure of his hateful fantasies these last few years. She was, so it turned out, human and flawed and fragile and all but falling apart in his hands. She, too, had suffered in the extreme. Maybe she still was to blame, but maybe she wasn't. Either way, he couldn't hate her. She wasn't that one-dimensional fiction he could conjure to help him through the bad times.

He wasn't here for revenge. He also wasn't here to save her. But he was beginning, badly, to want to.

'You still haven't taken her to your bed?' Rorks asked, somewhat gently.

Callum threw him a dark look. 'I told you that isn't in the plan.'

'Far as I can see, she's upended the plan start to finish.' He took a sip, pressing his lips together to enjoy the taste of the liquor. 'You and I were fucking for quite a while, don't forget. I know what you like between the sheets.'

'Rorks, fucking you is never something I'd forget,' he said. 'And we didn't have sheets in the salt mines. We didn't even have a bed.' He hesitated. 'You're not jealous, are you?'

'My General, I'd follow you into any battle you asked of me. You're the leader I will always obey. I'd die for you, man, you know that,' he said, with a soft smile. 'But we haven't been together like that for years and I don't have any claim on you to be jealous about. All I'm saying is that I know what you like, and you need to be in control in the bedroom, just as you do outside of it.'

Callum sipped at his whiskey, savouring the burn. 'Be careful where you're going with this. I'm your General. I could demote you for being a cheeky sod.'

Rorks laughed. 'I'm not complaining. I like a man who knows what he wants and is prepared to take it, the rougher the better. We both know how much I like to obey.' He paused, selecting his words with care. 'Have you considered that, maybe, so does she?'

'I wasn't like that with her five years ago,' he said, but he couldn't say he hadn't thought it. 'Not like I was with you.'

'She still knew you to the core. She fell in love with who you are and that's a part of you, whether you acted on it then or not.'

He sat forward, putting his elbows on the table and his head in his hands.

'God, Rorks, you think I don't want her in my bed?' he said, like it was some kind of confession. 'I have the woman in a collar, wearing one of my discarded shirts and nothing else, willingly obeying my every command. It's tough enough keeping my hands off her without you egging me on.'

'Is there any actual reason you're holding back?'

Callum gave him a very pointed look. 'After the salt mines, you really have to ask?'

Rorks visibly winced. 'Shit. Sorry. I never meant to imply it wouldn't be consensual. That's never what I meant.'

'I know. But I made her my slave, Rorks. That does tend to fuck up consent somewhat.'

He finished his whiskey, putting the glass down. He was tempted to pour them each another, but he didn't want to risk a hangover again tomorrow. Their celebration last night had been important, but they couldn't afford to let anything slip now. The whole situation was far more complicated than he'd hoped it would become when first going into this.

'You keep suggesting that maybe we could work together, or be together, or sort something out,' he said, fingers still on his glass. 'But no matter how cooperative she is, I still can't trust her, Rorks.'

'Maybe—'

Callum cut that off with a raise of the hand.

'Check out the servants. The local ones we sourced on arrival here,' he said, and his tone turned grim. 'Sal's been communicating with one of them secretly. I overheard them. I think it might be one of her former advisors. She gave orders to find some kind of vessel, spoke of research.'

'What kind of research?'

'Something dangerous,' he said, simply. 'Find me that servant, Rorks. We need to know what they're planning and we can't let them scuttle this.'

Rorks's expression looked troubled. 'Are you sure that's what they're trying to do?'

'No. But they're not working with us, that I am sure of.' He looked out over the valley. 'I don't actually believe Sal wants the demon to win. And maybe I do still care for her. But that doesn't mean I'm foolish enough to believe she's on my side.'

He looked back to Rorks, his closest friend, comrade, confidante. Former lover. Rorks would go back there, too, if he asked it. Rekindle their sexual relationship, if that's what Callum indicated he wanted. Some days, Callum was tempted. They'd been good together in bed, just as they were good fighting side-by-side. They were, simply, good together.

But what they'd had was fun, intense, and a reaction to their circumstances. A desperate need to connect with another human when trapped by the inhumanity of the salt mines. Neither of them had been exclusive with each other, nor would want to be, and Callum couldn't hold Rorks back from living his life to the full now they were out of that place. Rorks needed to explore and experiment and experience everything the free world had to offer.

Callum needed something different.

'I can't trust her, Rorks. It's that simple,' he said. 'Not even if I wanted to.'

CHAPTER 12

Salryanna

The nightmare was the same as it ever was. Every time she closed her eyes for more than a few hours, its black tendrils would wrap itself around her and squeeze. Until there was no breath left in her, until there was no *her* left inside her. Then she could no longer remember who she was or why she was, only that she was here to serve the demon and he would demand the suffering due to him. That was her purpose. That was all she was. Suffering.

Sometimes she thought it was the demon lashing out at her, these nightmares. Finding ways to destroy her peace even in her sleep. He didn't talk to her directly so much, not anymore, but he was always there. A weight across her shoulders, a stickiness on her skin. A fog breathed in and down her throat and inside her, constantly inside her, as if she were not made of bones and muscle and sinew and blood, and if they cut her flesh and opened her up, they'd find only blackness there, a rotting darkness. They'd find the demon.

He was there, always. It took effort to remember herself, even on the good days. At night, asleep, it was harder, and the nightmares were always intense.

She awoke screaming again. Falling, landing with a thump and a cry as the pain jolted through. She'd tumbled to the floor, accidentally landing on top of her already injured wrist, and a white-hot shot of agony flooded her entire body. At least it cleared the head of those black tendrils which otherwise stuck to her inside and out.

'Sal! Salryanna?'

Thumping feet accompanied the call of her name and Callum appeared in the doorway, as she found herself on the floor in front of the armchair. He wasn't alone. His friend, the Captain, appeared at his shoulder.

She couldn't speak for the moment, still trying to shake off the nightmare and get a handle on the bolting pain from her wrist, all at the same time. She cradled it with a grimace, but on sight of the two men suddenly crowding the doorway, she let go of her own arm and instead focussed on sitting up and not showing the pain.

'Sorry. Sorry,' she said. 'Nightmare. That's all.'

Callum frowned. 'Another one. You seem to have a lot of those.'

Every night. Only every time I close my eyes.

'Maybe,' she said, deliberately noncommittal, trying to find a graceful way of getting up off the floor without looking like a mess in front of both him and his friend. She could feel the red flush across her cheeks already.

He came forward, crouching to help her rise. She had to fight a momentary instinct to pull back, not let him help her. She could and would do it herself. Hyper-independence, or so Francis would call it, but only when they didn't think she could hear. She couldn't afford to let others close enough to help, and Francis knew that.

Only it would cause even more fuss if she pulled away and his hands on her arms were surprisingly gentle. These same hands that had delivered her a belting that still ached could be as soft and careful with her as they had been firm and unyielding.

That's why she shouldn't let him close, shouldn't let him touch her. Because it tore at her heart when he did and only left her wanting more.

He helped her to sit in the armchair. Which she did with a wince, because the bruises his belt had left across her skin had really come up now.

'Boss, if you don't need me, I'll go see to that other matter you asked about,' Rorks said from the doorway.

Callum straightened from helping her and nodded. 'Thanks, Rorks. Let me know as soon as you discover anything. As a priority.'

Rorks saluted and Callum returned the gesture with sharp efficiency, practised, habitual. It was comforting to see such everyday routines of his life, military and hierarchy and how in charge he was. He'd never been a supporter of the Light when she'd known him those years ago; he'd been as suspicious of them as she'd been cynical about her own order. But they were the ruling force and they had the army and he'd been a private then and that was his life. He hadn't minded the military bit, from her memory. The order and structure of it.

He thrived in it now. No matter the challenges he'd faced, and he'd been thrown to the worst of tortures, he'd risen to take control of his life for himself.

She'd never managed to do that. Take control of her own life. So it helped now, to see how he'd managed to do so for himself.

Rorks paused in the doorway, glancing back. His eyes were troubled as they shifted down to her.

'Have a think about what I said, Boss,' he said, deliberately vague. Something he didn't want her to know about, then. 'I reckon you deserve it. That maybe even you both do.'

'Rorks, enough. Out,' Callum ordered sharply, but Rorks' smile flickered and, still looking at Sal, gave her a wink.

Her eyes widened, unsure what to make of the gesture. Callum merely rolled his eyes, though he didn't look genuinely unhappy with his Captain, just exasperated. She was glad to know he had a friend he relied on, shared with. That he hadn't been so alone in the world, after she'd left him so awfully.

She knew what it was to be alone. She was glad that Callum had someone.

Callum sighed after Rorks left, looking down to where she sat.

'My back is stiffening up,' he said. 'I'm going to the bath to ease it. Come on. You can attend me.'

She followed him through without hesitation. She could use a bath to help wake her up and the throbbing of her wrist might be eased by the warmth of the mineral springs water too. Besides, she'd rather liked attending his bath so far, and maybe he'd liked it too, the massages she'd given him. Perhaps they'd helped. His scars were extensive and this kind of mineral pool would help with them.

She assisted his undressing, going straight to him in the bathroom to do so, because he'd had her do that yesterday and she didn't need to be told twice. Her fingers fumbled with the buttons of his shirt, though; her wrist was aching and her movement reduced due to it. She bit down on the pain to hide it.

He caught her hand by the second last button and stopped her progress. Turning her arm over, very gently, and frowning down as he held it in his own hands.

'This is still hurting you,' he said. It wasn't a question.

'I jarred it again when I fell from the chair. That's all,' she replied, effortlessly explaining it away. 'It's nothing to worry about.'

'Hmmm.' He raised disapproving eyes to her face. 'I don't like your tendency to be dismissive of your own body's needs. Sleep, food, you avoid both whenever you can. If this arm hurts, if there's any substantive injury, you need to let me know.'

She frowned. 'It's fine.'

'If I find out you're lying about that, I won't be happy. You'll get far more than a mere belting next time,' he said. 'Be warned.'

She pressed her lips together tightly, looking down and unable to keep his gaze.

'There was nothing *mere* about that belting,' she muttered eventually, unable to help the flush creeping across her cheeks.

Something flickered at the corner of his lips. Maybe it was even a smile. 'I do believe it made my point. So if you don't want another, behave.'

Amusement in his tone. Not that he'd hesitate to make her behave, nor was she certain she wanted him to. There'd been...a kind of peace, after he'd taken his belt to her. A calm she hadn't felt in a very long time. Everything had narrowed to a single point, the physical sensation, with everything else falling away. All the fear and anxiety and despair. All the guilt. For a little while she'd been free of a weight and had even managed to slip into sleep without struggle.

Of course, then the nightmares had come again and she'd woken back to a world as terrifying and painful as it ever was. But for a brief while there had been peace, of a kind.

She reached to his final two buttons, but he pushed her hands away and undid them himself, shrugging off the shirt. Then he reached out to hers as well. She tried to stop him and do it herself, but he gave her a pointed look and knocked her hands away, if gently with the injured one. So she could only stand there as, one by one, he undid the buttons on her shirt, before pushing it over her shoulders and letting it slip to the ground.

She found herself standing naked, so close in front of him she could feel his body heat, breathe in the scent of him. Almost feel the skin of him too, shirtless and right there in front of her. She could reach out and touch him, and for a moment her whole body yearned to do it. Put her hand out, rest her fingers on his chest. Trace the scars there; not the flogging scars of his back which she had massaged and was beginning to learn already. These were the more ordinary scars of a soldier, paler marks of past damage; that's what came with fighting for a living, she supposed.

The proximity of him was intoxicating. Overwhelming.

Out of desperation to keep her cool, she tried to step away. Her breathing was ragged already; she wasn't sure she could stop herself doing something stupid if she stayed so close.

He took hold of her arm and stopped her.

'Where do you think you're going?' he said. His voice was low.

'I...I just, I don't know, I—' She was even more flustered by the touch of his hand on her arm, and the way he'd pulled her even closer into him.

He cut off her stumbled words by leaning down and kissing her, ever so softly. Lips gentle against hers, a brief touch, a pause, then moving in again, more firmly this time. His fingers around her arm, holding her into him, the feel of his skin, his chest, against hers, the taste of him, mint and whiskey, the presence of him.

She couldn't help herself. She kissed back. She leaned into him. Though she knew she shouldn't, she should pull away, put distance between them, for this could only end badly. She'd already hurt him once before, she couldn't risk doing so again. It would destroy her if she hurt him again, but that's what she did, wasn't it? Harm people, even when she didn't mean to.

But oh, she wanted this. Wanted him. Opening her lips for him, feeling a slide of his tongue against her own, her hand going to his waist to grip him in return, pressing her lips upwards against his with genuine need. Her whole body heating and moulding against him, just like in the old days, just like—

He broke the contact, stepped back. A sizeable step. Suddenly. For a second he stood there, eyes wide and staring at her, and she could only stare back, stunned by this sudden ricochet of mood.

Then he turned away.

'Callum?' she called, quickly, and at least he stopped walking. His shoulders stiff with tension. He glanced back without quite turning around.

'I'm sorry,' he said, stiffly. 'I thought it might be—but no. I'm sorry.'

He spoke with as much firm decision as she'd ever heard from him. As if this were some grim error of judgement and he was acknowledging his accountability for it. While her stomach twisted with confusion and misunderstanding and a need she still couldn't reconcile.

'Why?' she said. 'What reason do you have to apologise to me?'

'The power here is too weighted against you,' he said, as if he had to force the words from between his teeth. 'So that wasn't fair. I knew that and did it anyway.'

She almost laughed. Fair? He was worried about whether this was fair? About what was appropriate or if she was being treated right? Of course he held the power here. He'd put a damn collar around her neck to illustrate that to the world. And she hadn't fought him for a single moment, for reasons of her own.

She looked down at herself. Naked, but for the collar she'd almost grown used to the feel of, and far too scrawny. Powerless. She couldn't even access her magic anymore. She had exactly nothing left that was hers, but that hadn't been his doing, it had been her own, five years ago.

Could she not have this one thing, just once? Was she not to even have something good in her life, however brief?

'Nothing in this castle is fair,' she said. 'That's been true since long before you got here.'

'Even more reason for me to leave you be.'

Leave her be? This was the man who only yesterday was threatening to have her raped if she stepped out of line. And yes, that was part of the persona he put on. The strong tough General taking command, his anger and pain lashing out to scare and hurt her, just as he'd been scared and hurt because of her. It was also because that's what he'd learned in the salt mines. How he'd been treated, so he knew how effective it was, and he the used the tools of his oppressors with dreadful efficiency.

She knew all that. But this seemed such a dramatic reversal, suddenly worrying about what was fair. She wasn't ready for it, didn't understand it. She was his slave. He'd made it clear he wasn't walking that back. So why wouldn't he call on her for such services when he wanted them? Wasn't pleasure part of what slaves did for their masters?

Or was that what worried him so much? Because he'd been through that himself and while he might be comfortable threatening it when his anger was up, he still balked before seeing the threat out.

'Surely you must know I want it too?' she said. 'Doesn't that count for anything?'

His drew back a breath, but at least he turned to face her properly. 'You tend to make decisions that aren't in your own best interests, so far as I've seen.'

She bit back a soft curse; he'd always been damn stubborn when he got an idea into his head. Instead, she took the risk and walked across to him. Slow enough that he could back off if he wanted. He didn't. He stood his ground and let her approach.

She stopped when she was in front of him, back in his personal space, so she had to tilt her head to meet his eyes.

'I am frightened of a lot of things,' she said. 'I'm afraid of what happens when your magicians try to break my binding. I'm afraid of what you will do to see out your aims here.' She hesitated. 'I'm desperately afraid I'll hurt you again, for I couldn't live with myself if I did.'

She reached out a tentative hand. Not daring to hold him or even touch his body, but finding his hand and gripping his fingers. He didn't shake her off.

'But I am not afraid of this,' she said. 'And I would like, for a few moments, to not feel afraid, even if only for a brief while.'

He raised his free hand, tracing a finger light down the side of her face, along her jaw.

'Do I not scare you? I rather thought I did.'

She pressed her lips together. 'Sometimes,' she admitted. 'But it is only with you that I have ever felt safe. Even when you scare me, you still make me feel safe.'

'That makes no sense.'

'I know.'

She leaned closer into him. He cupped his hand around her back of her head, wound his other around her waist, to hold her against him. Skin on skin. Warmth and stickiness. He was hard in his pants, she could feel him against her hip; he wanted her badly. Almost as badly as she wanted him. Her whole body hummed to be held against him, firmly within his hold, secure, possessed.

He leaned down to kiss her again. Lips on hers. Only momentarily, before resting his forehead against her own, breathing the same air with ragged intake of breath.

'Tell me what you want,' he said, almost a low growl.

'I want to know you're in control,' she said, without hesitation. 'I want to give up worrying for a little while. To not think for a while. Please. Command me and I will do.' She held onto his sides, hands sticky on his skin. 'Let me do something right for once. Let me at least try to be good for you.'

He almost pulled back again at that, she could feel the tension in him. So she clung on and held him closer still.

'This isn't you getting to apologise,' he told her. 'That's not what this is.'

'You've already told me no to that.'

The hunger in his eyes was real. He wasn't convinced, but he wanted to be, if her read of his expression was correct.

'You're oh so obedient, is that it?' He sounded breathless. Wanting. The desire in his voice was palpable. 'Such a good girl for me.'

Her limbs melted. The praise, as designed for seduction as it was, struck to the core of her. *Such a good girl for me.* Like she might even please, instead of hurt and damage and betray and harm. She desperately wanted to bring something good, if not to this world, then at least to him. It made her entire body feel boneless with want and need of her own to think that she might.

She hung onto him as an anchor. There was such strength to him, such drive and determination. He could hold her up when she could no longer do so for herself.

He brought his lips to her ear, her jaw, then back to her lips. Raising his hands through her hair and holding her head in place as he kissed her again, deeply this time, with real force and no longer hesitating. Tongue licking into her mouth and taking possession of her, just as she wanted. Leaving her breathless and unresisting and open for him.

He only paused one more time. 'Come attend my bath, slave,' he said, voice low, husky. 'You will see to my needs there.'

She followed him to the pool to do just that.

CHAPTER 13
Salryanna

The water was warm as they waded into it. She followed at his back, her fingers gripped in his, and he turned her as soon as they were standing waist deep in the centre of the pool, firm hands at her sides positioning her where he wanted.

There, he took her in his arms again, kissed her again, as if he couldn't get enough of doing so. Tongue deep in her mouth and hands on her body and there was no hesitation in him now. No second-guessing his own decisions or trying to determine the right or wrong of it, the good or bad. There was only want and desire and need and she fell into it just as deeply as he did.

It wasn't like the old days. It wasn't anything like the old days, those first early fumbles in the forest where neither of them really knew what they were doing, only that they wanted to do it. Somewhere in the intervening years, Callum had learned a thing or two. Good that at least one of them had, for it was far more than she could say for herself.

He held her with an arm behind her back and bent his head to her breast, tracing a tongue from her shoulder to the nipple and mouthing it until she whimpered with the sensation, leaning back in his hold. His other hand ran from her hip down her thigh and pulled her closer against him, so his erection pressed hard against her, and she wondered desperately if she could, or should, reach down to it. She wanted to. To feel him, to touch him, to make him shiver like he was making her shiver, despite the warmth of the pool. Only she wasn't sure what to do.

A moment of panic took her, that she didn't know what she was doing and was so very out of practice at being with him. But then he moved her again, walking her backwards until her calves hit the big steps at the back of the pool.

'Sit,' he said, and the command, light as it was, sent a thrill through her limbs.

She did, but he shook his head.

'Higher up,' he said, eyes dark with desire. 'Out of the water. I want to see you. I want you displayed for me.'

So she shifted to the higher steps, until she wasn't half-hidden by the water anymore. Her ankles were in it still, but only to her lower calves. It brought a tightness in her chest to be suddenly visible, though she'd been walking around his rooms mostly naked since he'd first brought her here and it wasn't like he hadn't seen the entirety of her before anyway.

He stood in the waist-deep water and narrowed his eyes.

'I said displayed. Knees apart,' he said, almost a growl. She could barely breathe as she forced herself to open her legs a little, the flush rising fast up her cheeks.

He gestured with his hand. Wider. Oh the stars. She did it, unable to meet his eyes, feeling so desperately wanton and reckless, vulnerable and needy. Her hands gripped the stone step on either side of her as she stared into the water and looked at him only out of her peripheral vision, trying to tell if this was good enough. If she was good enough.

He took his time. Standing with arms crossed and watching her with appraising eyes. Looking over every inch of her as she sat so shamelessly, legs wide open and naked for his view.

'Beautiful,' he murmured.

She jerked with the unexpectedness of it, looking up with wide eyes, because he didn't mean that. She wasn't the professional soldier here, who'd kept up fitness and athleticism and whose body reflected that. She was malnourished and underfed, awkward and all sharp angles. He was the beautiful one, not her.

Only his expression was soft as he gazed at her.

'You are beautiful,' he said, as if reading the disbelief in her face, and she had to choke back unexpected emotion, blinking away tears.

He came to her, running a hand along her knees and kneeling on the steps between her legs, tracing his fingers firm along her body to her face. Holding her there and leaning in for another kiss.

'Beautiful and so very good for me,' he said against her lips. 'Doing all that I ask and so obedient about it.'

She gasped, unable to help the sound emitting from her lips. A kind of whimper at the tumult of feeling. She raised her hands to his shoulders and clung onto him, but he took hold of them, placing them back on the step at her sides.

'No. I want you to sit there while I explore you,' he said. 'I've waited five years to have you back in my hands, through times I never thought I would. I will not rush this. I want to enjoy it.'

The sheer need in his own voice only spiked her own. The idea that he might genuinely find her desirable, beautiful even, was strange, intoxicating. It wasn't only words, his actions, his entire demeanour, backed that up. He ran his hands down her arms, along her thighs, then brought his lips to her shoulder, mouthing and nipping so slightly at her skin. Leaning into her, between her legs, but not touching her there, not yet. He was taking his time. He was in control.

Which she increasingly felt out of. The feel of him right there, the warmth of him. His lips against her skin, his teeth with the occasional bite that spiked a jolt of want inside her. By the time he was pushing her back so he could mouth her stomach, her hips, her thigh, she was desperate to have him and could not do a thing about it. He wouldn't even let her touch him or hold him. She was just to sit and be touched, be explored, as if he wanted to learn his new possession, until she was shaking with the need of it. Gasping with the strength of his hands on her skin, the feel of his mouth against her stomach, the trace of his tongue as he dragged it down, and down, and down, and—

'Oh. Oh my stars, oh Callum, oh—'

He chuckled, somewhere between her legs and traced his tongue right down the sex of her.

'You like that, my little witch,' he said and parted her labia with his thumbs and leant in again.

'Oh—yes—yes, sir, yes, sir, yes General—'

It made him laugh again, her inability to even speak a coherent sentence. But this sensation of him licking the very centre of her, using his lips and tongue and mouth to really taste her, it was beyond anything she'd ever experienced before. The care and dedication he put into it, the feel of his tongue sliding inside her, put her whole body desperately on edge.

'Please, I don't—I can't—I—' she whispered, not knowing what to do, where to put her hands, except he'd told her not to move, to just sit and let him do what he willed, and she tried, she really did. But when he was making her feel this way, how could she not move?

'Let it go, Salryanna. Let yourself go,' he said, pulling back just long enough to speak the words, before renewing his attention to sex, swirling his tongue around her clitoris.

She did what he commanded. She stopped fighting the sensations and instead let herself go.

The rolling orgasm that shuddered through her body was long and slow and all consuming. Head to toes, whimpers falling from her lips, wordless cries. Pleasure through her clenching limbs.

He held her through it. When her shuddering had calmed, she left shaking in the aftermath, he pushed himself up to sit beside her and wrapped his arms about her, holding her close.

'You did so well, my little witch,' he murmured, lips against her hair. 'You were so good for me. So very good.'

She buried her head into his shoulder and felt tears seep from behind her closed eyes. Tears for being told she had been good, for even imagining that was possible. For the sensations of pleasure. For knowing she was with him, and maybe it wouldn't last, but at least for these few moments she had him back with her again.

'Thank you,' she whispered. 'I...'

But she dragged her words off.

'Yes?' he prompted. He wasn't going to let her get away with not saying what was on her mind.

'It's been a long time, for me,' she eventually settled on saying, and maybe only because she could bury her head in his embrace and not have to look him in the eye when saying it. 'I'm not used to... to uh, feeling that way, to...'

'Hmmm.' He held her tighter. 'You're not used to receiving pleasure. Not around here, in this awful place. You're not used to feeling *good.*'

'I don't deserve good. That's not what I am,' she said, in a low voice she almost hoped was inaudible.

He stiffened. 'Say that again and I'll belt you. I won't stand for it, you hear me?'

So she didn't say it again, but that didn't change the fact that all she'd ever done was bring harm to others, to him most of all. It'd been a long, long time since she'd felt anything so purely pleasurable.

Instead, to cover the moment, she slid down a step and turned to face him, kneeling between his knees, half in the water.

He let her, head cocked as he waited to see what she'd do.

'Yes, sir,' she said, and didn't miss the catch in his breath when she called him that, the honorific. She knew she wanted him to take control, but it seemed he enjoyed being in control just as much. He liked it when she deferred to him.

'What are you up to, little witch?'

'Can I... I mean, would you let me do for you what you just... you know, what you did for me?'

His lips twisted in some amusement.

'I love watching you stumble over the dirty words,' he said. 'You'd make a hopeless soldier. You can't even swear.'

'I'm not a soldier. I'm a witch. One without even magic anymore,' she said, then frowned up at him. 'And now, I'm a slave. So I would like to...to suck my master's cock, if that would so please him.'

That got a laugh out of him. Which was good, because it had taken real effort. She wasn't good with the words, he was right on that, and just saying it made her cheeks flame with embarrassment and a flush of humiliation. All of which brought a renewed heat to her body not quite vanquished by the orgasm only minutes before.

He leaned down, putting his hands on either side of her face, and kissing her. She tasted herself on his lips, lost herself in the sensation of his mouth on hers, even as her fingers gripped hard on his knees.

When he sat back again, he gave her a nod.

'That would please me very much indeed.'

He leaned back on his elbows, legs spread and his words full of command. It brought her yet another flush of pleasure to hear the dark desire in his voice, and from knowing she might please him. From being given the chance.

He was hard, his cock long and curved. She remembered what he liked from the years before, even if she was somewhat out of practice. He'd no doubt had a multitude of lovers across the last five years, while she'd had none, there'd only ever been him. Well, only him that she'd chosen to be with. Nothing else had been her choice, so didn't count.

All of which meant he might know what he was doing, but she did not. And she desperately wanted to. She wanted this to be good for him, as good as he'd made it for her. She had done this before, of course, five years ago in the forest. She didn't imagine she'd been entirely good at it back then, she'd only tried a couple of times. But he'd seemed happy at the time. Surely she could make him happy now, too?

She placed one hand on his cock, then, experimentally, leaned forward to take the tip of it in her mouth. Swirling her tongue around the head. He tasted of sea water, mineral salts, and something sharper, more tangy, underneath. She got braver and put her whole mouth around him, sucking back lightly, and was rewarded by a sharp intake of breath above her as she did so.

It gave her a little confidence, so she tried again, pushing down as far as she could go. She didn't get far, gagging as soon as he went too deep. She pulled back, took a breath, tried again. Gagged again. Which tightened her chest, because she wanted, really wanted—

His hand snaked into her hair at the back of her head. Her new shorter hair, his fingers tangling in it, tightening just enough for her to feel his firm grip. The next time she went down, trying to push further, he guided her to it. Pressure on the back of her head, not forcing her, just teaching her as to how he liked it, and she went with it. Breathing out through her nose, feeling him slip further down her throat, and further again, until her lips reached his base.

He held her there for a moment, long enough for her to feel his hips shift, his cock twitch inside her, before he let her back up. She resurfaced with a gasp and a long breath. Then immediately wanted to do it again.

This time, it was easier. She was learning. His hand in her hair helped, though he didn't push her down again, just left his fingers firmly tangled there so that she could feel his hold. He gave her the space in which to figure it out, within the safety of knowing he would show her if she needed it.

And so she let herself explore.

Licking down to his base, then crouching lower to reach his balls, gently taking each in her mouth, before licking her way back up. Mouthing the shaft of him, the underside of him, then back over the head and using her tongue. Reaching her hand around his base and gently stroking. All the while, she listened to the sounds he was making above her, his breathing, the way it deepened, then shuddered. The occasional fast exhale or gasp. The moan that told her he was genuinely enjoying this. And that he was getting close.

His hand in her hair tugged slightly, then pressed down. Directing her speed, wanting it faster. So she sped up, following his direction, hollowing out her cheeks to suck back on him and using her hand at the same time now. His breathing ragged above her, a low curse vibrating through her ears. She sucked back again, one more time.

His spend hit the back of her throat, a salty taste she swallowed down as he cried out above her, his fingers clutching so tightly in her hair it stung, but she didn't mind that at all. It brought a buzz to her extremities, a need to the sex of her, for him to hold her down as he came, emptying himself into her mouth.

As his muscles began to relax, his fingers loosened in the hair at the back of her head. She slowly withdrew from him. Licking a little to ensure she missed none, then licking her own lips, pressing them together and swallowing. Relishing the taste. His taste. Still hanging on to his knees.

He pulled her to him, shifting down a step or two until they were both sitting in the water side by side. Cupping her face with one hand and kissing her deeply.

She clung to him. 'Was that okay?' She hesitated. 'Good?'

Oh the stars, but the vulnerability she could hear in her own voice was palpable. The shakiness of it. She'd wanted to sound certain and assured. She only felt inexperienced and awkward.

He put a hand to her chin and turned her head so she had no choice but to look at him.

'You were very good,' he said, a repeat of his words earlier, and she flushed, with a smile. 'My little witch. My Salryanna. My slave.'

'Yes, sir.'

She leaned her head against him and for the longest time just sat in his arms, allowing herself to enjoy the warmth of him, and the water, and, for a moment, to even let herself feel content.

For a moment.

CHAPTER 14
Callum

They took dinner on the balcony as the sun was setting. As promised—or was that threatened?—he supervised the meal to ensure she would eat. Vegetables, for the most part, so if she left the meat to the side he allowed that. He knew what extended fasting was like, and what it was like to come back from it. Though in his situation, it hadn't been self-inflicted.

Because he couldn't help himself, he didn't let her dress again after the bathroom. He had dressed, but he had her sit there naked just because he could. Because the flush on her cheeks told him she liked these kind of power games as much as she did. At least when they were games. There was a difference, of course, and for the moment she was consenting to this, obedience, obeying him. It couldn't last, and there could well come a point in the very near future when it had to become real, when he would have to enforce his control and command against her will, and she would not enjoy it so much then. Neither would he.

Those were challenges for tomorrow. He didn't want to think on them. Instead, he wanted to bask in the glow of the now, dwell on how it had felt when she'd clung to him, the way her trusting eyes widened every single time he told her she was good. Her need for the praise was intense. As if she'd never been told anything positive about herself in her entire life.

He was beginning to think that was the case. Except he had told her how wonderful she was, once, those days in the forest. He'd laid his heart bare for her there. Only for her to throw it away.

'You...you live in the capital now?'

She asked it, venturing the question while toying with some broccoli on her plate that, in a moment, he would insist she eat. Her voice so low he had to strain to hear it. She wasn't sure she should ask her questions, it was the first time she'd got brave enough to initiate conversation at all, and he couldn't help the way his heart pumped harder, as if that was progress of some kind.

'I keep a house there,' he said. 'A great big one, with servants and luxury and all the trappings, because what more could a man want, right?'

She bit her lip. 'You sound cynical. I thought it would've been nice.'

'I don't spend a lot of time there,' he said. 'I'm not particularly fond of it. It was a political move, no more. Part of the deal I made with the Light after coming out of the salt mines.'

Her eyes were wide and she risked looking up at him, rather than merely staring at her plate.

'You stormed the capital? You really did that? The stories are true?'

His lips twisted into a smile he couldn't help. He was allowed to be proud of his achievements, was he not?

'I stormed the capital.' He grinned at her. 'I led revolution in the salt mines, then I moved through the countryside forming an army of all those who could no longer stomach the command of the Light, and I stormed their capital, and I...'

'Won?'

'Well, so I'm told.' He shrugged. 'I'm a soldier. I know how to win a battle. The politics is something I've had to learn in the time since and I'm not so fond of it, frankly. Even if I've apparently proven good at it.' His smile tempered. 'The capital is all about politics. Hence my not spending time there if I don't have to.'

She looked out over the balcony to the slowly darkening valley beyond.

'It all seems so far away,' she said. 'I heard the news, of course. That there'd been a threatened revolution, a military coup. Only after you established yourself at top of the armies of the Light did I hear the name of the great General who had achieved so much on behalf of the people.'

He watched her face carefully, trying to read her expression in the growing shadows. Inside the lanterns were lit, but out here it was growing dark.

'Did it surprise you? To learn it was me?'

She shook her head. 'I always knew you would do great things,' she said. 'You were destined for leadership. I was glad when I heard your name. I was glad to know you were succeeding.'

'Did you not think then that we might meet again?' he said, softly.

'By the time I learned your name, the purpose of the General—to destroy the demon threatening trade routes to the south—was equally as known,' she said. 'I knew you would be coming here. It happened fast, after that.'

He let out a long breath. 'Yes. Of course.'

And just like that, they were back to their opposite sides. She was bound to the demon. He was the General of the Light sent here to destroy it.

It was growing too dark and she began to shiver as the cold dropped. He made her eat the last few bites on her plate, then took her inside to where it was warm, a fire already going. The servants doing their job almost invisibly, slipping through servant's entrances, half-concealed, then disappearing again. She'd been in contact with one of them, though he hadn't seen anything this afternoon.

A knock came at the door. Rorks. He sent her through to the bedroom with a pointed gesture, to which she frowned, but did as he instructed. He didn't want her overhearing his conversations with the Captain. She didn't resist, though by the troubled look in her eye, she wasn't so happy about complying either.

He waited until she had disappeared before he faced Rorks in the doorway.

'I'm only checking in, General,' the Captain said. 'I won't keep you. I just wanted to let you know I've a strong lead on...' He hesitated, eyes flicking into the room behind Callum, where Salryanna had just been. 'Well, that other matter. I'll have an update for you in the morning.'

'Thanks, Rorks. Your work on this is appreciated. Keep it confidential, okay?' he said. 'How are the men faring? How's morale? I'm aware I'm not as visible as I should be right now.'

'It's all good. The men are all enjoying the idea you are personally interrogating the Witch Queen and giving her a no good time about it.' Rorks grinned. 'I haven't dissuaded them of the notion.'

Callum huffed an amused breath. 'Yes, well. I suppose the last time they saw her I did have her sitting at my feet in chains. And before that, the collaring. If they're presuming brutality, I can't blame them,' he said. 'Fine, so long as things are under control. Let me know if anything comes up.'

'You got it, Boss.' Rorks's smile was knowing. He'd have seen the fact Salryanna was naked when he'd sent her through to the bedroom. 'So are you giving her a no good time about it?'

'You are entirely too free with your questions, Captain,' he said, before returning the smile. 'I took your advice, my friend. You were right, she does have tendencies similar to your own. It's been...fun.'

Rorks laughed. 'I knew it. Takes one to know one, see. It's the way she looks at you.'

'I'm not as rough with her as I was with you, mind. She needs careful handling right now.'

'You weren't so rough with me in the beginning either. Took me ages to convince you it was what I wanted,' he said. 'You do tend to hold back on your own needs out of care for your partners.'

'You needed careful handling in the beginning too,' Callum pointed out, firmly. 'You were a mess in the first days. Needed to be shown you were loved before anything else.' He paused. 'She needs it even more. You should see how she reacts when I tell her she's good. Like no-one's ever told her that before ever.'

Rorks's smile tempered. Something understanding, if more sombre, in his eyes.

'It's a praise kink, Callum. That's all. She's probably been starved of it for so long, stuck in this dreary place with that demon in her head,' he said. 'But I know from personal experience that if she needs careful handling, then you are the best man for it. You got me through some bad times indeed.'

'Likewise, my friend,' Callum said. Then he paused, narrowing his eyes. 'Are you seeing anyone right now? Because if you're still fucking Seth after that bullshit he pulled this morning—'

Rorks raised his hands to cut that off.

'I fucked Seth a handful of times a year ago, that's it. Not since, because the man is selfish as fuck in the bedroom,' he said. 'Anyway, if I were seeing anyone, you'd know about it, General. I always ask you to check them out first, don't I?'

Callum crossed his arms. 'Your tendency to like the rough ones can get dangerous otherwise,' he said. 'Just be warned, if you've hooked up with some guy I don't approve of, who doesn't treat you appropriately, then I will absolutely have something to say about it.'

'You never do stop looking after a chap.' Rorks's smile was warm. 'Never fear. I'm not seeing anyone right now because no-one of late has been good enough to meet my high standards. You taught me that. To never settle for anyone second rate, because I deserve only the best.'

'Absolutely right you do.'

'So do you, Callum,' Rorks said. 'And that woman has been the pinnacle of your desires the entire time I've known you. Let yourself enjoy this. For once, let yourself have something.'

Callum sighed. 'And tomorrow, when the magicians try to break the binding, and it all goes to shit?'

'So we worry about that tomorrow. Enjoy tonight first. Tomorrow can never be planned for. We learned that in the salt mines, right?'

'Right. Thanks, man.'

Callum gripped his friend's hand, then watched him go back down the corridor with a soft smile. They hadn't been partners for years, yet still Rorks came to him to vet any new relationship. Rorks could like things very rough indeed in the bedroom, to go with a tendency to want to follow another's command, so he relied on Callum's judgement as to whether a potential partner was trustworthy enough to put that much control into their hands. Sometimes it was like he was still asking Callum's permission to see someone. Like they'd used to, in the old days when they were still fucking, but weren't exclusive. He didn't need to anymore, but Callum took the responsibility seriously when he did, and Rorks came to him because he sometimes still needed it. The reassurance, the guidance, the care.

Just as he would always take Rorks's advice in his own relationships, for all he hadn't really taken up with anybody beyond one night stands in the intervening years. Not until now, with Sal. Maybe he wouldn't have her for long, maybe not even past tomorrow, if things went badly. This might even make it harder in the long run, cause them more pain, when they found themselves once again on opposite sides of a divide neither could cross.

But Rorks was right. Tomorrow could never be planned for. They had to take what pleasures they could, while they could, and worry about the rest when they got to it.

He found her in the bedroom, standing in front of the fire. Flickering orange and yellow hues lighting up her face, her skin, her body, reflecting off the collar around her neck. For a moment he just stood in the doorway gazing at her.

Enjoy the night, Rorks had said. Who knew what tomorrow might bring.

When he stepped further into the room, she heard the movement and looked up.

'Has your Captain gone? I thought you would be longer,' she said.

'He has work to see to. He was just checking in.'

He came across to stand behind her. Ran his hands down her arms, firmly, slowly, nudging her to lean back into him. Kissed the lobe of her ear with the faintest of touches and was rewarded by the shudder that passed through her body.

'He is very loyal to you,' she said, leaning her head back on his shoulder, practically melting against him. Interesting how his mere touch could do this to her. 'He looks at you with adoration in his eyes.'

An interesting observation. Not an untrue one either. Salryanna might be silent and fragile, but she was no fool and she paid attention.

'The feeling is mutual between us,' he said. 'Rorks and I used to have a thing. In the salt mines, a time after. We kept each other alive.' He snaked one hand around her waist. The other he ran down her shoulder, tracing fingers lighting across her breast, causing her to gasp. 'We haven't been together like that for a few years now, but the care is still there.'

She went still at that. He was observant too and he was watching her for reaction here.

'Are you...does he...'

'Are you jealous, Salryanna?'

She paused before answering. Perhaps considering her words.

'I don't think so, no,' she said. 'I am glad you had—still have—someone. But I don't like to think I'm intruding in another's space. I don't want to be in his way.'

He kissed her hair, continuing to trace his fingers down her skin, lightly. Circling a nipple, catching it between thumb and forefinger and squeezing gently, so that she inhaled sharply when he did.

'You're not. He and I were never exclusive, and we haven't been a couple, not like that, for a long time,' he said, not missing the way she relaxed again, tension seeping out of her limbs. 'But Rorks and I are close. We have our own rhythm. He looks to me for leadership, direction. I count on him for wise counsel. That's true of us professionally, as soldiers. It's true of us personally as well.'

She nodded. Her back arched as he played with her nipples with one hand, while holding her against him with the other. Her breathing growing ragged the more he did so, taking liberties with her body simply because he could.

He squeezed a nipple harder, twisted a little. She whimpered beneath his hands, without showing any instinct to pull away. The sounds from her went straight to his cock, hardening fast at having her like this.

'Did he give you...counsel, about me?'

He let go of her nipple and instead pushed his hand down over her hip, to the inside of her thigh. Then up, higher. Slowly tracing to the sex of her, parting the lips of her cunt with his fingers, even as she panted in his arms.

'Hmmm. He suggested I should not be holding back from having you in my bed,' he said.

'I agree with him.'

Her fingers reached back, gripped at the fabric of his pants and clung on, as he traced a single finger along the wet inside of her, up around her clitoris, circling it slowly, even as her hips began to shift, chasing friction, wanting more. He held her tighter with his other hand and didn't let her move. Forcing her still and holding her in place while he slowly traced his finger up and down.

'Uhhh...' she uttered, trying to say something, but gasping too hard in need. 'Please, please. Please.'

But he didn't move any faster or harder. He kept the path of his fingers agonisingly slow. Focusing on her clitoris now, but more around it than across it, until she was shaking in his arms, shuddering against him, but unable to reach the climax her entire body was clearly aching for.

'Please what, slave?' he murmured against her ear.

'Please let me...I need...please, can I, sir, please...'

'You still can't say those words, can you?' he said, if anything ensuring his touch went even lighter. 'I like you like this. Aching and shivering and desperate for my touch. Unable to think of anything else. I could keep you like this for hours.'

The whimper that escaped from her lips was divine. She was shaking all over, clinging onto him, entirely open for him to play with any which way he liked. He really could keep her like this for hours, the way she gave herself to him, the way she reacted and moved and touched and shook. The way she *wanted*, so desperately wanted.

But, careful handling. She was also incredibly fragile, vulnerable and, if he were being honest, scared and jumping at shadows. There would perhaps be a time when he could tease her until she could no longer stand and still not let her cum, but right now she needed two things more than anything: one, to know he was in control, and two, that he would look after her.

'My sweet, good slave,' he whispered and increased the friction and pressure just a little more between her legs. 'So good for me. Such a good girl for me.'

She all but cried at that, unable to speak.

He sped up slightly more. 'Come for me, my little witch. Show me how good you are. Let yourself go. For me.'

And she did. There, on command, without pause, the instant he allowed it. Crying out, her whole body shuddering through the orgasm.

And when she was done, he turned her to face him, and he kissed her. Deeply, firmly, with possessive need of his own.

'Now I am going to have you in my bed,' he said. And like the obedient slave she was, she followed him to it.

CHAPTER 15
Salryanna

'Undress me.'

The order shot a bolt of desire through the centre of her, despite the fact she'd barely come down from that last orgasm. She raised her hands to the buttons of his shirt, making sure she didn't fumble them this time due to her aching wrist. She didn't want him distracted by concern for her injuries, not now they'd come so far. Yes it could, and probably would, all turn bad again, maybe as soon as tomorrow. But she didn't let herself think on that. If this was all she could have, then she would enjoy it while she could.

There was only this room, this night. And his desire for her as strong as ever, matching hers for him. For a brief moment they'd found their way back together, to have one more time what she'd once thrown away. If it were temporary, so be it, at least she could have this moment.

She reached to his belt buckle next, then the buttons of his pants. His skin was warm as she pushed the shirt from his shoulders, the pants down over his hips. Stripping him of the garments piece by piece. When on her knees to remove his boots she wanted to stop there, take him in her mouth again, like she had by the pool. She swallowed her own salivating need and focused on the task to hand first, undressing him, sliding his pants over each foot, if unable to help her gaze sliding along the hard length of him as she did.

He caught her looking. His lips twisting amused as he put a finger on her chin and tipped her head up to meeting his eyes.

'So hungry,' he said. He ran a thumb over her lips and she parted them for him, tasting the tip of it with her tongue. 'You want this badly, don't you?'

'Yes, sir,' she said, without hesitation. She enjoyed using the honorific, and he seemed to like it when she did, and she had no other words to express exactly how badly she wanted this. To feel him with her, inside her, taking her away for a few moments of bliss. Helping her forget the rest.

She rose to her feet again and he put his hands on either side of her head, kissing her soundly. She would never get enough of that, kissing him, his tongue deep in her mouth, a slide of his teeth against her own, wet and hot. She gripped onto his sides to keep herself from swaying off balance, needing an anchor and relying on him to provide it. His erection was hard against her hip, already leaking at the end, and with a shaking hand, for it took all her courage, she slid her fingers down to it, touching him. Stroking him slowly while he kissed her, needing to hear those sounds from him again, the way she had in the bathroom. His breath catching in his throat when she used her thumb to smear the wet at the end and pressed her body against his, and was rewarded by his holding her even more firmly against himself.

He broke off the kiss with a gasp.

'Get on the bed. I want to fuck you.'

A shiver crossed her skin at his growled command and she climbed onto the ridiculously big bed this suite was furnished with. Soft and luxurious, was it any wonder she never chose this suite for herself? She'd have been lost in this bed on her own. She shifted to the middle of it now, lying back but propping herself up on her elbows as he came to her. Crawling over the top of her, then leaning down to kiss her again, like he couldn't get enough of that either.

When he reached down to the sex of her, still slick and wet from the orgasm of just before, he didn't hesitate or move slowly. He simply shoved two fingers inside her, hard and fast and as far as they would reach. She cried out with the suddenness of it, arching her back and bucking her hips upwards, losing herself at the feel of his fingers twisting inside her. He used his thumb against her clitoris while thrusting his fingers in and out, adding a third so she whimpered and spread her legs even wider.

'So damn wanton,' he said, finger fucking her hard. 'I know what you need, my slave, my little witch.'

And he did, too. Slipping his fingers out of her, moving himself on top. Forcing her legs further apart with his own and then finally, *finally*, sliding himself inside her.

She made some sound, some unintelligible whimper, as he buried himself deep. Arching her hips up to meet his, his lips back on hers too, her tongue in his mouth. She kissed down his jaw, then hung her head back with a gasp as he thrust into her with particular force. She could feel the collar around her neck and it turned her on all the more, because she really was his, even after everything. No matter all that had happened, the pain and horror of the past, the guilt and the hurt, she was his and that's all she wanted right now.

He moved them, shifting their bodies, his never leaving hers. Trapping one of her arms beneath the side of him and taking hold of her other wrist in a tight grip. Holding her down and thrusting into her harder, rougher. In control and hardly letting her move, and oh stars, but she could barely even think, she could only feel, the sensations of him.

When he moved a hand to reach between them, sliding his fingers across her clitoris, the orgasm burst from her without warning. She clenching and clutching around him, crying out with it.

'Sir, sorry, I'm sorry, oh the stars, oh I—'

He silenced her with his tongue and fucked her even harder through her climax, until she wasn't sure the rolling waves would ever calm. Then he was crying out through his own clenched teeth, muscles spasming, coming hard inside of her.

Breathing heavily and slowing to a stop. Collapsing to the bed, the two of them. He slipped himself from her and they lay, sticky and sweaty. Satiated.

He reached out to take her hand in his and pulled her over, tucking her under his arm. Holding her body against him.

'So what was that apology for?' he asked, after a long moment. 'I swear, I've never known anyone to apologise in the midst of orgasm before.'

She bit her lip, fighting an absurd impulse to say sorry for that as well.

'I wasn't sure if it was...allowed,' she said, very softly, feeling her cheeks flame red. 'So far, you've always, um, you know, told me it was okay to, ummm...you know.'

She was pretty sure her face went even more red when he chuckled.

'I'll admit I've got a thing for orgasm denial. But unless I've explicitly laid down the rule not to, always consider it alright to come,' he said, laughing under his breath. 'God, you get off on this control shit as much as I do. Only you like to give it up, whereas I like to take it. Five years ago, who would've imagined it of us?'

She pushed herself up on one elbow, so she could look at him.

'You were always so gentle with me five years ago,' she said. 'Did you ever want it like...to be in control like this, back then? Or is it only after...maybe because...'

His gaze was soft, meeting her eyes. He used one hand to tuck her hair behind her ear.

'I hardly knew myself then,' he said. 'You were my first. I didn't want to hurt you. I was afraid of my own impulses, so mostly tried to ignore them.'

'Now it doesn't matter. I am your slave. You have the right. You can do anything you like with me.'

A frown fleeted across his features. 'It does matter,' he said. 'I didn't enslave you for my own sexual pleasures. It was a matter of conquest, taking the castle and its queen.'

She ran a hand along his chest. Over the small scars, signs of previous battles.

'I think I wanted sex like this then,' she said, enjoying the warmth of his skin beneath her hand, the solid length of him against her body. His other hand trailed along her back and made her shiver. 'Only I didn't know how to how to ask for it.' She let her gaze shift to his face, then quickly looked away again, to his chest, not his eyes. 'Stars above, I can hardly say the words now.'

'I happen to find your inability to utter a single dirty word rather amusing.'

Her smile was fleeting. 'I always knew I was safe with you in the forest. I would've let you do whatever you wanted, no matter what, because I knew I was safe.'

It felt like his eyes were boring a hole in her. She couldn't meet them. She wasn't sure she knew what she was saying and it was probably confusing the hell out of him too. But she never did say things easily, she hadn't then either, and that was maybe the problem. Her ability to communicate what she was feeling had never been one of her strongest skills.

'And now?' he asked, very quietly.

'You can be terrifying now. You are so much stronger, so much harder, than you were,' she said, because she wasn't going to lie to him. 'I have seen your cruelty, Callum, and your ruthlessness, and more than anything else that tells me what you've been through these last few years, just how bad it was.'

'I'm not the only one who's endured a lot of shit, I think,' he said, grimly.

'Yet despite it all, the honest fact is I feel safer now, with this collar around my neck, with you having claimed your conquest, General, enslaved me and all, than I have at any other time in my entire life.'

His lips parted, as if he had a question, as if he wanted to say something, but wasn't sure what. She didn't blame him. It didn't make any sense to her, either. Anyway, what could he say? That yes she was safe? That he would not hurt her, but would keep her secure no matter what? That he would look after her and protect her and it was alright, they would be alright.

He couldn't say that because none of those things were true.

After a moment, he reached out, tracing his fingers lightly against her cheek.

'Maybe it's because for the first time you are not alone,' he said. 'Maybe because for the first time you don't have to face everything in this castle on your own. I could...*we* could—'

'Callum, stop,' she said, cutting him off as gently as she could. 'You cannot save me. That is not your purpose here and it is not your priority. Even if it was, you can't...it can't be done.'

Something turned hard in his eyes. A flash of flint. The man didn't like to be told what to do, and he really didn't like to be told when something was beyond his capacity. She should've remembered that. They'd sent him to the salt mines half dead from a flogging, expecting him not to last a two-month, no doubt. He'd defied them probably out of spite alone, simply because they'd tried to stop him.

Tell this man something he wanted couldn't be done and he took it as a challenge.

'I'll thank you not to tell me what I can and cannot do, slave,' he said, hard-toned, and oh the stars, she couldn't help but the way her entire body went liquid when he spoke like that. The rough command in his voice, edged with anger, a hint of brutality, that made her want to melt.

She nodded, lying down again against him, curling into his side. Because she couldn't help that either. He did make her feel safe. Even when she knew she wasn't, even when she knew she could never be.

Even knowing that what he planned here was the least safe thing for any of them and there was nothing she could do to stop him.

'You need to listen to me now, slave,' he said, still in that tone. 'I am not going to be stopped by that damned demon. I will succeed and I will take you out of this place with me once I have. I've claimed you and I'm not giving you up. Not again.'

All she could do was cling to him and tell herself this was the man who'd defied the salt mines. Who'd come back from that place of death to conquer half the world. Who'd forced the Light to negotiate and who now had control of their armies and he did the impossible, this man. He was strong enough, and ruthless enough, and determined enough, to change the world.

So maybe he could manage it. Maybe she was wrong.

'Yes, sir,' she said, then held onto him tight. Maybe.

Maybe not.

Just like a daisy, out in the forest.

~

She fell asleep in his arms.

Such a different thing to what she was used to, the never-ending nights when she would stalk the castle battlements just to avoid having to lie in her bed with her eyes closed. The days when she would exhaust herself simply so her body would collapse into sleep out of desperation. Her relationship to sleep was about on par with her relationship with food. Something her body needed to survive, but a difficulty to make herself succumb to.

Only here, in this bed, with him, she drifted off so easily. Warm and satiated and, yes, safe—and maybe it was an illusion, maybe it was only wishful thinking on her part, but she let herself indulge in the feeling regardless. Sleep was sorely needed and he made her feel safe enough to not worry about it.

It didn't last of course. The nightmares still came. Black tendrils of threat and darkness curling their way through her mind, around her heart, separating her organs and tearing through her body. The searing pain of it, the horrific consequences of it. She rarely remembered the details of nightmares afterwards, but the feeling of them, the emotion of them, the depth of her terror of them, that always stayed with her.

Screaming. Over and over, sobbing out her fear and screaming—

'Sal!'

Hands on her shoulders, at her face.

'Sal, wake up!'

She surfaced from the blackness with a gasp, like a drowning woman coming up for air. Callum was leaning above her, expression a picture of concern in the dim-lit shadows. The fire hadn't quite burned down across the room; there was light, but it was low.

It took her a moment. Callum. Bedroom. In bed with him. Her breath coming in shudders and tears still wet on her face.

'I'm sorry,' she whispered, body sinking back, rictus muscles slowly relaxing. 'For waking you.'

He lay on his side so he could face her. Reaching out to turn her so she faced him too and wasn't able to look elsewhere.

'I've told you before what I think about you trying to apologise for nightmares,' he said. 'So don't do that. Next time you try, I'll do something about it.'

She considered that. 'What?'

His eyebrows rose, a smirk touching his lips. 'I don't know. A spanking, perhaps.'

She considered that too. 'I'm not sure I'd be adverse to that. It might not have the effect you're looking for.'

This time, he outright grinned. 'That depends on the effect I'm looking for.'

His hand reached to her side, running down her hip, so she shuffled closer to him. She could feel him hardening beneath the blankets and, still dragged down by the lingering effect of the nightmare, she could only welcome his interest. Pressing her body up against him, it was a distraction, a way of forgetting the darkness, a comfort.

A desire.

'Hmmm. You have done a very good job of distracting me from asking about your nightmare,' he said, though she didn't think he was displeased, not by the way he pushed against her and held her close.

'Is that what I'm doing? I rather thought you started it.'

'Don't get cheeky, slave. And don't think I haven't noticed that you have these nightmares every single time you sleep,' he said. 'I want to know about them. Where they come from. Why you're plagued by them.'

Which were the last questions she wanted to answer, so she reached down under the covers instead, and found the hardness of him with her hand, stroking slowly. Rewarded by the long, deep breath he took and the clutching of his fingers against her hip.

'Perhaps you could give me something else to think about, then, so I sleep better,' she said, biting her lip and looking at him from under her lashes. All the while stroking his length.

He didn't reply, just pulled her into him, mouth crushed down hard on her own without preamble, just with sheer need. She arched back, gripping him to her with just as much force, desperately needing to wipe the awful taste of the nightmare from her mouth, the seeds of it out of her mind, and he could do that. That was absolutely something he could do.

It was a hard, fast pushing together, him rolling on top of her and forcing her legs open with his own, then shoving hard inside her without preparation or any of the gentleness he'd used with her previously. She gasped back from the force of him, letting it diffuse her, take her over, wanting it just like that, more like that, giving in and letting him have her. She was already slick enough from the sex earlier, more than ready for him and desperately wanting.

When he took hold of her wrists, the both of them, and forced them up high above her head and held them down hard with his full body weight as he slammed himself into her, she whimpered a desperate need. He was so damn strong. A soldier, a fighter, muscled and brutal and it took the breath from her, she couldn't move for his hold on her, the force of it. She dissolved beneath it, unable to think, unable to do anything but comply. The power of him took her apart.

When she came, it was with a rolling cry, her body not her own. It was all the more intense for being held down like she was. He was an unyielding force she could struggle against and know he would never let go, he would never lose. He could be relied upon to always be there.

She was still coming down from her orgasm when he let himself come, desperately spending inside her. A tightening of his grip; a slow dissipation as he came to a shuddering still. Falling beside her, and she found herself free, no longer held in place, desire satiated, warm and sticky and done.

She cried then. She wasn't sure why, exactly. Post-orgasmic bliss and all, maybe it was because it was too good, too nice. Maybe it was just the nightmare and all her fears returning. Knowing that no matter how strong or determined or forceful he was, no matter how powerful he made himself, he still could not protect her.

She would still lose him.

So she cried, tears seeping from behind her lids that she tried to hide, though he saw it, of course he did. Gathering her up in his arms and holding her close with gentleness now, soft kisses on her hair.

'Too much?' he asked, in a worried voice.

'Too perfect,' she answered, curling into him.

He didn't ask more. Just let her cry it out while he held her, kissing her and whispering how good she was. As if all he had to do was tell her that enough and she might even start to believe him.

CHAPTER 16

Salryanna

A nd the next morning, again. Waking up to his lips against her shoulder and his arm tightening about her stomach, pulling her back against him. The hardness of him already there and wanting and it was all she could do to lean her head back and find his lips with her own and spread her legs as he pushed her down face first onto the bed and took her from behind. Until she was coming in waves and undone under his hands and gasping. No tears this time, at least.

He didn't let himself climax, not yet, instead slipping from her still hard, lips still against her skin and hands trailing across her body.

'Good morning, slave,' he said, in an admittedly breathless voice.

She shifting around in his arms to face him with lazy movement. 'Morning, sir.' Gave him a smile.

'No more nightmares,' he declared, with something of a smug look, as if that were a victory he had won. 'Seems you can sleep peacefully, given the right conditions.'

She reached her hand under the covers to find him still hard as anything, sticky with her own wetness, stroking him slowly as she pressed her body against his own. It was easier to distract him, and herself, with that, than to respond to his words. He wanted to feel like he'd helped her and who was she to deny him that? He could not save her, but for the moment it wouldn't hurt to let him feel good about the possibility, just for a little while.

'Can I taste you?' she said, a question that took all her courage. But if she'd knelt before him yesterday and stated outright she wanted to suck his cock, then she could at least say that much.

He kissed her, hands by her face.

'Such a damn temptress you are, little witch,' he said, against her lips, before pulling back. 'Another time. I want to be inside you this morning. Come bathe with me so I can fuck you there.'

So they took it to the bathroom, and into the warmth of the mineral spring pool, and he led her into the water and sat on the steps and she crawled over his lap. Sinking down on top of him until he was deep inside of her. He held one arm behind her back, while the other clutched at her hip, as she shifted her hips against him and it was a slow burn, heated undoing this time, for he wouldn't let her speed things up and he kept the pace steady. Not fast and rough, but just as insistent, until she was whimpering and needy and clinging to him.

'Don't you come, not yet,' he said. 'Not until I say, this time.'

She all but cried, she was so close. 'I don't...know if I can stop it.'

'You can. You know you can. For me,' he said. 'Hold yourself right there for me, in this moment, this burning state of need, without going over.'

'I can't.'

'You can. You're a good girl for me. You can do it.'

And she did, because he believed she could, and she wanted desperately to hear him call her good again. She wanted to be good. So she held herself back from climax even as he kept the slow, steady movement going, until she was wrecked with need and seeing stars and unable to think. She simply knew she burned for him and that was her entire world, for those few moments. There was nothing else.

When he did let her come, it was with a command, an order. 'Now, slave. Come now, my good, good girl.' She cried out, clinging onto his shoulders, losing all sense of space and time. Only aware of him coming inside her at almost the same time, his lips against her skin as he did.

For a long time after she stayed sitting across his lap, holding onto him. He didn't seem to mind, just held her, and maybe he wanted it too.

They washed. She massaged his back to ease some of the stiffness from the scars, and he thanked her for it. Then, back in the bedroom, dried and cleaned, she watched him dress. Her sitting on the bed again, because he wouldn't let her help and it wasn't like she had any clothes to get dressed into.

'Do you need me to...'

She let her words drag off, because she wasn't even sure what she could do, only that it felt wrong to be sitting there just watching and not doing something.

He gave her a raised eyebrow. 'I appreciate the desire to serve, but exactly how much do you know about military uniforms?'

'Nothing,' she admitted. 'I didn't keep a standing army in the castle.'

'Maybe you should've. I might not have walked in and taken over quite so easily, if you had.'

Still, he opened both cupboard doors, displaying his excruciatingly neat organisation of clothes. Lacking in variety, of course. That was the military for you. He threw a thumb at the carefully folded under shirts, tops, and pants down one side.

'Working uniform,' he said. 'Battle dress. Informal, easy to move in. Easy to fight in. Also worn for non-combat everyday work or training, or when off-duty. More so for my men than myself; I'm their General, I never consider myself off-duty.'

Of course he didn't. He was a leader and a rebel soldier who'd taken over the biggest army in the land and conquered realms with it. The man was a workaholic, if nothing else.

The next section of cupboard was hanging buttoned shirts and well pressed pants; the kind of clothing he was in now, if still half unbuttoned.

'Service uniform,' he said, indicating these. 'Everyday wear, my standard. Unless I state otherwise, if I do ever send you to pick out a uniform, this will be what I'm looking for.'

She nodded, not sure why it gave her a sense of warmth that he would trust her with his things.

Finally he turned to the far end of the cupboard. More hanging, well pressed, carefully stored clothes.

'And dress uniform,' he said, indicating the elaborate jackets. 'Formal occasions, public addresses. The full kit.' He gave her a smile. 'Fancy dress, Rorks calls it. He hates the full regalia, says I made him my Captain just to torture him with it. That man is far more at home on the battlefield than he is at a formal event.'

She didn't say, *so are you*, though she did think it. Remembered him saying yesterday that the politics of the capital wasn't his preferred environment, that he didn't stay at his house there much. Did he even have a permanent place he considered home? His army had taken a lot of land, and won a lot of battles, since his time as their leader. Perhaps he had been on the move, shifting between one temporary place to another, ever since coming out of the salt mines.

He turned back to her with a shrug. 'And I wouldn't worry about learning the rank insignia or other pips. I'm the boss, that's all you need to know.'

He liked it. Being the boss. Not only with her, but with the soldiers as well. He fit so well into leadership, control slotting easily into his hands. At least that was something she could be glad of. That he had created a life for himself, he was a success, he knew where he was going and what he wanted and he had the ability to get there.

She pointed hesitantly to the formal jackets with the piping and gold and elaborate insignia.

'That's what you wore in the throne room,' she said. 'The day you had me brought to you, from out of the dungeons.'

'You don't publicly enslave the Witch Queen every day. That's a formal occasion if there ever was one,' he said, with only the barest hint of a victorious smile. He was still riding high on that victory over her. She supposed he would for a long while yet.

'It's nice to know I'm worth dressing up for.'

That was rewarded with a snort of laughter. He reached into the cupboard and pulled out another shirt, a standard uniform one, and threw it at her.

'There. That's your clothing for today,' he said. But then he also pulled out a pair of the working uniform pants and tossed those across to her too. 'You can also wear those.'

She raised her eyebrows. 'You're allowing me to wear clothing that actually covers my body to a decent degree?'

'Don't get smart, slave. Yes I am allowing you to wear more clothing today, but it is still very obviously *my* clothing,' he said. He was enjoying calling her *slave*. That was okay. She rather enjoyed it too.

She pulled the shirt on, doing the buttons up, if leaving the top ones undone in line with what he'd insisted upon yesterday. Rolling up the sleeves, because he was so much bigger than her and they otherwise fell over her hands.

The pants obviously didn't fit. She had to roll up the bottoms of them quite a way, and bunched it all in at the waist. There was a rope belt with the pants that allowed her to tie them tight just above her hips, and it would be enough to keep them up, though she wouldn't want to run or move fast in them, for fear they'd fall down from the activity.

When she was done, she faced him, feeling utterly ridiculous. He only gave her a nod.

'It'll do,' he said. 'It'll still send the right message that you belong to me and I've dressed you in whatever I had lying around.'

'You say you aren't fond of politics, yet I think you must be good at it,' she said. 'You know how to sell the message you want people to take away.'

'That's a hard learned skill, not one that comes naturally,' he said. 'I'd rather just fight an issue out, but that isn't always, or even usually, the most effective course.' He cocked his head as he considered her. 'Taking this castle by force was easy. It wasn't like you were protecting it to any degree. Holding onto power here, however, will require my achieving and maintaining a legitimacy in the eyes of the valley. Without it, I'll just be overthrown in a year or three myself.'

'Are you planning on staying?' For some reason, that surprised her. 'I thought this was just another conquest. That your point here was the demon, and once dealt with, you would move on.'

He was silent a moment. Maybe deciding how much to say.

'Success here is critical for my longer term plans,' he said at last, selecting words with obvious care. 'If I defeat the demon, I will secure this valley and save its people, bring a more peaceful existence to their lives. I will also secure a strategically important location for my purposes. Sea freight must move through this valley to the inland. There is no other way through the mountain range. It's politically valuable territory.'

'I'm aware of that. I was Queen here for five years. I know the political leverage of the geography, believe it or not.'

'You never used that leverage though. You barely seemed to pay attention to anything outside your castle.'

She pressed her lips together. 'I had other things to focus on.' She shook her head. 'But if you're just handing it over to the Light command anyway, why—'

She stopped. Suddenly. He said nothing, watching to see if she would make the connections.

Her mouth opened slightly as realisation came.

'You're not handing anything over to the Light command. You're setting yourself up in opposition to them,' she said. 'This is revolution by stealth.'

'This is revolution without bloodshed,' he said. 'I may be a soldier, but that only means I understand the consequences of battle better than any. When I marched on the capital after the salt mines, I could have challenged them then. I could have affected a coup and maybe would have won. But it would have been...bloody. And I'd seen enough unnecessary slaughter already.'

'So you negotiated with them instead,' she said. 'But now, if you do it this way, you will have a strategic base of operations from which to challenge the capital, the army behind you, and the people's good will and support.' She paused. 'Do it this way and...you can't lose.'

'Oh, I can lose. I'm staking everything on this. And I have to defeat your demon first. Save this valley from him.'

The breath went out of her. It was audacious. It was risky. It was all Callum, just the kind of thing she would have expected from him. Aim for the stars. He'd always been like that, while she had been the more pragmatic one, the practical one. The one who saw the difficulties inherent in his grand plans.

He had asked her to run away with him once with only his dreams to back them. And he'd fallen because of those dreams, because she had dashed them and he'd suffered for it.

Now he was back with even bigger dreams. And an even bigger distance to fall, should he fail.

But to just imagine it...

'You asked why I was prepared to clothe you more decently today, and that's the reason,' he said. 'What we go to this morning is likely to be difficult enough as it is. You being severely underdressed is a distraction neither of us need.'

She swallowed, her mouth suddenly dry.

'Why is this morning different to yesterday? You had me in only your shirt out in front of petitioners and your senior captains, then.'

His expression was serious. 'This morning my magicians begin their work,' he said. 'This morning, they attempt to break the binding upon you.'

And in that, all her own dreams came crashing back down. Because that was why this was going to fail, and where this would all end, and she couldn't even warn him about what was to come.

CHAPTER 17

Salryanna

The magicians had set themselves up in one of the empty halls of the castle. There were plenty to choose from; after she'd sent everyone away, that's all there was: empty spaces. Now, Callum was filling them again, bringing in his men and associated hangers on, servants, tradespeople, and others. It gnawed at her to see so many inside the castle walls.

But it was the magicians in this big stone hall that worried her most. At least they'd kept others away; this room was fairly isolated and mostly empty apart from a few chairs and a table against the wall. There were three magicians in there, all men of course. The Light Command didn't value women and it hadn't taken her more than a glance at Callum's army to notice the officer class were all men. Yet she had glimpsed women among the ranks, which had to be new. Callum didn't think the same way as the Light Command. He'd said to her five years ago that women were equally effective soldiers as men and he'd happily fight beside any. It was only the Light Command who didn't allow it, but he was already changing that, slowly, in small ways. What else might he change if he no longer had to answer to them at all?

One magician, an older man, stepped forward when Callum led her in. He didn't even glance at her, only looked to Callum. She'd hardly be important to him as a person, or even as a fellow magic user. She was simply the Witch Queen, a position and an enemy to defeat.

Someone to break.

She surreptitiously scanned the room while Callum spoke to the man. The other two magicians were younger, but not too young; they'd all be experienced and she knew from the collar around her neck that they had real power. There were sigils already marked out on the floor, large painted circles with arcane symbols she could well read, and could tell from that alone they knew what they were doing.

Her hands were sweaty, she wiped them against her pants, trying to calm her racing pulse. There were only a few possible outcomes from this and all were very bad. She'd had no further contact from Francis and no backup plans she could be sure would work.

Contain the damage, it's all she could do now. And if she was to do that, then there was only one real option before her.

She tried to blink back the prick of tears, because this was inevitable, dammit, and she had no right to self-pity now. She'd chosen her path five years ago. Now she had to commit to the reality of it.

Keep Callum safe. Keep the others in the castle safe. That was her only focus.

Once Callum had spoken to the magician, he turned to her. His expression was sombre. He nodded to the single wooden chair in the centre of the room.

'You should sit down now,' he said.

She swallowed unease, eyes scanning the floor again, the sigils and signs marked upon it. Three concurrent overlapping circles with the chair in the centre space. It was a prison, of sorts. Once she stepped in, and they began their rituals, she would not be able to step out again.

She raised her chin and straightened her shoulders, then stepped over the lines drawn on the floor. Walked directly to the chair and sat upon it.

'The Witch will need to be tied down,' the older magician announced. One of his juniors was holding a rope and came towards her with it.

She couldn't help it, she shied back with a quickly caught breath and a defensive shake of the head. She didn't want that man anywhere near her.

Callum cut the man off. 'I'll do it,' he said, taking the rope from him and coming to where she sat. Walking over all those sigils and signs as if they meant nothing, and to him, they didn't. He wouldn't be affected. Even after the magicians began all he had to do was stay out of the way and he'd be fine.

For a man who'd happily enslaved her and paraded her around as his property, he certainly looked reluctant when approaching with the rope. She put her hands on the arms of the wooden chair to show him it was alright, she wasn't resisting this. She just hadn't wanted the magician to come near her.

'This is not how I imagined myself first tying you,' he muttered when he took the first length of rope and wound it around one of her wrists. Which made her flush because, well, he had imagined it. Much like she had.

'It's okay. This is necessary,' she said. 'Nobody can be sure how I'll react once they start the ritual. Even if I try to remain in place, I may not always be in control of my physical self.'

He didn't look like it was okay, he looked like he was hating this. But he moved to tie down her other wrist anyway. He made the ropes firm, the knots tight, without being cutting or painful. She couldn't move her arms at all. There was something almost comforting in that.

'So who will be in control of your body, if not you?' he said, a trace of bitterness in his tone. 'As if I couldn't guess.'

She bit her lip. 'Callum, it's okay, really. This is the right thing to do.'

His eyes flashed flint; the man really didn't like to be told what was the best action, even when she was trying to tell him he was right. She wished she believed it herself, but there was no other choice now. This was the only way, as much as it broke her heart to know it.

'I don't like not understanding the process,' he said. 'I don't like not being across the full detail. This magic, it's not my thing.'

'You're a soldier, I know,' she said. 'But this isn't a battle that can be fought with swords and fists. That's why you have magicians working for you. Trust in them.'

She didn't, of course. She wouldn't have trusted those men if they'd offered her salvation on a plate. Still, they worked to the cause of the Light and that would be enough here; Callum could trust them to the extent that they would further his overall aims. The rest was only minor detail.

He bent to tie her ankles to the chair legs, one then the other. She was in bare feet still, his trouser legs rolled up the calf. The rope was tight around them. She was glad for the feel of it, the strength of the bonds he tied her with. She would not be able to get out and that was important. Once this started she may well try, unable to help herself, and she couldn't let herself do that. She had to stay in place. She had to see this through.

She blinked back the tears again. She couldn't let him see them. She couldn't let him question this, not now.

'You better tie my body down as well,' she said and his eyebrows went up.

'Sal, is this really—'

'This is the only way,' she said, and took a long breath. 'You must defeat the demon.' Then, more of a whisper. 'I want you to defeat the demon.'

He paused, rope still in hands. 'I don't know whether to believe we're on the same side or not. I don't know whether to trust you.'

'You don't have to trust me. Tie me down and your magicians will do their work. This is what you came here for.'

So he did, winding the rope around her chest and the back of the chair, until she was firmly held in place. There would be no escaping these ropes and that was important. She didn't want any escape here.

When he straightened, he looked grim indeed.

'When this is done, the binding will be broken,' he said. 'You will be free to tell me the secrets of this castle. What I need to know to destroy the demon.' He paused. 'If you so choose to.'

'I know.'

'You need to know that if you choose *not* to, if you don't collaborate with me, then I will need to do what I can to get that information from you anyway,' he said, voice tight. 'I will need to see this through.'

Which was a long way of saying he'd need to interrogate her.

Torture her, even. Whatever was needed to make her talk. He might not want to use those exact words, but she knew what he meant, and if she were a better person she might even assure him that she would tell him willingly, when she could. That if he broke the binding, and she was free to, she would give him all he needed.

She couldn't tell him that. She would not lie to him. That wasn't how this was going to go.

'I know,' she said instead, and did not miss the way his jaw clenched at her vague response.

He took a step away. Before suddenly turning back and slamming both his hands on the arm of the chair, over her wrists, and leaning forward. His face close to hers with a tight expression.

'Sal, if there is anything, *anything*, I should know before we do this, you need to tell me now,' he said. 'Don't hold back on me. Not again.'

She could feel her eyes go glassy. She wanted so desperately to reassure him. She wanted him to kiss her and hold her and tell her it would be alright, that he would make everything okay. He would save her and protect her and love her and they would all be fine, because he would make it so.

But that wasn't how this was going to go.

She tried to smile, but it failed.

'I know you don't want me to apologise,' she said, and could hear the waiver in her own voice. 'So I won't. But I will bear the guilt of what I did to you with all-consuming regret right to my dying breath. You didn't deserve any of it. You need to know that.'

'That's not what this is about, Sal.' He shook his head. 'There is something you're not saying, something you're hiding. I know you. Work with me here. Please.'

She blinked fast, tears too obvious, wet on her cheeks.

'You need to keep your focus on your end goal. Defeat the demon. Overturn the command of the Light,' she said. 'Save this land, Callum, please. I believe you can do it. You are the strongest, bravest, most clever man I have ever known.'

'I don't know what you're trying to tell me, Sal, but this ritual, it's not going to be easy, is it?'

She shook her head. That was the understatement.

'It's going to get very rough,' she said quietly. 'And that's okay. It is okay. You need to focus on your purpose.' She gasped back a breath. She was so scared and he must see that. If she wasn't tied down, she'd be shaking. 'Just...please, if you could be in the room? Don't come near me, don't come in the circle, it's too dangerous. But...just be somewhere I can see you? I just need to know you're nearby. Then I'll be okay. I'll have the courage to see this through, then.'

It spooked him, her saying that. She could see it in his face. But how could she not? He nodded, hesitating, not wanting to do this. He knew he was about to hurt her badly. Even if he didn't know anything else, he knew that.

It was going to be so much worse than that. She wished she could warn him. She wished she could tell him she was sorry.

'I'll be here,' he promised and straightened. 'I'm not leaving you. Keep your eyes on me.'

'Thank you.'

He turned away to step out of the circle, but she couldn't help herself. She had to call him one more time.

'Callum,' she said, and he looked back over his shoulder. 'I...I just wanted to say, I'm glad you came here. I'm really glad, more than you could possibly understand, to have had this chance to see you again. Being with you has been the most blissful and most wonderful experience of my life and I wouldn't change my time with you for all the world.'

A frown settled deep across his face. She'd made it sound too much like goodbye. Because that's what it was. Only she couldn't tell him that.

Then the magicians were asking him to move right back, ushering him out of the circles and to the edge of the room, and the candles were lit and the ritual initiated.

It was begun.

The low intonation was a pressure in the back of her head. Not difficult at first, more like a buzzing, an insistent annoyance. Compared to all else she'd experienced these last five years, that was almost nothing.

It didn't stay at nothing though.

The magicians chanted their spells from the three points of a triangle marked across the circles, of which she was in the centre. The candles produced a smoke and a scent turning sour. She grimaced at the fetid smell of it, worse when she could taste it, shifting her head side to side as if that would ward off the smoke. It didn't help. Gritting her teeth wasn't any better.

She coughed when it went down her throat. Strained unwittingly against the rope tying her to the chair. The volume seemed to rise, a chanting that brought actual pain now, a burning heat inside her bones. Like the chair was hot, like the very air was hot. A temperature that rose fast until she had to bite down hard to conceal her cries.

Her eyes flicked upwards. Searched for him, knowing he must be there. There. Standing against the wall far back, but directly in her line of sight. His eyes were wide, his expression worried. Watching her.

She looked to him to help her keep focussed. To remind her of what this was and why she must let it happen.

A whimper escaped from between her teeth anyway and her fingers curled in as she tried to ward off the pain.

The magicians around her moved and something ramped up with them. A rushing, an invisible piercing. Like a sword had run through her, but there was no sword and there was no one near her. This time, she couldn't disguise her cry.

He jerked forward as he heard it and so she determined to fight harder.

A magician appeared to her left, close enough in his protected circle to land in her sight. She snarled at him, animalistic and aggressive. A growl that threatened. She would tear him apart if he got too close. She would rip the very flesh from his bones.

He was not stupid enough to come close.

Instead, he raised something, a token, a cup of liquid, and splashed it at her. It landed across her face and shoulder.

She screamed.

The burning. She pulled at her bonds, trying to rip her limbs from the ropes, anything to get away, get out of this. But she was tied tight and there was no escape to be had.

She looked for him again, to give her courage. To remind herself of why. He stood stiff, hands clenched into fists at his side, and she wished then she'd asked him to leave the room after all. So he didn't have to see. She'd been so selfish asking him to stay, simply because she was scared to face this alone. She should've thought better, she should've realised how it would be. She should have asked him to go.

'You don't have to—' she tried to say, but the words wouldn't form, she couldn't make her mouth work. Her body was hardly her own.

And the magician threw more of the water, the liquid, whatever it was, and she cried out an agony at the top of her lungs.

'Is this really the best way?'

Callum. Urgent in tone. Questioning them, perhaps questioning himself.

It took everything she had within her to whisper. 'Keep. Going.'

She didn't know if he heard and either way the magicians didn't stop. The burning was going to take her, she couldn't hold it off. She just had to hang on. That's all. Hang on long enough, give them the time enough, and it would be okay. She could do this. She could do—

Something tore inside her. A ripping of flesh under the skin. A blackness across her sight and she could not see for the darkness and not hear for the infernal roar and her skin tore and there was a tearing, a cutting, inside.

'Sal!' Callum's voice, raised loud. She couldn't see. She could barely hear him.

'Keep.' She had to gulp back breath. 'Going.'

Her words got lost in crying screams as the tearing inside her contin-ued. But the chanting continued louder. The burning water and the magicians doing their work.

Choking. She was choking. Coughing. On fire. If it wasn't for the ropes, she'd have tried to run. If it wasn't for him somewhere there, she'd have begged to be let go.

She had to see this through. The agonies were white hot and ever-lasting.

'Stop!'

A new voice.

'Boss, Stop!'

'Rorks?'

She tried to force her eyes open, but there was only darkness.

And a familiar voice.

'Oh stars, stop, you bastards! You're killing her! Don't you see you're killing her!'

She tried to say it. *Keep. Going.* She tried, but the words were lost in the choking darkness and the pain and the burning. She tried to tell him that it was okay, she was supposed to die, that was the point.

But the pain became too much and she was lost in the darkness and then there was nothing else. There was only agony.

CHAPTER 18
Callum

Callum didn't like this. He really didn't like this.

It escalated so fast. One moment he was tying her wrists and ankles to the chair, and she was giving him cryptic statements that sounded way too much like *goodbye*. The next she was screaming in the kind of pain he hadn't heard uttered since...well, since the salt mines.

All he had to hang onto was his own determined purpose and her own words telling him he must stick to it.

Keep going.

She said it, between screams. And though it tore into him, ripped at his heart, he let it continue because even she had warned him this would be rough. The breaking of a bond between the demon and his witch queen. That was not going to be easily severed. They'd both known there would be pain.

He couldn't stand still. He tried to keep in front of her, in her line of sight. But he stood stiff, his hands clenched, and hated not knowing what the magicians were doing. Hated not knowing what any of this was.

And then she screamed and her eyes...her eyes went black.

He almost stopped it then.

Keep going.

He let it continue because she had told him he must, because his purpose here was set. The demon was no ally of hers. She'd suffered these last five years too and that was due to the demon. If he was to help her, he had to ensure this bond was broken. Only then could he free her, and the rest of this valley, from that creature's yoke.

Her cries were piercing and made his heart break.

'Stop! Boss, stop!'

It was an unexpected voice. He turned on instinct, frowning. 'Rorks?'

His Captain came rushing in, dragging with him another Callum didn't recognise. A tall, blond servant, who took one look at what was going on, and tried to rush into the circles.

'Oh stars, stop, you bastards! You're killing her! Don't you see you're killing her!'

Callum grabbed the person and hauled them back before they could step into the circle. 'Stop, you'll die!' he hissed, but they only struggled in his arms.

'You're killing her! Can't you see?' They turned to face him, pulling away. 'You've got to stop this. It's destroying her. She can't heal, her magic is cut off. The demon is eating her from the inside!'

Something like a spear pierced the insides of Callum's chest. 'What?'

The newcomer looked panicked. 'Stop it now or she'll die!'

And in the same moment, Salryanna uttered the most blood curdling, pain-filled scream that went on and on. Even Rorks backed away at the sound.

Callum twisted to look back at her, tied to the chair by his own damned bonds, to see blood spilling from her mouth and several long bloody lines appearing across the shirt she wore. As if there were gashes opening up in her skin. As if she were being torn apart.

He made an instant decision.

'Stop!' he demanded, with such force and command that the magicians turned to him with shock. Only then, they resumed the chant. They didn't actually stop. And he couldn't step into the circle, he'd been warned of that already.

So he grabbed the closest one and shook the man hard.

'Stop this now or I'll have your head!'

The man gasped and stopped the chant. Gestured to his fellows. Salryanna's screams quietened the instant the magicians chanting stopped, though the blood still poured from her mouth, and her shirt was dripping red.

Callum took the risk and presumed it was safe enough.

He ran into the circle. Nothing harmed him, so he went straight to Sal in the chair. She was shaking wildly and breathing a gurgling breath as the blood spilled from her lips, soaked through his shirt from her body.

'Sal? Sal, can you hear me?'

He dove to his knees in a panic, pulling at his own damn knots to let her free. She didn't open her eyes, she didn't stop shaking. Didn't seem to recognise he was there.

'The collar!' the newcomer called out. 'You have to take off the collar, so her body can heal.'

At that, even Callum hesitated. Since he'd got here, the only thing saving him and all his men and everyone in this castle from the wrath of the Witch Queen was that collar dampening her ability to use her magic.

It was only a moment. Then he reached into his pocket and pulled out a key and unlocked the damn thing. Wrenched it from her neck, blanching to see that it had left a brutal burned ring all the way around her throat.

As soon as he pulled it off her, her gurgling whimpers stopped. And she slumped, into his arms, utterly unconscious and covered in blood.

He'd almost killed her. This was his fault. She might not even live yet.

He'd near killed Salryanna.

The medics met him in his rooms, two of his best, so Rorks must have been the one to send them. He had picked her up from that awful chair in that awful room, crying out for someone to get the medics, before carrying her back to his suite. Stalking through the corridors and practically kicking the door open. Placing her so gently on the bed, then immediately trying to clean some of the blood from her, inspect her wounds.

The medics rushed in without preamble. They didn't even give a basic salute. That was fine, it's what medics did and Callum didn't give a fuck about protocol right now. He stood back to give them space, breath tight in his chest, and watched as they stripped his bloodied shirt off her.

'Oh god.'

Rorks came in at that same moment, following the medics and dragging that damned servant with him. The horror in his voice echoed the sensation in Callum's chest at the sight of Sal's body. Her chest was covered in deep gashes, long and brutal. Like someone had taken to her with a serrated knife, except the wounds weren't that clean cut, they were more like claw marks. Like she'd been torn by a beast.

A beast clawing at her from the *inside*.

All Callum could do was stand back and hope the medics were able to do something. His muscles stiff, hands clenched into fists at his side, but otherwise unable to act. The activity around the bed was fast, urgent and expert, wounds being cleaned, bandaged. She wasn't profusely bleeding anymore and he wasn't sure why, for they were deep wounds, but they had a seared look to them. Like they'd been cauterised.

What could have done that?

What kind of pain must that have caused her?

But he knew the pain she'd been in, he'd witnessed her suffer it. He'd heard her cry it out loud. While he'd stood and watched and let it happen and now had almost killed her.

A hand, warm, felt its way around his arm and squeezed. Rorks. He was glad for the surreptitious gesture of comfort, even if he couldn't react. All he could do was watch the medics and desperately wait for news.

When it came, it was almost positive, but also not. She was not in immediate danger, her wounds were not bleeding out, there was no reason she shouldn't heal. Yes she was unconscious and they weren't sure why, but it was probably a good thing, for it would allow her body to rest, maybe recover.

They couldn't tell him what had made those marks, what had clawed and torn through her flesh. Nor could they say what further damage it might have inflicted inside her. But they did not need to tell him what it was, he already knew.

The demon had done that to her. And it was Callum's own fault that he could.

'Boss?'

Rorks's voice was low, careful. Callum made himself turn from where the medics were making Sal as comfortable as possible, having done all they could for now. She looked like she was sleeping. She looked almost peaceful. Except she was never at peace, not even in sleep, she was plagued by nightmares constantly and her days weren't much better and had the woman any peace at all? Ever?

It wasn't like he'd made that any easier for her.

There was nothing to do now but wait and hope she healed and woke up.

'Boss, did you want to...'

Rorks dragged his words off, but gestured to the servant brought with him. Tall, blond, androgynous, and staring daggers at Callum.

'Yes, I most certainly do,' Callum said, through his teeth. 'Other room, not here. I want to ask our new friend some extremely pointed questions. Bring your sword, Rorks.'

He waited until the medics had given him all the information they could and left, and that he was sure Salryanna was comfortable and breathing, and then he went out into the sitting room. Rorks brought the other, the servant who was no servant.

Callum pulled a hard-backed chair from the dining table, plonked it in the centre of the sitting room, and gestured to it.

'You,' he said, directly to the stranger. 'Sit. You're going to answer my questions.'

They pursed their lips, chin rising. 'Just so you know, I don't recognise your authority. I serve only my Queen.'

'Your Queen isn't in any condition to answer my questions right now, so you're going to instead. Sit the fuck down.'

Rorks backed up Callum's furious words with a raise of his sword and a hand on the other's shoulder, directing them to sit. Thank the gods for his Captain, who knew when to back him up, what he needed, always. The two of them worked together seamlessly.

The other sat. Primly, stiffly, unhappily. Callum stood in front of them and crossed his arms.

'Right. What's your name? Who are you? Because you're sure not a servant,' he said. 'And don't think to hide anything. I know you've been communicating with Sal, I've seen the two of you together.'

They at least had the grace to wince at that revelation.

'Francista Jeremiah Solsten Quinze,' they almost spat out. 'Francis, if you will. I'm her governor. When she became the Queen, she assigned the governance of the valley to me.' They paused. Shrugged with some petulance. 'I'm also the closest thing she has to a friend. The Queen doesn't exactly let people close.'

Which, for some reason, tore even harder at Callum's chest, kind of like the wounds across Salryanna's.

'She said she sent most of the castle away when she took over,' Callum said.

'Most? She sent everyone away. Almost no-one came here except me, a couple of day staff who never stayed overnight, and deliveries,' they said. 'She wouldn't let anyone near. She didn't want to endanger them. She was afraid of others getting hurt.' They exhaled a suddenly weary breath. 'It was just her in this damned place. Her and the demon she can never escape.'

Callum sucked back air. The worse part was, he could imagine it. He could see that she would do that. Send everyone else away until it was just her, no matter it made it all the worse for her, no matter how awful it was. Rorks didn't look any happier than he felt, holding his sword on Francis in the chair, but his eyes on Callum. Worried.

'She was determined to bear the burden of this place on her own,' Francis said, into the silence following their last words. Some of the stiffness had gone out of them, their own despair showing through. 'And nothing I could do, nothing I could say, would change her mind on that.'

I belong to the demon.

She'd told him that all along. And he'd refused to countenance it. How much had she tried to say in half-truths or oblique references? Never telling him anything outright. Never trusting him.

But he had stormed her castle and taken it by force, enslaved her in the most humiliating fashion he could devise. That didn't exactly lay groundwork for trust.

None of these thoughts swirling through his head would help right now. He had to focus. He had to keep his eyes on the end game.

'What happened back there?' he said. 'What happened to her? Explain this to me, because I'm bloody tired of being kept in the dark on critical points of fact.'

Francis gave him the nastiest look he'd seen on them yet.

'You almost killed her by attempting to break her binding, that's what happened to her,' they snapped. 'That collar stopped her from being able to heal. The demon was eating her up from the inside and she couldn't heal herself with magic. Your damned ritual to surface the demon was destroying her before your eyes and all you did was stand there and watch her fucking scream the agony of it.'

Callum's whole body pulled back, as if he'd been hit, because that's what it felt like. A full body blow, a nausea in his gut, because what part of that wasn't true?

He couldn't let it distract him. He couldn't focus on his own emotional turmoil right now. He had to know the reality of what he was dealing with once and for all.

Focus.

'That wasn't what I asked,' he said, firmly.

Francis clenched their jaw. 'She didn't tell you anything, did she?'

Callum shook his head grimly. 'No. I can't say that she did.'

They sighed. 'That's typical of Salryanna.' Something of the fight seemed to go out of Francis. 'Why do you think the Witch Queen exists? What is her purpose?'

Which was not the question he'd been expecting. He straightened, exchanging a glance with Rorks, who was as confused as he was. But it hadn't been asked with rancour or refusal, and so he met it with a genuine answer.

'The Witch Queen serves the demon on this plane. She protects the demon's interests in this world. She is his earthly handmaiden,' he said, deliberately choosing to repeat the standard understanding as taught by the Light Command. He knew it wasn't the truth, but he wasn't prepared to venture a more nuanced response yet either, not when he didn't know why, or what exactly, he was being asked.

Francis gave him a dour look. 'And you believe that?'

'No. It's a propaganda line from the Light.' He shrugged. 'But the Witch Queen is bound to serve the demon, that much she told me herself.'

A look of pain crossed Francis's face.

'The Witch Queen doesn't protect the demon,' they said. 'The Witch Queen protects us *from* the demon. Do you understand the difference?'

Something sour stirred in the back of his throat. 'What?'

'She isn't bound to the demon, the demon is bound to her. She acts as the constraining vessel. Restraining it.' Francis hugged their arms about them. 'She is the sole reason the demon has not turned this entire valley, and all the lands beyond, into a burning hell on earth. Because she exists to trap him inside of herself, in order to protect all other life.'

Silence. Callum felt like the breath had been ripped from his lungs. *I was sacrificed to that creature long ago.* Was that what she meant? It wasn't just watching other novices burn up and knowing that if she didn't step up someone else would be harmed in her place. It was knowing that if she didn't step up, nobody else would be strong enough, and the whole valley, and all the lands beyond, would fall prey to the demon.

Had she really seen it that way? Was it really that way?

I don't want to be strong anymore. I don't want to always be the strong one watching while others burn.

Dear god. Whether it was actually the truth, or if there'd been other ways, or any other option, he didn't know. But that Sal had seen it as the only way, that she'd had to sacrifice herself, was something he could believe.

'It can't be true,' Rorks said. He sounded devastated. 'She would have said something to Callum, she—'

'No she wouldn't,' Francis cut him off with an exasperated huff.

'Salryanna doesn't want anyone else getting involved, in case they're at risk. She's determined to bear this alone.' They sounded softly cynical and extremely worried. 'It's killing her, of course. Slowly, over the years. She's the strongest Witch Queen I've seen in my lifetime and I've been here for three of them now. But the destiny of the Witch Queen is to contain the demon until she is consumed entirely by him, at which point he passes to the next host.'

'The novices,' Callum said. 'She sent away all the novices. There's no one else to pass the demon onto.'

'And no-one to share the load, either,' Francis said. 'Previous Witch Queens would use the novices as fodder to feed the demon, so they'd burn up and enable the Queen to survive longer. Each of them thought only of their own power of course; there is intense power in being the Witch Queen. They'd extend their own lives through the sacrifice of the novices. Only Salryanna never wanted to hurt others. So she bore it alone.'

Callum closed his eyes. 'Fuck,' he said, softly. 'Fuck.'

'Wait. If it's killing her, but there's no novices and no-one to pass it onto next, what did she think would happen when she finally succumbed?' Rorks asked. He sounded haunted, but he was thinking the clearest of them all right now. 'Surely she had some kind of plan?'

Callum's head shot up. 'Her research,' he said, staring at Francis. 'I heard you two talking about some kind of research.'

'It doesn't matter.' Francis shook their head. 'It didn't work. She's been trying to find a way to trap the demon in a non-living vessel, something that wouldn't be harmed by it. So that when she can no longer continue, she doesn't have to find another sacrifice to become the Queen.' They shrugged. Bitterly. 'Only we never managed to figure it out.'

Callum stood straight. Ran his hands over his hair and tried to think. She'd seen herself as damned. Everything she'd done or said, it was from someone who had no hope for her own future. Not eating, not sleeping, hiding away alone from the world. Her own suffering was unquestioned, by herself most of all.

When he'd been flogged, when he'd been in the salt mines, when he'd suffered, he'd never once considered himself deserving of it. Nor anyone else suffering alongside him. No matter what the others in the mines had done to be thrown into that pit, and some of them had committed heinous crimes indeed, nobody deserved that. So he'd fought against that suffering, he'd rebelled against those who inflicted it.

She'd never once fought for herself in all that time. She'd only ever fought to save others, sacrificing herself to do so.

'She never said.' He looked down at his hands, as if regretting not being able to draw a sword and fight this out. He could understand how to fight. He wasn't sure he understood Salryanna's choices. 'She never told me. Not five years ago. Not now.'

'She didn't know five years ago,' Francis said, wearily. 'They don't tell novices anything. She only learned as she tried to run, to come to you. That's when they gave her the only choice she's ever had: run away with you, or stay to sacrifice herself. And if she'd chosen the former, every living creature in this valley would be long dead and the rest of the lands enslaved to the demon. So it wasn't much of a choice really, was it?'

He ran his hands over his face. 'She should have fucking told me.'

He couldn't help the anger in his voice. Perhaps it was driven by fear and heartache and hurt and worry and guilt, but he was angry too. If Sal had just told him he wouldn't have tied her to that chair and tried to break the binding. He would have tried to help her.

Which was the problem, wasn't it? She didn't see herself as able to be helped. Best she just make the noble sacrifice without ever letting on.

'Yes, she should've,' Francis said. 'But if she had, you wouldn't have done what you did. And she needed you to do that.'

'I almost killed her!' Callum shot at him.

'You don't think she wasn't aware of that?' they replied. 'That's what she wanted. The power of the demon heals her body. With that collar cutting access to her magic, she was hoping it would kill her after all, and with her, the demon. That the collar would stop him escaping, so he'd be dragged down with her. She wanted you to destroy the demon.' Their voice dropped 'Even if you had to destroy her to do it.'

Now her words as he tied her down made sense. They'd unsettled him badly, because they had sounded almost like a goodbye. Which was exactly what they were. A goodbye.

It was such a complete fucked up mess. He could barely make sense of it. So he clung onto the one thing he knew more important than any other.

'Will she survive?' he said. 'Will she wake up?'

'I think so,' Francis said. 'Her body will heal fast without that collar on. Give it a few hours and she should stir.'

Which was all he could focus on for the moment. He nodded, a kind of thanks, and turned away. There should be other questions. He should properly interrogate this person. But right now, he didn't have the energy or the will. He had to get things clear in his head, figure out what this meant.

He had to decide what to do next.

He ran a hand over his face and looked to Rorks.

'Find Francis a room, ensure they have food and whatever else they need to be comfortable, then lock them in,' he told Rorks. 'Set a guard.'

Francis straightened with protest. 'I've told you everything I know! I'll answer more questions if you need. I want this resolved safely too.'

Callum turned a glare on them. 'Until I decide otherwise, you're my prisoner. Be glad it's not the dungeons,' he said. 'You will be looked after and you won't be hurt, not unless you force me to it. But I won't have you wandering free around the castle until I've figured this out.'

'Sal was right not to trust you.'

'Sal deliberately kept me ignorant of critical information, lied to me by omission and manipulated me into almost killing her,' he snarled back. 'Collar or not, that woman is no longer Queen here, she's a slave who belongs to me. And I will deal with her over this, you can be sure of it.'

'You don't—'

'Enough. You don't get to dictate anything here,' he cut the other off. 'I said you would be looked after and I meant it. When Sal is awake, and well enough to take visitors, I'll allow you to see her. Until then you will remain in your assigned room and you will give me no goddamned trouble, or else I will revoke such privileges. Understand?'

Francis stood, chin lifted high. 'I fully understand. I will be informing the Queen of this treatment when I see her.'

Callum turned from them before he could be tempted to true fury.

'You do that.' He waved a hand to indicate for them to go. 'Rorks, get this person out of my sight.'

'Yes, General.' Rorks saluted, then grabbed Francis by the shoulder and marched them out. Leaving Callum alone.

He slumped down into the chair and put his head in his hands and wondered what the fuck he should do now.

CHAPTER 19
Callum

'Boss?'

He didn't shift when he heard Rorks return. He wasn't sure how long the Captain had been gone, not all that long he didn't think. Maybe he already had somewhere prepared to hold Sal's advisor. Rorks was organised like that, Callum could rely on him.

So he stayed where he was, which was standing in the bedroom leaning against the wall, arms crossed as he watched the rise and fall of Salryanna's chest. She was still breathing. She was still alive. Covered in bandages and a blanket, but alive. The startling red burned mark of the collar still circled her throat.

Had it been burning her all this time, that collar? Or had the burn only come from the ritual? Would she have told him if it was hurting her? She always dismissed her own pain as if it were unimportant, not worth thinking about. As if she somehow deserved it.

Would he have taken it off her even if she had told him?

He couldn't have said he would. Before the debacle of the ritual he'd assumed that collar was the only thing keeping the demon at bay. The collar on the Witch Queen was stopping the demon destroying them all through her. Or so he'd thought.

Now he knew *she* was what was keeping the demon at bay. And he hadn't exactly been helping her do that.

She hadn't told him. How could he have made better decisions when she hadn't told him?

Yet why would she tell anything to the General of the Light, who had taken her castle and herself by conquest, and treated her with such brutal cruelty?

He couldn't keep the thoughts straight in his head.

Footsteps sounded by the door to the bedroom. 'Callum?'

'I'm here, Rorks.'

Rorks stepped into the dim shadows of the room. Coming to a stand beside him and for a moment looking down at Sal on the bed himself.

Then, after a moment of silence, he sighed.

'Come on,' he said.

'What?'

'Just come on. You're not doing anybody any good in here, least of all yourself.'

He took Callum's hand, which he hadn't done in a long time, and tugged him away from the wall, then led him into the other room. Into the brighter light, with sunlight streaming through the big glass windows from out on the balcony. Callum grimaced against it, preferring the darkness of the bedroom right now.

Rorks pointed him to the lounge and Callum went to one of the arm chairs, falling back into it with distraction, while Rorks busied himself at the cabinet by the side of the room. The drinks cabinet, where he poured two whiskeys, bringing them back over to where Callum sat.

'Bit early in the day for it, isn't it?' Callum said, but without any real energy.

'It's a minute after midday, at least. And you need something to help you relax right now,' Rorks answered, firmly.

The Captain put one glass down on the coffee table and brought Callum's across to him. Instead of handing it directly over, he went down to his knees. Kneeling in front of Callum's chair, like he'd used to in the old days when they were together. Only then did Rorks hold forward the glass.

Callum took it.

'It's been a long time since you waited on me,' he said, rather fondly.

'I'm always here to wait on you, whenever you need it,' Rorks said, putting a hand on Callum's knee, probably just to steady himself as he knelt. 'We might not be lovers anymore, but you will always be my General and I will always bow to you. You know that.'

Callum reached out his free hand to cup the other man's cheek. 'I do. Thank you, my friend.'

Rorks leaned into the touch. 'And if it were any other circumstances, I'd totally offer to blow you as well, to help you relax,' he said, almost as if he were joking. Almost. Only there was a little too much need underlying the forced humour, and the expression faded fast from his face. 'But I know that's not what you need right now, General.'

'I'm afraid it's not,' Callum agreed quietly. 'But is it what you need, Rorks? It's been a long time since we were sexual. Is there a reason you're offering now? Are you doing okay?'

Rorks gave him a tired smile.

'Get back to me on that. My needs are not top of the priority list right now,' he said, then raised a hand to cut off the protest he obviously knew Callum would make. 'I'm serious, General. I'm doing fine. I'll admit I've found myself feeling a little unmoored of late and I'm not sure why. But I'm okay.'

'You don't think it's because Sal is back with me?' Callum suggested gently, though Rorks waved that away.

'No. Well, I mean, maybe? But I really don't think so. I am too glad to see you with her, Callum. I want it too much for you,' he said. 'And it doesn't change anything for me, for us.' He shrugged, self-consciously. 'I think it's mostly because I'm worried. About you, about everything. But I am okay, really. Just a little unsettled and we can talk about me once we've got things sorted here. I'll keep.'

Callum pulled him in close. It'd been a long time since he'd allowed himself to do so. Holding him, lips against his hair.

'Rorks, please. If you're not doing well, please tell me,' he said. 'I've already failed her. Don't let me fail you too.

Rorks pulled back only so far that he could look him in the eye, not leaving his hold.

'You have not failed her. And you couldn't fail me if you tried,' he said, in a hard tone. 'Don't think it.'

'I almost killed her, Rorks.'

'Because she wanted you to. Because she deliberately didn't tell you what you needed to know to avoid it,' Rorks said, expression torn. 'I understand why, you know. Why she did it like that. I don't even blame her. But I do think she was wrong, and you cannot blame yourself for it.'

'If you understand why, that makes at least one of us.'

Rorks gripped Callum's hand.

'She hurt you five years ago and she's never forgiven herself for it,' he said. 'Bound to the demon, she sees herself as unforgivable, as damned. It doesn't matter what you do or say, she's determined to punish herself.'

Which made little sense to Callum, but it did align with so much he'd seen of Sal these last days. Punishing herself, blaming herself. The self-loathing under her skin was intense, even when she hid it most of the time, never letting anyone see, never letting anyone close. He'd only caught glimpses of it himself.

But Rorks seemed to understand it and had been his wise counsel too many years for him not to pay attention to what the man was trying to say now.

'I didn't let her apologise,' Callum said. 'I told her I'd never grant her absolution. God, Rorks. I wish I'd told her she was forgiven. Would that have helped?'

'I actually don't think so.' He sounded very pragmatic, like he knew what he was talking about. 'It's not about whether you forgive her. It's about whether she forgives herself.'

Callum frowned, trying to wrap his head around it. He couldn't conceive of loathing himself to such a degree that he'd willing add to his own suffering. He'd only ever fought against the trials others had put him through. He'd known he hadn't deserved any of it.

She seemed to think she did.

Rorks shifted where he knelt, still holding onto him, and Callum knew he wouldn't move until given clearance to do so. In other times, he'd have left Rorks there despite the discomfort, and ordered him to be still and bear it, which would have made Rorks burn for him.

But this was not those times, and it was not a time to indulge in such things either. He leaned forward to kiss the man's forehead, something he hadn't done in years, then nudged him upwards.

'Get up off your knees, my friend. You can serve me just as well sitting comfortably on the couch.'

Rorks's cheeks flushed a little. 'I happen to like being on my knees for you.'

But he did take the chance to push himself up and move to the couch. Picking up his whiskey and taking a significant gulp, an indicator of just how much courage it had taken him to kneel. To confess such a need at such a time, what with everything else going on. Rorks had that same tendency as Sal to put his own needs last, but he was better at communication than she was. At talking his emotional state through. He didn't usually hide his pain from Callum, not unless he was really struggling. Not like Sal could.

'You know I'll always listen to your counsel, Rorks,' he said. 'But you barely know Sal, you haven't had a single direct conversation with her.'

'I know *me*, General. I know how my mind works. And I know the likely path I would've gone down if I had been in Salryanna's place,' Rorks replied. 'I would have done just the same as her, only I wouldn't have managed to survive it quite so long. She's a lot stronger than I am.'

Callum gave him a dark look.

'You are one of the strongest people I have ever known and if you dare undermine yourself with such statements again, I will get out my belt, I don't care if it's been years since we did that,' he said, and Rorks went red. 'I will add also that you have always been a strong communicator. You can talk to me about your needs. Sal cannot.'

'I had you, Callum. You taught me to communicate. You gave me the strength and the courage to do so,' he said, softly. 'She's not had that. She's had...a demon in her head, and nobody to support her, for five long years.'

He closed his eyes. Taking a shaking sip of the whiskey and lingering with the burn. Rorks was right. He did need the liquor. He needed this conversation. He needed his Captain on his knees reminding him of his willingness to serve, and of Callum's own need to lead and control.

Rorks wouldn't let him doubt himself. Which was undoubtedly what Rorks intended to show him here.

'Thank you, Captain. For sticking by me. Even when I'm not sure of what to do next.'

'You will know what to do, General. You will make the best decisions you can in the moment, based on the information you have, as you have always done,' he said. 'And I will follow wherever you lead.'

'And when she wakes up? How do I even begin to untangle the mess of where she's at?'

'The same way you untangled the mess of where I was at in the salt mines. By being you,' he said. 'That's all she needs.'

'What about your needs, Rorks?'

Rorks paused, as if choosing his words with some care.

'I need you too. I won't deny that. But she isn't my competition.' His smile was soft. 'I have listened to your stories about Salryanna the entire time I've known you. I've held you through nights where you've cursed her, and nights where you've cried over her. If I speak like I know her now, it's only because I do so through you.'

Callum took a long breath and another sip of whiskey.

'Then we better hope I know what I'm doing. Or else we'll all fall prey to the demon.'

CHAPTER 20

Salryanna

Everything hurt.

She didn't want to open her eyes, it was so bad. Aching head to toe worse than ever, not an inch of her spared. Worst was her chest and when she shifted sharp pain flared, and she hissed from between her teeth.

It got her eyes open, anyway. Above her was the canopy of the bed, dim-lit shadows, curtains pulled, if with sunlight sneaking through the cracks. It was daytime, then. She wasn't sure what day. She wasn't sure of anything. Except that the last thing she remembered was Callum tying her down to the chair in the ritual room, and the magicians starting their chants, and then...

Pain.

'Oh stars,' she breathed, and tried to push herself up in bed, but failed as an agony shot through her. Tears seeped out at the corners of her eyes, because it hadn't worked. She was still here. And so was the demon.

'Even now, you still can't swear properly.'

The voice was grim set and tired. She turned her head, or tried to. It hurt, so she winced, but managed to slow down and turn more carefully until she could see him.

Callum.

He sat in a chair at the side of the room, an armchair which wasn't there before and must have been dragged in from the main sitting room. He wasn't wearing his usual uniform—*service uniform*—but was wearing the more informal one—*working uniform, battle dress*—that he said he rarely wore because he was so rarely considered off duty. He looked exhausted. How long had he been sitting there?

'Callum?' she said. Or tried to. Her mouth was dry and it was hard to form words. She needed water, and to sit up, and to get her head clear. To face him. To figure out this situation before she could make it worse.

As if she could make things worse by this point.

She tried again to push herself up, stealing herself against the pain this time, but there was a weakness in her muscles as well and she didn't quite have the strength. Only then there were hands under her arms, gentle ones, assisting her and providing the strength she currently lacked. He helped her sit. Finding pillows to push behind her so she could rest back. Reaching to a pitcher of water by the side of the bed and filling a cup and handing it to her, then helping her hold it because her hands still shook.

The water was a balm.

So was he. But as she handed him back the cup, it took every ounce of her flailing willpower to make herself look up at him and meet his eyes. He didn't look happy.

'Thank you,' she whispered, hoarse, still trying to find her voice. 'Um...how long... was I...?'

'I'm not sure you should talk yet,' he said, as if refuge could be found in practical facts. 'I'm told your recovery will be fast, and considering it's only been about six hours since you were practically bleeding out, clearly that's the case. But you need more time to regain your full strength.'

She looked down at herself. Blankets, his bed. Bandages. The memories threatened to return too fast and she tried not to let them, but it was hard not to recall Francis's voice somewhere in the mix, Callum's crying *stop!*, panic and disorder and...

Her recovery should be fast?

Oh. Oh the stars.

Her hands went to her throat, even as her eyes shot back to him. There was...no collar. She was not wearing the collar. She stared at him, though he said nothing, simply stood there and watched as she made the realisation.

'You... you...' She still couldn't speak properly. She wanted to swear at that more than anything. 'My magic. You gave me back my magic.'

'You would have died otherwise.'

Her hands dropped to the bedclothes. 'You should have let that happen.'

'God damn you, Sal.'

He turned away, running hands through his hair. Like he wanted to stalk out of the room. Like he didn't know what to do with his limbs. She felt the tears come, she didn't mean to hurt him, yet she had done so all over again. It was the last thing she'd wanted to do, but what other choice had there been? It would have destroyed the demon.

He had made the other choice.

'I'm sorry,' she croaked, desperately.

He span back around. 'No. Do not apologise. Not to me.'

She raised a shaking hand to wipe at her eyes. Then she looked at her hands again. Waved one in a gentle gesture to see what was even possible in her current state.

There was a blurring of the air just in front of her, and a translucent scene, indistinct figures playing back like a hallucination made real. One of them, familiar from when she looked in a mirror, tied to a chair and screaming. Others rushing in to call stop. The last, diving to his knees to rip the collar off her throat, then holding her when she collapsed into his arms.

The illusion vanished as her strength did and she gasped and fell back against the pillows, panting heavily with the effort.

Callum was at her side again in an instant, bringing the water to her lips.

'At least try to recover before draining yourself with that...magic,' he said, tone dark with disapproval, helping her drink. He sat on the bed beside her and she was glad for him being closer, for all his dourness.

'I wanted...wanted to know what happened...' she said, between gasps.

'You could have asked me.'

She frowned because...he would have said? If she'd asked? Yes, she supposed he would have, and it hadn't even occurred to her. Because she'd always just done it with magic and there'd never been anyone here to ask anyway.

She fought off the urge to say sorry again.

'Francis,' she said, her own tone turning low. 'They were there. That's who told you to stop.'

'That's who told me the truth of what was happening, so I could make fully informed decisions. Something you never did.'

He was angry, but it wasn't the righteous fury she was used to. It wasn't even the tough General determined to enforce his control, either, which she had come to rely upon. Callum here, now, reminded her of the boy she'd left in the forest. The hurt on his face as she'd turned her back on him and left him to the merciless Light, all those years ago.

It was like that all over again. No matter what she tried, no matter what she did, she always ended up hurting people. She always hurt him worst of all. And she couldn't even apologise.

His shoulders slumped where he sat, as if he wasn't sure what to do now. Or that he knew what do to, he just didn't like it.

'Tell me, Sal,' he said, after a moment. 'How afraid do I have to be for the welfare of my men now that the Witch Queen has her powers back?'

Her mouth opened with surprise, dismay. She shook her head.

'Not at all,' she said, or tried to. Her voice was still so damned croaky. 'Callum, please. I'm not challenging your conquest here. You want this castle, you have this castle. You took it, you claimed it.' She swallowed, trying to find some kind of voice. 'Just as if you want me as a slave, you have me as a slave.'

'Hmmm. All about what I want. But what do you want?'

She frowned. 'Me? I don't understand...'

'What do you want, Sal? Because while I think we both want the same thing, I cannot be sure,' he said, then dragged back a sardonic sigh.

'We do many things well together, you and I, but communicating was never one of them.'

'No,' she agreed, quietly.

He gave her a pointed look. 'That can't go on. You need to talk to me. Be honest with me. Work with me, Sal,' he said. 'You know what my end game is. Tell me yours, honestly. So we both know where we stand.'

The breath went out of her. She'd thought he was about to turn away from her all over again, that she'd hurt him too badly once more, cornering him into a situation where he'd almost killed her, orchestrating that to happen.

But his words weren't those of a man about to turn his back.

'I want...'

She had to stop, take a breath. What she wanted never seemed to matter. Thinking like that wasn't something she was used to.

He said nothing, only waited in silence, as if he knew she needed time to work up to this. She gave it a second go.

'I want the same thing you do.' Her voice was quiet. 'For the demon to be gone.'

'Right. That's a start, at least.'

She took a risk, drumming up every ounce of courage she had. She reached out to his arm, where he sat on the side of her bed. Her own was shaking and weakened, but she put her hand on him anyway.

'I want you, Callum,' she said, quietly.

He didn't pull away. For a moment, he didn't shift at all. Then he moved to take her hand in his, winding his fingers through hers, looking down at them, her small hand engulfed in his larger one.

'I believe you,' he said. 'I'm not sure yet that I can trust you. But I believe you enough to try.'

'I understand.'

He gave her a troubled look. 'There's going to be some ground rules to this. The first is you need to communicate with me,' he said. 'And I, you. It goes both ways. But if we're going to do this, take on the demon together, then we need to talk to each other properly.'

She nodded, her chest tight with a swirl of relief, of wonder, of fear it would go wrong. Desire for it to go right. To not lose him after all.

'Yes,' she agreed.

'Good.' He turned his head to look at her. His lips twitched at the corner of his mouth, almost an exhausted smile. 'Rule two is I'm still in charge. Collar or not, I took you by rightful conquest and I plan to keep you. Slave.'

Relief flooded her limbs, because he was playing with her now, he wasn't running from her, he wasn't hating her. He might still be angry, even hurt, but he wasn't leaving her.

Her smile bloomed. 'Yes, sir.'

'Don't look too pleased with yourself. I'm still furious with you for not telling me what I needed to know,' he said. 'I will be dealing with you about that, once you've recovered well enough to face just punishment. You won't be so happy about it then.'

Which brought a flush to her cheeks, she could feel them flame red. She wouldn't resist that either, when the time came.

'I also don't want you using your magic without my permission.'

She looked up with a sudden tension. 'What—'

'Yes, I didn't think you'd like that,' he said, grimly. 'When I said I was in charge, I meant it. This isn't a game. That magic drains you and it's demon-derived; I don't know how much it takes out of you to feed the demon, or how much it ties you to that thing. I don't trust it.'

'You could ask me,' she said, sharply. 'I happen to know somewhat more about it than you do.'

'Either you agree to only using magic with permission, or I put the collar back on you,' he said, hard toned. 'Your choice.'

He wasn't going to budge. The breath was tight in her chest. Her magic was a core of who she was. It was part of her. And it wasn't all demon derived; she was trained in magic from all sources, the demon was just the most powerful one.

But he was serious.

'Fine,' she said, tightly. 'Sir.'

'Mmmm. You can keep the attitude to yourself, thank you,' he said, something of a warning, to which she frowned. 'But your agreement is noted. And that will be enough for now, I think. You need to rest more. Recover. We will determine our next move once you have.' He paused, expression and tone softening. 'Together.'

The tension went out of her, the irritation at his rules when she didn't like them. Together. They would work on this together.

She wasn't alone in this anymore. She wasn't alone.

'Callum,' she said. 'Thank you.'

He squeezed her fingers, then let her hand go and stood up. 'Rest, my little witch. When dinner is brought up, we'll see if you're ready to eat something.'

He went to the door, but there he paused. Looking back, still exhausted, if appearing a little lighter now than when she'd first woken up.

'Sal, when I say you're not to apologise to me, it's not because I'm refusing you absolution,' he said. 'Not anymore. You don't need to hang onto your guilt. The reason I don't want you apologising is because you haven't done anything you should apologise for.'

'I betrayed you,' she said. 'I hurt you, I lied to you, I manipulated you.'

'Perhaps. All in your efforts to protect others. While I treated you with cruelty and malice when you never deserved it, simply because my heart was broke,' he said. 'We have both done things to hurt each other, and both imagined ourselves hurt by the other. So maybe it's time we move past that. Maybe we both stop pointing fingers of blame and start talking it through instead. Okay?'

There was a hard knot in her chest she couldn't shift. 'Okay.' She swallowed. 'But. I don't know if I... Callum, you're right. Only I'm not sure how to...I've never blamed you, but I do blame myself and I can't see how not to. I'm no good at this. I've never been any good.' She dragged a panicked breath and said in the smallest voice, 'what if I mess things up?'

He smiled. 'Then I'll give you a belting and we'll start over.'

'Promise?'

'We'll work it out. I promise.'

He left her to rest. And she sank down into the pillows with the first ounce of hope she'd felt in five years.

~

He allowed her to get up for dinner. She was feeling much stronger by then, recovering fast, because her body would heal without that collar. Still, he was being careful. He probably didn't trust her healing, considering it derived from the same source as her magic and he'd been very clear about his thoughts on that.

She still wasn't happy about it, but it was that or the collar and at least this allowed her some chance to use her magic. She just had to convince him of it first. The fact he had a soldier's distrust of magic to begin with didn't help, but they were only just starting to learn how to trust each other, and she understood his need to move slowly. He was a man who had to be in control and to do that he needed to understand his environment, his people. He took a conservative line when he wasn't sure he understood.

She could work to his speed. To gain his trust again. To learn to feel worthy of it.

He dressed her in one of his shirts again. He was going to need a lot more shirts if he wanted to keep dressing her in his clothes. She didn't resist, she liked the comfort of being clothed by him, to his taste. It was like a warm embrace.

She looked at herself in the bathroom mirror upon getting dressed and tried to get used to the fact one thing was missing. No collar now. Instead, something new: where the collar had been was a burned red mark, almost a brand. It would have happened in the ritual, though she could barely remember the pain of that in among all the other agonies. The collar turning hot, searing, as her body tried to access her powers to heal, but the collar stopped it.

Maybe she wasn't wearing the collar any longer, but its mark remained upon her nonetheless.

She wasn't upset by that, just curious. Her fingers tracing the red band around her skin; it didn't hurt now, it had simply scarred. So be it. That was the last of her concerns.

When she came out of the bedroom, she found dinner laid out on the balcony table as usual. He wanted her to eat, though it was the last thing she felt like. Fortunately it was only broth and some bread, so she managed it, slowly. He supervised the whole time, making sure she finished it all, though he finished his meal in a third of the time it took her to eat hers and he'd had a lot more on his plate than she did. He didn't rush her. He just wanted her to finish. So she did.

'Explain something to me,' he said, as he watched her eat. 'The demon is slowly burning you out and there will come a time when you are consumed by him. That's the point he'd ordinarily be transferred to one of the novices, right? Except you sent them away.'

Her eyes flicked up to his, then quickly down again. Francis must have explained a great deal indeed. She wished they hadn't, she wished Callum didn't want to discuss this. None of it left her easy, especially not others knowing the truth of it.

But he'd said they were to talk openly, communicate. Though it went entirely against her long-ingrained habits, she had to try.

'Yes,' she said. 'The Queen before me, she used the novices to extend her own life, sacrificing them to save herself. The ones before her too, I'm told. But the Queen's destiny is always to be consumed by the demon in the end, we can only last so long, even the strongest of us.' She paused, meeting his eyes again. 'Even me. It's my destiny.'

His jaw tightened. 'I don't believe in destiny. And I have other plans for you.'

'General, it may still happen, we both need to accept that,' she said softly. 'Destroying the demon is set to destroy me. It is...likely. That's the way the binding was devised.'

It was as strong as she dared put it. She wanted to say it was far more than likely, it was certain, but he wouldn't react well to that.

'I don't accept any such thing,' he said, firmly. 'And what I don't get is this—if when the Queen's body expires because the demon has burned it out, then the demon moves to the next vessel, why did you think the ritual might destroy the demon via destroying you? I know it's something to do with the collar, but I don't understand it. Tell me about that.'

She winced, trying to find the words.

'The demon's power heals my body from external wounds or harm. What it can't do is heal me from the physical harm of restraining the demon itself,' she said quietly. 'That is, the harm done by the demon being constrained within me, slowly eating my physical self from the inside.'

A troubled look crossed his face at that. She wished she could lighten the terminology, but that was the most gentle way she could put it. Burning her slowly over years from the inside out might not be easy to hear, but it wasn't easy to experience, either.

'The ritual was supposed to break the binding upon me,' she said. 'Which you, and your magicians, assumed just meant the demon had bound me to keep his secrets. But that's not what the binding is. It's a binding on the demon, to force it to protect my physical self. To enable me to constrain him.'

'If I'd known that before, it would have made a lot of difference,' he said, darkly.

She nodded, looking down. 'I know. I'm sorry.'

'No apologies, remember. And I've already warned you I'll be dishing out consequences for that offence in due course,' he said. 'Now go on. Explain why all this made a difference. Why you thought it might work to let yourself be destroyed in this way, when I know you didn't have any novice or other vessel lined up to take on the demon should you perish.'

She sighed, looking out over the valley. 'The collar,' she said. 'As the binding weakened, the demon tore at his prison—me. And the collar stopped me healing. I thought the collar might also trap the demon within me for long enough, so if I was destroyed, he wouldn't be able to transfer. I was betting on it taking him out of this world, this plane of existence, with me.'

'What do you mean, plane of existence?' he asked, with a tone suggesting he wasn't sure he'd like her answer.

She knew he wasn't going to like it.

'The demon would be banished to the afterlife, to the hell from which it came, and I...would be bound with him,' she said very quietly.

Callum stood up in sudden shock. 'You have got to be fucking kidding me. Sal, you're talking about eternal damnation.'

He stood tall and furious on the other side of the table. She bit her lip, but couldn't lie to him.

'We don't really know of the planes from which the demon came,' she said. 'The concept of eternal damnation is a belief of the Light. I don't subscribe to it. There are many who don't believe such.'

He threw up his hands in frustration. 'You risked your eternal soul ending up in some hell dimension,' he said, as if that wasn't the sacrifice made of her when first bound to the demon five years ago. She had always been facing such.

He pointed a finger at her, a hard expression on his face.

'No more of this, you hear?' he said, a command with all his military force. 'I won't put up with your constant willingness to sacrifice yourself as if you don't matter. Whether it's punishing yourself by refusing to eat, or trying to get yourself destroyed by the goddamned demon, it stops now. Enough!'

The power of him was a force she could barely resist. Such strength, as if he might be able to will this reality into a shape he preferred, instead of what she knew it was; that she had been damned five years earlier.

It was hard not to be swept up in his determination to control even reality itself.

'Yes, sir,' she said, a whisper.

'Dear god. If you weren't still recovering, I've have my belt to your arse right this very minute, I swear,' he said, with no small measure of fury. 'You matter, Sal! You don't deserve this, you never did.'

'Yet if I'd had true courage and selflessness, I would have destroyed myself five years ago to kill the demon with me,' she said softly. 'Only I couldn't. I was scared. I don't want this, Callum, it terrifies me. So I tried to find another way. For five years, I've tried to find another way. Only I failed. That's why I...encouraged you to follow through with the ritual. Because I didn't have the guts to do it myself.'

His teeth gritted.

'Enough, slave. I will not leave you to that demon. I won't allow you to sacrifice yourself,' he said with such force she winced. 'Your research. That governor of yours mentioned it. You were trying to find another vessel, a permanent, non-living, one?'

'It didn't work.' She sighed. 'I thought I got close a couple of times, I created a kind of box lined with magic and runes. Only I couldn't manage to complete the spells, not with any success.'

He crossed his arms. 'You ran out of time. Because I arrived with an army at my back to take this place by force.' He paused only long enough for her to nod acknowledgement. 'So what if you had that time? What if I put resources to it too?'

'It was such a long shot already, Callum. I don't know...'

'We have to start somewhere.'

He sounded so practical, pragmatic. So determined to believe in a possible future, and she wanted to let him convince her it might work. She wanted to believe with the strength he believed. It didn't surprise her that he'd been the one to conquer the salt mines, to rise up from a literal point of death to rebel, then raise an army and march on the capital of the Light. That he then pulled back from full scale war to instead negotiate, because he knew the consequences of battle and that bloodshed was never welcomed if it could be avoided.

He had energies to save worlds, this man. He made her gasp and maybe, even after everything, he could even make her hope.

She nodded. 'Yes. Okay.' She breathed it, because she couldn't believe, and she couldn't quite hope, not yet, but maybe there was a spark of something that might turn into that. Maybe.

Oh, she had thought five years ago she loved this man. That was a mere childhood infatuation compared to what she felt for him now. He might not let her sacrifice herself for that demon, but she would for him, if he asked it. She would for him.

The doors opened in the other room. A voice called out. 'General?'

'Out here, Rorks,' Callum called back, and went to the doors to meet his friend. There was a salute, because there were always salutes, and something exchanged with the man inside, some kind of gesture. Then a nod from Callum as he stood back and waved the newcomer through.

Newcomers. Plural. The Captain had brought another.

Salryanna stood up. Or tried to. She wobbled on her feet and had to hold onto the table for support. Her balance was still off, her legs still weak.

It didn't stop her calling out.

'Francis!'

They came forward, and for all she was angry with them for intervening in the ritual and giving all away to the conquering General, she was also filled with relief.

'My Queen, you must sit, you—'

She surprised them by throwing her arms about them, with the kind of hug she never allowed before. To be touched was to let people close and she didn't do that. Francis took a moment to hold her back, clearly stunned. Both of them too glad to see the other alive and here.

'Please, sit down, my Queen,' they said, possibly only seconds before Callum, by the glowering look on his face as she faltered again.

She let Francis help her to the chair. 'I'm fine, Francis. I'm okay. Still tiring, but I'm healing.' She looked back up to Callum, who crossed his arms with a pointed look. 'I'm doing rather well, all things considered.'

'Hmmm. Indeed,' Callum said. 'You need to stay seated. You've barely recovered at all. This is a visit only, a supervised one. You're both still my prisoners, do not forget.'

'How could I forget your authority, General?' she said, with a dry smile.

'Watch your tone with me, slave,' he shot back. Probably enjoyed the dark expression crossing Francis's face at it, too.

She only nodded acknowledgement. 'Yes, sir,' she said, without hesitation, and didn't miss the way he turned to hide a smile.

'Behave and I'll let you both talk out here,' he said, somewhat mollified. 'I've business to discuss with my Captain. And do not move, Sal, I mean it. You don't have the strength back yet.'

'I won't. Thank you.'

He gave her a nod, then ushered his friend back inside and left her to speak with Francis.

CHAPTER 21

Salryanna

Francis wasn't happy, but that was not unexpected. In point of fact, neither was she. They had intervened when she hadn't wanted them to and yes, it may have saved her life, and yes, it may even have saved her eternal soul, should Callum's Light-influenced beliefs have any merit, but that wasn't the point.

She didn't have the energy or the will to berate them for it. Her body still ached, though her open wounds were fast healing over; her lingering exhaustion remained very real. Besides, she was too happy to see Francis and not have to hide it. She'd never been any good at subterfuge.

'You are being cared for, my lady?' Francis asked for maybe the twentieth time. 'He is not abusing you?'

'Francis, I am being well looked after. I'm not even getting away with skipping meals.'

Their expression was dubious, with a low sideways glance to the doors leading inside, then a glance to her throat. The collar may not have been there, but the red branding of it was.

'He does not treat you like a Queen.'

That was said as if it were the greatest sin possible to commit. Francis couldn't even bring themself to say the world slave, probably.

Not in relation to her, anyway. She could remind Francis they'd owned slaves when she had first come to power, but it probably wouldn't help now. It'd been one of her first, and only, acts as Queen, to banish slavery in the valley, and Francis hadn't been so happy at the time.

'To him, I'm not. At best, in his eyes I am a deposed Queen.' She shrugged. 'Considering I never wanted to be Queen and never actually acted like one, handing all governance over to you, it hardly makes much difference to me.'

'But your status, your position, must be respected. He cannot simply...'

'Put a collar around my neck and enforce victory by conquest?' she said. 'Actually, he can. And has. It's not only the way of this world, it's a conquest I'm not resisting, Francis.'

'It doesn't feel right, Your Majesty.'

She sat back in her chair, considering the governor.

'The General cares for humanity, Francis,' she said. 'He wants a governance in place that works for the people of this valley, which helps them, improves their lives. If he were some dictator despot here only for his own vainglory, I would have a very different response. But he is genuinely a good and caring ruler. The valley could do a lot worse.' She gave them a soft smile. 'It had worse in me. The people were just lucky they had you as a buffer.'

Francis still couldn't help tut-tutting, but they also were forced to nod. Salryanna had been disinterested in ruling, even while she'd understood the needs of it. She'd wanted the people protected, mostly from her. While her predecessors had all been tyrants.

The Valley had suffered for a long time and not merely because of a demon. Those who'd ruled hadn't been any help either.

'His man, that pretty-faced Captain, has been asking my advice on the governance of the valley,' they said, a little mollified. 'Requesting my involvement. And I...well, my lady, I didn't like to refuse, though they are the enemy. It didn't seem the best for our people if I rejected them outright, and...'

'It's okay, Francis. You should work with them. Please do,' she said, gently. 'I never paid any attention to the people, I handed over my responsibilities. You are betraying nobody by working alongside them for the benefit of our people here.'

It obviously still didn't sit right with Francis, but they gave that a sharp nod.

'Well, my lady, I have always put the needs of the people first,' they said. 'I will accept their offers to continue in my role under the General's leadership, if you so recommend.'

'I very much do.'

Their expression turned troubled. 'I worry for you, Salryanna. What of you?'

'Francis, I love the General. I always have done.' She smiled sadly. 'I may also be somewhat afraid of him, and only just learning again to trust him, but I do believe I am safe with him. Safer than I've ever been on my own.'

Francis's eyebrows rose. 'You? Safe? If I could see you safe, my lady, I would be very happy indeed.'

'Well. I'm as safe as can be for now.' She looked down at her hands with a sigh. 'The General believes he can destroy the demon, without destroying me. He thinks he can save me.' She looked back up to them. 'He can't, of course. But I will let him try.'

Francis was silent a moment. 'And when he fails?'

'Then I will do what I must and hope that he does not resist the inevitable, any more than I'm resisting him now,' she said. 'Until then, we work together.'

Francis reached across the table to take one of her hands.

'You deserve more,' they said.

'But I won't get more. So I will savour these moments with him while I can and then face my fate as I always was going to,' she said. 'If he can continue on to heal this world afterwards, then please help him, Francis. He is a leader to follow. He might have hardened armour, but he is a good man underneath.'

Francis did not try to suggest she might be wrong, that maybe the General might save her after all. Francis knew better, just as she did.

In the meantime, she would give Callum what he wanted and would work with him and let him try. Even if she knew it wouldn't work. So much of her yearned to believe like he did, if not in the possibility of his goals, at least in himself. There was such energy to him, such drive, such passion. He sort to change the world, by force if he had to.

There was an optimism to him. He believed he could make the world a better place, and set out to do so, and so far he had succeeded. He saw himself as hard-bitten and cynical and a dark realist, but he wasn't. Underneath, he was a believer in hope and beauty and positive change. And he had the innate energy to make such things happen.

So maybe he could manage to do the impossible. Maybe he could save her, and the rest of the land with her.

Maybe.

Callum led his Captain back out to the balcony long before she was ready to finish speaking to Francis. It seemed time was up. Callum looked serious, his expression tight. Rorks looked...unsettled. She wondered what they'd been discussing.

She was glad Callum had this friend, the Captain who meant so much to him. Who'd been his lover at one time and she still wasn't sure she hadn't somehow inserted herself between them, and worried that she might have. But Callum had reassured her, and Rorks had only ever looked on her with a welcome and warmth. On her part, she felt only intense gratitude for Rorks having been at Callum's side, someone Callum could lean on and be with and rely upon. Share with. Care for. Love, even. Callum needed to look after others, it was part of what drove him, that need to protect, save, defend.

The last thing she wanted was to take anything away from Rorks or his relationship with Callum, just because she'd found herself back in the General's life.

Rorks gave her a flicker of a smile as she met his eyes. She realised she had been staring and looked away again quickly, though she tried to return the smile before she did.

To cover, she tried to stand, but Callum gave her a sharp look and a gesture to stay where she was. She stayed, not without gratitude; her body was starting to sag, and it hardly mattered she'd spent all day in bed, her energy was drained.

'Do not move,' he ordered her, so she sighed and sat back.

Francis, however, stood. They squared their shoulders and faced Callum directly.

'General, a moment of your time?'

Callum raised an eyebrow, but gave them a nod. Turning his attention fully onto Francis in that way he had, which told you he was listening, he was paying clear attention and hearing what you said. She'd seen him do it with the petitioners too, and with his men. A manner which demonstrated that for those few minutes, you were the only thing of importance and he was listening.

'Go ahead, Governor Quinze.'

Francis glanced momentarily to her, before turning back to Callum.

'Your Captain indicated that you may be prepared to negotiate my position,' they said, if stiffly. 'If I were to publicly recognise your rule here. Add my voice to its legitimacy.'

'I am open to negotiation on such matters, certainly.'

'Then...' Francis took a deep breath. 'You need to maintain constancy of governance. I have been the face of governance in this valley for five years now. If you do indeed care for the welfare of the people, as I am told you do, then I would recognise your authority. Work under your command in providing continued governance, as I have previously been doing for the Queen—' They paused. 'Former Queen.'

To his credit, Callum didn't once look her way.

'Governor, I would welcome such a development and I thank you for your...adaptability in the current circumstances.' He glanced at Rorks. 'Captain, see our friend back to their rooms, please. Ensure they have anything needed to be comfortable and I will come by in the morning to negotiate terms.'

He held out a hand. And Francis shook it.

As Callum walked with them to the door, Rorks manoeuvred his way past Salryanna.

'Your work?' he whispered, leaning down by her ear to keep his voice low. She bit her lip, nodding. 'Well done.'

He even squeezed her arm before heading over to the other two and saluting to attention before Callum.

'Captain, ensure you sign off duty after seeing to the Governor,' Callum ordered Rorks. 'You've already worked a double shift and more besides. Assign others to any outstanding tasks for the night, you are to take some personal time.'

'General, it is unnecessary and at this juncture, I—'

'I said sign off, Captain. That is an order.'

Callum's tone turned commanding indeed, and exceedingly impatient. Sal recognised the tone from the one he'd used with her in the study when he'd called her out for not eating, right before giving her the belting. Even though it wasn't directed at her now, it still made her wince.

Rorks stiffened. Reacting instantly, just like she did. He hid the reaction as best he could, expression tightening and eyes lowering, with a short nod of acknowledgement. It wasn't much, but she saw it, because she knew how it felt to be subjected to that tone, and that demanding, commanding stare.

She knew what it was to *need* it.

'Yes sir,' Rorks said, and his voice sounded almost even, if you weren't listening for the shake. He saluted again, probably unnecessarily, though she didn't exactly understand military protocol.

Callum didn't return the salute, he just gestured out the door, to which Rorks went with Francis in tow, the two of them disappearing out of the suite.

When Callum turned back to her, he looked no less impatient than he had with Rorks. She didn't think it was to do with her, but something had put him out in the conversation with his Captain.

'How are you faring?' he said, words solicitous, but his tone was not one to be denied. He wanted an honest answer. She had to bite back the instinct to obfuscate.

'Fatigued,' she said. 'Mostly just fatigued.'

'Pain?'

'Not really. An ache, all over. But the sharper pain is gone.'

'Hmmm.'

He gestured her to stand, holding her arm to help her do so. She didn't really need it, but he insisted and it was strange, this sense that someone was genuinely trying to look after her. She'd never had that before. It was a new thing to think she didn't have to gut it out and push on regardless of how she was feeling, that she could actually say if she was hurt, and take time to recover.

It had been a long time, maybe not ever, since she'd experienced that. She wasn't sure what to do.

He didn't seem to have any compunction or hesitation, and always knew what to do. He undid a couple of the buttons on the shirt he'd bade her wear, while she stood very still and let him do so. If he wanted to strip her, he could. Part of her wished he would. But that wasn't his intent here.

He inspected the bandages beneath the shirt, winding one back slowly to view the wounds beneath.

He sucked back breath when he did.

'Bad?' she said, quietly.

'Only from a certain point of view,' he answered. 'They're almost fully healed. It hasn't even been twelve hours.'

He wound the bandages back anyway, as if she still might need them. Perhaps it was simply something he could do with his hands.

'The demon heals me fast,' she said and didn't miss the clench of his jaw.

'The demon is what hurt you to begin with.'

'I know. And it will be the demon that kills me in the end.'

He didn't like that. A hand to her chin, tight clenching there, forcing her head up to look at him, meet his eyes. A fury in them.

'Not if I have anything to say about it, slave.' He shook his head and dropped his hold on her. 'If you have enough energy to come through to the study, I would like to show you something.'

'I can, I will,' she said, just glad for anything to focus on that wasn't his anger or the demon or her doomed fate ahead.

He helped her. She couldn't stop him and a traitorous part of her had to admit she still needed it. Her balance was so off she would have stumbled otherwise. But he took her arm in his, and put another around her waist, and guided her across the sitting room and into the study, to the large armchair she'd fallen asleep in the day before.

It was warm, his touch. It was solicitous and caring and gentle. This man who could be so rough and so hard and so cruel when he wanted, could also be kind and soft when he chose, too.

She watched him from her chair, as he went to the desk and the several unrolled pages there, large ones. Maps. She could see a little from where she sat, but her eyes were on him. Never wanted to leave him. No matter what he insisted, she didn't know how long she might have with him, and she didn't want to lose a second of it.

He selected a map and brought it back over to her, placing it haphazardly on the little side table. It was a plan of the castle. Ah. She'd been hoping with the distraction over the failed ritual that he might have forgotten about his desire to map out the place.

Apparently not.

He gestured to the map.

'Here,' he said. 'What's in this tower?'

She tried not to hesitate. 'There's nothing of importance there,' she said, with genuine honesty. Nothing he would find important anyway. 'It's just a back tower.'

'My men haven't been able to get close. There's magic protecting that tower,' he said. 'They've managed to access most other parts of the castle, even those magically protected, yet not this place. Can you tell me why?'

'Um. It's not demon magic protecting it.'

His eyes narrowed. 'Then what magic is?'

He didn't sound like he was prepared to put up with any excuses, notwithstanding the fact he was being careful with her physical health right now.

'It's not important, Callum, I promise.'

'Be warned, Sal,' he said, hard-voiced. 'I've just had Rorks in here telling me he absolutely must continue working through the night when I know the man has hardly slept for days. So I'm not in the mood for your games right now on top of his, got me?'

Oh. She looked up, surprised. She knew how much Callum relied on his friend for counsel, companionship, support. She knew how much Rorks meant to him.

'Is there anything wrong?' she asked.

He exhaled a terse breath through his teeth, throwing up a hand in a gesture of uncertainty. But he didn't brush off her question.

'I don't know. He says not. But Rorks avoids time off like you avoid food; when he's anxious, he'll bury himself in work,' he said. His shoulders dropped; he looked tired himself, almost as weary as she felt. 'Not quite a couple of years ago, I discovered he was working himself round the clock for close to five days running. He'd had some bad relationship breakup and was falling apart. Hiding the truth of his emotional state from me.' He gave her a pointed look. 'Like someone else I could name.'

She pressed her lips together. 'I won't do it again. I promised you that.'

'Yes, well so did he. Only I'm starting to see the same signs in him now,' he said. 'I'm trying to head it off before he gets to crisis point, but it's hard to know how far to push.' He ran a hand through his hair. 'Rorks is like you in many ways. When he's struggling, he tries on some pretty unhealthy coping mechanisms. Only I'm not sure what's behind this and it's not like we have a lot of time right now to stop and figure it out.'

She reached out a hand and, perhaps surprisingly, he took it. That he was sharing this with her, his concern for his friend, letting her hear his worries, meant everything to her.

'You're worried about him,' she said quietly.

'I'm worried about him,' he agreed. 'But he keeps telling me he's fine. I could be jumping at shadows.'

'It's not because of me, is it? Because I'm here with you and...'

He cut that off with a raise of his other hand, even as he stood by her chair and rubbed his thumb along her knuckles.

'No. That much I'm sure of,' he said. 'He could just be having a hard time in a relationship, that's what it was last time. But he usually gets me to vet his lovers and he tells me he's not with anyone currently.'

Her mouth opened in surprise. 'You approve his partners? Really?'

'He wants it that way. Rorks likes it pretty rough and it's safer if he gets them checked out first. He knows I won't withhold approval without solid reason.'

Something about that felt a little bit thrilling. If Rorks was like her, she was pretty sure it wasn't only for reasons of safety that he sort

Callum's permission for his own personal relationships. Perhaps they weren't still together, but there remained a certain dynamic and it wasn't only born of military hierarchy.

'But you do withhold approval when you deem it warranted,' she said, also not a question.

'That's the point. Hasn't happened often, but I'm not giving him permission to fuck around with someone I believe might hurt him.' He cocked his head as he looked at her. 'Why all the questions, witch?'

She shrugged, running her thumbs over his hand, enjoying the rough feel of his fingers around her own.

'You like talking about your Captain,' she said. 'And you were worried. I would like to be someone you can talk to when you have concerns.' She kissed his knuckles. 'Thank you for sharing.'

'Hmmm. You also managed to avoid answering my question.' He gestured back to the map. 'What's in the south tower? Who's magic protects it, if not the demon's?'

She sighed. There was no reason not to tell him. Except that he would want to go see, and that left her feeling...vulnerable. Which was silly, considering he'd collared her publicly and threatened her with rape and done his best to emphasise the powerlessness of her situation all the way along. Even if now he had recanted on some of that, and she did trust him, or was learning to again.

'Mine,' she said at last. 'My rooms are there.'

His eyebrows shot up. 'So that's where your personal suite is found. I was beginning to think you didn't have a bed in this place.'

'That's about all that's in there. A bed. A wardrobe. Not much more.'

He narrowed his eyes, arms crossed. 'And your research.'

This time, he wasn't asking questions.

'Yes. I could go fetch it, bring it here for you to study...'

'I will go,' he said, cutting her off. His tone was firm indeed.

She tried not to look reluctant. 'You won't be able to find it. The illusions hiding it are carefully woven.'

She knew what would come next, of course. She just wasn't sure how to avoid it.

He crossed his arms, not prepared to put up with her prevarication. 'I'm sure the witch who wove them can undo them just as easily.'

'It's not that simple. I wove them over years to admit only myself and those in my company, it will take time for me to unweave—'

'Fine. We will both go. In the morning, after breakfast, presuming your health is up to it,' he said. 'I will brook no argument on this.'

He was serious. And it wasn't a battle to die for. There was nothing that really mattered in there, it was just her personal things, and there were few enough of those.

She was tired, exhausted. She didn't want to fight. She wanted to give in to him, let him win. She wanted him to be right, because if he were right, then the future might not be so utterly damned.

She nodded. 'Yes, sir.'

He put his hand to her chin and tipped back her head, stopped her looking down to the ground. Made her meet his gaze.

'Now you are going back to bed. You almost died this morning.'

She thought about protesting. Decided she was too tired for that, too.

'Will you help me?' she asked, softly.

He reached down hands to help her stand. 'Of course, little witch. Come on. Let's get you to bed.'

CHAPTER 22

Salryanna

The South Tower was the furthest, most remote, most isolated tower in the entire castle. Nobody went there. Most of the time nobody could find it due to the protections she'd woven, but even if they could, they wouldn't have. There was nothing up this way. It was too remote to be of use for anything but storage and didn't even have the views of the valley that the other sides of the castle enjoyed.

All you could see from the windows of this tower was forest. There was a reason she'd chosen this place to make her home.

She walked slowly, carefully. She was feeling a great deal better, for all it was only twenty-four hours since she'd been torn up by the demon. A reminder that no matter how powerful she was, it was not her power, and she wielded it for a reason: to contain the demon, to be the barrier protecting the world from it. Such had been sold to her as an honour, but she'd known even five years ago that it was the end of her if she agreed. Only what other choice was there? She watched as her two fellow novices, her friends, burned up screaming, because she wouldn't step forward to do her duty. Their deaths, agonised and awful, on her hands. Of course she'd accepted her fate, then. Of course she had.

Callum didn't accept fate. Callum fought against impossible choices. Callum might even change the world.

But she was not Callum.

He walked beside her and she held onto his arm as they went. He didn't rush her, though perhaps he suspected it wasn't only her recovering health that kept her steps slow. It wasn't like there was anything here to be reluctant about. There were no secrets, no shame, and no excitement either. It was just her rooms.

Maybe that was the reason. Because these were her personal rooms and nobody had ever been in them beside her.

The tower was silent, so far from the main activity of the castle, bustling now that the General had brought an army and community to it. Which still left her anxious and worried, but at least he hadn't insisted she go out into it again, not after that first time with the petitioners. Even without her concerns that people here meant fodder for the demon, she wasn't used to crowds and they made her uneasy. She wanted to hide away. It was all she'd known for five years, she wasn't sure any longer how to be with others.

They climbed stairs, narrow and cold. Then onto a landing, with an unremarkable wooden door down the far end. She took a long breath.

'I'll need to use magic to open the door,' she said quietly. 'Is that okay?'

'Go ahead,' he said, and she raised a hand to begin. Before she could, he put his own hand on her arm and pulled it down again. 'This isn't the demon's power, you said? This is magic of your own?'

'Yes, I was trained in all sorts. I had a kind of natural affinity, could use many types of magic, when I was younger,' she said. 'The demon's power is by far the strongest, that's all. It eclipses all else.'

'Why didn't you use the demon-driven magic to hide this place, if it's so strong?'

She opened her mouth to give him a quick or easy answer, but stopped herself. Let her shoulders drop with a kind of shrug.

'This is my space,' she said. 'I can't separate myself from the demon, but I wanted...something. Something that was mine. That wasn't so tainted like everything else in my life.'

He put a hand to her face, a troubled look behind his eyes. But what could he say? It was the truth of her existence.

Eventually he nodded. 'Go on, then. Take us in.'

She turned to the door and made a series of gestures with her hand, along with a murmured incantation. There'd been a time when she'd been taught never to allow others to overhear her words of power, but she was long past caring what anyone else heard or saw of her magic. She was strong in it, she always had been even before the demon, and once she was bound there was no other more powerful. Let them try to steal her tools, or her power itself. If anyone could, they were welcome to it.

Callum distrusted magic like the good soldier he was. He was hardly going to steal anything of that kind.

The door unlatched, creaking open an inch. She gestured him through.

He led the way, keeping a hold of her hand and pushing into her little sitting room study. There were only three rooms and a tiny balcony; it was like a smaller, less ornate, less luxurious version of the rooms he'd taken for himself. Her study, bedroom to one side, and washroom to the other.

Light streamed in from the windows looking out over the forest. It wasn't much of a view compared to the one from his suite out over the valley, all that could be seen were the trees. But it was the only view which mattered to her.

She walked to the window, clinging onto the sill. Her desk was to the side and the door to the balcony on the other. He stood in the middle, frowning around, as if it wasn't what he had expected.

'Um, this,' she said, reaching to a small wooden box on her desk. Unadorned, not special. Beside it, a series of papers.

Her research.

'This is all I have,' she said. 'I was trying to get the magic right, seeing if I could turn this box into the next vessel, but I couldn't make it work. Those are my notes. You'll need me to translate them, but maybe your magicians might make more of it than I could.'

He stepped up to the desk to consider the box, and the notes, nodding, though his expression remained tight.

'We will bring them to my rooms. I'll have the magicians look over it,' he said, then looked back up to her. 'And you. They will need to consult with you.'

She winced, thinking of the men from the ritual, the nasty expression in the eyes of the elder, their complete lack of engagement with her. Even if they'd been here for other reasons entirely, they wouldn't have liked her; she was their enemy, and she was a woman, and she knew their kind too well.

'If you think it will help,' she said, trying not to sound reluctant.

'Sal, you're the heart of this. You know more of this than anybody. My magicians are powerful, but I hardly trust what they do,' he said. 'I don't like magic, you know that. I need you to speak to them. They—'

He broke off.

'They?' she prompted after a moment.

'They almost killed you. Following my orders, I'm not blaming them, but they had no idea it would end that way, no more than I did. You were the only one to know,' he said. 'You need to speak to them, so that all our knowledge can be pooled and all our resources can be put to this task.'

She sighed. 'Yes. Yes, of course.'

He turned, looking about him. Curious, maybe. Or perhaps it was a duty he felt he needed to see to, checking the rooms of the Witch Queen to be assured there were no dark secrets hidden away in them.

If so, he held back on his scrutiny, though his interest in her space was written across his face.

'You can look wherever you like,' she said. 'Feel free to check the suite. There's not much here. I did tell you.'

He did look, checking the other rooms, which were spartan enough. While he was in the bedroom, she went out onto the balcony. Her plants were out here, big pots of small bushy green shrubs just beginning to flower. She waved a hand to produce a small watering can out of nowhere, before remembering she wasn't supposed to use her magic without permission. Oh well. It was a small slip, she'd confess and bear it.

She watered the plants, glad to see they hadn't fared too badly in her absence. Then she put the can down and stood by the balustrade, looking out over the forest.

It didn't take him long to get his fill of inside before she heard him step onto the balcony behind her. He approached to stand with her, though she kept her gaze focussed on the forest.

'You chose the smallest set of rooms, in the most isolated back corner of the castle, when you could have had your pick of any,' he said quietly. 'You could have had the rooms I'm now in. They were made for the Queen. Why did you live out here?'

'It can't be considered isolated when the castle was empty regardless,' she said. 'There was nobody else around anyway.'

'All the more reason to take the better appointed rooms.'

She sighed and nodded to the view. 'The forest. From here I could see the forest.'

His hand came to rest on top of hers on the balustrade. 'You keep daisies on your balcony.'

He meant her plants. They were all daisies. She nodded, pressing her lips together. For some reason, she could feel the prick of tears at the back of her eyes and tried to blink them away.

'The only time in my entire life I have ever felt safe was in the forest with you,' she said, so softly she wondered if he could even hear her. 'It was the only thing I ever wanted. So I made my rooms here, where I could see the forest, and I filled them with daisies, because the flower reminds me of you.'

'Ah, Sal,' he said, then put his arms around her and pulled her into him. Tucking her head under his chin and pressing his lips to her hair. 'I wish I'd known. I wish I'd understood all you were going through. You were so alone.'

'It was my fault. The only reason we weren't together was because I betrayed you,' she said. 'You were suffering the horrors of the salt mines, and I was here, bound to a demon. Maybe my reasons weren't what you thought, but I still chose that for the both of us. I still caused it.'

'Enough. We agreed we were no longer pointing fingers of blame. That means at ourselves, as well as each other,' he said, firmly. He didn't let her go, his arms remaining tight around her. 'I spent many nights in the mines cursing your name, but all the more missing you with every fibre of my body. I tried to hate you. But I never could. I loved you too much.'

He leaned back, bringing his hands to her face and tipping her head up to look at him. She knew her eyes were glassy. His weren't much better.

'I still do,' he said, then leaned down to kiss her.

His lips were soft against hers, his arms around her warm, and safe. And despite knowing she could not have this forever and that it all would have to end sooner than she would like, she leaned into him and let herself have this. Just for a little while. She could allow herself something, just for a little while, surely.

Even if it meant it was only going to hurt so much more in the end.

They gathered the box and her notes to take back to his rooms. He even agreed to let her seal her rooms again, though he asked if she could weave in the ability for himself to return if he should want. She could and did. It was simple enough and she didn't want to keep him out of her rooms.

Before they left, he stood in front of her wardrobe with a frown.

'I suppose I should allow you some of your own clothes,' he said.

She looked at the dresses and skirts and blouses hanging there. They felt like something from a long time ago, from another life, or for another woman.

'It is your choice, sir,' she said, quite deliberately. 'I am your slave, I belong to you.'

'Hmmm. I like dressing you in my things,' he said, not quite biting back a smile. 'I like seeing you in my off-cast clothing. I like displaying you so the world can see you like that. So that everyone knows you're *mine.*'

She felt the heat rise to her cheeks, just as she heard it in his voice. So she gathered her courage and stepped forward to stand in front of him. Close enough that she could put her hand on his chest, looking up

'Then I like being dressed as I am,' she said. 'As you like me.'

He shifted closer to her, an arm snaking around the back of her waist to hold her against himself.

'Still, there may be occasions when it suits me to have you dressed more appropriately,' he said. 'We will take back some of your clothes. But you will only wear what I tell you, when I tell you. I will continue to dress you to my pleasure.'

She drew back a shaky breath, gripping onto his shirt. She could feel him hardening in his pants, so she shifted her hips to press back against him. The look he gave her was pointed; he knew what she was doing. He didn't stop her though.

'And does it please, how you have dressed me now?' she said. 'Or would it please you better to undress me instead?'

'It would indeed,' he breathed and caught her lips in a kiss. His tongue licking into her mouth, his hands around her tight. She felt like she was held on this earth entirely by him. Held up by him, caught in the force of him, swept away by him. She wanted nothing other.

He broke off the kiss first, with a growl and a shake of the head.

'No,' he said. 'Stop tempting me, witch. You're not fully recovered. You were almost dead, this time yesterday.'

'I am recovered.' It came out more pleading than she meant it. 'Please, Callum. General. I...I need this. I need to know I please you.'

I need to know you think I'm good...

She didn't say the last. It was too difficult to put into words and in the end, she didn't need to. It seemed all the reassurance he needed, for his lips were back on hers in a bare moment, and then sliding down her jaw to her neck and throat. Kissing and biting, so that she hissed with need, but could do nothing except hang onto him and give herself over.

His hand went to the buttons of her shirt—his shirt, that she was wearing—twisting them undone with deft fingers and pushing the garment off her shoulders. She'd abandoned the bandages this morning; her wounds were a little pink in skin, but otherwise healed. All except the burned ring around her neck, the mark of the collar. That scarred. She did not even regret it, for it had been made by the collar he'd put around her neck, and she did not want to be anyone else except *his*.

His tongue traced it, the mark. His lips, then his teeth biting into her shoulder, even as his other hand ran down her side to her hip, then to her breast, finger flicking across the nipple. Such hung onto him and lost herself to the sensations, to the feel of him, the warmth of him. All of him.

He walked her backwards, until her calves hit the bed behind her. Her bed, so much the smaller and more modest than the furniture in the suite he had claimed.

'Down,' he growled and a thrill pulsed through her at the command. She immediately sat on the bed, looking up with wide eyes.

He stood between her legs, holding her gaze as he pulled his own shirt off, then undid his belt. Slowly, right by her face, not giving her any space, pushing his pants down over his hips and freeing his cock. He stroked it himself, eyes never shifting off hers, hard and glistening at the end with pre-cum.

Her mouth salivated, her whole body flushed. She didn't look away from him, but opened her mouth and leaned forward and let him feed his cock between her lips and over her tongue. She swirled her tongue around the head, tasting the tartness of him, closing her lips and sucking back. All the time keeping his eyes held with hers.

His breath shuddered and his hand crept around the back of her head, fingers winding into her hair. Tightening, pushing down. She breathed out through her nose and didn't fight him, let him push further into her mouth. She focussed on not gagging, on taking him as far as she could, a slow but hard and uncompromising slide into her throat, back out, then in again. While he held her head in the position he wanted it and used her mouth at his will and her entire body went weak, bones turning to liquid, with the need for it like this.

When he pulled back out entirely, she gasped back breath, clutching at his thighs, but tried to move in to take him again. He held her back by the hair.

'No. Move back up the bed,' he told her, so she did, pushing herself backwards onto the bed which had never had anyone in it except herself, in this room which had always been lonely, but hers. He came forward, shaking his pants all the way off and crawling to kneel over her. Leaning down to kiss her again, then kissing down her throat, her shoulders. Her breasts. Reaching with one of hand between her legs.

She gasped at the feel of his fingers lightly tracing the outline of her sex, reaching up with her own hands to hold him.

'No,' he said sharply. 'Hands above your head, hold the bedhead. I'm exploring here, you don't move.'

'Yes, sir,' she breathed, wobbly at the commanding tone as she put her hands against the headboard. Whimpering aloud when he pushed her legs apart with his hand, then shoved his fingers, two of them, inside her without any further preamble.

She was so wet already it didn't hurt. She arched under him, until he shot her a look and she fought instead to lie still, just like he wanted, while he finger fucked her hard.

'Good girl,' he said, and she flushed. 'So good for me.'

'Sir... sir...' She could barely remember how to form words. His hand between her legs was a revelation.

When he moved his thumb to her clitoris while adding a third finger inside her, she almost came then and there.

'Don't you dare,' he said, seeing the signs already. 'You wait for my permission.'

'Please, I need...'

'No you don't. You just lie there while I explore and have fun with you,' he said, a slow, dark grin forming across his features. 'We're going to play a game.'

'A game?'

'Mmmm. I ask a series of questions. You answer me whether you want to or not. And when I'm satisfied, then—and only then—will I give you permission to come.'

Her eyes flared wide. She was already so close she wasn't sure how she would hold out. And she didn't like the sound of those questions. She didn't think they'd be ones she'd want to answer.

She also wasn't going to refuse this game, no more than she would refuse him anything. Her whole body burned to play.

'So my little witch, will you be a good girl for me and answer my questions?'

'Yes, sir.'

His grin flashed dark. 'This was your bed. Tell me, have you had anyone else in it with you, these last few years?'

His fingers scissored inside her as he asked and she uttered a desperate sound, but managed to shake her head. No, of course she hadn't, and he would know that. He knew she had kept away from everyone.

'I want to hear your answer, slave.'

'No. No-one.'

'So you lay in this bed alone.' His grin twisted, as did his fingers inside her, and she gulped. 'Did you touch yourself, when in this bed, witch?'

She didn't want to answer. He'd known she wouldn't. She wasn't comfortable talking out loud about such things, she couldn't say the dirty words, she couldn't even swear. Which was why he was doing this. Enjoying making her squirm and turn red with embarrassment, asking her intimate details, all while fucking her with his hand.

'The truth now. Tell me if you touched yourself.'

She nodded fast, pressing her lips together.

'Out loud, I said,' he reminded her.

'Yes,' she whispered. 'Oh, please, can I..?

'No. Not yet. How often did you touch yourself? How often did you make yourself come?'

She screwed her eyes closed, desperately trying to stay still, her whole body like hot liquid, hands pressed against the backboard. She couldn't think, she couldn't move because he had said not to. The sensations were too much, the commands overwhelming. The world dropped away, almost like it had during the belting. Everything falling off except for him, his touch, his words, his orders.

'At night,' she said, a breath. 'And morning.'

'How many nights? How many mornings?'

'Every night. Every morning.'

His chuckle was low, delighted. 'Oh my hungry little slave. Can't say the dirty words, but craves the sensations still,' he said. 'Tell me what you thought about, when you were making yourself come. Tell me the fantasies in your head.'

She was long past denying him any answers. His face was above hers, his breath warm on her cheek, as he held himself up on one arm above her, while the other hand moved inside her, along her sex, and took her apart. Her every muscle hummed, her body floated, she couldn't think except to answer him.

'You,' she whispered. 'In so many ways.'

'Tell me some.'

'Coming back for your revenge, forcing me to pleasure you,' she whispered. 'Coming back to claim me, to teach me the errors of my ways. Coming back to—'

She cut herself off.

'What?'

'Save me,' she whispered. 'Please, may I? May I...'

'Yes, sweet slave. Yes, my Salryanna. Come for me. Come for me, my good girl, my love.'

And she did, waves of it rolling over her, muscles tensing and spasming and her entire body coming undone in his arms.

Then, when she was still again, his arms went around her and he held her as she cried, for somehow she always seemed to cry during sex now, and was she so damaged as all that? It seemed she was. But he only kissed her, and told her she was good, so good for him. He told her how much he loved her.

'I love you. Callum. I always have. I'm so sorry I hurt you. I love you.'

'Hush. I know you do, my good girl. I know. I'm here now.' He lay with her, just holding her, lips against her hair. 'I'm here and I will save you. I *will* save you.'

She closed her eyes. She wished it could be true.

'That was a fantasy,' she said, burying herself in his arms. Breathing in the scent of him. 'I know you want to, I know you will try. But that was a fantasy.'

'I came back, didn't I?' he said, then exhaled a long breath. 'Yes, for revenge, no matter I swore I it wasn't. We both know I took every opportunity to lash out at you, trying to salve my wounded pride. I made you a slave, I forced you, I claimed you as mine.'

'The real is different from the fantasy I had in my head,' she said. 'And you never forced me. I had to back you into a corner before you took me to bed.'

He ran a hand through her hair, along her scalp. A nice buzzing touch that left her tingling.

'The fantasy in your head is one you still have control of, even if you're fantasising about not having any control,' he said. 'Whereas when I arrived, I allowed you control of nothing. I was hurt and trying to hurt in return. You were right, I was cruel.' His eyes closed a moment. 'I wish I hadn't been.'

She put a hand up to his face and turned so she could kiss him. 'If we are no longer blaming ourselves, we must also give up the regrets born of it, I think.'

His eyebrow raised. 'Is that your way of telling me to cut out the self-pity, slave?'

Her lip twitched into a smile. 'It would be quite presumptuous of me to imply any such thing, my lord.'

'Yes, it certainly would. Wouldn't stop you though.'

She smiled, lifting herself up on one elbow so she could look at him properly. Running a hand over his chest and the myriad of small scars and marks detailing his fighting history across his skin.

'Tell me of you, General. I want to hear about you. Did you have all sorts of lovers over the last five years?'

That earned her an amused huff.

'I was too busy conquering the world to take lovers,' he said. 'There was Rorks. He was the only one. Well, apart from a few transactional arrangements, paying my way in some brothel or another.'

'I'm glad you had Rorks. I'm glad you weren't alone.'

'Mmmm.' He pulled her back to him and kissed her, slow and deliberate. 'Now neither of us are alone.'

She quieted him with her tongue, kissing him harder, until he rolled her over and moved atop her, opening her legs with his own. Sinking down into her, and she still so wet and slick and ready for him. Gasping when he entered her, still kissing, tongues in each other's mouths. She wanted to move quickly, push the pace, but he held them back. Slow, steady, a build down low in her body, and it didn't seem to matter she'd just had one orgasm, for he built the need within her again. Until she was panting, needy and lost in the sensations of him, taken apart and wrecked beneath him.

He let her climax as it naturally came to her this time, her body clenching around his own, which must have spurred on his own peak, for he was coming inside her all too soon afterwards. Groaning into her throat as he gave a final thrust inside her, then slowed to a still, then slipped carefully out.

He kissed her softly in the after of it. 'I will save you,' he whispered as he did. 'I *will*.'

As if he could make it happen by sheer force of his will. As if he could convince himself of it, as well as her, if only he declared it so.

As if he had any chance at all.

CHAPTER 23

Salryanna

Afterwards, they went back to his suite. She only just managed to make it there before her energy really faded. Stumbling through the doorway, so he had to catch her arm and steady her.

'Hmmm. To bed with you,' he said. 'You're still recovering. I've pushed you further than I should have.' A smirk surfaced, one she didn't think he could help. 'Right to letting you seduce me in your rooms. Temptress.'

'You're the one who dresses me in no more than your discarded shirts,' she said, as he helped her across the room. 'If you find me tempting, it is your own fault.'

'You're getting cheeky. I should do something about it.'

'You should,' she said, unable to help her own smile. 'I rather like the sound of that.'

He laughed softly. It was good to hear him laugh. It had been so very long.

She wasn't going to resist his instruction to rest, though. He was right, the fatigue was catching up with her.

Only before they were halfway across the room, a knock came at the door. Powerful and unhesitant. She glanced sideways to him and found a terse frown cross his features, but as they were just passing the sitting area, she reached out to one of the armchairs. There was possibly a second or two where he hesitated, perhaps debating whether to send her to the bedroom instead, but if so, it was only momentary. He helped her to the chair.

It was progress, she decided. Only the day before he'd have sent her to another room entirely in the attempt to keep his conversations private. Not that it would've stopped her listening in.

'Wait here,' he ordered, before returning to the door.

When he opened it, she wished she'd gone to the bedroom after all. At the door was one of the magicians.

Her stomach tightened. She neither trusted nor liked the three men who'd performed the ritual yesterday, a feeling she knew well was mutual. This was the older one, the strongest of them and most senior, grey through his hair and beard, blue and gold down his robe. When his eyes turned over her, there was a disdainful sneer in them, before he ignored her completely.

'General, may I have a moment of your time?'

Callum looked coolly at the magician, not dismissing him, but not welcoming either. 'How long do you need?'

'A minute only, I assure you.'

'Then go ahead.'

He gestured the man in, but remained standing just inside the door-way, not inviting him to sit down. Nor did he send her to the bedroom even now, which meant he either didn't mind her hearing, or actively wanted her to.

The magician didn't even look at her.

'I believe breaking the binding remains possible,' the man said. 'If we conduct the ritual in a place of greater significance to the demon's power. The location was an error last time, the cause of what went wrong.'

Her mouth went dry. She fought not to give visible sign of the nervousness in her limbs, she didn't want the magician to see it. The fact was, nothing had gone wrong in that last ritual, they simply hadn't understood what they were doing and she hadn't informed them of the truth of it.

If they knew to target a place of power now, did that mean they were learning?

Callum crossed his arms, sceptical. 'Where would such be? We're in the demon's castle, for god's sake.'

'The alter room. We need to locate it,' the magician said. 'It's the centre of the demon's concentrated power and if we conduct the ritual there, we can raise the demon. Destroy it in physical form.'

'And kill Salryanna, like almost happened last time?' Callum said, hard voiced. 'No. That is not an option.'

'The witch doesn't have to die. If the demon is manifested physically, outside of its host on this plane, as we could do in the alter room, then it could be defeated without killing the witch.'

Her eyes closed. It was perhaps true, theoretically. The magician wouldn't care for the exceedingly long odds of it though and wouldn't bother to inform Callum of those.

Callum wasn't foolish. He looked no more convinced than she felt.

'Salryanna has been researching options for capturing the demon for several years,' he said. 'I want you to review her research. It may assist.'

The sorcerer's eyes fell on her at last. Cool and full of judgement. Not appraising; the man had appraised her worth long ago, before ever meeting her, and had made his judgements then. They held. She was the enemy. She could not be trusted.

But the General he reported to had instructed him to engage with her ideas. So he looked to her, he gave her a solemn nod, then just as firmly looked away from her again.

'Of course, General,' he said, calmly. 'May I have the opportunity to question the witch?'

Callum's eyes narrowed. 'I'll have her work sent to you and if you have questions afterwards, you can ask them here, in my presence,' he said, firmly. 'In the meantime, work with my Captain to find the alter room. He's been mapping the castle, all its secret ways. He knows the layout better than anyone.'

A moment's silence met that. She looked down, aware of the glances to her, of the untruth in Callum's words. Yes, Rorks knew the layout best of anyone in his army, but there was one other who knew it far better.

Herself.

'General—' the magician began.

'I will enquire of the witch,' he said, cutting the man off hard. 'You speak to my Captain if you would like to know more.'

The man stepped back with congenial acquiescence. None of which Salryanna believed for an instant.

'Of course, General.'

He took his leave without a further glance her way. Yet she could feel his animosity as he went. The magician would happily see her sacrificed to kill the demon.

Callum wouldn't want to hear it. He already understood those men did not like her, but he wouldn't see the threat. Would they find the alter room? Could they? It would take them time, but Rorks was mapping this castle and maybe if they told him what to look for, he might be able to do it. She'd never kept up the strength of magical protections because there was never any other here to protect it from.

Her stomach turned with the concern. If they actually found it, what then?

Callum faced her, concern troubling his features. *I will enquire of the witch.* Would he ask?

What would she say if he did?

'General?'

It was another voice at the doorway, a more familiar one. A more welcome one. It broke the moment, her breath releasing, Callum stood straighter and turned at the call.

'Rorks? Come in. I just—'

He stopped when the Captain stepped into the room. She was alerted first by that, the sudden cutting off of Callum's words, even before she looked up to see Rorks slipping inside, slowly closing the door behind him. The man was hesitant in a way she'd never seen him before; usually he'd swan into the General's suite confident he was always welcome into Callum's spaces and company. Now, he came in tentative, looking away. Keeping his head down, angled to the side.

It didn't quite hide his face, though that was clearly what he was trying to do.

'What happened?' Callum's voice was half-strangled. He stepped forward, then stopped, as if he wasn't sure if he should rush straight over or give the man space. 'God, Rorks. Are you okay?'

Down the side of the Captain's face was the most awful bruising. Black eye, swollen cheekbone with split skin. His lip split and blooded. His face, those pretty features full of sunshine, had been beaten black and blue.

It wasn't fresh. She straightened with her own gasp. The blood had been cleaned up and the cuts had clotted. The bruising had really had time to bloom, so it must have been a few hours at least. Most likely it'd happened the previous night.

She looked to his hands on instinct, to see if his knuckles were equally bruised. Signs that he'd been fighting an equal fight. She couldn't see any indication of it.

'I'm okay, General, really,' Rorks said, still not quite looking at either of them. 'It's just a few bruises. Nothing to worry about.'

The man's voice was hoarse. Even she could see he was underplaying the severity of his wounds. This was a bashing, good and solid.

'Nothing to worry about?' Callum gestured straight to him. 'Your face! Rorks, what the fuck happened?'

She pushed herself up to stand, despite her own fatigue. 'Your bruising looks severe,' she said, as gently as she could. 'Did you see any medics? I could perhaps look over your wounds, I was trained as a healer.'

Rorks's expression tore at that and he looked at her direct for the first time. His eyes were glassy. Close to tears.

'Thank you. Medics aren't needed, really. Thank you. No. I'm okay. I really am.' He sucked back a breath. Then he straightened his shoulders, lifted his chin, and stood practically to attention. 'My apologies, General, but I made a poor choice and suffered its consequences. That is all. I will be fine. I just—'

Callum's eyes narrowed and he crossed his arms. 'Tell me what happened, soldier.'

The order was plain and simple and not to be denied. The firm direction was palpable, as was the underlying anger behind it, coming from the growing realisation obvious to both of them that Rorks was trying to avoid telling him something important.

Rorks closed his bruised eyes.

'I thought it'd be okay. I was off duty, as you ordered. But my mind wouldn't stop. I needed...well, you know me.' He tried a tight, pained smile that quickly disappeared. 'I just needed to be taken out of my head for a bit. Just a little while. So I went looking for something. You know. Just for a once off. A few hours to distract. No more than that, I promise.'

Something dark settled across Callum's face. As if he perfectly understood Rorks's stumbling, reluctant words and the meaning behind his upset confession. She didn't, not exactly, but she could see the men did and neither of them looked at all happy about it.

'Rorks, why didn't you come to me?' Callum said and there was something almost devastated in his tone. 'I would've kept you safe. I would've—' He broke off, then simply repeated, 'Why didn't you?'

Tears appeared in Rorks's eyes that he couldn't blink back.

'I didn't want to bother you, sir. Not with Salryanna here,' he said softly. 'You've only just got her back after all these years. I wasn't getting in the way of that. I just needed to get out of my head for a few hours, that was all. I can deal with the rest, I...'

He swallowed the words and looked to her with the most apologetic expression she'd ever seen. It made her want to go up and throw her arms about him, tell him it was okay, that he was always welcome. He could never get in the way. She was the one worried about doing that. He should always know he had space and a place here.

He looked down to his hands, shoulders dropping in resignation.

'I fucked up, Callum. I know I did. I'm sorry. But it's not hurt anyone else except me and I'll heal, it's only a few bruises.'

Callum's jaw was a tight ball. 'Who did this to you, Rorks?'

Rorks struggled to find his voice. Eventually he managed to whisper, 'Seth.'

The breath went out of her. Seth? The man who'd tried to rape her? Callum had said he was demoting him, punishing him. She'd assumed he'd been banished somewhere, but clearly he was still about the castle.

And Rorks had...what? Fought him? Confronted him?

No. She only realised now, so much later than Callum had. Rorks had gone to Seth willingly, looking for something else again.

The cold fury on Callum's face was almost as bad as those first minutes she'd faced him in her throne room, after she'd been dragged up from the dungeons. While Rorks could only stand before it, miserable and hurt.

'Tell me what happened,' Callum said, in a low, tight voice. 'In full detail.'

'It was off duty. It's not important—'

'You goddamn tell me, soldier!'

Rorks drew back a shaky breath. He must've known this was inevitable as soon as he appeared.

'I went to him. I initiated it,' he said. 'I thought...we'd messed around in the past. A year ago. And it was okay. He never went too far. He stopped when I asked him to back then. I didn't think...'

Callum's entire body was coiled, like a spring wound so tight it could snap.

'You went to Seth even after I warned you not to,' he said. 'Even after what he did to Salryanna.' He paused, but the only answer Rorks could give was to nod. 'And it went bad.'

'I'm sorry, General. Callum. Sir. I'm...'

Callum gestured to his face. 'Did you ask him to do this? The bruising?'

'No!' Rorks shook his head fast, then had to wince with the pain of it. 'I didn't submit to him. I just thought he'd be up for something, a bit of rough sex, that's all. I'd never kneel to a man like that.'

'You went to him.'

'I know I shouldn't have.' He wiped the dampness off his cheek. 'You'd told me not to and it was all I could think the whole time. So I tried to stop.' His shoulders dropped, defeated. 'That's when it went bad. He didn't like me changing my mind halfway through. Lashed out. Which is on me for going to him in the first place, when I already knew better.'

Salryanna felt like she might be sick. Her whole body sweaty and faint. She held onto it, gripping onto the back of the chair so she wouldn't sway. Rorks looked physically beaten, but emotionally far worse. She wanted to hold him and tell him it was okay. She wanted to remind him that this wasn't his fault, it wasn't on him at all and he could not be blamed for the harm inflicted by another. He had every right to change his mind, no matter when it was. It was the other who was guilty, not Rorks. She wanted to tell him that Callum would help him and she would help him too.

Only he didn't need that right now, her insisting on truths he wasn't yet seeing himself. What he needed was Callum and his very particular way of taking care of those he loved.

'Don't you dare say that,' Callum said in a hard voice. 'You do not compound the errors you did make by taking the blame for another's violence! Seth did this, not you.'

Which didn't seem to make Rorks feel any better. 'I went to him after you'd told me not to,' he said. 'I went against your orders.'

And she knew, then, what Rorks really needed to come through this. She knew, because she would feel the same. It wasn't gentle words from her and certainly it wasn't a hug. It was to be reminded of what he actually was responsible for, and to pay the price for that, so he could let go of blaming himself for everything else. He couldn't judge himself clearly right now and she knew what that was like. To assume blame for everything because your guilt felt so overwhelming. To never be able to forgive yourself anything at all.

She knew. And she knew who'd helped her with it. Rorks needed someone to judge him fairly, someone he trusted, and to punish accordingly, so he could let go of the rest.

He needed Callum in full, furious General mode.

Only Callum looked torn himself. Desperately angry at what had been done, but holding himself back. Why? Was it simply because he wasn't sure how much he should push on this, like he'd said to her yesterday evening, when opening up about his worries for the other man? Was it because of the ambiguous nature of the relationship between them, former lovers who clearly still cared?

Was it because of her?

'You didn't come to me,' Callum said, and ran his hands through his hair. A gesture of hurt and worry. She'd never seen him show it so openly before. 'Goddamn it, Rorks, you know you can always come to me. You don't have to risk yourself with low life rapists like fucking Seth.'

She bit her lip, looking between the two men. Callum as distraught as Rorks. She wanted to hug him too, but it wouldn't help. She couldn't fix this for them. They had to do that for themselves.

Rorks wiped hard at his eyes, no matter the bruising.

'I never knelt for him. You know that, don't you? Callum? General?' He stopped himself, with a desperate gasp, and turned to her. 'Salryanna, I'm sorry. I'm making such a mess of this, I'm so sorry. Since the first day I met him, I've understood how much he loves you. You're the centre of his everything. The last thing I ever wanted was to get in the way, not now he's got you back, I didn't want—'

Enough.

She stepped across to Rorks. She might not be able to fix this, but Callum could. And if this were the old days between he and his Captain, he'd have acted already. He would know what was needed to ground the man, to help him and calm the swirl in his head.

Rorks hadn't come to Callum because she was there. If Callum was also restraining himself for the same reason, she couldn't let that go on any longer. She had to stop such foolishness and not let them do that to each other.

So she went to Rorks, right up to him, until she stood directly in front of him. Taking his hands and holding them. He was a tall man, taller even than Callum, and she had to look up to meet his eyes as she held his fingers in hers.

'You're like me,' she said and it wasn't a question. 'You need him, don't you? To feel his control, so you can feel safe. To help define where your responsibility starts and ends, so you can let go of the rest.' She paused. 'Yes?'

Rorks stared at her with wide-eyes and obvious surprise. She wasn't sure why, for it seemed only obvious to her what he'd been going through. Why he'd chosen as he had, made the mistakes he had because of it, and took on guilt he shouldn't bear at the same time.

'Yes,' he breathed.

'Then know he is there for you whenever you need him. He will always be there for you,' she said, with genuine warmth and care. 'I can't change that. I wouldn't want to. I would never take him from you, no more than you'd take him from me. Okay?'

Tears pricked Rorks's eyes anew. 'Okay.'

'He is yours as much as he is mine. And we are both his,' she said, with a squeeze of the hands.

And then she let his hands go and stepped back. Straightened her shoulders and adopted a professional, neutral expression as she turned to Callum.

'General, if you need to discipline your soldier, please do not hesitate on my account,' she said, with formal rigour. 'I will go rest, as you wanted, and you leave you to deal with your man.'

Callum's face was peaked, a tight expression of upset and concern and utter fury at the way Rorks had been hurt. Underlain most of all by the guilt of not keeping him safe. He was holding a tight rein on it, but she could see it. She always had been able to read Callum.

He looked at her, perhaps trying to read her face as she was reading his. Then he gave her a grave nod and looked back to Rorks with a much darker expression indeed.

'You. Get in there,' he snarled at the Captain, pointing towards his study. 'We are going to discuss this in fine detail.'

Rorks still looked somewhat stunned. 'Yes, sir,' he managed, then ducked his head and all but stumbled in his rush to get into the study.

Callum waited until he had disappeared, before turning back to her. Shoulders still stiff with suppressed emotion.

'You are sure?' he asked her. 'It's okay if you're not.'

'I am very sure, my love. He needs you right now, desperately so. And you need him,' she said. 'I would not have the two of you separated, not because of me.'

He stepped across to her, cupped her face his hand, and kissed her.

'Thank you, witch,' he said. 'On his behalf and also on mine. Go rest. When lunch arrives, come fetch us.'

She nodded, then went to the bedroom to lie down as ordered, and left him to go see to his Captain.

CHAPTER 24
Salryanna

Lunch arrived sooner than she expected. She saw the movement out on the balcony from the bedroom where she was lying down. She hadn't slept, but she was feeling more rested, so she got up to watch the servants lay it all out. Fruits, sweetbreads, soup.

He'd said to fetch them when lunch arrived, and she would have to or else risk his lunch getting cold. Had there been enough time for whatever Callum planned, for the conversations they needed to have and their consequences to have played out?

She hesitated a moment, but there was nothing else for it. She had her orders, enough time or not.

She padded across to his study, bare feet on thick carpets, then hovered outside the door. She couldn't hear much from inside, so she lifted her hand and knocked, tentatively, on the wood.

'Come in, Salryanna,' he called.

She opened the door and stepped inside. They were both standing, but Rorks was looking away and only just pulling his pants back up over his hips, doing the buttons up. His face was red, where it wasn't black and blue, and his eyes bore a tell-tale glisten.

Callum stood far more calm and composed, but his belt wasn't in the loops of his pants, it was in his hand.

'You said to fetch you when lunch arrived,' she said. The under-standing of what had just happened in here brought a sense of order and control. It helped when her life had always felt beyond control. Hope-fully it had done so for Rorks as well. And for Callum.

'Thank you.' Callum turned back to his friend. 'Captain, look at me.'

Rorks finished the final buttons on his pants and came to stand before Callum, looking up into his eyes so much more easily now than he had out in the other room, when he'd first come in and hadn't wanted to face either of them. There was a looser sense to his limbs, a more relaxed tone to his whole body, and even though he'd been obvi-ously crying, still wiping at his eyes even now, he was no longer shaking or cautious or worried. Rather, he looked up at the General with adora-tion and awe.

Callum handed him his belt without instruction, as if he knew very well that Rorks understood what to do with it. And Rorks did, taking the curled leather and feeding the belt back through the loops of Callum's pants without hesitation, like he was finishing dressing him of a morning, while Callum stood still and allowed him to do so. The Captain reaching around him with care to ensure it carefully went all the way around in the right position, then buckling the belt the front, and only ever dropping his eyes for an instant when he needed to ensure it went in the right loop, otherwise holding Callum's gaze directly the entire time.

It was...intimate. A raw thing to watch. It brought a heat to her stomach, down low, and a flush of her own need, a warmth throughout. There was experience in the way Rorks did this, and command in the way Callum received the service, like they had both done this before.

'You won't disobey me again,' Callum said, in a firm voice.

'Never, sir.' Rorks buckled the belt and let his hands drop to his sides again.

Callum raised his hands to the Captain's face, careful of his bruising.

'And you won't take any responsibility for that other's violence either,' he said. 'What he did was not your fault. If I even hear a hint of you blaming yourself again, I will take out my belt again, understand?'

Rorks, face held close to Callum's in such gentle hands, nodded. 'Yes, sir.'

'I approve your partners. You are *my* Captain,' Callum said. 'Nobody else gets to touch you. Nobody I don't approve of. I will keep you safe, Rorks. Haven't I always?' He leaned his forehead against Rorks's own. 'You come to me if you're struggling. I'll look after you. You are mine, dammit. *Mine.*'

Rorks reached to his sides, gripping his shirt. 'Yours. Always.'

Callum kissed him softly on his bruised lips. Lingering on the contact, if carefully, for the man was still injured and sore. Split lip or not, Rorks leaned immediately into the touch, kissing back and clinging onto Callum all the harder.

When they finally stepped apart, Callum looked to her. She smiled, wanting him to know it gladdened her heart to see them together.

'Salryanna, would you see to my Captain's injuries, do what you can to assist his healing?' he asked.

'Of course, General,' she said. 'Am I allowed to use healing magics?'

A darker look pierced his expression. 'Not if it draws from that damned demon.'

'It doesn't, I promise. Healing is my magic, not the demon's,' she said. 'It won't fix everything. It may not even help much. It's not the strongest of magics. But it could assist in soothing some of the worst ache.'

'Then yes, permission is granted,' he said. 'For the injuries to his face and body as inflicted last night. Not any pains inflicted by myself on him just now. Those I want him to feel in full.'

'Of course. I understand.'

Rorks stood self-conscious as they spoke, cheeks flaming red around the bruising. Standing very close to Callum, reaching out to his hand and holding it tight.

Callum turned to Rorks again. 'Stay here with Salryanna. There's lunch on the balcony, I need you to supervise her meal, ensure she eats, then allow her to see to your wounds. Both of you are to stay here in my rooms until I return.'

Rorks looks vaguely uneasy at that.

'Do you not need me to accompany you?' He spoke carefully,

perhaps not sure how the question would be taken right now. 'We were scheduled to speak to the governor, and—'

Callum's eyebrows raised. 'Did I not just give you an order, Captain?'

'Of course, sir. My apologies.'

'I'm not putting you back on active duty right now, Rorks, so don't even think of it,' Callum said. 'I want you here by my side, where I can keep an eye on you, until I decide you're ready to return to work.'

The Captain nodded, gazing at Callum with wide eyes full of reverence. Even she could see just how much Rorks idolised the man. How deeply he loved his General.

It made her smile. She could understand why someone would love Callum, it only made sense to her.

Yes, sir,' Rorks said.

'I will speak to the governor,' Callum said, before his expression darkened. 'But first, I have another matter to attend to.'

She stepped forward, especially when Rorks didn't ask. 'What are you going to do?'

Callum didn't look angry she asked. He did, however, look grim.

'I am going to deal with Seth. Once and for all.'

He sent Rorks to the balcony, but bade her bring him his sword.

He hadn't worn it since he'd arrived and successfully taken the castle. The last time she'd seen it on him was when she'd been dragged before him in the throne room and that had been full dress uniform, or so she'd subsequently learned.

It wasn't a dress sword, though. This was a real weapon which had seen real battle, dark and stained, well cared for. She wondered uneasily what his plans for Seth were. This castle had its dangers, particularly when it came to violence. Things escalated here in ways not always expected. It was one of the many reasons she'd sent everyone away.

She watched him strap it on, so it hung from his waist.

'Do I want to ask what you're going to do?' she said, quietly.

'No,' he said, simply. He didn't sound like he would brook any questions about it, either.

She nodded, looking down at the sword on his hip. It seemed long, dangerous. A weapon of death and destruction. He was a soldier, he led an army, he knew death and destruction very well. He did not shy away from such things.

But she was not him.

'I wouldn't dream of advising you on the running of an army, General,' she said. 'But...can I ask a favour?'

His eyes narrowed. He wasn't in the mood to be challenged, not after what had happened with Rorks, but this wasn't merely a professional concern. This was personal. He was going to see to Seth not only due to what that man had done to Rorks, but also to her.

'You can ask,' he said. 'I do not guarantee I will grant it.'

'If your plans for Seth are something...final,' she said, eyes on the sword. 'Would you consider imprisoning him first, if only for a few days, and making your decision on his fate after a little time has passed?'

She could tell by his expression he wasn't particularly happy with that. He crossed his arms and stared her down.

'Is this your way of suggesting I give it time and decide with a cooler head?' he said pointedly. 'Because I do not appreciate the interference in my affairs, slave. Seth is a soldier who disobeyed orders and harmed others. Discipline in my ranks is my responsibility.'

'It's not that, I promise. Well, maybe, a little, but...' She tried to find the right words. 'What you decide to do in retribution for what he did to your Captain is none of my business. But you are also seeking retribution on my behalf. For what he did to me. And... I don't want anyone else hurt due to me.'

'Sal, you cannot be defending him. He was going to rape you that day in the throne room.'

'He was going to the day before, too. That time on your orders.'

His expression darkened. 'That was a threat used to keep you in line before I understood your full situation.'

'Perhaps. Perhaps you would never have let it actually happen. Or perhaps, had I been the enemy you expected to find here, you might have,' she said. 'It doesn't actually matter. To me in that room, there was no difference. In my experience, both were the same threat. And both were real.'

His jaw was a solid ball. She knew this was a challenge, a difficulty. He didn't want to hear it. She didn't even want to make it. But he was not a man to shy away from hard realities. He'd known exactly what he was doing when he chose his strategy of conquest here, the taking of the castle, and the taking of her as its Queen. Just as he'd known exactly what he was doing when he'd had her threatened with public rape. It wasn't pretty or nice, it had been cruel and ruthless. But he'd never denied his ability to be that, either.

She put her hand on his arm.

'It is your decision and I am your slave,' she said gently. 'I have never resisted that. I'm simply uneasy with vengeance sort on my behalf. I have experienced too much pain, and caused it too often in others, to be comfortable with being the reason behind it for anyone. It doesn't matter who they are, this is about who I am.'

'It's not vengeance. It's discipline in my ranks,' he said. She didn't call him out on it, on the fact that it was as much revenge for the hurting of those he cared for as anything else. 'I will make my own decision on that.' He paused. 'But I will consider your words before I do. That's the best I can offer you.'

'Thank you.'

She reached up, standing on tip-toes, and kissed his cheek.

He wound a hand around the back of her head and pulled her into him and kissed her lips, firmly, tongue against hers in her mouth and she melted against him as he did.

'Go eat,' he said, when he let her go. 'And look after Rorks for me. He needs a kind hand now.'

'I will. Don't fret about him. I'll look after him until you get back.'

She watched him go, the door closing behind him, that sword on his hip, and tried not to wonder what he would do when he found Seth. It would not be pleasant, and she was glad she would not be there to see it, even if all he did was throw the man to the dungeons. She suspected his choices would be a lot more brutal than that, however.

She found Rorks on the balcony, leaning on the balustrade and looking out over the valley. He must have heard her approach, for he turned when she stepped outside, and even gave her a slight, if melancholy, smile.

'He's gone, has he?' he asked. 'I guess he took his sword?'

She nodded. 'I asked him to consider putting Seth in the dungeons first, before making any final decision. I hope you don't mind.'

Rorks sighed. 'I don't think that will change anything. Callum will probably execute him regardless,' he said. 'He has to. If he lets Seth get away with disobeying his orders and harming his favourites, he'll have rippling disrespect and disorder in the ranks. He has to come down hard after this. I've forced Callum's hand on that as much as anything.'

Maybe she understood that. She didn't disagree. But she had needed to say something to Callum for her own sake, and was glad she had, even if he chose differently.

She cocked her head. 'Favourites?'

Something lighter twisted at the man's lips.

'You and me. Welcome to the club. It's a bit more complicated than you might think, being the recipient of the General's affections,' he said. 'His world is a political one. That means ours is too.'

She felt a kind of thrill at his unconscious wording. *Ours*. As if it really were a club. As if they were in this together, not just her and Callum, but her and Rorks too.

As if she wasn't alone.

It was a euphoric feeling, to not be alone. To know there were others by her side, even if they couldn't change the ultimate outcome and her fate would still be what it was always doomed to be. She wouldn't have to face it alone and uncared for. That was a miracle she'd never dared to hope for.

'Oh, I don't know. He made me a slave. All I have to do is let him make the decisions.' She grinned. 'He can have the complications. I'll just follow orders.'

Rorks snorted amusement. 'You could be a soldier, sounding like that.' He nodded to the table laid out with food. 'Come on. I'm supposed to make sure you eat. So please do so because I don't want to cop another belting.'

She sat, and so did he, across the table from her, carefully. He was probably pained, bruised from the belt as much as Seth's fists. She ate some soup, as did he, and some fruit following. Found she was actually hungry in a way she hadn't felt for a long time. She ate even more than him, which was astounding given how little she usually took, though admittedly he didn't eat a lot.

'Are you okay?' she asked, over the soup.

'I am now. Well. Getting there,' he said, and gave her a small smile. 'Thank you. For making me feel welcome. I hadn't realised how much the impact would hurt. Feeling like I had to step out of his life.'

'Oh, Captain. Please don't think that. You are welcome, I want you here as much as he does,' she said, urgently, because she couldn't have Rorks feeling like that, not because of her, not for anything. 'He loves you. You know that, don't you?'

He paused before answering, as if he had to think about it.

'Yes, I think. I think I do know that. But it's always been unspoken between us,' he said, at last. 'For my part, I adore him. I'd die for him. I have been in love with the man since the day we met. He saved my life, more than once, but there's no debt there. It's simply who he is, a man who saves others, even at risk to himself.'

She looked down into her soup. Remembered his words, *I will save you.* He wouldn't, he couldn't, but he would try. Even at risk to himself.

It left her stomach turning uneasily.

'I was always alone,' she said, not looking at him directly. 'I couldn't let anyone near. It was too dangerous. I've been alone for so long that... I'm not always sure how to be with others now.' She looked up to him, meeting his eyes. 'He thinks he can save me. He can't. But he thinks he can.'

Rorks eyed her with some speculation, sitting back in his chair.

'Don't underestimate him. He rose from the depths of the salt mines. More than once he's done what others considered impossible.'

She was not surprised the Captain would have such faith in Callum. She felt the pull to it herself, and she knew the reality of just how impossible his aims were here.

'I believe he can change the world,' she said quietly. 'But to do so, he needs to survive this castle first. He needs to defeat the demon. And he won't be able to do that if he's focussed on saving me.'

A troubled frown crossed Rorks's eyes. His bruising was so stark against the paleness of his skin, the blond of his hair; he looked almost fey, with his colouring, so different from the darker tones of Callum and herself. He was like a picture of an angel of the Light. What had Francis called him? The one with the pretty face. And Seth had taken to his face with his fists.

Surely Seth would know Callum's fury would come after that? Perhaps his attempted assault on her could be read as a soldier not knowing where the unspoken lines were; Callum had all but encouraged such a thing in the way he'd set up her enslavement, even if he didn't like to acknowledge it. But an attack on Rorks? The General's favourite? A Captain of high rank, while Seth had been demoted for the attack on her.

Or was that the point? Lashing out in anger for his demotion, targeting the man Callum openly cared for, his long-term offsider. Perhaps not daring to do it outright, but when Rorks had gone to Seth, it must have seemed like a genuine opportunity for revenge.

'Callum doesn't make idle claims,' Rorks said. 'If he says he will save you, he means it. The man has been through hell on earth and not only survived, but come out victorious from it.'

'I've seen the scars on his back,' she said, looking down at her plate. 'I caused those scars and the hell on earth he suffered through.'

'No, you didn't. The command of the Light did that to him,' he said, and in that moment, he sounded as firm as Callum ever did. 'You broke his heart, that's true. But you didn't order his flogging and you didn't send him to the salt mines. And I think his heart has mended somewhat, now he has seen you again.'

He gave her a smile. There was something friendly and warm about Rorks. Something genuinely empathetic. No wonder Callum had taken to him, cared for him so much.

'The scars still hurt him sometimes. Massage helped, I was able to do that for him, at least,' she said. She bit her lip. 'Can I ask you something? About...back inside? Before.'

He took a piece of fruit, picking at his plate.

'You mean about me and Callum? You can ask anything you like. I'll not hide anything from you.'

'Only...when I came into the study, and I know he um...'

'Gave me a fucking good hiding?' he said, with clear pragmatism, even when her words stumbled. 'I deserved it. He'd told me not to go near Seth and I did so anyway. That's what the belting was for. The disobedience. Deliberately putting myself in harm's way when I'd been warned already.'

She nodded, looking down at her own plate. He was so matter of fact it made it easier to ask.

'There was a thing you did,' she said. 'He gave you the belt, afterwards, and you put it back on him, and it looked so intimate. And I wondered...well, I'm not sure what I wondered, but what was that?'

Rorks considered a moment before answering. 'He and I have been side-by-side for close to five years. Off and on sexually, and we were never exclusive with that, but I have always looked to his leadership and followed his direction, and I always will.'

'Not just because you're a soldier and he's your General?'

'I'd obey that man if we were shepherds in a field, Sal. It's very different to the demands of military hierarchy,' he said, then gave her a smile. 'You know this. You know what it's like. You're like me, when it comes to Callum.'

She raised an eyebrow. 'I'm a slave. I don't get a choice.'

'The most willing slave I've ever met,' he returned, with an amused snort. 'I bet you wouldn't be so obsequious if he sold you to another. It's him, not the slavery, that you're here for.'

She sighed, but there seemed little hope in pretence with this man.

'Yes, okay. If he were anyone else, or thought to sell me to anyone else, I wouldn't still be sitting here. I'd have...disappeared.' She shrugged. 'I'm not entirely defenceless, not even when I had that collar on.'

'Exactly,' Rorks said. 'I've been through this castle end-to-end, I've seen how many hidden towers, passages, secret doors, and protected places it has, and I don't know it half as well as you do. You could've taken yourself off at any point and we'd never have found you again, not if you didn't want us to. And I'm pretty sure you'd have found a way out of that collar too, given enough time, had you really wanted to.'

She pressed her lips together. 'Yes,' was all she said.

'So. You're here, like this, because you choose to be,' he said. 'You do this because you want it. Like me.'

There was no point claiming otherwise, not when Rorks saw into her head in a way not even Callum managed. Because they were the same like that, Rorks and her. They were both adoring of the General, to start with.

She gave him a nod and he grinned at her for the concession, like it was an argument won.

'Anyway, the thing with the belt was just a habit we fell into, years ago,' he said, with a shrug. 'If he'd punished me for something, it was part of showing respect for that process, for the need for it, for the implements he chose to administer it. To acknowledge, for the both of us, that this wasn't something resented or unwanted, but willing, consensual, desired.'

She nodded to that too, because she understood.

'Nothing changes because he found me,' she said. 'Okay? Nothing between you and him should change at all. Sex included, if you choose it. Your relationship with him is too important. I don't want him to lose you. I don't want you to lose him.'

'What about you?' Rorks said, softly.

'You won't change what is between Callum and I,' she said. 'I lose nothing by his having you. Yet I may gain a friend myself.' She looked out over the valley, the incredible view of it. 'I've been alone a long time, Captain. I hardly know how to deal with other people. Crowds scare me. My own power scares me, for how it endangers others. Yet Callum understands me. He makes me feel safe. And maybe it's because he loves you, or maybe it's because you're like me, but you feel safe too.'

'I would no more hurt you than he would. He loves you and I really don't want to get in the way of that.'

'You don't. That's the thing,' she said. 'If my world consisted of just these rooms and the both of you, I would be quite happy.'

He smiled. As if the thought made him happy too. There was a relaxation to his shoulders, as if she'd finally convinced him it was okay. That he could have a relationship with Callum, that if they chose to return to a sexual relationship that would be okay too, whatever was needed between them. He was so desperate not to hurt her, and not to harm her relationship with Callum, but he wouldn't, couldn't, do that.

Of course, her world didn't consist of just these rooms and the two men. And she could never be happy because she knew that it would not end well for her. That wasn't Rorks's fault, or Callum's. It wasn't even hers. It was just the way things were.

Her world revolved around a demon more powerful than either of the men really understood. And her only objective now was making sure that they were safe and saved from it, and Callum could see out his aims for the world, with Rorks by his side.

Even if she had to betray them both to do it.

CHAPTER 25
Salryanna

S he took Rorks back into the sitting room to see to the healing. Callum had given her the okay to use her magic to help ease the ache from his bruising, and if that was one good thing she could achieve, then she was glad to do so.

He sat on the couch, looking wary as she knelt in front of him so she was eye height.

'I'm not the one you should be kneeling in front of,' he said, trying to make a joke, but only sounding nervous. Soldiers and magic, they just couldn't get their heads around it.

She gave him a pointed look. 'I'm a healer. It's not that kind of kneeling.'

'I know. Sorry. I'm just...not good around magic.'

'You and every other soldier.' She gave him a smile. 'Don't worry. It's gentle, it's natural. You won't feel anything adverse, hopefully the opposite. It won't fix everything, but it might bring down the swelling a little and make your face feel less tight.'

'That would be good.'

She inspected the bruising carefully, and took a cool wet cloth, which she'd prepared already, to his face, to sooth the swelling. He was still tense as anything, especially as she put down the cloth and instead held her fingers against the bruising around his eye. It was swollen to the point where he could barely open it and coloured a nasty black-purple. His cheek bone was also swollen, the skin split.

'Did he use his fists?' she asked, gently.

'And boots.'

She stiffened. 'To the face? That's a deadly act.'

'To the body, mostly.' He looked away. 'He knocked me about until I wasn't struggling anymore, then he held me down and finished taking what he wanted, until he was done.'

Her hand against his face stilled. He must have noticed because he let his gaze travel back to her face.

'It's okay. I survived the salt mines. It's not the first time I've been fucked against my will.'

'That's rape,' she said. 'It is not okay at all.'

'Yeah. It wasn't uncommon in the mines.'

She took hold of his hands and held them tight. Callum had told her that already, it shouldn't be a surprise, and yet the horror of it still sat sour in her stomach.

'I'm so sorry,' she said. 'Are you hurt, physically, for it?'

He shook his head. 'I don't think so. Not this time. We'd already...' He winced. 'I changed my mind after we started. I was already pretty ready for him, physically I mean.'

'That doesn't make it any better,' she said quietly.

'No. It doesn't.'

He sounded like he knew what he was talking about, which only made it worse. The implication that he had been physically damaged before. The pragmatism when he said he was physically prepared, even when it was still rape. She would not pry further, no matter his tone of practicality, for she could also recognise a mask when one was being worn. The defensive armour of cynicism.

'I will focus on your face, and...where on your body did he damage most?'

'Ribs, I reckon. Not that he broke anything, at least. And gut. It's all bruising, far as I can tell. Nothing more.'

As if that was nothing. As if the purples and blacks down the side of his face meant nothing for not being broken bones or torn skin.

Soldiers. If it wasn't gushing blood or falling off, they didn't count it as important.

She was a healer, however. Before the demon ever entered her life, before anything else, she had been trained as a healer and maybe her natural magics weren't as strong, but they were still there and still real. If they were all the power she had, she would be happy. She would give up all the rest in an instant, if she could.

'Don't touch the bruising from before. From Callum,' he said, as she sat back and prepared to work. Perhaps he meant it as a reminder.

'I know. I wouldn't.'

Because she knew how fondly she had held the sensations close to her, before the collar was taken off and her body healed itself, bruises from the belting included. She'd revelled in the twinge and ache of them, because each moment had felt a comfort, somehow. A reminder that she didn't have to feel guilty anymore, because she'd already paid a price, one he deemed enough, even when her incessant self-reproach wouldn't let up. She could trust him to be fairer on her than she was on herself.

Now the collar had gone it was as if he'd never taken his belt to her skin at all. Only the red mark around her throat, the burn left by the collar, remained. And that took some effort for her to retain, when her body wanted to heal.

She knelt back and raised her hands in the air in front of her, making a complicated gesture before his face. A whisper of a word, two, not his language, not even her own. He watched with widened eyes, stiff where he sat on the couch, not liking this, but letting it happen without interference because...well, because he must trust her. Because Callum trusted her to do this, he had asked it of her, and Rorks would obey his General. He would trust her too.

When had Callum started to trust her like that? Not when he'd first arrived; the distrust between them then had been palpable. Yet it seemed to take hardly any time for them to find each other again, even in this most dire of circumstances. Callum trusted her even with his favourite. And she relied on him, believed in him. Hid herself behind his protection.

His protection could not last, of course, no matter how much he wanted it to.

Just as she should not be trusted.

She healed Rorks's face with gentle hands and gentle magics. The body blows too, bruising on his ribs and hips. She carefully left the impact of the belting alone, as both men wanted. Whispering and moving her hands before him and watching the swelling recede, the bruising fade. Not completely, but enough to get him through the worst of the injuries. It drained her doing even that much, something she had not mentioned to Callum, because if she had he would not have allowed her to do this. She wasn't fully back in strength and this took quite a bit out of her.

She got him to the best point she could, satisfied she'd done some real good to heal the harm done to his body. Then she smiled, shifted her hand in another direction, said another word, different ones again, and watched as Rorks instantly fell asleep.

She caught him as he slumped over. Laid him carefully, gently, upon the couch.

He was comfortable there and would not be hurt. She would keep him safe, as she would Callum. They needed each other, those two, and she would make sure the General of the Light could see out his plans for the future, and would have his favourite by his side as he did. Even if that couldn't be her.

Callum needed to succeed here. She would make sure of that, too.

Once she had settled Rorks, she stood up and stepped back. Glancing only once at the door, before heading into the bedroom. This was best done in another room, away from the gentle Rorks, and the bedroom was large enough.

She walked past the couch and the armchairs, the coffee table and the fireplace. The cabinets and the bookshelves still half-empty. Callum hardly had time to fill them yet. Still, the fact they were partially filled, books he'd brought in already, suggested he meant to stay. He really had claimed this castle. He meant to use it as his base, while he challenged the command of the Light and control of this land.

He meant to free the people. Of all the impossible things in this world, he would take that one on and he would succeed. She would make sure of it.

She went into the bedroom and stood in the centre of the room, where there was a decent amount of space. Then she stood still, taking long breaths to centre herself and find her courage.

Once she was centred enough, she raised her arms. And called down the demon.

The darkness overwhelmed in an instant.

She gasped it back, the room falling away, the world disintegrating around her. Nothing to hold onto, so she was scrabbling in the ether, falling, floating, unmoored. Filled with terror, for she was always filled with terror at this moment, she'd never become used to it, not once in all the years. Perhaps that was appropriate.

She wasn't the only creature here. That was the point, of course. She reached out, not so much physically as psychically. Stretching to see if she could find—

The searing pain doubled her over, then bent her back almost in two. It took every sound from her, so she could only gasp, and sound-lessly beg, which of course was useless. Even if she'd yelled out words of submission, it wouldn't have helped.

Instead, she rallied what little strength she had, cursing herself for having to do this while still recovering and weakened from the demon's attack during the ritual. With a final effort, she forced herself upright and still.

It took all her willpower to manage it. Even after she stood still, unbent, unbroken, bones unsnapped, she panted with the force of it.

'My Queen.'

The demon's voice was not human and surrounded her. She swallowed at the way it grated along her bones in the darkness.

'My Lord.' She dragged back another breath, got herself together. 'Perhaps a little light to appease my human eyes?'

He did nothing, but when she raised her hand and conjured such for herself, it was not opposed. She even created a floor, walls, lanterns upon them. Not a whole room, but enough of a structure to ease the way her mind still balked at the impossible proportions of this space in which the demon was bound.

This was not the demon's dimension or home. This was his prison, and one of her creation. Within it, he was all powerful. She stepped into this place at considerable risk. But it was not uncalculated. The demon still needed her, after all.

Something slithered around her leg. She fought to stay still; to fight such things only made them worse. She swallowed as it gripped her ankles, one then the other. Maybe a snake. Maybe nothing so obvious.

'There are people in my castle,' the demon said, speaking in her language for once, rather than straight into her head. It was undoubtedly for a reason, probably a trick. 'You have brought back the sacrifices for me, my Queen.'

'I have not,' she said, standing her ground. 'That is not my doing.'

'You rule all powerful in your world.'

'I do not. There is another. There are complications. I have been deposed.'

A kind of laughter echoed about her brain. About the emptiness of the space and between the flickering walls that faded in and out of view.

'What do I care for human structures of power or rule. You have all the power you could want, Witch Queen. You could use it, if you chose. You could rule your entire world. You are more powerful than any other of your kind.'

Her eyes closed. 'I know. I choose not to use it.'

'That is your choice. I care little.'

The voice was indifferent. He was so beyond her world and its petty squabbles. So beyond anything the minds of humanity could envision. The slithering continued up her leg, wrapping its way around her. Around her waist too, and arms, pulling them back. She didn't fight it. She wasn't here without purpose and the trick with the demon was to pick appropriate battles.

Tendrils of black wound around her throat, through her hair. She gave herself in to them and let them have their way. It was give and take with the demon. She gave some, so she could take some. That was a language the creature understood.

'I will take them as sacrifices anyway,' the demon said, almost idle about it.

'You will not,' she said, through clenched teeth.

'You are waning, my Queen. You won't have the strength to stop me soon.' There was a flash in front of her. A kind of face, all sharp teeth and bloodied terror.

'I can still stop you now,' she said, trying not to shy back from the image. The demon's visage was not something that could easily be held in a human mind, not even her own, so far beyond her comprehension it was. But it gave her flashes, moments, images to hang understanding on. Mostly what she understood was that it was terrifying and vicious and awful.

'I have come to ask for a boon,' she said, while she still could. The slithering, curling darkness was wrapping its way around her in black tentacles. They squeezed, here or there, threatening to take the breath out of her.

'There will be a price,' came the answer.

'There is always a price. I'm here to pay it, am I not?' She tried to lift her head. Show some pride. 'You will take me soon. I could fight that, I could maybe last for years yet. Then pass on my knowledge to the next, to continue to trap you still.' She gasped back a breath as a tentacle slithered along her stomach, then around her breasts. 'But I will not, I will not fight you any longer. I will give in to all you require of me. If you leave the General and his people alone.'

Laughter echoed so loudly it hurt her head. 'I will take this world for my own. I will eat their spirits so they dance in pain for eternity.'

'No.' She gritted her teeth against the force of his will and matched it with her own. 'He intends to take on the Light. To oust them from the world.'

'I care not for petty human struggles.'

'I am your Queen. You want me. Give me this, and you will have me.'

'I will have you anyway.'

She snarled her response, pushing all her will outwards, and in doing so, shaking off the curling, slithering coiling black tendrils slowly crushing her body.

'You. Will. Not.'

She stood alone, standing up to the demon, not trapped, not harmed, and he could not have her, not like he wanted. Not unless she let him.

'I defy you now and I will defy you always,' she cried out in a fury. 'And maybe I will wane, but another will come in my place, and then another, and then another. You will be the one trapped for all eternity!'

She paused, but he gave no answer. She could feel him still there in the darkness.

'Or...you can give me this boon,' she said into the silence. 'And I will give you myself.'

She let the breath go out of her. Shoulders slumping with it. She wasn't sure it made any sense, only the demon didn't see the world in the way she did, or other humans. The demon was too large to consider reality as they knew it. She was bound to the demon and her fate was destined due to it. None of this would change that.

The demon would have her anyway. But for some reason, the free offering of herself meant something to him.

The snaking tendrils found their way back around her ankles, holding her in place. Then her wrists. Then her body, around her waist, her thighs. Her throat. She did not fight, she gave in to them. Closing her eyes and letting it happen. It was not the first time she'd experienced this. She wasn't sure she could survive it again.

A sliding slickness along her stomach, between her breasts, around them. A tightness as the coil around her throat wound harder and threatened to take the very breath from her lungs. She didn't need air here, but her body didn't know that, breathing was an instinct and the panic began when her airways constricted. She could not move, tentacles holding her in place, pulling her limbs wide, which made the panic all the worse for her immobility.

Tears pricked her eyes, she could not help it, as a slippery black length snaked across her face to her lips, pushing them apart and sliding into her mouth. Like a tongue of darkness and foul intent. Pulsating in her mouth and tasting sour, tendrils in her hair pulling back her head, she could not scream now, she could make no sound. She could only exist as the creature took from her, over and over again.

When the snake climbed her leg and pushed into her sex, she tried to scream regardless, but the sound was lost to the thing in her mouth. It pushed in deep, a sliding wetness fucking into her. Smaller bursts from it spreading across her skin, to her arse, and inside there too, like fingers in and out.

The room she had created fell away, the lights snuffed out. The floor and the walls dissipating back into the nothing that was here. Until she was lost to the void, voiceless, motionless, only a vessel for the demon to hurt, over and over again. As the tendrils of it, the tentacles of it, shoved inside of her deep and hard and rough, into her body, but mostly into her mind. A black horror that took her over and infused her every pour and crushed any sense of self until there was nothing left of her. There was only the pain and the suffering.

She was only suffering, that was all she was. Just as the demon wanted her to be.

CHAPTER 26
Callum

It was almost dusk when he returned to his rooms, grim faced and tired, but at least satisfied enough had been done to manage the immediate issues. Seth was not dead, no matter how fiercely Callum wanted it. Instead, he was thrown to the dungeons and would stay there until Callum had more time to decide what to do with him, something that approximated justice rather than mere revenge.

If Salryanna's words had left their mark upon his leaving to see to the work, so be it. He hadn't liked her way of comparing what Seth had done with what he himself had threatened her with, though he wasn't fool enough to deny her experience of it as being equal. He had created the allowance for such behaviour in his own men; he had loosened the boundaries by permitting, even encouraging, the threat of it. Which meant it was at least partly on him that the likes of Seth began to take more liberties than meant. Callum didn't regret his choices, except maybe not dealing more finally with Seth when he'd shown his true nature upon first assaulting Salryanna, but he did acknowledge their consequences. All of which meant it was also partly on him that Rorks had been hurt the way he had.

He was exhausted with thinking around it, wondering how much he had left the two people he loved most open for attack, when he was the one supposed to protect them. His heart still twisted to recall the bruising on Rorks's face. Worse, the hesitation and hurt in his eyes when he'd described what Seth had done to him. The way Rorks had blamed himself, which had sealed the consequences really. Callum hadn't wanted to punish the man, but Rorks needed someone to judge him fairly, because if left to judge himself he would never forgive himself. Rorks had needed to know Callum was there and in control, just as much as Callum needed to know he had Rorks within his control. That he could protect, and discipline, and make everything right for him again.

It was quiet when he first came in the doors, closing them behind him with a soft click. He was about to call out, before seeing Rorks asleep on the couch. For a moment he stood there, watching the man's sleeping face. The swelling around his eye had gone down significantly, the bruising visibly faded. Whatever Salryanna had done, it had a genuine positive effect.

Salryanna. He looked up, towards the bedroom; she must be in there. Resting, with any luck.

He turned to go find her, but as he did, Rorks shifted on the couch. 'Boss?'

The Captain's voice was muffled, half asleep. Callum went across to him, crouching down and reaching a hand to his face to brush away the hair that had fallen in his eyes.

'I'm here, Rorks,' he said quietly. 'How are you feeling?'

'Like I'm hungover. Or half-drugged. That was one hell of a sleep,' he said, trying to rub his face, and push himself up. Callum helped him sit. 'What time is it? Where's Salryanna?'

'Late afternoon. I've just walked in. I'm about to find her,' he said, trying not to show the curl of unease in his gut at Rorks saying he felt drugged, and Sal not in sight. It was magic, that was all. He didn't trust it, though even he had to admit Rorks's face looked much better.

'The gods, but my head is fuzzy,' Rorks said, grimacing.

'Sit there for a bit, don't get up too fast. You—'

There was a thump, loud, from the bedroom. Like something hard falling to the floor.

Callum was standing in an instant. Rorks also, though he staggered.

Callum steadied him, their eyes meeting in equal wariness. They hadn't worked together so closely for so long without being able to read each other, especially in times of stress.

'Go,' Rorks said. 'I'm right behind you.'

Callum did, rushing through to the bedroom, not even sure what his urgency was, only that he felt it. A burning fear that something had gone wrong, something he hadn't been ready for. Something unexpected. He'd learned to despise the unexpected. Five years ago, he'd never seen Sal's betrayal coming. In the salt mines, they never gave warning, they simply pounced. These days, he liked to know where he stood. He liked to be in control.

This felt increasing out of his control and he wasn't even sure why.

He slid to a stop in the door to the bedroom. 'Sal.' Then he dived forward to get to her.

She lay in the middle of the floor, naked and bleeding from a myriad of scratches and cuts all over her body, eyes closed and shaking. Shivering. Sweat covered her, as did some kind of substance, an oozing sticky muck, translucent black and grey that clung to her, and the carpet, and his hands too as he reached for her, turning her, trying to get her to look at him.

'Sal! Salryanna?'

She didn't respond, perhaps couldn't. Her teeth were clenched as if in pain, her hands balled into fists, but as he tried to reposition her, her body resisted. Her limbs twisted in awful, unnatural ways, until he thought her bones would break, and he couldn't make them stop. As if something he couldn't see was tying her body up. Pulling her head back, her mouth opening and her eyes too, staring wide and terrified but not seeing him. Tears falling from the corners of them.

As her mouth opened, she seemed to be choking on something, like she couldn't breathe. It wasn't only her limbs being manipulated. Her whole body seemed squeezed, twisted, blood and ooze all over her.

Even as he tried to calm her, she was flung onto her stomach and there was a sound like rushing air and her back opened up in a long, bloodied welt. She screamed, or tried to, but could make no sound, choking on something invisible shoved down her throat. Another welt, her entire body jerking. Another. Nothing he could do would stop it. It was like a flogging by an invisible presence.

This wasn't natural. This was demonic.

'Oh god.' Rorks's voice, as the man staggered forward and dropped to his knees beside Callum. Reaching out to help, but no more able to do that than Callum was. This wasn't some battle, and it wasn't some political confrontation, and it wasn't anything that could be dealt with by a sword or a fight.

This was coming from inside of her.

'Stay here. Stay with her,' he ordered Rorks, then he pushed himself up and dashed out of the room.

Across to the study. Diving for his desk, pulling open the top drawer. His fingers slipped, they were covered in the gunk that was all over Sal, black ooze and her own blood. Ripping the drawer open until it almost fell.

Taking the golden collar out of it.

In the half-minute it took him to get it and return to the bedroom, diving down to the floor beside her again, she was almost blue. He met Rorks's eyes. There was no telling if this would make things worse or better. He'd torn this damn collar off to save her, let her body heal itself.

He had no other ideas.

'Hold her down,' he ordered, knowing Rorks was potentially still too weak, and that if her body was being manipulated by that demon, she could well lash out. It was all he had. Rorks tried, but it took the both of them to pin her down and still he struggled to get it around her throat.

The instant he clasped the lock shut, she fell still, in a crumpled heap.

He sat back slowly, as did Rorks, the three of them on the floor of the bedroom covered in a vile black ooze. She was on her stomach and he couldn't see her face, but her body wasn't shaking, or choking, or moving in unnatural ways. She'd collapsed down.

'Sal?' he ventured, and carefully reached out a hand to her head.

She turned, shifting at the touch, to look up at him. Her eyes seeing him at last.

And then she burst into tears. He gathered her up in his arms and held her tight.

~

He didn't want to ask what that was or what had happened. She didn't seem capable of speech just yet anyway. So he held her close where they were for some minutes, until she had stopped sobbing, and only then did he move. Gathering her up in his arms and standing. Carrying her through to the bathroom.

'Rorks, you too,' he said, noting just how pale his Captain was, even with the remaining bruises. 'Come on.'

They went to the pool and Rorks undressed to get in first, then Callum handed Salrynna to him in the water while he stripped his own clothing and joined them. Sal didn't seem to want to talk, but she clung to them, one or the other, as Callum began the slow and careful task of washing her down and checking her wounds.

He could get a healer. He probably should. But right now she didn't need that most. She needed him, she needed a sense of protection and safety and care. And Rorks was so gentle with her when Callum went to get cloths to help wash her limbs and get that gunk off, he was better than any healer right now.

Maybe later. Maybe once she'd explained. If she would explain.

The cuts and scratches over the body were mostly superficial, except for the welts across her back and buttocks. He held her while Rorks saw to those, washing her carefully down, disinfecting every wound.

'They didn't all break the skin,' Rorks said. 'They'll heal okay, with time. I don't think she'll need bandaging. I've seen far worse.'

Neither of them mentioned that they'd heal easier if he took the collar off her and let her magic heal her body. He wasn't prepared to risk that just yet.

'Thanks Rorks.' He reached out with one hand from around her, to grip the other man by the arm. 'It's appreciated.'

Rorks gave him a tired smile. 'I know what I'm doing with this kind of thing. I did this for you, remember?'

'I could never forget. You saved my life.'

'And you mine, sir.'

All the while, Salryanna sat between them, clinging to him, or to Rorks when he had to get up for something, she not saying a word. The black gunk took a while to clean off her, and from themselves. It was a sticky muck he pushed straight into the pool's filters, those pipes ever-renewing the water here, refreshing the filthy water with fresh.

The warmth of the mineral water helped, though. That and gentle persistence.

'What even is it?' Rorks asked.

'I don't know.' He shook his head. 'Something inhuman.'

'It's the demon.' Sal's voice was croaky, sore. 'It's his darkness. It's—'

Her words cut off with the strain of making sound. He put a careful hand to her face and turned her head up so she would look at him. Her eyes were red-rimmed from the crying, but at least clear now.

'Don't try to speak, your voice is still too raw,' he said. 'Rest. Let us care for you.'

Tears appeared at the corners of her eyes. 'I'm sorry—' she tried to say, but he cut her off.

'Enough. I told you not to speak. You already know what I think you apologising,' he said, if gently. 'The demon can't get to you right now. You're safe.'

Her hand rose to the collar round her throat. An unreadable expression passed across her face and she looked away, but she did give him a nod. He helped her sit straighter at the edge of the pool, running a cloth down her arms, while Rorks helped with her legs. When he'd cleaned off one arm and moved to the other, her hand reached for him, his shoulder or forearm, always holding on, as if afraid to let go.

He'd seen Sal scared before. He'd seen her resigned to her fate, or outnumbered and accepting of it. But he'd never seen her vulnerable, not like this. Not when he'd had her threatened with rape, not when he'd attempted to break the binding. He'd been cruel to her and kind to her both, yet at no point had she ever looked so desperately weakened as she did now.

'It doesn't work like that,' she whispered.

'I told you to not speak. Obey me please.'

Her lips pressed closed. Rorks took pity on her, moving around in front so he could clean off her feet and giving her a grin as he did.

'He forbade me from speaking once. If for entirely different reasons, mostly because I'd been talking utter bullshit all night,' he said. 'Wanna hear that story?'

Callum knew the story, of course, and rolled his eyes, but gestured it was okay to continue when Sal looked to him for the go ahead. So Rorks spun an only slightly exaggerated tale of entirely inconsequential foolishness he'd got into when out drinking of an evening during the march to the capital. A story involving Rorks pushing boundaries way too much until Callum had been forced to reign him in. It was all self-deprecating humour, Rorks making himself the only target of it, in which nobody got hurt and all was in fun. It was the Captain's way of putting others at ease. Callum had seen him do it before.

And it worked. That was the thing. Salryanna perhaps didn't laugh loud, but she was smiling by the end of Rorks's story and it had allowed Callum time to clean the rest of the gunk off her, and even wash her hair. What was left of it. All that long hair she'd chopped away that first day, as if it were nothing. Her only vanity. Because to her it was nothing, because she saw herself as nothing, and it broke his heart to understand she still held that view even now. That she wasn't important. No matter how many times he told her, or showed her, or tried to convince her otherwise. It was just as Rorks had already told him: it wasn't about his forgiveness, it was about her ability to forgive herself. And that remained a long way off.

'That was where he finally snapped and ordered me back to camp,' Rorks said, grinning as he came to the end of the story, or at least where he usually ended it for most people. He glanced at Callum, then back to Sal. 'You don't want to know what happened after that.'

'I might—' she tried, a hoarse whisper.

He squeezed her shoulder firmly. 'No talking.' Then paused, before adding, 'what happened after that was Rorks got tied down to my bed, gagged, and properly fucked, if I recall. Which shut him up pretty well, from my point of view.'

Rorks turned bright red, but he did give her a wink with his good eye. 'It was really hot.'

She smiled and opened her mouth with her eyes on him, as if deliberately tempting, which was probably the place to call an end to that
conversation.

'And no,' he told her, before she could even try a bit of wilful
disobedience just to get her rocks off. 'You've been too hurt to fuck
around, so don't even think about it. Your injuries aren't going to heal
in some incredibly fast way this time, not now I've put the collar back
on you.' He stood, reaching a hand to her. 'Come, slave. I want you to
lie down. To sleep. When the evening meal arrives, we'll see if you can
eat.'

He didn't ask what had happened to her or what any of it meant,
though that was a priority. The priority, really. The demon had taken
her in some way and he still wasn't sure how or why or what the consequences might be. He needed to know. They had significant detail to
discuss, in order to determine how best to proceed.

But while her voice was still so raw and damaged, and while she
looked still so vulnerable and hurt, he didn't want to push her.

'Rorks, wait here. You're still recovering yourself, rest in the pool
longer. I'll be back,' he ordered the Captain, who nodded without
comment and even looked someway thankful.

He led Salryanna out of the bath and helped her dry off, patting
down the injuries and welts across her back and her skin, while she clung
shakily to him. Her balance was still off, muscles wavering, so he picked
her up again once she was dry and carried her through into the
bedroom.

He laid her down upon the bed, helping her find a position on her
side which wouldn't hurt the worst of her wounds. Then he leaned
forward to kiss her cheek.

'Rest,' he said. 'I'll come find you when there's food. We'll talk after
that.'

She reached out to his arm to stop him rising. 'Sir...'

'If you try to say a single word more, I'm doubling the strike count
for when I finally judge you well enough to cop the belting you already
have coming,' he said, dourly. 'Just so you know, I don't forget about
such things.'

'Please. Time is running out. We need to... we need to do this, to...'

He put a finger to her lips.

'I know time is short, Sal. I can see how much it's draining you. Every second you're still bound to this place is a damaging one,' he said, seriously. 'The sooner I can get you away, the better. But you can barely speak and it will keep for another hour or two.'

She sighed, but nodded. Didn't try to say anything, which was a good sign.

He pushed the hair from her face, running a gentle finger down her cheek. 'I need to know what happened here. I need to know what happened to you. What hurt you like that.'

'Demon,' she whispered and he nodded, for he knew that much, he just didn't know why. Or why now.

He let his hand run down to the collar around her neck. 'This isn't making anything worse, is it?'

She hesitated, then shook her head. 'Not worse.'

Not better either, though from what he could tell, it had saved her life. But that was a conversation for when she could speak. He needed the full detail.

He could not ask, not yet, not now. Instead he forced a smile, thinking of Rorks and his foolish, frivolous stories, just to distract and ease tension. Running his thumb over her lips.

'I like having you in a collar,' he said and it wasn't a lie. He'd hated owning slaves for the brief period he'd done so in the capital, but Sal was not the same. This was personal, not commercial. 'I like the sense of ownership it gives me over you. You are mine. *Only* mine.'

And not some demon's bride, or whatever else she was meant to be. Not some demon's *lover*, which is what he suspected had happened to her just now. The way the gunk covered her and the injuries she'd incurred. Her lips were bruised, like something had been shoved inside them. Her cunt was bruised too.

He knew the signs of rape when he saw them. He'd had to care for Rorks too often in the salt mines after just such a thing. Only in the mines they'd been human predators. She was dealing with something else again.

'Yours,' she managed to whisper, but it sounded like wishful thinking. Unconvincing.

He leaned over and kissed her bruised lips. 'Rest. I'm going to check on Rorks.'

'Take care of him. He was...' She grimaced with the effort of speaking. 'What Seth did...like in the mines. He—'

'I know exactly what Seth did,' he said. 'I'll take care of the Captain, don't worry. Thank you for looking after him while I was gone.'

'If you want to, need to...' She was really struggling to speak now, barely any sound to her voice. 'You and him. You know, sex. Don't hesitate. Nothing changes. I want you to be together.'

'I know that too,' he said. 'Will you please stop trying to talk now? My arm is going to get tired with all the beltings I'll have to give you.'

She pressed her lips together and nodded. He left her to rest, because she needed it. The last few days she'd been deposed as Queen, thrown to the dungeons, publicly collared and enslaved, threatened with gang rape, and abused verbally and emotionally by just about everyone, most of all himself. Then he almost killed her and now...whatever this was.

He couldn't question her yet. But he couldn't shake the nagging feeling he needed to. That there was something she didn't want to say, something she was hiding behind her conveniently ruined voice.

Something that would say how this ended and if he didn't know, he'd already lost.

CHAPTER 27
Callum

R orks was still in the pool and, because he desperately needed
something to relax himself as well, Callum waded back into it
once he returned. He rolled his shoulders, stiff after carrying
the sword and swinging it today too. Carrying Sal herself. Not to
mention the tension he couldn't shake.

He must have made it too obvious, because Rorks swam to the edge
and held out a hand to him.

'Let me massage your back,' he said and, when Callum raised his
eyebrows in surprise, just shrugged. 'Salryanna told me it helped.'

'It does, somewhat. But the warmth of this pool helps on its own,'
he said. 'You don't have to.'

'I want to, General,' Rorks said, with a flash of his own vulnerability. 'Please?'

'As you like, Captain.'

Honestly, it was welcome, the service Rorks wanted to provide,
the feel of the other man's hands on his back. Working out the
tension in his scars and the muscles beneath. His touch wasn't as firm
as Salryanna's when doing this, a less confident, more hesitant sensation. Rorks hadn't been trained in massage as she had and wasn't as
adept at it. But the touch, and the reconnection of it, was welcome.

It'd been a long time since he'd felt Rorks's hands upon him, skin on skin.

He leaned into it, let his other cares go momentarily. For now, Salryanna was safe in bed and Rorks was safe in this pool with him and the battles to fight were for tomorrow. They could wait until another day. He could, just for this moment, let himself indulge in the affection of those who cared for him. If they were to defeat the demon, it could only be together, surely.

'Is Salryanna okay?' Rorks asked from behind him, hands across his shoulders.

Callum wished he could answer yes to that.

'I don't know. She seems okay for now. But I don't know what happened,' he said. 'The demon. It was something to do with the demon.'

'Her bruising. Did you see?' Rorks's voice was very quiet.

'I did. It was pretty clear what was done and undoubtedly not the first time,' he said. 'The demon's lover. That's what they call the Witch Queen, isn't it?'

'I don't think that had anything to do with love.'

'It certainly wasn't consensual.' He dragged back a long breath, arching back with Rorks's touch. 'Not that I imagine she fights such things. She's been resigned to her fate, her so-called damnation, a very long time.'

'When you don't believe you have a choice, that's not the same as consent,' Rorks said, hard voiced.

'No, it's not. The collar cut it off, anyway. Physically at least,' he said. 'But I don't know what's going on in her head. She's not good at letting me know that.'

'She's never had anyone she could tell that to before,' Rorks said, as if it were simple. 'It will take time for her to learn that she doesn't have to bear all the pain of something alone. That you can help.' He hesitated. 'We can help.'

Callum couldn't help the smile that brought to his lips. The warmth of the thought.

'She is very taken with you,' he said. 'She wanted to make sure you were looked after, my friend.'

He felt, rather than could see, Rorks's shrug.

'She's afraid she won't live through this,' he said softly. 'She's making sure you don't have to be alone once all this is done. That's why she's so determined to see us together.'

Callum sighed. The same thought had crossed his mind. Sal didn't believe she could be saved and he hadn't yet been able to convince her that he would do it. He was not leaving here defeated. He would destroy that demon and save her and see out his plans for the longer term.

But she couldn't see a future for herself. She could only see that she was damned. She'd told him that too many times.

'Perhaps. I don't think it'd change anything if she did consider she had a viable future,' he said. 'You showed her warmth when no-one else, not even myself, did. You understood her when even I struggled to. She has a great deal of fondness for you, Rorks.'

The hands on his back stilled a little, but didn't lift. If anything, they pressed further into him. Callum could feel the man's hesitation. The want for himself, but the fear of doing wrong by others. By Sal. Rorks had always been like that. He put other people first, even to his own detriment; he didn't even realise he was doing it half the time. Callum had learned to look out for him in such ways, make sure the man didn't lose out entirely in his effort to make everyone else happy.

Callum turned to take one of his hands, then tugged the man around in front of him. Rorks came willingly, as he always did; he never resisted anything Callum wanted. Then he sat back on one of the large steps at the side of the pool, water to his chest, and pulled Rorks onto his lap, put his arms around him, and held him.

The way Rorks clung to him, instantly putting his head on Callum's shoulder and holding him back with such intensity, told Callum that the other man needed this. God knew, he needed it himself.

'I've got you, Captain,' Callum said quietly. 'I'm here and I'm not going anywhere and I've got you. You're safe with me. Okay?'

Rorks's breathing was a little ragged and he nodded rather than verbalise an answer. Sometimes, this was all it took: holding him. Back in the salt mines, Callum had learned fast that what Rorks needed in the worst times was to know he was seen and understood by someone who genuinely cared for him. That he was safe with at least one person, with him, even if the chaos around them was unrelenting. They'd both been brutalised in those salt mines, to the point where you learned to be dismissive of it. Externalising a blasé bluster. It happened, assault, rape, and sure, it was bad, but it didn't matter, it couldn't damage you further, it was over. It was done. Whatever. That's what you told others. That's what you told yourself.

It was a mask, an armour, of course. A pretence that such things didn't leave a lasting mark just because the scars weren't always visible. They all dealt with it in their different ways.

'What did you do to Seth?' Rorks asked softly, after a long time.

'He's in the dungeons. I'll leave him there a few days, until I can judge his fate with a clearer head,' he said. 'Not that I expect it'll change my decision. The man's life will be forfeit. I'll swing the blade myself.'

'Even though I was the one to go to him?'

Rorks's voice was so quiet it was almost a struggle to hear it.

'Seth disobeyed official military orders and harmed an officer in doing so. He will be dealt with in official ways,' he said. 'While you, my Captain, made a personal decision that went against my private orders to you, but I've already dealt with your disobedience in a far more personal way.' He ran a hand over the man's shoulder. 'Let it go now, Rorks. You've paid the price more over than you should need to for it. None of it is your fault.'

'Yes, sir,' he said, with a nod. 'Thank you.'

'I will always be here for you,' he said, softer now. 'I'll give you what you need, always. Sometimes it might be a belting, and you might not enjoy it, but trust me to know what you need.'

'I always have. Always will.' Rorks lifted his head from his shoulder. His lips ghosted Callum's cheek, face held close to his own. 'Why did we stop being physical, General? I've missed this.'

'We just drifted. You needed space and time to play around with a variety of partners. After the salt mines, you needed to find yourself again, and know you could do that, and enjoy it, and that such enjoyment wasn't taken from you by that place,' he said, leaning his forehead against Rorks's own. Breathing in the scent of him, the warmth of him. The feel of him under his hands. 'While I was too busy to think of much beyond the most transactional of encounters. I didn't want to wrap emotion into any of it.'

'We never stopped being us, though,' Rorks said. He shifted a little in Callum's lap. The man would have to feel his hardening erection against his hip. 'I always came to you for command. I have always craved your orders, General.'

'Mmmm.' Callum ran his hand down the man's side, then over his thigh. Reaching it up the inside of his leg, until he found Rorks's own stiffness, his cock fully hard beneath the water.

He cupped Rorks's balls gently; was gratified by the soft gasp of the other man.

'And I have always desired your service, Captain,' he said. 'Your obedience and fealty given.'

Rorks shifted his hips to push himself harder against Callum. 'Will you take me, sir? Will you hold me down and fuck me hard? I need you to fuck me.'

'No. Not yet. You're still recovering from last night.'

'But—'

Callum reached up with his other hand, the one not gently massaging Rorks's balls beneath his rock-hard cock, and wove it into his wet hair. Then he grabbed hard and yanked his head back.

'I said no,' he growled. 'I will have you when I choose, soldier. My timing, my choice.'

Rorks sucked back a breath of desperate want, shuddering in his hold. So responsive, full of need. Callum hadn't been planning on taking this sexual, not even when he first agreed to the massage, but Rorks needed it. So did he. A desperate want to take this man apart until he was a begging mess stole over him, a forceful need to control and demand.

He moved his hand around to Rorks's cock, long and thin and familiar, even after all this time. Gripping it beneath the water, running his thumb along the head. Slowly beginning to stroke the man. Rorks, head still pulled back in the hold of his other hand, whimpered, and thrust his hips for more, but Callum kept the pace even, slow. Maddeningly so, until Rorks was all but shaking in his arms.

'That's it, soldier. That's what you need,' he said, in a calm, firm voice. 'I'll fuck you when I'm ready to. Right now, just give me this. Show me the beauty of you, laid out so splendid across my knee.'

He leant his head, his lips to Rorks's exposed throat. Licking and kissing the water-warmed skin there. Biting, so that the Captain's entire body shuddered and he uttered a series of small cries, the sound of each going straight to Callum's cock. To know he could make this man produce those sounds, that he could play this man's body to his own will, touch where he liked, as he liked, as long as he liked.

Sucking on Rorks's shoulder, leaving his own bruise, his own mark. And all the while stroking the man, firm and long, until he was helpless in Callum's arms, until he was writhing and whimpering and a total mess of need and desire and want.

'My General, my lord, I—'

'Come for me, soldier.'

Rorks did, in rolling waves and with a cry, his entire body stiffening and spasming within Callum's hold.

Gently now, Callum released his grip on Rorks's hair, and on his cock, once he'd pumped all there was to come from it. Washing his spend away to the filters of the pool and manoeuvring Rorks gently to sit between this legs and rest his head on his chest. Arms about him once again. As Rorks's settled, shaking still from the orgasm, and holding on to him tight.

'Better?' Callum murmured, into his hair.

'Better.' He buried himself even further into Callum's arms. 'Thank you. I needed that.'

'I know you did. I've got you.'

'You could have... if you wanted, I would've been alright if you'd wanted to fuck me.'

Callum eased the man back by the shoulders, then reached a hand to his chin, tipping it up to make Rorks to look him in the eye.

'You offered only because you thought it was what I wanted. Yet you know it wouldn't be good for you, physically or emotionally, so soon after last night,' he said. 'I will fuck you Rorks. When I judge the time is right. I am already looking forward to it. But not until I deem you're ready.'

Rorks shifted until he was kneeling on the step between Callum's legs. He reached up to ghost his lips with a kiss, soft and willing.

'Will you let me do something else for you instead?' he said, almost tentatively. With such a plea, a need to please. There was no way Callum could say no to that.

He sat back with his elbows on the step behind him and his legs spread. 'See to it, soldier. Make me feel good.'

Which brought a flush to Rorks's skin and a smile to his lips, before the man brought his lips to Callum's chest. Licking and lightly sucking, not bruising him the way he had on Rorks's skin, just tasting his body. Sucking gently on a nipple, and when Callum pushed himself up a step so that his hips and cock were out of the water, Rorks moved down to put his lips on that too.

Rorks's mouth around his cock was fucking heaven. The tongue of the man was divine, swirling around the head, leaving a trail of sensation that made his entire body throb. The Captain knew what he liked and hadn't forgotten a trick in all the time since they'd last done this, sucking back on him like his life depended on it.

Callum wove a hand into the hair at the back of Rorks's head, knowing how much the soldier liked having his hair pulled. Not doing so now, not hard anyway, just resting his hand there, like a kind of threat, he could if he wanted to. When Rorks started going deeper, taking Callum further into his mouth, into his throat, Callum tightened his hold just enough, and then on the next thrust, *pushed*.

Rorks went right down over him, until he was deep in Rorks's throat, and oh fuck, oh god, but the sensation was so fucking good. To be holding the man over him, to have that power, only made it more intense. Rorks didn't struggle, he was an old hand at this. Instead he breathed through his nose until Callum lifted him, then held him by both hands and fucked his face at his pace, to his desired depth, taking full control.

He wasn't going to last long, not like this. It'd been too long since he'd last had Rorks's lips around his cock, had the man naked on his knees desperately sucking him down. He let Rorks's hair go and gave the man back some control, who then went to his work with renewed gusto.

As if he wanted nothing more than to have Callum's cock in his mouth. As if all he wanted was to swallow Callum's come.

Which he did. Callum gave him no warning about it, they both knew each other too well, and Rorks would know he was expected to drink him down and be grateful for it. Callum crying out through clenched teeth as the orgasm took him in waves. The shudders of his muscles rolling for the longest time, until at last he relaxed down into the aftermath.

When he could, he pulled Rorks up to sit on his knee again and kissed the soldier deeply. Tasting himself on the other man's tongue. Holding him close.

'I do love you, Callum,' Rorks said. Something he'd never said before, such had always been unspoken between them. It had been dangerous to verbalise affection in the salt mines and they'd always let the habit remain after. 'I just wanted you to know that.'

'I know. I've always known.' He hesitated. 'You know I love you also, don't you?'

'Yeah.' Rorks looked up with a twisted smile. 'Sal told me.'

Callum huffed a bittersweet laugh. 'Of course she did.'

Of course he loved Rorks. Just like he loved Salryanna. Even when he didn't let others close, didn't engage with relationships or sex beyond the most commercial. He hadn't been able to conceive of caring for another after the betrayal of Salryanna five years earlier, his heart too broken, he imagined beyond repair. Only Rorks had repaired it. Rorks had ensured he was whole enough, and healed enough, to be able to come back to Salryanna and love her again too.

He couldn't live without either of them. They were wound together for him. And for the first time in all these years, he began to wonder if maybe it might be possible to keep them both.

If he could defeat the demon first. If he could save Salryanna, and Rorks too, and keep them all alive long enough to do that.

CHAPTER 28

Salryanna

She slept. And as always when she slept, came the nightmares.

Long black tendrils creeping over her skin, pulling her into the darkness. Wrapping themselves around her, forcing themselves inside her. She unable to fight, unable to see, unable to feel anything except the demon claiming her.

Was this what her eternity would look like? Callum's god, his religion, they spoke of eternal souls and damnation forever. That wasn't her belief, yet it terrified her all the same. Damnation. What else could even await one like her?

She tried to scream but it was hard to make it sound. Her throat felt already raw, like it had been ripped through, and she thrashed about, but the bindings were too hard, the demon too powerful, and it was all she could do to just sob as it came again and—

'Sal, wake up!' His voice. A command she almost instinctively followed. 'Sal, open your eyes. Look at me. It's me.'

She made herself do so, his hands upon her, she holding onto him as he leaned over her in the bed. She gasped back breath into lungs that didn't want to take it. Her fingers clutching onto the sheets, her heart still pumping, the fear in her every limb, only slowly dissipating.

'Nightmare,' she said, or tried to. Her voice still sounded raspy and thin. 'Nightmare.'

A troubled look crossed his eyes. 'Deep breath now,' was all he said, and sat on the bed beside her to hold her until she stopped shaking.

He wore his battle uniform, everyday wear, but his hair was wet, as if he wasn't long out of the pool. She tried to push herself to sit up, but struggled, limbs aching. Her throat hurt, as did the rest of her. The understanding of why made her look away, unable to meet his eyes.

'Where is your Captain?'

This time there was more sound to her voice, at least.

'Balcony. The meal has been served, I sent him out to eat, then came to get you,' he said. 'Even if it's only soup, you need to have something. You need the sustenance.'

Of course he'd make her eat, even if her throat felt closed over and her stomach nauseous and her body as if she might crumble away. To him, it was taking care of her physical self, eating properly, paying attention to her body's needs. A soldier thing, she supposed. Whereas she struggled to see the point. The demon would burn her up either way.

'Yes, sir,' she managed, spurred to make the point she was eating only because he wanted her to, which was contrary and foolish of her, because the man would only get stricter if he thought that was needed. Maybe that was why she said it like that.

'Hmmm. The only question is if you're okay to get up and eat with us, or should remain here.'

She looked up. 'I'd like to come out. Please? I...don't want to be alone.'

His expression softened. 'Well. We can do that. Your voice is sounding a little better, anyway.'

She let her contrariness fade in the light of his concessions. 'Is he okay? Rorks?'

Callum smiled gently. 'He asked the same of you,' he said. 'Yes, he's okay. He's been through worse. Your healing efforts helped a great deal, so thank you.' He reached to the collar about her throat, fingers lingering upon the metal. 'I wish I could allow you to do the same for yourself.'

'You could. There is not the danger you think there is. Not from that quarter.'

But he shook his head. 'I don't trust the demon or its hold on you,' he said, simply. 'And I can't trust your word when it comes to the demon's impact upon yourself. You've too much a habit of concealing it when you're hurt.'

She pressed her lips together tightly. Piqued mostly because he was right. It would leave her more vulnerable if he took off the collar and she couldn't actually say what would happen. But she was vulnerable regardless, collar or not.

So she didn't say anything. Looking down at the bed in silence.

'Are you going to tell me what happened?' he said, when she maintained the silence. 'Explain how you were left in this state?'

'I am bound to a demon, General. That's all that happened.'

A hard looked crossed his face. 'You will come out to eat with us. But then you will tell me, slave. I need to know.'

He wasn't going to let her remain quiet. She nodded, to acknowledge he would insist, even that he was right, he did need to know, if without promising she would actually tell him. She needed him to defeat the demon. And she would need to do what was necessary to ensure he could. That was all that was important now.

'Come on,' he said, standing, but holding his hands down to her. 'Let's see if your balance has returned, or if I need to carry you out there.'

She frowned. 'I can walk. I don't need to be carried everywhere.'

'Oh, so now your pride kicks in. After everything I've put you through, all of which you've taken without resistance, it's this you suddenly rebel on?'

He was teasing her, which helped as she had to hold onto him tight and let him assist her even just getting out of bed. The demon had taken more from her than she'd expected, but the price always was higher than planned when you bargained with that creature. She leaned on his arms, swaying a little with the room turning. Only for a moment. After a few long breaths, she steadied herself and, so long as she clung onto him, managed to walk forward.

Rorks was out on the balcony by the table and his face lit up as they appeared in the doorway, Callum helping her with one arm around her waist, the other holding her hand. She gripped him hard just to stay upright, already exhausted just by walking three rooms. Stars, but the demon really had pulled strips off her this time, worse than anything before.

It was the collar, the people in his castle, the attempt to break the binding. All of it was empowering the demon, putting cracks in the restraints she kept on herself; it always had been a creature who found a fissure and blew it wide open.

She closed her eyes, but all she could see were the novices burned up before she stepped forward to do her duty and be bound. Before she managed to contain the demon and keep it controlled. Choosing damnation and a demon's hell, all paid off with a bit of transitory power she hadn't even wanted.

Rorks jumped up to pull out a chair and Callum guided her to it. She sank gratefully into it, shaking from the exhaustion. All hells, but how was she going to see this through, if she couldn't even walk by herself without collapsing after a few dozen feet?

'Thank you,' she murmured, feeling her cheeks flush red. She wasn't used to being so in need of assistance. There'd never been any help to ask for, in the past. Now she wasn't sure how to ask for it or what to do when she needed it.

'Here, soup,' Rorks said, putting a bowl in front of her.

She nodded thanks and peered up at him, his features still bruised. Such marks seemed wrong on a face otherwise so angelic, the black and purple, though the swelling had gone and he didn't appear to be in any pain from it. The black eye was healing well and he could open it fully again.

'Your face is feeling okay?' she asked and he smiled. He had a lovely smile. She could see why Callum had fallen for him.

'It is amazing. Thank you. I've never recovered from a beating so fast,' he said, even if beating was severely underplaying what happened to him. 'All armies should have healers like yourself. I'll have to remind the General of that.'

The General himself sat down at his own seat with a far more cynical expression.

'We have magicians. They don't do a hell of a lot when it comes to real world battlefield injuries, so far as I've found.' He looked to her with eyebrows raised. 'I've not seen magic like that before. So excuse my suspicions.'

She shrugged, looking down at her soup. When she picked up the spoon, her hand still shook, betraying the physical weakness still in her body, so she put it down again fast. The last thing she wanted was to appear too weak to feed herself, especially in front of these men.

'Most magicians are focused on their own power,' she said. 'Healing magics aren't particularly powerful and don't get you far. They're all about helping others. Our world doesn't value such.'

'And yet it should,' Callum said. His head cocked, considering her. 'You're weakened now. Did the healing magic take something out of you? Is that the cause?'

She shook her head. 'Healing doesn't hurt anyone, not that kind.'

'Hmmm. So it is the demon draining you. Harming you.'

She looked down into her soup and wondered how to explain. If she could, even if she wanted to. Yes, it was the demon, but it wasn't like she'd suddenly been hurt. This was a process that never stopped. It had been accelerated, but it was simply life for the Witch Queen, and it had only one end.

He wouldn't want to hear it. She wasn't even sure how to say it.

'If you take off the collar, I will heal,' she said, instead, and received a dark look in return.

'You'll heal the usual way without it,' he replied. 'Without risking the demon taking even more from you.'

She didn't say it would make no difference in the end. The demon would breach the collar eventually. For the moment, there was almost a relief in not having that open connection threatening to tear her apart, the constant fight against giving in to it. That was the contradiction she couldn't explain to them. The more power of the demon she used, the stronger she became; previous Witch Queen's had revelled in it, thrived from it. All had sort power of immense kinds.

It had burned them out all the faster. By not using it, by stepping back from it, she weakened herself, left herself more open to the demon's use and abuse, but she also maintained a stability in the control she managed. The demon could reach her, hurt her. It could not hurt others.

Callum's arrival had upset the balance. The collar around her throat had changed things, it blocked the connection. Everything that had happened had altered the careful balance she'd kept for five years now, by being alone, by taking the hits alone, by not taking the power on offer.

'Five years,' she said. 'I've kept the demon at bay for five years without any collar.'

But Callum wasn't stupid and he wasn't buying it.

'You've kept the demon at bay from the valley, from all others, for five years,' he said. 'By putting yourself in its way instead. By sacrificing yourself. How many times has that happened, what happened to you earlier? How many times has that been done to you?'

She pressed her lips together, looking out over the valley. Her soup going cold before her. Callum's eyes were hard on her face, not shifting her from out of his sights. Rorks was quiet, looking to his General, then to her. Not going to interrupt.

'I don't keep count,' she said at last, which was as much an admission as anything that it was often. Yet it was also true enough. She didn't keep count. She'd long lost count.

Callum leaned forward over the table.

'You see, Sal, in the salt mines, they'd take us at any time. Day, night, it didn't matter,' he said and his voice was calm, pragmatic. Objective, even. 'Most of us learned fast to get out of the way, even if that meant pushing others into harm instead. It left us turning on each other, never trusting one another. We were made enemies of our own fellow sufferers in trying to save ourselves, and as such, we suffered alone.'

He paused, looking away at last. Off her and to Rorks, who was silent and watching his General. Rorks gave him a soft, sad smile, and a nod, as if there was some question asked and an answer given.

'Only then there was Rorks,' he said. 'Because this man is a fucking angel that the rest of us can't compare to. He sees the good in everyone. Even to his own detriment sometimes, as you've already seen, his trusting the likes of Seth when he shouldn't.'

'I'm not so gullible, General,' Rorks said. 'And I'm not that much of a saint. Seth was was a fuck up on my part, that's all.'

'You're too smart to be gullible. But you do trust, Rorks, and you want to see the best in people, even those who might not deserve it,' he said. He looked back to her. 'I was still half dead from the flogging when thrown to the mines. I shouldn't have lasted a fortnight. Except Rorks took the hits for me, he gave me time to heal. He didn't even know my name, he simply saw a stranger in need of help, and so he helped, putting himself at risk to do so. I didn't even realise what was happening at first, but once I did, I swore to protect him with everything I had.' He paused. 'I failed.'

'General,' Rorks broke in, very gently. 'Are you sure she needs to hear this?'

'Yes, I think she does.' Callum considered his Captain. 'But I will stop if you prefer, Rorks. It is not only my story to tell.'

Rorks sighed. Looked to her with an almost apologetic expression.

'Not on my account,' he said. 'I don't mind for myself. I only wondered if Sal was ready for some of the detail. It's your call.'

Callum gave him a nod, but met her eyes. 'Rorks's protective instincts are strong, as you can see,' he said to her. 'I take his advice seriously. Only I do think you need to know this. I don't always succeed, Sal. My victories are famous. My failures I live with more privately.'

'You didn't fail,' Rorks said, firmly.

'I did.' Callum didn't look at him as he said it. 'I let you be hurt. I couldn't stop them.'

He gathered himself, the guilt he made no effort to hide, and she wanted to say he didn't need to tell her, but knew it was only because she didn't want to hear the details Rorks was trying to protect her from. She wanted to think of Callum as the General of the Light who accomplished impossible victories and hadn't yet been beaten. Yet she knew why he was telling her this. He wanted her to know he was human. And being human, he failed sometimes too.

'They'd take me Sal, and I'd let them, because by then I was strong enough to endure it,' he said and she made herself nod acknowledgment, though the understanding of what that meant tore up her insides. 'They would never break me, no matter what they did, beatings, rapes, tortures. I could face all that. But then, somehow, one of us fucked up. They learned Rorks and I were close. That we cared. That's when they stopped targeting me directly and went instead for him in my place. Because that way, I could be broken.'

'But you weren't, General. And neither was I,' Rorks said. 'We kept each other alive. And we're here now, strong, thriving. That's all that matters. '

'Perhaps.' He didn't sound convinced, but exhaled a long breath. 'One night, they waited until well after midnight, and then they burst in and literally dragged him out of my arms. There was nothing I could do. They held me back and made me watch while they...' He stopped, gritting his teeth. 'I begged them. I offered myself. I told them I'd cut my own hand off if they wanted, to show my submission to their rule. Anything, if they would just stop hurting him. All they did was laugh. For that was the point, wasn't it? To use us against one another. To weaponise our affections against each other.'

She felt like throwing up. It wasn't as if she didn't know he'd suffered in the salt mines, and Rorks too, and exactly what had been done. He'd been open about that all along. It was the way they were used against one another. The way any connection, any care, was made into a weapon.

She felt the tears prick.

'They wanted you to suffer alone,' she said. 'They wanted you isolated, alienated from everyone. Too afraid to care.'

'Because alone, we could be controlled.' He reached over to wipe the tears from her cheeks. She hardly recognised they were there. Being extraordinarily gentle with her, despite telling her a tale that was anything but. 'That was the point where I decided *no more*. Enough. That was when I first rebelled. I decided in that moment that if they would use my care for one man against me, I wouldn't retreat from that. I would do more of it. I would care for all the men in those mines. I would fight for all of them. Take the hits for all of them if I needed to. And I would convince them to look out for each other while I did so.'

Rorks smiled. 'As I said. They didn't break you, boss. Didn't break me either, because I'm still standing. At your side, always.'

'You brought everyone together. You created a cohesive force,' she said. 'That's how you managed a revolution in the mines.'

'And then a march on the capital. And a bargain with the Light Command,' he said, leaning forward again, this time taking one of her hands in his own. 'Which brings me here, Sal. To you, who insists on suffering alone, who won't let me close enough to take the hits or to help. Who won't tell me what I need to know in order to save you.'

She closed her eyes, aware of the simmering frustration under his skin. His attempts to understand her position, his failure to do so. He thought he knew what this was because he had experienced the horrors of the salt mines. But those horrors had been all human.

'This isn't the salt mines,' she said at last. 'I couldn't have survived what you describe. They would've broken me in an instant. I'm not like you, either of you. I'm not that strong.'

'You need to tell me what I should know, Sal,' he said. 'What do I need to know to defeat the demon? Stop cutting me out.'

For a moment, a wisp of a minute, she wanted to tell him. She wanted to believe he could do it, he could destroy the demon if only she told him the right secret, the leverage, the arcane knowledge only she knew because she was the Witch Queen. This was what he had come here for, wasn't it? Why he'd enslaved her, what he'd tried to break the binding to achieve. Discover the secrets of Castle Ravenswild.

The secrets that would let him destroy the demon.

The secrets that would destroy him at the same time. She couldn't do that. She couldn't.

'The alter,' she said, staring out across the valley. 'Your magicians were looking for the alter because they think they can manifest the demon there, on this physical plane, and then destroy him.' She paused. 'I know where it is.'

Both the men straightened, watching her. She didn't look at either of them. She kept her eyes firmly on the view out to the valley.

'You think this is the best way forward also?' Callum asked, carefully.

She pressed her lips together, selecting her own words with care.

'There is a room in the lowest basements of this castle. Below the throne room,' she said. 'It's the heart of the demon's power. The alter.

The earliest worship of him occurred there, causing the breach between our planes that allowed him to come through to this world. It is there, if anywhere, you might contain him. Trap him. Maybe even force him back and close the breach.' She exhaled a tight breath. 'If your magicians know their work.'

He reached to her, put his hand on her chin and made her turn to look at him.

'I will not trap that demon in this castle if you are also trapped inside,' he said. 'So tell me you will not be imprisoned here too. Tell me, if we do this, that you will come with me after.'

He wouldn't let her look away. He was such a force of a man.

She wished she didn't feel so much like crying.

'I will come with you,' she lied. 'I promise.'

CHAPTER 29
Salryanna

Callum allowed her to sit in the lounge with them after dinner, though it wasn't his first choice. He'd wanted her to return immediately to bed. This was the compromise, because she didn't want to be alone, to sit quietly in their company instead. She was happy enough with that.

The two men spoke and planned and made decisions. They called in the magicians at one point and discussed the plan with them. She almost wished she had retired to the bedroom then, she didn't want to face those magicians, especially their leader, that narrowed-eyed man who held only enmity for her.

At least he had no interest in engaging with her directly. She listened as Callum insisted saving her was part of his plan, that they were not to unduly endanger her as part of this. The magician gave him all the assurances that it was the demon, not the witch, their magics were targeted upon. He didn't mention that in his belief the demon and the witch were inseparable and two sides of the same being, bonded and merged. She knew it, but she didn't tell Callum either.

The magician did warn Callum that it would be a powerful ritual and it could rock the entire castle. At least he gave that warning.

When he saw the man to the door and returned, grim-faced after the conversation, she could only reiterate the point.

'The demon will lash out at every chance,' she said, quietly. 'The castle itself is at risk.'

'So we clear the castle,' he returned. 'Every person in it will be evacuated first. Whatever is needed, we will do.'

He and his Captain planned it out. Deciding on strategy, efficiency. Keeping soldiers ready on the periphery, far enough away to be safe, and able to protect the valley if required. The roles each of them would take. Rorks would see to the evacuation and the organisation of the castle. Callum would see her to the ritual. It was all organised and they sounded professional, competent. Skilled. Experienced in the ways of the world, both good and bad, and for someone like her, who was not experienced and barely knew the world, it was a comfort to listen to them. They were a protection. An armour she could hide behind, knowing they genuinely cared.

But sometime after the fire had died down, she felt arms under her knees and shoulders, and realised she was being picked up. She'd fallen asleep in her chair as they talked, and now Callum was lifting her, carrying her through to the bedroom.

She didn't protest, instead holding onto him. Trusting him. She didn't want to let go, not even when he laid her down on the bed and kissed her softly on the corner of the mouth.

'Sleep now, my love,' he said.

She reached out on instinct, taking hold of his wrist. 'Wait. I don't—'

—*want to be alone*. She cut her own words off. She couldn't place that burden on him, he had the Captain to look after as well. He had a whole castle to protect and the valley too.

But he only put a single finger to her lips to quieten her and, when he stood, Rorks came over to him and undid his shirt, assisted his undress, like she had done on other occasions. Stripping him off and serving him in those small, intimate ways, that made her feel warm to see. An informal ritual, one both men were obviously familiar with, no matter they kept saying it'd been a long time since they'd been together.

Rorks turned towards the bathroom, arms full of the General's discarded uniform.

'Where are you going, soldier?' Callum said, if gently.

The man hesitated, clutching the clothes like they were armour. 'Take these to the laundry chute.'

'Leave it for the morning. Stay, Rorks,' Callum said, reaching out to his arm and squeezing softly. 'Please stay.'

Rorks's uncertain eyes flashed to her, perhaps unwittingly. She gave him a smile and a nod. His mouth opened, maybe to ask if she was sure, if they were sure, but then he closed it again words unsaid and instead simply placed the clothes in a neat pile in the corner. When he straightened again, he took a nervous breath, but began pulling off his own clothes.

Callum waited until he was done, then gave the other man a wordless, fierce hug. Rorks held him back just as tight. He was smiling when they parted to come crawl into bed with her.

'You're not alone,' Callum told her as he pulled her into him, without even needing to hear what she'd been going to say before.

Rorks curled up on her other side and even slid a tentative arm about her waist. She could feel his hesitation, and his distance kept, the light touch of his hand. So she reached to him and wound her fingers in with his, then pulled his arm right around her. Pulled him closer to her in doing so. He relaxed at her back, then. At the invitation, the clear welcome. It was warm, comfortable, to be cushioned between them. She felt safe.

There was no sex. Not this night, she was too weakened, too raw still. It was simply a night spent together and maybe it was an illusion, maybe it was only temporary, but she allowed herself to take comfort in their obvious care. For her, for each other. Surely she could be allowed that much, before the morning and the darkness it would bring?

There were no nightmares. She slept solidly, and when she awoke, still cocooned by the two of them, she thought that at least she'd had this one night. She had this to hang onto, when everything else fell away.

Callum was awake when she opened her eyes. Lying on his side, watching her and Rorks, who was still at her back with an arm around her waist, snoring softly. The feel of him was a comfort.

Callum smiled when she met his eyes, reaching out wordlessly to brush his fingers lightly over her cheek, her lips. She parted them for him, trying to taste his fingertips, but he shook his head and wouldn't let her take his fingers into her mouth. She could almost see the argument forming on his tongue; she was still hurt, still recovering, she was not ready for sex and games yet, he needed to ensure she was okay.

But she wanted the connection. Needed it. She didn't want to leave this bed where she was so protected and surrounded with care. Love, even.

Behind her, Rorks stirred. His body shifting and she pressed her lips together to contain a smile, because she could feel the hardness of him at her back. He pressed himself into her, arm tightening around her waist, and she knew he'd take her side in this, even if Callum was determined to be careful.

She reached a hand to Callum's shoulder and pulled him closer to her, straining forward herself to brush his lips with her own.

He let her, but only for a moment.

'Not this morning, Sal. You're too hurt still,' he said, half a whisper so as not to wake Rorks. She could've told him the Captain was already very awake.

As if to prove it, Rorks's hand firmed further about her and pulled her back against himself.

'Morning, General,' he said, with his face against Salryanna's shoulder, before he raised his head with a smile. 'It's been a long time since I awoke in your bed. I've missed it.'

Callum's expression softened at the greeting. She took a risk and moved her leg, just enough to brush against his own erection, hard under the blankets. He wanted it. She wanted it. She knew Rorks wanted it, because he was not hiding that, holding her tight and pressing against her.

The Captain reached over her to find Callum's hand and wind his fingers in with the General's. Then he pushed himself up on one elbow, leaned across her and kissed him, much as she had done. It pulled Callum closer, so she pushed against the hardened sex of him.

'You are a temptress, witch,' he said, with a reluctant growl. 'But no.

You are still recovering. So is Rorks. I'm not fucking either of you right now, or letting you fuck each other. Not while you're both still hurting.'

As if to emphasise his point, he pulled back, putting space between them. It only made Rorks wind his arm back around her middle and pull her against him again, lips on her shoulder. She leaned back into the embrace, eyes on Callum. She knew the view he would have from his side of the bed. The man he loved and the woman he loved, naked, entwined, displayed for him, and Callum did like a display. She kicked the blankets down further, so he could see all of her stretched out, and Rorks behind her, their long limbs tangled together.

Rorks ran a hand down her hip, the outside of her thigh.

'Callum, I'm fine, I promise,' Rorks said. 'Sal healed me.'

'Physically, perhaps,' Callum returned. But he didn't do anything to cover them back up and his eyes roamed her body, Rorks's too, with open appreciation for the view.

'And you heal me emotionally,' he said. 'Being with you, giving myself to you. That's what I need right now, that's what heals me. And I can't speak for Sal, but I reckon she and I are much the same, like that.'

Callum said nothing, lying on his side of the bed, his eyes taking his fill. The hardness of his cock was very obvious as he took his time to look over them.

Rorks's hand came back up her thigh and over her belly, then to a breast, which he cupped. She breathed in deep as he played with the nipple, like he was doing so for Callum's entertainment, which made it all the hotter.

'Don't fuck her,' Callum said, and it sounded enough like an order that it made her burn between her legs for the denial. 'You might be physically improved, Captain, but she hasn't had the same healing.'

'Sir, I would be ok—' she tried.

'Silence from you, slave,' he cut her of hard. 'You don't get a say. I decide. The Captain will do. You lie there and take it.'

The denial, and the way he said it, a firm command, had her body arching against Rorks. As if to prove that point, his fingers flicked the nipple, and he brought his lips down on her shoulder, trailing his tongue along her skin. Using his teeth just enough to scrape, for her to feel it.

She gasped, pushing back. All while Callum watched with darkly hooded eyes.

'Squeeze her nipple, Captain,' he told the man holding her. 'Hard enough to hurt. Make her squirm for me.'

Rorks did and she squealed even as it brought a wetness to between her legs and pushed back against him.

Callum nodded approvingly. Lying back and watching, clearly enjoying the sights.

'Run your hand down her body. Down her thigh. But don't touch her cunt,' he said and Rorks enthusiastically complied. By her ear, his breathing was increasingly ragged also. She could feel him hard as rock at her back, desperate to be touched himself, but Callum would decide, and the both of them desperately wanted that to be so.

She almost whimpered when Rorks hand skated around her sex without touching it. She could feel how wet she was; he'd be able to feel it too, on her thighs.

Callum licked his lips. 'You want to fuck her, Captain?'

'Yes, sir,' Rorks breathed, pressing hard against her. 'If you would let me.'

'Not this morning,' he said, something hungry in his voice. 'I like seeing you both denied right now. It's a fucking beautiful sight.'

Warmth rushed up her entire body. Even Rorks put his lips to her shoulder and dragged back a ragged breath, continuing to caress and trail his hand along her skin, her legs, her hips, her belly, but never where she most needed it. Pressing hard into her back, so she knew just how badly he needed it himself.

'When there is a day with more time, I will keep you both like this for hours,' Callum said, with heated need in his own voice. 'Displayed for me. Touching each other for me. Never coming.'

'Yes, sir,' Rorks whispered. She said nothing, only bit her lip with a soft whimper.

'Touch her cunt now, Captain. Slowly though. No penetration,' he said. 'Explore her.'

It was a struggle not to come the moment Rorks's clever fingers slid between her labia, along the sheer wetness of her. She uttered a groan of a sound, utterly unabashed and entirely full of need. Like a sob, but with pleasure, as his fingers found her clitoris and ever-so-lightly circled it. She needed more friction, was desperate for more pace. But it wasn't up to her, it was up to Callum, and Rorks to see out his General's orders, and that made it so much hotter, and so much harder to hold on.

Her whole body shook with the burning need for it, but the touch of the man behind her wouldn't give her enough to go over. She could barely think. Held open and displayed for Callum, who watched with care and careful appreciation, hunger obvious in his face.

She tried to throw out a hand, to find him, because she needed to feel his touch and physicality too. She got nowhere near him, but he reached out to take her fingers and held them hard.

'Take it, my good slave,' he said softly. 'Take it for me. You're so beautiful like this, shaking with need and want, all for my entertainment. Such a good girl for me.'

Thought went right out of her head. There was only the sensation, only him before her, and Rorks behind her. Then Callum shifted forward on the bed to lie in front of her. Kissing her, as Rorks continued to play symphonies on her sex. She gripped onto Callum, and pushed back against Rorks, and was captured, secured, held between the two.

He lifted his head, moving to kiss Rorks above her, pressing her between them. It was almost too much to hold back

'Please,' she whispered. 'Please let me...'

He bent his head back down to kiss her again, before leaning back.

'Make her come, Captain. I want to see her come.'

So Rorks did, increasing the friction, the speed with which his fingers moved across her clitoris, just enough to take her over the edge. She cried out, both of them holding her through the orgasm until the shaking of her limbs began to ease, and her gasping calmed, and her shuddering muscles came to a still. Panting between them, trying to hold onto both.

'Well done, my sweet slave,' Callum said softly, kissing her again.

'Thank you, sir.'

He reached over her to Rorks, running a hand down his arm. 'And as for you, Captain. You can get over here right now. I'm going to fuck you.'

Rorks eagerly exchanged places with her, but Callum didn't give him any time to get comfortable. The General manoeuvred the other man with a far rougher hand than he'd ever used on her, even when holding her down. He showed Rorks no gentleness and in turn, the Captain didn't seem to expect—or want—any. Callum immediately shoved Rorks into the mattress, turning him so he was facing her, then gripping his head by the hair at the back and shoving a knee between his legs. Rorks whimpered, tried to reach back, but Callum shook him by the hair.

'Don't you dare touch,' he growled. 'Sal, take his hands. Don't let him move them.'

She wouldn't be able to hold a man of Rorks's strength in place, but that wasn't what was being asked of her. She took his hands in hers, holding them and shifting so she was close enough in front of him that he'd feel her body heat, the shift of her skin as she moved. She even gathered the courage to kiss him, if gently. It was Callum's place to be rough with the man, but that wasn't her.

Rorks pressed his lips back on hers, kissing more firmly and she opened her lips for him, tongue against his. It felt indecent, in the best possible way, to be kissing him like this while Callum held him. Rorks was hard as anything, his cock long and curved and she wondered, if she asked, if Callum would let her suck his man. At another time, she thought he would.

Callum reached over Rorks and took hold of her chin, turning her head. Then he placed two fingers at her mouth, pressing in.

'Get them nice and wet, slave,' he said and she knew what for, so she sucked on his fingers and ran her tongue around them, between them, while Rorks remained trapped between the two of them. When his fingers were wet with her saliva, Callum took his hand back and reached down between Rorks's legs.

Rorks gasped, his hands squeezing hard on her own, as Callum's finger must have penetrated him. She watched Rorks's face as Callum worked him open, the flashing emotion and sensation, the way his breath came in caught snatches. The gasps and little noises he made of need. Pushing back against Callum for more, pushing forward against her for friction on his cock. She kissed him again, holding his hands.

'General, my General,' Rorks whispered. No more than that.

'I've got you Captain,' Callum said. 'It's been a long time since I've had the chance to fuck you. So beg me. Beg me for it.'

Rorks whimpered. 'Please, sir. Please fuck me. I need you inside me. Hurt me. Don't be gentle. I'm yours to take. Please.'

A gabbled, rambled litany of need and desperation.

'Mmmm. So fucking wanton.' Callum kissed Rorks's shoulder, then bit down hard and sucked on the man's skin, bruising it and marking him. 'You're mine. Both of you. Only fucking mine.'

He spat into his hand and reached down to his cock. Positioning himself to enter Rorks. He was not gentle about it. Shoving right into the other man, who he held down with his full strength, so Rorks cried out and gripped onto her hands, reacting to the rough treatment with greater arousal and need.

Callum fucked the Captain hard. Rorks uttered small cries on each thrust, his own cock twitching, untouched, as Callum rode him and took his pleasures, just as Rorks had begged him to.

'Slave, stroke his cock. Not fast. Slow. Very slow,' Callum ordered, darkly, a breathless quality to his voice. Rorks all but cried at the command. She didn't hesitate, following orders and reaching down to take a firm grip on Rorks's long cock and stroking it, base to head, slowly, all the while never breaking eye contact with him.

He was whimpering and begging in whispers, near incoherent with sensation, between Callum riding him and not giving him any chance to move, and her stroking his cock.

Callum kissed the man's shoulder, dragging back his own shuddering breath.

'You take me so well, Captain. I love being inside you. It's been too long,' he said, mouth against Rorks's skin, mouthing and biting at his neck and ear and shoulder. 'I love the way you give yourself up to me. Offering yourself up for my pleasure.'

'I love you, General,' Rorks whimpered, gasping.

'I know, my love,' he said. 'Come for me. I want to feel you clench around me. I want to feel you orgasm with me inside you.'

She firmed her touch and stroked that bit faster and Rorks didn't take long, after that. Barely half a minute and he was crying out and spending in her hands, it hitting her belly and breasts and if she thought Callum would have allowed it, she'd have taken it in her mouth too. But he hadn't wanted penetration with her, had decided she wasn't healed enough yet, so she didn't push and instead stroked the Captain through his orgasm, as Callum continued to ride him, even after Rorks came down from his climax.

She shifted forward, pressing the front of her against Rorks, the mess sticky between them, and kissed him as Callum kept fucking him towards his own climax. Reaching out and holding them both. Knowing how much Callum liked to watch, so showing him, her and his Captain kissing and holding each other, until the General was coming himself, deep inside Rorks, crying out and gripping onto them.

Until they all came down from the high of climax, and Callum carefully, gently now, took himself from out of Rorks, who exhaled in the moment. Then Callum wrapped his arms around them both, holding them close in.

'I love you,' he said, and maybe it was to her, and maybe it was to Rorks, but it didn't matter. It was true for both of them.

She smiled. Because at least she had this. This night, and this morning following. No matter what happened today, she'd had this.

CHAPTER 30
Sabryanna

They got up, they bathed, they dressed, they ate. They spoke carefully and with care to each other, but anticipation of what was to come underlay every interaction.

She realised as they sat for breakfast that she didn't want to lose this. After five years of being alone, after all the guilt and the resignation, she had found a kind of redemption in Callum's arrival and the return of his love for her. In Rorks coming with him and slowly understanding they weren't losing anything by her interruption in their relationship; if anything, she'd helped them to reconnect again. That they could be together, all of them.

She didn't have to feel guilty anymore. She didn't have to loathe herself for the pain she'd caused others. Callum had forgiven her. Maybe, if they'd been able to continue like this, she might even have learned to forgive herself.

Of course, that wouldn't come to pass. But the loss of the new potential for it hurt in ways she hadn't been expecting.

Still, she would make amends for the harm she'd caused these last few years. Dismissing the needs of the valley folk by palming off the responsibilities for governance to others, not even paying attention to them. Betraying Callum, lying to him, sending him on the path that led to the salt mines and all that followed there. Breaking his heart.

Yes, she'd felt trapped into the choices she'd made, but she'd still made them. Now would be a chance to put things right.

Rorks was the first to leave. She gave him a hesitant hug, kissing him softly, chastely, on the lips. He only grinned and swept her up into a much bigger kiss, lifting her from her feet in a bear hug, before plonking her back on the ground again.

'Look after the boss for me,' he said, with a grin.

'I will,' she said. 'Please be careful.'

He screwed up his nose. 'I'm going to lead soldiers. It's what I do. I've got the easy bit.'

'Just keep a good distance back. Don't come near the alter room,' she said. 'You need to get people away.'

Including yourself. You must stay safe. Callum will need you...

But she didn't say that last out loud. Rorks knew what he was doing.

He turned to his General, cheeky grin fading into something more contemplative as Callum came to stand in front of him.

'Good luck, Captain,' Callum said to him.

Rorks stood to attention and saluted formally. 'See you on the other side, General.'

Callum saluted sharply in return. Between them, the gesture was almost as intimate as a kiss.

Rorks left, closing the door behind him with a solid click. Callum gestured to her to fetch his sword. She had her balance back and her voice too. She still didn't feel physically strong, but she wouldn't need physical strength for this.

She retrieved the weapon and brought it to him. Stood before him as he strapped it on. He in his service uniform, her dressed in his clothes still, if with full pants and shirt that covered her properly. They stood looking at each other, ready to go do their part. Go to the alter of the demon.

He raised his hand to the collar around her neck.

'What will happen if I take this off you?' he said.

'*When* you take it off? This won't work if you don't,' she replied, as gently as she dared.

'I don't like attempts to force me down a particular path,' he said. 'It is my decision. Not yours. Now answer my question.'

'I'm not entirely sure. Nothing, hopefully.'

'So you won't start choking? It won't take you back to where you were yesterday, when I put this thing on you again?'

She opened her mouth to say *no*, but didn't want to lie. 'I don't know. I don't think so.'

'Hmmm.'

He didn't move to take it off her. Instead, he walked to the drawers against the wall and retrieved the chain he'd kept her at the end of, that day he'd received petitioners and wanted to display her as defeated and enslaved.

He clipped the chain to the collar. She opened her mouth with some confusion.

'You don't need—' she began.

'Sal, right now, I want the world to understand who you belong to and that it's not that damn demon,' he said. 'Most of all, I want *you* to know it. Maybe I'm being petty and extreme, maybe I'm even being cruel, but I don't care. I'm not letting you get away from me again. You're *mine*.'

She wanted to argue. To tell him that wasn't fair. She wanted to remind him that he had to take off her collar or they wouldn't be able to finish this. She wanted most of all to say he didn't need to put her on a chain to keep her with him because she was his, she would always be his, and she never wanted to leave.

But she couldn't say that. And in the end, perhaps the person he most wanted to convince was only himself.

She closed her mouth again.

'Yes, sir,' she said.

Then she followed him out the door.

∾

She could taste magic in the air as they stepped down the cold stone staircase that led to the lowest basement. To the room at the centre of the castle. The alter room of the demon.

The steps led to a short corridor and at the end were two large wooden doors. Every fibre in her body resisted walking into that place, but she forced herself onwards nonetheless. This had to be done. Besides, the magicians were already in there, all three of them, preparing the space.

The Light's magic lay over the surface of everything. She grimaced at the sour tang, it made her less want to interact with these sorcerers than ever. They ignored her, she was only a slave, and a witch, and not worth their notice. Even if she was the entire reason they were here.

Underlying their magic was something darker, nastier. She could taste that too. A thrumming that never went away. It was strong here. She was amazed they could withstand it, then realised they couldn't feel it. This was the demon's alter room, deep in the castle, at its furthest depth. She avoided it mostly, it wasn't as if she needed to be here to reach the demon. This was a place devoted to the worship of the creature, but she did not worship the demon. She corralled him, at her own cost.

The large, cold space was dark. In the centre of the room was a small black alter. Vaulted ceilings threw shadows from the candles and lanterns on the walls; the air buzzed with power and promise and threat. She wanted suddenly to tell Callum not to take the collar off her, anything might happen, she could guarantee nothing except that the demon would have free passage through her again. She didn't know what would happen, only that it'd be something bad.

She forced her lips shut.

He led her to the alter. The glower as he glanced at it contain furies.

'So we raise the demon and we trap it in here,' he said. Even his tone sounded tense. She wondered he hadn't drawn his sword already. 'Within these marks?'

He gestured to the thick lines drawn on the floor his magicians had prepared.

The lead sorcerer stepped forward, indicating the wider circle in the centre around the alter, and then smaller ones at three separate points, conjoined by a triangle. Signs and sigils were painted throughout.

'The demon will be trapped within the inner circle,' the magician said. 'Once we begin, General, you must not cross inside it yourself. It would be your damnation.'

Callum nodded with a terse expression, eyes flickering to her.

'What about you?' he said. 'You'll be in this circle.'

She cut off the first words that came to her lips. *I am already damned, what difference does it make for me?* He would not respond well to that.

'If they can get the demon to manifest separately to me, and trapped within the circle, then hopefully I can cross back,' she said. 'That's the idea.'

His eyebrows shot up. 'The idea? I want this based on more than just some vague fucking idea.'

'Callum, General, please,' she said. 'We don't know, nobody knows, how this will go. All we have are ideas. Researched and theorised by the best experts you have. That includes me.'

'Sal, I don't like this.'

'I know. But you must defeat the demon,' she said. She gestured around them. 'These lines are important. This ritual is different to the first, I won't be tied down this time, because they want to manifest the demon in a separate physical form. Within the circle will be the demon's domain and he won't be able to step out. You must stay back, outside of all the lines, at all times, so he can't reach you.'

He frowned down at the floor. 'The magicians are in connected circles. Aren't they at risk?'

He asked good questions. The man was no fool.

'They will be protected by their magic. Their smaller circles are bridge spaces, both the demon's plane and ours merged, but they are also filled with each man's own power to keep him safe,' she explained, because clearly the magicians never had. They did watch her with narrowed, suspicious eyes though.

He exhaled through his teeth. 'Okay. So we do this. The demon manifests. The magicians trap him in place.'

'Then you get out,' she said.

'And you, slave,' he returned sharply. 'I'm not leaving without you.'
She tried not to look distressed.

'Sir... Callum...' She took a long breath. 'I promise I'll try. But if things go wrong, if this doesn't go to plan, then you need to promise that you'll do what you must to defeat the demon, no matter the consequences for me.'

He crossed his arms. 'I'm not leaving you behind.'

'This is too important. The world needs you to do this. You must see out your plans.' She wrung her hands together. 'You have a future.'

'And it includes you, Sal.'

Her shoulders dropped. They were words she wanted to hear and was most terrified to hear, all at the same time.

Instead, she leaned forward, up on her toes, to kiss him. 'I'm glad you came back. No matter how this goes. And I know you don't want to hear it, but I am sorry for all the pain I caused you. I am so desperately sorry. '

'Don't you apologise.' He shook his head. Then he kissed her again. 'Don't you dare.'

For one moment more, they kissed.

Then he stepped back. 'Okay, let's do this.'

He took the collar off her.

The power surged through her veins in an instant. She gasped with the feel of it. Not like before, with the choking and the tearing of her body, after she'd given herself to the demon without a fight and he'd taken her. This was something different.

She struggled to hang onto it. Then she stepped back to the alter and nodded to him to step away in the other direction.

One of his magicians put a hand on his arm and tugged him back. Outside of the circles. Each sorcerer then took his place in the smaller circles joined on the outside to the larger one. Their chanting began, like it had last time. Only this time, she wasn't wearing the collar from the first.

Callum was pulled right away, to the edge of the markings at the side of the low room. Dark, shadowed, only candles and cold stone and that black alter in the centre, which she stood beside. Taking deep breaths.

The magicians wove their enchantments. Some of them, heard at the edge of her awareness, were meant to bind her to this plane and to their will. Did Callum know that? That his magicians were working to their own agenda and felt more threatened by her than he realised. They would happily see her destroyed along with the demon. She was the witch.

The Witch Queen.

And this was her castle.

It rose up from her toes. Through her limbs. A force, an energy. Would this have happened last time if she hadn't been in the collar? Maybe? Or maybe the demon would have chosen different still; trying to destroy his prison, instead of use it.

Maybe, now she had offered herself, had promised not to fight him, he decided on other ways forward. The demon did not think like they did. The creature was not human. It was a mistake to consider otherwise.

This was a sensation beyond anything she'd experienced before. The demon always had promised ecstasy, but she wasn't foolish enough to consider the price worth it. Now she wondered.

She wondered.

She felt her body turn, arms akimbo. Her head fling back. Mouth open. A gasp. Aware of the other presences in the room, she could sense them just by their living essence. Little glows of green flickering flames for the magicians. A bright golden for Callum.

And in the centre of the room, herself, burning red. More powerful than any.

Somewhere, deep down, she felt a laugh. Then she heard it. Bubbling up from within her. Sound slipping from her lips. As the chanting increased and the candles flickered and the men in the room, because it was always fucking men, attempted to keep her controlled. But they were so small, so insignificant. So powerless. Compared to her, they were nothing, they had nothing. They were insects she could flick away.

She laughed.
And the demon laughed with her.

CHAPTER 31
Callum

Salryanna laughed. And Callum's entire world twisted in a truly awful way.

It was *her* laugh, that was the worst part. It wasn't some unfamiliar, previously unheard sound, some demon he could instantly recognise as not her, even if it wore her face or took possession of her body.

It was her laughter as he'd always known it and so loved to hear.

He hadn't heard her laugh since he'd returned. Not once. That fact hit him now. He'd gained a few smiles from her, if mostly melancholic ones full of regret or resignation or acceptance of a dark fate. He'd certainly seen tears, and despair, and upset. And fear, of course. He'd come to know her as terrified, constantly, sometimes of him, mostly of something else. A future that was damned, perhaps.

Or maybe of herself.

Now, she laughed, that sound from five years previous, from the forest. The sound of her happy, which he hadn't genuinely heard since before she betrayed him to take on a duty she'd felt condemned to shoulder alone. No matter he'd tried to tell her she wasn't alone, or show her he could help, that he would save her. She'd still not been happy.

Not like then.

Not until now.

Her laughter bounced off stone and overrode the chants of the magicians and she smiled, so dark, so alive and alight and bright. Looking around her, standing by the alter in the middle of those circles, while the magicians wove their magic at three points around her.

She grinned and looked at him.

Then, eyes held on his, she flicked a hand like she might swat an insect and all three magicians lifted a foot into the air.

There were strangled screams, the chants stopping instantly as they cried out. Callum staggered backwards a couple of steps out of the shock of it. The sorcerers' heads were forced back in unison, each man reaching for his throat, kicking his legs wildly, and uselessly. It was as if they were being held up by some unseen forced tied about their necks. As if they were being throttled by it.

And all the while, she laughed.

Callum cried out. 'No!' He started forward, only to be stopped by the edge of the circle he'd been warned too many times not to cross. Almost pinwheeling to keep his balance and not over-step that critical line.

'Salryanna?' he ventured, warily.

'General,' she replied, idly, and it was her voice, even if it came in an unfamiliar tone. The hint of a snarl, something he'd never heard from her before. 'Oh my dear, General. You are such an idiot.'

His stomach twisted hard.

'Sal, I know that's not you.'

She only laughed again. 'Of course it's me.' She lifted her hands and the magicians turned in the air, each of them audibly choking, eyes wide and legs kicking. 'I am the Witch Queen. This is who I am. It's who I've always been.'

She walked around the alter, running a hand over its black, smooth wood, then leaning her elbows upon it and looking back at him with that dark smile.

'You led your armies to my castle, General. You took it over by force. Conquest, wasn't that your word?' Her head cocked as she considered him from over the alter. 'You threw me to the dungeons, publicly humiliated me, threatened me with rape, and put a damned collar around my neck. You led me around on a fucking chain.'

She straightened, losing the laughter, and the sly smile which had come with it. Her expression now turned vicious.

'After all that, you didn't really think I was on your side, did you, General?'

He rocked on his feet. Conscious of the magicians hovering in the air. Their magic was meant to protect them, but a single flick of her wrist and they were trapped, strangled, prone. The most powerful sorcerers of the Light had nothing compared to this power in her now.

It was not Salryanna. It was not.

'Yes,' he said back. 'Yes, I do know Salryanna was on my side, and I will not believe otherwise.'

She laughed a low, dark chuckle.

'What if I told you I betrayed you so gladly all those years ago?' she said. 'The pain on your face that day was delicious. As you realised I was leaving you to rot in the hands of the masters of the Light. You suffered so delightfully.' The laughter dissipated. 'You were meant to die.'

'Well I didn't.'

She snarled a dark sound. 'Yes. A right fucking cockroach, aren't you? Just won't fucking die.'

She threw out a hand in his direction and something—something he couldn't see, couldn't try to dodge, wasn't able to detect coming—slammed into his chest and threw him backwards with force.

He collided hard with the wall at his back and only just managed to keep his head from slamming into the stone. Taking the brunt of the collision with his body, fighting to stay conscious. He had to stay conscious. He had to fix this.

He had to save Sal.

Still, it took him a moment. Dragging back breaths into his lungs winded and heavy, nausea threatening to drag his breakfast up and over the tiles. Struggling to his hands and knees as the room span around him.

While she snarled down.

'You thought you could take my castle by conquest. You thought you could take my throne. My power!' She cried it out at him. 'And you think I was in support of all this?'

He spat onto the floor, bloody gunk. Looking back up at her with narrowed eyes.

'Yes,' he said.

'You really think I wasn't going to ever resist?' Her teeth bared. 'I was biding my time. Learning what I could from you, before choosing my moment to act.' She chuckled darkly. 'But don't feel too bad, we had a few fun times. You're not that bad a fuck, you know.'

He tried to let it wash over him. Slide off his skin. 'It doesn't matter what you say. I know it's not you.'

Her eyes widened, her expression turning almost innocent once more, into something he could almost recognised as her.

'Please, sir, let me come. I need you to tell me I'm a good girl.' Her tone sharpened and the laughter turned mocking. 'Fuck, you were so easy, falling for that shit. I played you from the fucking start.'

She walked forward, stalking toward him. But stopped still a distance away. At the edge of the circles marked out on the floor. The circle he'd been warned multiple times not to cross.

The circle that was meant to trap the demon.

'And you, so surprised I didn't resist,' she continued. 'All ready for my fury and resentment, like you were fucking gagging for it. So I didn't give it to you. I stored it up for the right moment, so I could enjoy it all the more.' Her lips twisted into a stiff, rictus expression that might have been a nasty smile. 'Now you've handed me the most perfect opportunity.'

He forced himself to his feet, trying to ignore the words, not let them hurt. It wasn't Sal saying them. No matter it was her voice, her face, her mannerisms, her intonations. Her laugh. That laugh he hadn't heard for five years and which had once been only for him, so was it any surprise he hadn't heard it since his return? What had he given her to laugh about? Slavery and defeat? Cruelty and abuse?

He would have resented. He would have fought and howled with fury. He would have hated. It never had made sense that she didn't, that she claimed to accept her fate and obeyed without question. What did make sense was the idea she was pretending, calculating, biding her time—

No. This was not Sal. Not his Sal. He couldn't allow himself to believe it. It was only the demon's lies.

The three sorcerers still hung in the air. As he stood, he tried to edge around to one of them. He could reach into their circles without stepping across the line, and maybe he could pull one out, and beyond her power?

She could not breach the circle she stood in. The trap actually held.

'Want to see what I can do, General?' she said, as he came within a few feet of the closest magician.

Her words were sultry, almost purring. The tone alerted him in an instant. Even as his head shot around, warned by her words, she lifted a hand and the man he was closest to was yanked high into the air, right to the ceiling. Crying out in a desperate panic, arms flailing and legs kicking.

'Wait—' Callum tried to call out, but there was no time. Before the word even left his lips, she gestured downwards, almost lazily.

And the man high above was thrown to the stone floor at intense speed.

His body hit the flagstones at such a rate his limbs crumpled and his head split open. Blood and brain matter splattered across the dark tile. Limbs practically snapped in two. Callum had seen broken bodies before. He'd seen blood and gore and death on the battlefield, almost too much of it to count. He'd led armies and fought wars and those horrors were familiar to him.

This was worse than any of it. This single man, whose body was broken in a bloodied mess, seemed in that moment the worst thing he'd ever seen.

Maybe that was because the woman responsible simply stood there and laughed.

'I am the Witch Queen,' she said, then gestured to a second magician. Not even looking at him. Simply jerking him to the ceiling, then throwing him down again, without even going near him.

'No, Sal,' Callum breathed, but there was no way for him to stop her. He didn't even have time to take a step towards the second magician, too high, up by the vaulted ceiling, before he too was thrown to the floor.

There was a crunch and too much blood. Callum shied back, an arm across his face to protect himself from the splatters of it.

'While you, General, are *nothing*.'

He backed away. Each of those men had been in the smaller circles connected to her own. Sal herself had said those circles were filled with each man's magic, which would protect them. Only their magic hadn't a chance against hers.

But she'd also said the overlapping circles increased their risk. He was outside of them all. She couldn't leave the larger circle with the alter now. She was trapped inside it.

He inched around towards the third man. The leader of the magicians, the strongest, watched him from wide-eyes, unable to move or speak, still hanging in the air. He was careful as he crept closer, going slowly so as not to trigger her to act, though she watched him with amused eyes.

He didn't go into the circle, but he got close enough. So that this time, when she gestured upwards like she had two other times before it, he could move first.

He shot his hand out and gripped the edge of the man's robe. Careful not to step into the circle, but yanking him out of it. Or trying to. The force of the movement upwards almost lifted him from his feet and it took all his strength, his entire body weight pulling back, to intervene and stop the man flying to the ceiling.

With a final pull, the man instead came with him. Both of them falling back in a tumble to the floor. Callum pushing back and dragging the magician with him as fast as he could. The man was unable to speak, his throat ringed a dreadful black-purple and almost crushed, so his breath was a choked wheeze.

Only before he could get the magician far enough away, the man was yanked out of his hands. Whisked back into his circle on the floor.

'No!' Callum said and tried to hang on, but the force of it was too hard. The man's foot had still been within the circle, he'd still been within Salryanna's reach.

She was not making the same mistake twice. With a growl, she threw the magician into the air, but instead of tossing him straight into the floor, she hurled him hard right at Callum instead.

He rolled out of the way, diving down with arms up over his head. Only just making it with a gasp as the other man's body flew over him and then crumpled around a pillar. Bending in ways a human body was not meant to bend, with a crunch of bone and tearing of flesh. He was dead in an instant, which was perhaps a mercy.

Callum remained panting on the ground. Lying on the stone after rolling back. When he looked up, he found himself right in front of the doors leading away.

Promise you'll do what you must to defeat the demon. No matter what the consequences for me.

She was trapped in the circle. Her power was immense, the strongest sorcerers of the Light hadn't even made a dent on her, she'd swatted them like flies. But the circle held. The trap held. That was her research, wasn't it? The research she'd spent five years on, then handed over to him, so his sorcerers could implement it here. It worked. Maybe not for long, maybe eventually she'd get out, but for now, she could not move beyond it.

Which meant he could leave now, and collapse the castle, seal this place up. Destroy it. Just like she'd advised him to all along.

Seal it up with her still inside.

The bile rose up from his gut. His hands shook.

'Callum!'

The call came from the doors. His eyes widened as he turned fast. 'Rorks? No. Stay back! Stay out of here!'

Rorks hovered in the doorway, horror written across his features as he took in the bodies, the blood on the floor.

'What—' he breathed. 'Callum?'

'Get out Rorks. Evacuate the castle and get out. That's an order.'

'Everyone's out. There's only us.' His expression firmed and he rushed to Callum, helping him up, arms around him. Callum leaned hard on him as he struggled to his feet.

'General? Do we run?' Rorks breathed, close to his hear. 'What do you want to do?'

Callum dragged back breath, gripping on to Rorks. Closed his eyes.

I'm not leaving you here.

I belong to the demon.

You belong to me!

Then he opened his eyes, took Rorks firmly by the shoulders, and kissed his lips. Hard. Sudden. With desperate need.

'I love you,' he said. 'Now go. Get out of here.'

'Callum, no. I'm not leaving you.'

'I can't leave Sal,' he said. Rorks eyes flickered over his shoulder to the woman in the centre of the room, whom Callum had no doubt was smiling. 'The demon's taken her. I've got to save her.'

The laughter from her at that was amused indeed. The blood drained from Rorks's face at the sound and his hands gripped Callum's arms harder.

'Then I'm staying too,' he said, no matter the terror in his eyes. 'I'm not leaving you or her.'

'No, Rorks. Get out. That's an order. She can't move beyond the circle, she can't reach anyone outside of it,' he said. 'You've got to—'

'Oh, General.' Sal's laughter filled the room. 'Is that what you think?'

She flicked a wrist and Rorks was yanked into the air, then pulled right to her.

CHAPTER 32
Callum

N o. No, no, no.

Callum didn't hesitate chasing after him. Rushing back, crying out with the shock and awful understanding of it. Maybe she couldn't physically move from out of the circle, but her magic now extended beyond it.

Rorks hung in the air. Struggling and terrified, at least a foot off the ground, his legs kicking at nothing. But he was still outside of the circle, she hadn't dragged him into it.

He didn't appear to be choking, like the magicians had. There was no grip about his throat and he wasn't being strangled, instead, his arms were pulled back hard behind him, like he was somehow bound, and he couldn't move them. His teeth were clenched, maybe to contain the pain of the position. Or his fear.

'No, Sal, please!' Callum tried, hearing the desperation in his own voice. The panic rising. 'Please, let him go.'

Sal laughed. Then she gestured with her hand and Callum's heart clenched with sudden fear. Rorks wasn't pulled upwards like the others had been. Instead, his head was yanked backwards to expose his throat, as if by an invisible hand tugging in the back of his hair.

'Do you think he's enjoying this, General?' she said. 'He does like a bit of pain. Gets into some bondage. Do you think this is turning him on?'

'Sal, don't.' Callum could hardly hear her taunts over the roar of panic in his ears. Distantly, he knew it wouldn't help. He had to think clear. But this was Rorks and his terror overtook him in an instant. This was the salt mines all over again. This was the worst of every trauma he'd experienced, right back in the now.

'You don't need him, Sal. Let him go. Please.'

'I don't want to let him go. I'm going to have fun with him.' She grinned at Callum. 'While you watch.'

'No.' He reached out a hand, desperate. 'Have me instead. Let him go and you can have me. I'll give myself up, I won't fight. You can torture me until the end of time. Take all the revenge you want. Please.'

It only made her laugh again.

'General, surely you realise that this is the best way to torture you?' She giggled, like a girl. 'You told me that yourself. They never broke you in the salt mines, not until they took this man from you. That's what you said. Not until they held you down while they hurt him in your stead.' Her smile turned dark and sly. 'Hurt him very, very badly, while you watched, and oh, I'm going to enjoy hurting him so very, very, badly.'

Rorks swung in the air. Body bound by invisible forces, his head pulled back and arms yanked hard behind him. His jaw clenched. He looked for Callum, eyes turning to the side, but he couldn't move to see properly. The terror in his expression was palpable.

Callum was afraid to step any closer in case she killed him, like she had the others. Those whose bodies which even now littered the floor, their blood making the stones slippery. His heart was in his throat.

'I like your angel, General,' she said. She made a series of gestures with her hand in the air. 'Let's see if he really does get off on pain, shall we?'

One by one, the buttons on Rorks's shirt popped open and the material pulled away to expose his chest, with unseen hands. Then, another gesture, something long with her nails.

Deep scratch marks raked slowly down the flesh of Rorks's chest. He sobbed out the pain of it as they did.

'Sal, please!' Callum cried.

'I think I'll keep him,' she said, with pleasant decision. 'I'll play with him a while and you can watch. Then, when I'm bored of that, well...' She shrugged. 'Then I will kill you, General. So you will die knowing the woman you loved has dragged the man you loved down to eternal damnation. Torture everlasting for both of us. All because of you.'

'No!'

Callum tried to run for Rorks, but her hand swatted and he was hit away. Thrown back against the wall, only luck seeing his head not crack against it or his brains splatter over the stone. Even still, he knocked hard and the room span so he had to clutch at the ground until he could see straight.

Rorks's cry came again. He tried to get up to reach him, only to fall, stumbling as the room span from the blow of landing against the wall. Not able to do a thing as more deep, bloody claw marks seared down Rorks's torso.

'This is my revenge, General. The revenge of the Witch Queen you thought you could best and control,' she said. 'You thought you could defeat me, enslave me, but you have no power that could match mine.'

'I thought I could save you.'

He said it rather quietly, still clinging to the floor. Swallowing and tasting blood. He said it because it was the truth.

Then he pushed himself to his knees and managed to lift his head.

'Do you want me to beg?' he said. 'Here, I'm on my knees for you. Do you want me as a slave? I'll be it. Anything you like. I'll do all you ask. But please, Sal, take me and not him. Please don't hurt him.'

Her laughter was louder than ever.

'Will you offer to cut off your hand for me, General?' she said.

'If that is what you want, yes.'

'But why stop there? Your human masters, they had no imagination,' she snapped. 'What if I tell you to take your own eye out, for if you don't I'll take his instead? An eye for an eye. Shall we play that game?'

'Anything you want, I'll do it. Just let him go.'

'No. He's staying with me forever. Eternally damned.' Her expression turned malicious. 'You can watch his tortures before I kill you, then you die knowing he'll be dragged to hell with me.'

And something in that didn't quite catch.

His mind was a whirr, a panic. Rorks held hostage, Sal possessed, or something, he didn't know. And he couldn't get close, because of that circle. The circle she was trapped inside of, which she hadn't made any move to breach. Maybe her magic had extended beyond it, but she still couldn't pass out of the circle.

He'd been warned—she'd warned him herself—don't cross the lines. Because to cross it was to invite damnation.

'Why kill me?' he said, suddenly.

Her eyes, blackened, pinned him. 'Because you don't deserve to live.'

'It's me you profess to loathe so much. It's me who's hurt you, who humiliated you, who enslaved you. Me who stands in the way of your demon,' he said. 'Yet you offer me a death so final? Even knowing that upon death, as a good soldier of the Light, I will go to paradise.'

She snarled. 'That's your faith. I do not subscribe to it.'

'Yet you use threats of eternal damnation and that's my faith too,' he said. 'If Rorks is a tool to hurt me with, why threaten him with eternal damnation, but allow me to ascend to paradise?' He pushed himself up, shaky on his legs. 'No. No, I don't think so.'

'Stay back General. I have your boyfriend in my power. I could take his ear, his tongue, his balls,' she said, grinning as she did. 'Wouldn't that be fun?'

Yet she didn't do it. For all her words, her laughter, her threats, she didn't do any of it.

'You can't reach me. You can't cross the circle,' he said, testing out an idea. She only hissed.

'While you don't dare to cross.'

'No. Because you warned me yourself. That for anyone to cross into that circle was to meet their damnation.'

He looked to Rorks, who hung terrified, chest bleeding from those awful wounds down the length of him. Shaking his head, as if to tell him *no*. Because Rorks knew Callum too well and he'd know now what Callum was thinking.

'I'm not leaving you, Captain,' he said. Then he looked back to her. 'And I'm not leaving you either, Salryanna. If you're going to hell, and if you're taking Rorks with you...' He smiled. 'I'm coming too.'

He stepped across the line. He stepped inside the magical circle.

CHAPTER 33
Salryanna

From somewhere deep down in the dark, she screamed. *No.* Somewhere beyond the world and all sense of it, a distance gone, a life she'd given away so as to save others, she screamed. No.

If you're going to hell, and if you're taking Rorks with you...I'm coming too.

The words cut through the chaos in her head. That wasn't the deal. It wasn't part of her deal. She struggled to open her eyes. To come forward, to grab hold of something in the world. Something beyond the darkness and the black suffocating nothing that she hung in.

'I know you're in there, Sal.'

The words came out of nowhere, but they were *his* voice. There was something strangled to it, something hurting. Why? What?

'I know I can't save you,' he said, somewhere beyond the black. 'I want to. I desperately want to. But you always told me I couldn't and I never listened. So I'm sorry. I'm sorry I didn't listen to you.'

What? What was it? The words, that voice. It cut through the darkness, the horrific black tendrils that held her in place and suffocated her and pressed inside her body and were all she was conscious of.

There was nothing but darkness and the demon. But now...words.

His words.

'I'm sorry.'

Why was he apologising?

There was a groan somewhere. A bitten off cry. His? Please no. Was he hurt? She twisted in the black, fighting against the loops holding her in place.

'I'm sorry I wasn't there for you when you most needed me. That you had to suffer alone all that time.'

Where was he? Why did he sound breathless as he spoke? Like he was struggling to get the words out?

'I'm sorry I didn't understand what you were going through and that I treated you so fucking badly. More than anything, I'm sorry I can't save you.' A pause. A dragged back breath, like he was in pain. 'But you can, Sal. You're the only one who can.'

It didn't make sense. The words, they made no sense. They made her want to cry, but there was no crying in the darkness, there was only the demon and herself crushed within it. She was no person, had no significance, she was only the demon's thing.

'You can save yourself, Sal. You just have to fight for you. For once, fight for yourself.'

The sob that arose out of her was unwitting and full of pain. She tried to move, as if she even had a body anymore. She tried to scream. Soundless.

Try smaller. She tried to blink. Just blink. Focus on that. Blink. Maybe there was a flicker. Maybe an eyelid.

A flash of something bright beyond that eyelid. A room. Stone. Circles on the floor.

Callum, inside the circle, fallen to one knee as black tentacles tried to coil themselves around his limbs and drag him towards the alter. The breach, the portal to the demon's plane.

No!

Darkness took her again. The vision vanished.

But he was still talking.

'You always saved others,' he said. 'You put yourself in harm's way, gave up everything, to protect other people. But there's one thing you've never done, Sal, and that's stand up for yourself. Now you need to.'

This wasn't the deal. She struggled in the darkness. He was inside the circle with the demon. No. He was meant to be saved. Him and the Captain. No-one else was to get hurt. Everyone else left alone. That was the deal. They would be safe.

She turned, twisted. The darkness smothered her in total. There was nothing else. Her writhing subsided.

But then, more words.

'Sal, you must hear me. I know you're in there and you need to hear me.' His words were so far away. 'Fight, Sal. Fight for yourself. I'll be right here with any help you need. I'll support you, I'll never let you be alone again. But I can't save you. Only you can do that.'

She cried then. Not even screams, but sobs. Wracking, awful sobs that required physicality and so she found the physical for it, the body she had lost, the worldly presence she had sacrificed. She felt it as she sobbed, and if she could feel it, she could move it. Surely?

She fought. She struggled. Fingers shifting. Sobbing into nothing.

'You have your own power. You healed Rorks,' he said, with a gasp of breath. Pain from him.

She tried to shake her head. What power? Healing? Her power, that not derived from the demon, was weak, meaningless.

He kept talking.

'You also healed me. Did you know that?' he said and he sounded so strained, but so determined too. 'I was so full of anger and hate, so desperate for vengeance. I'd stopped caring for the world. I even pushed Rorks away. I cared too much for him, but I was too damaged, I couldn't keep anyone close.' He gasped, a strained cry he bit down on quickly. 'But you healed me. By refusing to give me the fight I was so pushing for. You refused to play my game my way and instead offered your own strength and purpose. You saved me, Sal. I learned I could love still. I could care again.'

A shuddered breath. A cry not-quite-suppressed.

She wanted to say something. She wanted to speak. She couldn't make any words sound, she couldn't find lips or a mouth or a tongue. She had no voice.

'Now you need to save yourself,' he said instead. 'You have the strength, you have the will, you have the power. You just have to believe it of yourself. You have to stop hating yourself and know that you deserve to live. You deserve to be happy.'

Another blink and she could almost see him. Wavering, a beacon in the darkness. On his knees and being slowly pulled down by those awful, black tendrils. This man who was so strong, who could do anything. Who could change the world.

Telling her that she was the strong one.

She focussed on her lips. On her tongue. On her throat. 'Go....' she croaked out.

And her hands, reaching out. The tentacles receded at her fingertips, at her movement.

The translucent, wavering vision before her in the darkness jerked straight at the sound of her voice.

'Sal? Sal, fight. Keep fighting.'

She forced the black on him to fall away, somehow, with healing, maybe, or just herself. It exhausted her just to get that much through. She could see him yank it off himself as it weakened, grimacing as he did.

'Get. Out.' She forced the words to sound. 'You must...'

'I'm not leaving you, Sal. I'm right here with you, I always will be.'

She cried. And felt real tears on her physical face.

'Heal yourself, Sal. You healed me, now heal yourself. That's your magic, it doesn't belong to any demon. It is yours alone.'

Her healing magic was weak and soft, it couldn't hurt anything or anyone, it could only heal and save, that was all. It had never been considered worth anything, not by anyone she'd ever known.

But he had said she'd healed him. And that maybe she could heal herself...

From deep down inside, she found something. The healer part of her. The part that she'd always been told didn't matter. As a novice, it was dismissed, ridiculed. As the Witch Queen it had been abandoned. What use had she for healing after she sent all others away and she'd been already sacrificed, already damned?

She found it, she whispered, words with new meaning.

Swimming up through the darkness. Throwing out her arms. And *pushing* the dark away.

The world came rushing back. The room, the alter, the basement.

The body, this body, her body, physicality, reality, blinking in the light and gasping and dragging back breath, air, actual air. Staggering with the weight of it.

And him, right there, the last of the black leaving him too. Pushing himself up on staggering legs. Coming to her, holding her.

'Run,' she managed to croak out even as he tried to hold onto her. *'Run!'*

She pushed him out of the circles marked on the floor, pushing him away with hands and body, and when that didn't work, with magical force that threw him back hard. He landed on a shoulder on the floor, skidding along it. Unhurt, at least no more than he already had been. That was all she could manage.

Then she staggered upright, alone in the circle now, and turned to face the demon.

The creature arose, black smoke, curls of darkness, from out of the alter. Forming into a shape that might, vaguely, have approximated human. Or maybe it didn't. There were tentacles, and claws, and a dripping black wetness to the form. Curling up from the black wood, as a spinning centre opened in the alter, and from it, this thing conjured out of nothing.

Those tentacles reached straight for her.

She fought them. For the first time in her life, she fought the demon. Though she was sure to lose to its power, she wasn't giving in anymore. Not this time.

'Sal!' Callum's voice. Crying it out desperately from across the room, where he lay on one shoulder.

'Stay back,' she managed to call. Her throat was too croaky. 'Get Rorks.'

She was vaguely aware of the other man having fallen sometime before. When she'd been dragging herself up from the depths of darkness, when Callum had been caught inside the circle. Now Rorks lay where he'd fallen, curled up and bleeding, but breathing and alive and that was what mattered.

Right now, it was all that mattered. Getting them out alive.

In her peripheral vision, she saw Callum push himself up and run to where Rorks lay. Kneeling by him and Rorks responding, struggling up, blood all down the front of him and in obvious pain.

She couldn't focus on them. The demon pulled her close in, tentacles wrapping around her waist. A long, black tongue, no longer ethereal or thin as smoke, but now forming hard and physical, wet and dripping and impossibly elongated, reached out and licked down the side of her face. It tried to push itself between her lips, so she pressed them together and turned her head away, even as other tentacles wrapped themselves about her arms and legs.

'Run, Callum!' she got out when she could risk it, even as that black tongue tried to wrap itself around her head, then went for her throat.

Callum straightened, pushing Rorks behind him, furious determination settling across his face. He drew his sword. Oh, stars, no. The man was a soldier and thought this could be a physical battle. He thought he could fight.

The man had also said he'd learned to listen to her.

'No swords. No battles,' she called, urgently. There was no way to battle this creature with weapons; if they tried, the creature would only feed on the violence and the blood.

And Callum, the great General of the Light who had won wars and led rebellions and planned revolution, didn't hesitate to drop his sword to the floor.

It gave her the strength to struggle. To grit her teeth. 'No,' she snarled at the demon, even as it dragged her towards the alter, and the spinning opened up hole in the world turning around it. A gap, darkness beyond. She knew that darkness. She did not want to go back to it. There'd be no return for her if she did.

It was a portal, of a kind. A doorway. It connected this world to the one where the demon existed. A whirlwind, a prison.

She kicked out with all she had. 'No more,' she said, and looked to Callum, where he stood defending Rorks, trying to see how to help her.

'Collar,' she cried out. 'The collar!'

His eyes widened, confusion in them, maybe even an attempt at understanding. He couldn't understand, of course, but he also didn't question her. Without hesitation, he reached to his belt where the golden metal circlet hung.

She managed to wrench a hand free and stretched it towards him, nodding. He threw the magical, metal, golden collar towards her, and she caught it because she always would. The magic of it, calling to her own. A fission in her hand.

Behind her, the demon laughed.

'Do you think you can escape me with that?' The demon's voice slid across every surface of the vaulted room. A scraping darkness. *'Do you think to put yourself back in a collar to belong to a man, when you already belong to a demon?'*

The words were inhuman, suffocating, demeaning. Callum and Rorks both shied back, hands to their ears, Callum pulling Rorks into him to protect them both.

'You are my Queen. You belong to me, witch!'

In that moment, she twisted around in the demon's grasp, a creature made physical so as to hold her.

'I belong to no-one!'

She slammed the collar around the neck of the thing in front of her, then with every healing sense in her body, she pushed her magic outwards. Her own magic, healing magic, which couldn't hurt anyone, not even a demon. But it could heal. With everything she had, all the power she could find within her, leaving nothing back.

If she could heal Rorks, if she could heal Callum, if she could even heal herself, then maybe she might possibly heal the world.

With a furious cry and a rattle of stone, the tentacles slid away. The blackness turning in on itself. Sucked into the whirlwind portal as it collapsed, imploding, inwards, that old breach born of dark worship and the evils of men that had once long ago let a demon into the world. Healed now with the magic of a single woman.

It closed into nothing. She dropped to the ground.

Free.

CHAPTER 34

Callum

There was an explosion.

That's the best way he could describe it. Something exploding out of nothing, and blinding light, or maybe darkness, and a force that knocked him over, so he went sprawling to the ground beside Rorks.

The other man grabbed him and pulled him out of the way just as something crashed down from above. Stone from the vaulted ceiling. Shards of it scattered and he threw his arms up over his face and his body in front of Rorks to protect the man.

The whole castle shook. His vision blurred and he wiped hard at his eyes, his hand coming away red. He'd copped a sharp to the forehead, but it scraped past. Lucky. For now.

'We've got to get out of here. The place is coming down,' Rorks said. He was pale. Bleeding still from the wounds down his chest.

Callum looked around. 'Can you run?'

'Out of here? Definitely.'

Callum turned to the centre of the room. Sal. She was lying in the circle before the alter. There was no sign of the demon. He got up and staggered to her, not caring for circles on the floor anymore. As the ground shook and he almost fell, near sobbing with relief to find her breathing. She even stirred, not quite conscious, not entirely unconscious.

'We're going,' he told her. 'You're coming too. I'm not leaving you.'

He thought her lips moved, but he couldn't be sure. Anything she might have tried to say was lost in the noise. The roar, the crashing. Somewhere beyond this room, there was an alrighty bang, an explosion of some kind maybe, and collapsing of stone. It sounded like walls coming down.

He gathered her up in his arms and staggered back to Rorks. Together they ran for the doors. Making it out just in time as something crashed behind them and a single glance back told him the alter was gone, the roof caved in above it.

They bounded up the stairs as fast as possible given their physical state and the fact he was carrying Sal. The cascading destruction of brick and mortar behind them trailed their every step. Rushing upwards and almost falling into a collapsed hole.

Callum turned towards the main part of the castle, but even as he did, another wall came down in front of them.

'This way,' Rorks said, pulling him in the other direction. Callum followed, trusting in the Captain to know the best, fastest routes to save them all. Rorks had mapped this damned castle end to end, he knew it better than anyone. Except Sal herself.

So he didn't question the twists and turns and dark little corridors Rorks led him down, simply trusted the man to know how to get them out. Putting the escape in his hands, as the ground shook and stone crumbled about them.

Rorks turned down one corridor, then had to double back as it collapsed ahead of them.

'Down here,' he said, sounding certain, and turned into a dark little hall that looked like it was already coming down in pieces. He didn't pause to follow Rorks into it. Gripping Sal close, blinking back the blood that kept getting in his eyes. Ahead, Rorks didn't look any better, covered in blood down his chest, but he kept going and so did Callum.

In his arms, Sal didn't move, not once, not even to cling on around his neck.

A door. There was a door, black wood and old. Rorks ran right to it, as if he knew it. Hauled open the old iron locks and shouldered his way through.

Sunlight. Dear god, it was daylight outside. They stumbled into a secluded courtyard, a gravel-lined back alcove that had probably only been used by servants before, but it got them out of the castle. Running from it and only just missing being crushed by falling stone and a wall collapsing.

'Further,' Callum choked out, breathless. 'Out of the grounds. Keep going.'

'I know the way.'

Rorks waved him to follow and they ran, across the gravelled court-yard and then into gardens. Then paddocks. Further even, heading for the tree line beyond.

The forest.

Callum almost wept with relief for it.

'There,' he called. The forest had always been saviour and safety. The one place Sal had always felt safe.

Rorks didn't waste time in asking for clarification. He just led them across the paddocks and cleared ground until the world stopped shaking and they reached the first of the trees.

Which is where they stopped, just inside the tree line. He couldn't keep going. Rorks was in even worse condition. Gasping breath and stag-gering, the both of them. Callum leaned against a tree, using it for balance as he managed to fall to his knees without letting go of Sal. His chest ached, he suspected at least one broken rib, and that was going to fucking hurt once the adrenaline wore off. His forehead wouldn't stop bleeding.

But for now, he let himself drop, still cradling Sal carefully in his arms. He didn't put her down. Just sat at the base of the tree holding her close.

Rorks staggered to the ground on her other side. His chest was a bloodied mess. His expression was tight and, worse, full of horror and desperate fear. But he said nothing and together they watched from a distance as Castle Ravenswild fell in on itself.

Collapsing stone and a building imploding, until there was nothing left standing, just a pile of rubble on the ground.

'The men,' Callum said, in a raw voice. 'Did you get them out? Was anybody...'

'Everyone was evacuated,' Rorks said. 'I got them all out before coming back for you. Even Seth from the dungeons.'

Callum couldn't find the energy to care for a man who was only alive because Salryanna had asked it of him. But Rorks would never leave anyone behind, not even a brute who deserved it.

Callum wanted to reach across to him, but couldn't let go of Sal.

'Rorks. Rorks, are you okay?'

There were tears on Rorks's face, a silent crying, but he did manage to nod.

'I think so? I will be.' He groped out a hand and found Callum's around Sal, clutching his fingers, and Callum held his back just as hard. 'I need you, Callum. Is that okay? I know she does too, but is it okay if I need you as well?'

'Rorks, always. Always.' He gasped back breath. 'I'm sorry I let us drift. I'm sorry I wasn't always there for you. I cared for you too much, but I was broken, I was too damaged to give you what you needed. I—' He stopped his own words, stumbling over them. Took a long breath. 'I am not that now. I am here for you. I'll never, ever let you stray from me again, I promise.'

Rorks gulped back his own tears, pushing himself forward. Pressed his lips to Callum's over the prone form of Sal still in his arms. Callum wouldn't stop clinging to her. Not even to lay her upon the ground. She hadn't stirred. Hadn't spoken, hadn't moved. He wouldn't let her go. He would never let her go.

When Rorks sat back, his eyes flickered down to her.

'Sal...' the Captain began, but dragged off, perhaps not wanting to ask.

'She's breathing,' he said, his voice tight. 'I can feel it. When I hold her close, I can feel her breathing.'

Rorks didn't answer immediately. The silence was telling, the tension in Callum's arms too tight, too frightened. He couldn't let her go. He had to cling on. He had to hold onto her, so she would stay with him, so she would be there. And he would be there for her. For her and for Rorks and he would never let either of them down again. So long as she stayed with him. So long as she was still there.

After a moment, Rorks reached out a tentative hand.

'General, may I see to her? Check her over?' he asked softly.

Callum tensed and pulled her back into him.

Rorks laid a calm hand on top of Callum's, where he held Sal.

'I promise you don't have to let her go,' the man said gently. 'Just let me see to her. Make sure she's not got any wounds, doesn't need aid. Okay?'

'She's breathing,' he said. 'She's breathing, Rorks.'

'I know, sir. Let me assist you.'

Slowly, very slowly, Callum willed his arms to relax. To open just enough to let Rorks see to Salryanna. Check her pulse, her heart, her breathing. Look for wounds. She was sleeping. That was all. That was all it was.

'She breathes, sir,' Rorks said carefully, as if Callum hadn't just told him that. As if the relief Callum felt wasn't a gut-punch force simply to hear someone else confirm what he so desperately willed to be true, and Rorks knew he needed to hear it. 'She breathes and her pulse is steady, which means her heart is beating normally. Her colour is fresh, her skin warm. She lives, sir. She lives.'

He spoke with calming reassurance and Callum felt the tears on his own cheeks, leaning back against the tree, still holding her, but loosely, watching Rorks as the man checked her over. Rorks knew what he needed to hear and that he needed to continue hearing it. Attending to his needs, even as he attended to Sal's.

She lived. She was sleeping, but she lived. A steady inhale and exhale, with a pulse and a heartbeat, and she lived. She lived.

She just wouldn't open her eyes.

Rorks checked her over for the usual vital signs, like they would any battlefield injury. Callum couldn't. He was too afraid. But Rorks did what was needed, took the professional role, did what should be Callum's responsibility and Callum let him, because he needed the Captain right now.

In the shade of the trees, beside a burning, collapsed castle, Rorks ascertained Salryanna still had all the vital signs as strong as ever. She lived.

'She will wake up,' Callum said.

Rorks reached over to him, across her prone form, and pulled their heads close. Rested his forehead against Callum's own.

'She will wake up,' Rorks repeated his words. 'And until then, we will take care of her.'

Callum closed his eyes. Breathed in the other man. Nodded. He leaned forward and brushed his lips against Rorks's own. Then he pulled Sal into him and leaned against Rorks's shoulder, the man's arm slipping around him. A warmth, a comfort. A love.

He let himself rest, for the first time in five long years.

CHAPTER 35

Salryanna

Birds were singing.

Nearby. She had often listened to them from her rooms in the castle, the little balcony she'd filled with daisies and from which she could see the forest beyond the cleared paddocks surrounding the place. Only there the birds had been distant, far away. They never came near the castle, not even the big black birds the place was named for. Like all else about it, even the castle's moniker was a lie.

Now, there were birds singing and they were somewhere nearby. And... fresh air. Fresh air that brought scents she'd never quite forgotten, not even after five years.

She opened her eyes. Rubbed them to get rid of the sleep caught in her eyelashes and found herself lying on a cot by a large open window. While outside, not a dozen feet beyond her window, was...

The forest.

Something turned inside her. She twisted to look further around and figure out where she was. It wasn't anywhere she knew. It wasn't the castle.

She was not in the castle. It took her a moment to comprehend that.

She was still in the valley though. Near the forest. Was this a small cottage, perhaps? Her body felt achy and stiff, but not otherwise hurt. She even felt rested. She just had no idea where she was.

Her heart thumped and she tried to push herself up. She was alone in what was a large room. There was a fireplace, currently unlit; the warmth of the day was felt even inside. A kitchen stretched along the back and there was a meals area and a little sitting space next to the fire. A bookcase along the wall closest to her. It was homely, understated. Warm.

Worn in. This was somebody's home.

She managed to swing her legs around until she was sitting on the side of the cot. There was a small table beside it with a mug of water, a book, a candle. The book was marked at a page halfway through. Poetry, of all things. She had never read much poetry.

Callum had always liked poetry.

Callum...

Another sound made its way through to her. A thudding, not rhythmic, exactly, but regular. Like someone was chopping wood. It was coming from outside, drifting in through the window, but maybe from the other side of the house?

There was one external door leading out towards the forest and another, an internal one, leading further into the building.

She made herself stand and found her balance settled, though her legs were a little wobbly. She managed to shuffle over to the table, gripping onto the back of a wooden chair and catching her breath. Her muscles were definitely weakened. She didn't like the sensation, but at least she felt grounded and not about to sway or fall. A long woollen night-dress dropped to her ankles. She didn't recognise it, but it fit her and was comfortable, and there was a shawl across the bed. She reached for it, snagging it with her fingertips to pull around her shoulders.

Her feet were bare, but that was okay. It wasn't cold. She walked carefully across the room to the internal door first, rather than head for the one to the outside where she might have to walk around the house to find whoever was chopping wood out there. If there was someone, she wanted to find them as a priority. Even above figuring out this place and where she was and who's home it might be. She needed answers. She needed reassurance.

She needed to know what had happened.

Carefully, she opened the door and found herself in a long hallway with stairs leading up and other doors leading off it, but also, at the far end, an external door. A more formal entrance. She went to it, padding along the polished floorboards of the hall. It was a cosy home. Sweetly decorated. Welcoming. She had no idea who it belonged to. She desperately needed to know.

She opened the external door and found herself stepping onto a large, covered veranda, looking out onto a cleared space at the edge of the forest. A well-graded road led away, down a steep hill. Farmland stretched in the valley below, but they were high up here and while the valley stretched into the distance, the road that led away from the house turned and twisted down the hill, and quite a way down she could just see the outline of a few buildings. A town, in the distance.

The chopping sounded again. Around the side of the house. But another sound now too, equally as unfamiliar, from the road. Horse's hooves. Slowly coming closer. She saw the figure a distance away, someone riding a horse which veered off the road once they were nearer the house, coming through cleared paddocks. Not arriving formally by the front, but taking a smaller track. She lost sight of the rider through the trees.

She followed the veranda around the house, which was larger than she'd expected. Turning the corner to find the people she'd heard.

And there...

There.

He was chopping wood. While the front of this home looked across the valley and down the hill, the side here was cleared for a small yard with the forest beyond. He wore working uniform, well, the pants at least. He'd stripped off the shirt, which hung over the veranda railing near her, undoubtedly due to the sweaty job he was attending to. A pile of logs sat next to him and he was splitting them into smaller pieces suitable for a fireplace. He reached down to another even as she watched, placing it on the cut trunk of a felled tree, and swinging the axe to split it.

Callum.

He was alive. She was alive. She didn't know how or why or what had happened. She wasn't in the castle, she didn't know where this was, but they'd not left the valley. And he was alive.

He was alive.

She almost cried out with the sheer relief and wonder of it. Only before she could, the horseman she'd spied earlier came riding around from the other side. He vaulted off the animal, throwing the reigns around a branch of a tree at the edge of the forest, before walking across to meet with Callum.

Her heart leapt on sight of that angelic face. Rorks.

'Sir!'

Callum put down his axe and held out a hand.

'Welcome home, soldier,' he said, warmly. Rorks took his hand with a smile, then Callum pulled the man in closer and kissed him. Hands wrapped around his waist, not rushing the greeting. Neither of them did, lingering in the moment.

'You're all sweaty,' Rorks declared when he was finally let go.

'That's the first time I've heard you complain about that.'

Rorks's smile turned wicked. 'You do look pretty fucking sexy. You should go shirtless more often, sir.'

'Mmm. Behave and I might,' Callum said, with a grin. It was all so easy, so familiar. Such a simple care and humour and love in their voices, and an openness she didn't think she'd seen before, not even when they'd been together in the castle.

'I should assign this job to you, now you're home,' Callum said, but it wasn't a genuine threat. He picked up the axe again and swung it at the log. Rorks took the chance to admire the man's body. Salryanna couldn't blame him. This was certainly a sight to wake to, the muscular definition of Callum's torso as he swung that axe.

'I've been riding all morning,' Rorks's protested. 'But I'll happily sit and watch you do it.'

'I bet. Tell me about the city while I work, then. What's the mood? Did you check in with the town on your way up the hill?'

Despite his protests, Rorks picked up the split wood and put it into the stack of smaller pieces, while Callum readied another log.

'I did. You might want to go into town tomorrow,' Rorks said. 'Francis has a list of things to run by you. They would come here, but the townsfolk would like to see you and Francis says it'd be good for you to be visible right now.'

'Okay. It'll give you a chance to rest tomorrow, after riding today. I'll go see to the town,' he said. 'What of the city? What of our men?'

'The men are ready to fight the moment you need them. Until then, they're carefully keeping under wraps. Revolution by stealth, right?' he said, and listening from the veranda, she felt a buzz along her extremities. That was what she had called it, his plans. Revolution without war, in his words. 'Politics in the capital is worse than ever. It's been noticed you haven't returned to your place there. I think the timing on this will be pushed faster than we might like. Unless you want to spend some time in the city to waylay concerns—'

'No.' Callum cut him off. 'Even for the briefest visit, it's at least two weeks travel. I can't leave her for that long.'

Rorks reached a hand to the General's shoulder and slipped another around his waist. Pulling him close, rather than letting him see to the next log.

'I know. So we work our plans around it,' he said, calmly. 'She's the priority. For both of us.'

Callum leaned his head against the other man's. 'Thanks, Rorks.'

They kissed again and for a moment she stood watching, warmed by the small scene, the reunion of the two of them, a surge of affection in her chest. She almost didn't want to interrupt it. They'd clearly been in this place for long enough to settle, to create a home, routines, familiarity. They were together. That was the important thing. She smiled to see them together.

She waited until they separated again before she took the couple of steps leading down from the balcony. Hanging on to the handrail for support, her body still a little weak. She must have made some kind of sound, because both men across the yard turned.

They saw her. They stared. Then, in an instant, Callum dropped the axe and ran.

'Sal!' He cried out, a desperation. 'Sal!'

Then he was with her, his arms around her and pulling her into him, holding her, gasping breath. She clung to him, holding him back, as hard as he held her. His lips on her own, only momentarily, because he had to pull back to look her in the face, to check she was okay. As if he had to see her with his own eyes, as if he couldn't take his eyes off her for fear she might disappear.

'I'm here,' she said, on instinct. He seemed to need to hear it.

'Sal, dear god, you're awake, you're awake.'

Rorks was there barely seconds after him, arms around her also, unexpected, welcome. His lips on her cheek, kissing her, holding her too. The two men half-crying, half-laughing, both.

She tried to make sense of it. Decided just to go with it.

'Where am I?' she asked, looking from one to the other.

Callum laughed and held her to him.

'Home, my love. You are home.'

They helped her back inside the house. Refused to tell her anything until she was sitting down and they'd checked she was okay. Back to the kitchen sitting room in which she'd first awoken, the one with the beautiful large window looking out onto the forest, with the cot she'd slept in positioned against it. So she could wake up and see the forest, Rorks told her. So that when she awoke, she would know she was safe.

The kindness of that stunned her. She wrapped their arms about her even closer.

Callum wanted her to lie down again, worried as he fussed over her. She told him she'd been lying down long enough and what she wanted now was to be up. Aside from a slight weakness in her muscles, she felt healthy, whole. Better than she had in a very long time.

In five years, even.

They compromised. Rorks pulled a chair out at the kitchen table for her to sit in, and Callum sat beside her as she did, his arm around the back of her, his other hand holding one of hers. She was grateful for the continued touch.

'I'm out of the castle,' she said, and almost couldn't believe it. 'For five years I haven't been able to leave it. I've been bound to it. Now I'm out of the castle.'

The men exchanged a glance, but it seemed a positive one, and when he looked back to her, Rorks smiled the warmest smile.

Callum squeezed her hand. 'Is there any of that soup left, Rorks?' he said. Apparently unnecessarily, for Rorks was already starting a fire and pulling out a pot to heat over it.

'Onto it already, sir.'

She shook her head. 'It's okay, I'm not really hungry. I just want to sit and be with you. And maybe, you can tell me what's happened?'

'You need proper sustenance, it's been so long,' Callum said. 'We'll talk through everything, I promise. But you need to get your strength up.'

'I feel strong already,' she said. 'I haven't felt this whole, this healthy, in...' She dragged off, looked from one to the other. 'Five years.'

The reality of what all this meant only slowly caught up with her. Five years trapped in the castle because she was bound to the demon. A creature that was slowly consuming her from the inside. Her body had felt that, the gradual decline, even as it tried to heal itself. It could never truly heal from the increasing burn of the demon. Not while the demon was still bound to her.

She wasn't in the castle anymore. And this home they had made was well established.

'How long was I sleeping?' she asked.

The silence which met her question was telling. Eventually, Callum shifted to take her hand in both of his.

'Just over three months,' he said, simply.

The breath went out of her. She stared at him, then around to Rorks, who nodded in mute agreement. Three months. No-one survived a coma of so long, she knew that because she was a healer. It became impossible to get food or water into them, without which nobody could survive. If a comatose patient couldn't even swallow water, they were usually gone in a week.

'How...' she breathed.

'The medics said it was dehydration we had to defend against,' Rorks said. 'But you could still swallow. They reckoned it was only a reflex, but either way, it was a good sign. It meant we could feed you. Make sure you wouldn't starve or suffer of thirst.'

'You've nursed me this long?' she said, still stunned.

Rorks smiled. 'Of course,' he said, as if there would never have been any doubt. 'Admittedly, the Boss did the most. I just ran around following orders and getting what he needed.'

'You ran yourself ragged keeping my army operating, my political negotiations in check, and securing us a stable base in the valley,' Callum cut in firmly. 'Not to mention being my eyes and ears in the world. All so I didn't have to leave here. You kept me going, Rorks. You held me together.'

'We held each other together. I had my fair share of nights where I wasn't coping, but you got me through,' he said. 'Anyway, that's what I'm here for, Boss. Making sure you've got all you need. Which includes making excellent soup.'

He grinned as he ladled soup into a bowl and brought it across to the table, putting it in front of her. It smelt amazing and she had to admit to a stir of hunger in her belly as she looked down at it.

She reached for a spoon and carefully took a sip. The taste was as good as it looked.

'Oh. That's wonderful,' she said, and took another sip.

Rorks looked pleased. 'Thank you. I'm not too bad a cook for an army brat, so it turns out.'

'We'll work up to solid food,' Callum said. 'You've been living on liquids for three months. We'll get the medics in to check you over and work out the best recovery steps.'

She ate more of the soup, glad he sat so close, and that he returned his arm to over the back of her chair again. She wondered whether to tell them the swallow reflex wasn't usually retained in comatose patients. They must have watched over her around the clock. Feeding her, caring for her, nursing her through it.

Setting her up by the window so she could awake and know she was safe.

'I don't think the medics will be needed,' she said. 'I'll see them if you wish it, of course I will, anything you want. But I am well. I...I think that's why I was unconscious for so long. I think my body was healing itself. That it needed a deep, deep healing, and you gave me the chance for that.'

He raised a hand, pushing the hair from her face and tucking it behind her ear.

'Do you remember anything?' he asked gently. Across the table, Rorks sat down, with a more worried expression.

She sucked back a breath and considered her memories.

'I remember you taking my collar off,' she said. 'And then...darkness. Only darkness and the demon.' She could have said more, her eyes clenching shut, but they didn't need to know what it was like down there in the dark. They didn't need to know the suffering of it. They'd already been through enough. 'Until...you.' She looked up again at Callum. 'You stepping inside the circle. I remember you...you told me I could save myself.'

Memories flashed in ragged pictures and fragmentary moments. She couldn't piece it all together. She suspected that was partly her own mind protecting herself from the truth of it. But she remembered enough, because the demon had shown her, down in the darkness. The demon had taken great pleasure in showing her the threat to Callum and Rorks, and what he'd made her—or not her, only the demon in her form—say to them, do to them. What the demon had put them through.

That had been part of the suffering. But only part.

That had been the deal, had it not?

'He showed me,' she said quietly. 'The demon, when I was in the darkness. He showed me what was done. What was said to you. To hurt you, to harm you. And I'm sorry.'

'A demon's tricks and I knew that from the start,' Callum said calmly.

She raised her eyes with hesitation to meet his. 'I told him to say those things,' she said very quietly. 'I told the demon what to say that would hurt you most.'

Callum only shrugged.

'Honestly, Sal, before Rorks was taken, I wasn't sure if you weren't still in control someway and saying such things yourself,' he said. 'To make me leave. To make me abandon you. Seal up the castle and leave you to your fate.'

Fear swam in her stomach, but she wanted to be honest with him. She'd always tried not to lie, but she'd never tried being genuinely honest before. She wasn't sure she knew how.

'That was my deal,' she said. 'With the demon. To save you, the both of you. He wasn't to hurt you and I would remain, I wouldn't resist any longer. But I knew it would never hold, the risk would always remain while you were in the castle. So I told him what to say so you would leave. To make you go.'

'Except it was never going to work,' Callum returned, dryly indeed. 'I was never leaving you, no matter what you said. Not then and not ever.'

She exhaled in a rush. Reached out to find his hand, groping for his fingers, needing to feel his grip on her, needing him to anchor her.

'Me neither,' Rorks added, with a smile.

She didn't know what to say. Callum pulled her into him and held her, while she tried to comprehend what all this meant. She was out of the castle. She was no longer bound to place or duty or obligation. There was no more demon.

'What now?' she asked in a quiet voice. 'I've never known life outside of the castle. I've never known life without the obligations of my duty.'

Callum's lips ghosted against her forehead. 'Now we take time to recover and we take a breath and we see,' he said. 'You're free, my love. Now you can do anything you like. And you can take however long you need to decide what that might be. Recovery should not be rushed.'

She curled up in his arms and wondered why the very idea could terrify her so much.

Callum didn't want to leave her side even for a moment. Rorks made him some soup as well, and her some more, because it turned out she truly was ravenous, now she had finally woken up. He then got himself some and they all ate, heartily, thoroughly.

If the three months sleeping was her body healing itself physically from the damage that had been done to it by the demon over so long, it would take longer to heal the mental scars. But Callum, who admittedly knew something about emotional trauma himself, was determined to ensure she had the time for that as well. This was their home. A safe space in the forest, a short walk to the town, but isolated enough to give them space. She never need leave it if she didn't want. Or when she was ready, she could go anywhere she wanted. It was up to her.

She couldn't comprehend that. The world seemed too large and terrifying. The chance to stay here, away from the world for a little while, was a lifeline she clung to, but the men seemed to understand that too.

'Boss, if you want to bathe outdoors, we should do so now before we lose the day's light,' Rorks said, once they'd finished their meal and he'd cleared the dishes.

Callum threw him an amused look. 'Is that your way of telling me I need a bath, soldier?'

Rorks grinned. 'I would never, sir. But I have ridden a long way today and I'd like one,' he said. 'I thought maybe Sal would enjoy it.'

Callum brushed his lips against hers. 'I think she would too,' he said. But he looked back to Rorks. 'I'll take her out with me, while you—'

Only Rorks stepped forward, took the General's hand in his own, and pulled him gently back from Salryanna.

'Let me take her for a few minutes, sir,' he said. 'I won't let her alone, I promise. You go out while we get towels and things, then we'll meet you there.'

Callum frowned, clearly not wanting to leave her side for even a second. But she could see Rorks wanted it, and she suspected if she didn't ease Callum into an early understanding that she didn't need to be continually hovered over, he wouldn't stop.

Not that she minded. But it would also be nice to speak with Rorks.

She smiled at Callum and squeezed his hands.

'I'll be safe,' she said. 'I'll be with Rorks. I'm not going anywhere, I promise.'

To which he looked uneasy, but obviously couldn't find an argument to resist. He couldn't be glued to her side every second of every day.

'I'll just be outside,' he said, at last.

She pushed him up gently. 'And we will just be a few minutes.'

He leaned down to kiss her, before straightening. Rorks came around the table with a smile.

'Call if you need anything particular bought out, sir.'

'Thanks, Rorks.' He kissed the man as well. 'Your service is, as ever, appreciated.'

Rorks flushed with the praise, visibly pleased. His cheeks were still pink when Callum left and he turned back to Sal, biting his lip, almost sheepish.

'Um. Want to have a quick tour of the house, while I get the stuff?' he said, and her eyes lit up.

'Yes please.'

He helped her stand and they tested how strong she was on her feet. She was fine. Three months of sleep left her feeling all the better for it. The initial weakness in her limbs wasn't even lingering now.

He gave her a quick tour. Said he'd show her around in more detail later, but for now she could at least orient herself. Downstairs was the kitchen and informal sitting room where she'd been, and that was where they spent most of their time indoors, he said. Sitting with her and with each other.

Across the hall there was a more formal drawing room, and a dining room, and Callum's study, which was lined with bookshelves and had a big desk and a window that also looked out onto the forest, like hers had done.

There was a daisy bush in a small pot in his window. She lingered by it, fingers brushing the soft leaves.

Upstairs was the main bedroom, dressing room, washroom, and another couple of guest rooms. Rorks had his own study up here, but said he didn't use it much. Mostly stored things and that was all.

In the main bedroom was a very large bed, while the dressing room contained more military uniforms than one could imagine possible, in two sizes for the two men, and complemented by some less than official looking clothes as well. Non-uniform wear. She pressed her lips together as she considered the space, then back out into the bedroom. The wash-room was large, with its own large fireplace where water could be heated and, again, two sets of men's things, razors and the like.

'None of the indoor plumbing here that the castle had, of course,' Rorks said. 'But I'm working on that. I've got ideas. Give me six months and I think I could make it work.'

She turned with eyebrows raised. 'Really? The castle was built on the seams of the mineral springs. The place was founded with magic.'

'Plumping and mechanics aren't magic, they're science,' Rorks said. 'The mineral springs flow through this entire mountain range, including right behind this house. I think I can work something out, given time.'

Which sounded so clever and suggested so much about what Rorks might be capable of. She looked around her with a tight chest and bitter-sweet eyes. It felt like such a home. The home of the two men and this their bedroom, their intimate spaces, and suddenly, all at once, she felt quite the intruder.

'He made this place for you,' Rorks said, eyes on her, as if he could read her mind.

'Huh?'

'The boss. When we got away from the ruins of the castle, we managed to get to the town. Walked in half dead, him carrying you, blood all over us. Francis and the townsfolk came out to meet us,' he said. 'They celebrated him for defeating the demon. He told them that was your work, but they still see him as some kind of hero. They gave him this place to be his own. It'd been neglected for years as too isolated from the main town, but I think Francis took one look at us, at you, and knew you'd like to be near the forest. That this location was perfect.'

'Francis,' she said with a sigh. 'I'd like to see them.'

'I'll get them to come up and visit, if you're not ready to go into town just yet,' Rorks promised. 'The General has fixed up the place over the last three months. There was a lot needing doing, it was a bit of a wreck, but he's repaired everything and built it back up. A home, he said. He wanted you to have a home when you woke up. A home you could love, and where you'd be safe, and not simply a place you were trapped in.'

'Oh.' She felt tears prick and wiped at her eyes. 'Oh, Rorks. It's beautiful. But this is your space with him. Please tell me I'm not intruding. Please tell me I'm not going to be in the way.'

Rorks put hands on her shoulders and turned her to face him. Then, if with a not-quite-hidden breath for courage first, pulled her to him and kissed her firmly on the lips.

He let her go with wary eyes on hers, as if not sure that had been welcome and waiting to see.

She smiled. 'What was that for?'

'Because we're a relationship all three of us, and this is our home, for all three of us,' he said. 'Surely we're beyond worrying about stepping on each other's toes, you and me? We're as much together as we are with him, aren't we?'

She pulled him closer and kissed him back. 'Yes. We are. All three of us. Together.'

His grin was broad. Then he turned to pick up a stack of towels and dumped some in her arms.

'Come on. Let's go find him before he starts fretting for being away from you for too long.'

He led her back down the stairs, always being careful to keep an eye on her, which she noticed, but didn't say anything. The care was welcome, even if it wasn't needed. She felt stronger than ever. She hadn't felt like this since she'd been a novice.

Instead of going back to the kitchen, or the front door, he turned and led the way past a pantry and cool room, to a mud room with a door leading out the other side. It opened onto a partially constructed wooden deck. Beyond was a side of the house she hadn't seen yet. The ground sloped downwards just a little and a hundred feet beyond was a series of natural warm mineral springs pools, fed from within the mountain.

'Oh,' she said, smiling, her eyes wide.

'Pretty awesome, hey?' Rorks said. 'Come check it out. The boss has fixed up the house, but out here is where I've been doing some stuff.'

A stone path led down to the pool, where Callum was already in the water, watching them approach. Someone had built a small, enclosed rock pool hived off from the main body of water, and a path that led around it. There was even a long wooden bench, upon which Callum had thrown his uniform before jumping into the pool. Steam dissipated off the top, suggesting warmth.

'I've been building the rock edge up, so we can access it easier, without the mud or dirt,' Rorks said. 'This was the other reason we settled on this place, though it needed so much work. The warmth of the spring helps his back a lot. I've been trying to massage his scars, like you did, but I don't think I have the same clever touch.'

'I've been trained, that's all. I'll show you what to do, if you like.'

'I'd like that.' He smiled. 'Do you want to swim, or do you want to just sit on the edge and dangle your feet in?'

She gave the Captain a pointed look. 'I am going all the way in, Rorks. I'm not just dangling my feet like an invalid.'

He grinned and began stripping off his shirt by the long bench. She turned to spy Callum, swimming back their way, hoisting himself up on the clear rock edge and she didn't even mind when he put his hands about her and kissed her and got her nightdress wet in doing so.

He held her to him. 'So what do you think, witch? Is this place okay?'

While his tone was amused, there was a need underlying it. A suggestion he needed to hear it from her, out loud, just what she thought of the home he'd built for them. The safety he'd tried to create here, so when she awoke she'd find herself comfortable. All while never knowing if she'd ever actually wake up.

'It is beautiful, General, and I adore it,' she said. 'Thank you. I've never had a true home before. Not until now.'

'Our home,' he said.

She nodded and didn't ask for how long or what next or about the future. She'd heard enough from his brief conversation with Rorks, before they'd known she was awake, that he'd not given up on his plans, even if he had put them on pause. Slowed them down in order to prioritise care for her. Rorks had been out judging the mood of the city, the readiness of his army. They'd been shoring up relationships with the Valley and she was pretty sure when she got to speak to Francis that she'd find Callum was actively in command. The Witch Queen was no more and the demon was gone, but the General of the Light was in control and setting up a power base. One from which he hoped to rival the Command of the Light and the Capital itself.

Revolution by stealth. He always had long term plans and he'd not given up on them. How long would this tranquil escape for the three of them last? How long before a more political future interfered?

She didn't ask. It would come, in time, and she'd decide what part she wanted to play in it, if any. Until then, they were here.

He helped her strip the nightdress off, even as Rorks finished undressing himself. When she turned back to the blonde man, she startled, eyes widening.

'Rorks? Your chest...'

'Ah.' Rorks looked down at himself. 'Sorry. I'd forgotten.'

Along his chest were what might have been called scars, if they had ever actually healed. Claw marks ripped into him. A demon's claw. The wounds were still open, if not actively bleeding. Cauterised. Bright red slashes across his frame that looked dreadfully painful.

Oh the stars. Her heart thumped with the knowledge he carried lingering marks, unhealed injuries that never got better.

Callum turned her head so she would not look.

'Don't fret, my love,' he said. 'We keep an eye on his wounds. They don't heal, but they don't fester or get worse either. I make sure he is looked after.'

She couldn't help but look sideways at them, despite Callum's attempts to shield her.

'Do they hurt you?' she asked Rorks, in a small voice.

She didn't miss the way Rorks looked to Callum first, for permission to answer. From the corner of her eye, she saw Callum's nod to go ahead.

'Sometimes, yes. It comes and goes,' he said. 'There are times it can be...quite bad. Other times, I hardly even notice.'

'The demon did this.'

Rorks reached a hand to her arm, squeezing gently.

'The demon did a lot more to you and to Callum,' he said. 'If this is all I bear from the experience, then I consider myself lucky for it.'

She bit her lip, considering his chest. Then, experimentally, she raised a tentative hand.

'Do you mind if I...?'

She didn't finish the question, but Rorks, eyes wide now, looked again to Callum, this time maybe for reassurance. Callum took his hand and nodded that he should.

'Um. Okay,' Rorks said.

She placed a hand on his chest. Not over the wounds, but near them. The other she lifted half above his damaged skin, close, humming something under breath. She didn't know if this would work. She hadn't tried magic yet. But healing magics had always been her own, not the demon's.

With her eyes closed, she moved her hand in a complicated gesture. Then put both back on his skin, his sides, focusing hard. Breathing deeply through her nose. Willing it to work. Willing herself to find something, anything, inherently good within her, that might help and never harm.

When she staggered, exhaustion catching up, Callum caught her.

'I'm alright,' she said, clutching onto him. 'Just pushed it a little too fast. But I'm alright.'

She looked back at Rorks. And smiled. All but the deepest of the wounds across his chest had closed up, while the two remaining were so far more visibly advanced in their healing now. They had scarred, she could do nothing about the that, but they had healed.

Rorks looked down at himself and blinked.

'Oh my god, Sal.'

'I couldn't do that much. I'm still not quite as back to strength as I thought I was. But...it's helped?'

Rorks leaned forward with a grin, taking her face between his hands, and kissing her. 'It's helped. Thank you.'

Then he whooped a joyful sound, loud and echoing to the forest. And ran to the end of the rocky outcrop, then jumped into the water with a splash and a laugh.

Sal leaned against Callum, grinning as she watched him.

'Thank you, witch,' Callum said softly, by her ear.

'Will you help me into the water, General? I don't think I'm up to jumping in like the Captain.'

'Of course, my love. Come on.'

He held her hand and, at the edge of the water, he got in first, then helped her slide in. It was a shallower depth here and they could stand. Along the rock edge, someone—probably Rorks—had built rocky steps and they sat in the warm, fizzing, steaming water, Callum holding her to him closely, while they watched Rorks further out swimming and messing around.

'He can be quite the clown,' Callum said as they sat quietly. 'There were times in the past you would have never realised he had such capacity for joy. Not only in the mines, but afterwards too. I wasn't always aware of how much he struggled in those years. I was too caught up in my own pain. Too blind to anything but my own rage.'

'You cannot blame yourself for it,' she said. 'You both had to recover from what was done to you in the mines. You might have physically earned your victories, but it takes time to emotionally recover too.'

'Yes.' He sighed. 'I'm trying to make amends now, to be there for him as he needs me. To see him laugh is a sight I'll always treasure.' He looked down to her. 'You need your time to recover as well. I am here for you too, my love.'

'I know.' She leaned her head on his shoulder, glad for his arm around her. Watching Rorks in the water. 'He only ever calls you *sir*. Or Boss. He looks to you for approval for things. For permission.'

'That's just Rorks and I. We have our own rhythm,' he said. 'He likes to serve, I like to be in control. We choose it to be this way.' He looked down at her. 'Why do you note on it? You know this about us already.'

She shrugged. 'I just wondered what I am now. Am I still your slave?'

'No.'

His voice was firm, so hard in tone she tensed. Frowned up at him, until his expression gentled and he raised a hand with a soft touch to her face.

'You belong to no-one, Sal. No-one but yourself,' he said. 'You are free.'

'I'm not sure I know how to be free. I've always belonged to some-thing or someone. My order, when I was a novice, with all its strict rules. The demon.' She paused. 'You.'

'It was all the rest of us who tried to tell you where you belonged, that it was to one thing or another,' he said. 'But you never belonged to anyone but yourself and in the end you found that truth. I am proud of you for it. I'm in awe of you for it.'

She took a breath for courage. For luck.

'Well if I am free, then I am free to choose for myself,' she said. 'What if I choose to... I don't know how to say it. Be like Rorks is with you?'

He didn't say anything at first, his eyes never leaving hers. Then he tipped up her chin and kissed her lips softly. A lingering touch, hand against her face even after he leaned back again.

There was a kind of need in his eyes, but a reticence too.

'You don't have to,' he said. 'I know it seems terrifying to be suddenly free, and I will help you, I promise, I will always be here to support you. But you don't have to—'

She raised a hand and put a gentle finger to his lips, to stop those words right there.

'If I am free to make my own choices, then this is a valid choice for me,' she said, firmly. 'I know you, Callum, and I know myself, and maybe I've never been able to choose before, but I can now.' She lifted her chin, proudly so and unashamed about it. 'I know what I want.'

His eyebrow raised. 'You sound just like Rorks.'

She couldn't help but smile. 'He and I are much the same like that, you know.'

It made him laugh. 'God help me,' he said. 'The two of you will be ganging up on me before I know it.'

She leaned her head against his shoulder again and he wrapped his arm around her, pulling her close in. His fingers moved soft circles through her hair, a tingling against her scalp.

'If it is a choice you freely make, then I won't lie,' he said. 'It is one I would welcome. I cannot deny my own nature.' He paused, considering. 'I need to feel in control, I think. I need to feel I can keep you, the both of you, safe and protected, even when the world is dark around us. That's how I cope. But you can change your mind at any time, I will be here for you no matter what.'

'I know that,' she said, then looked up from within the warm circle of his hold to meet his eyes. 'Callum, I fell in love with you knowing your nature. Maybe you were only gentle with me in the forest all those years ago, but I knew who you were then, just as I know it now. And your nature appeals to mine.'

He leaned his forehead against her own. Breath mingling, warm.

'If you need structures and rules, I can and will provide,' he said. 'But be warned, I can be strict. Just ask Rorks.'

'I don't need to ask him. I was your slave, remember.'

'I will never forget. But I don't want you as a slave, forced and compelled. I want you, Salryanna, willingly mine, choosing to be mine. Because you want me just as much,' he said and there was something of a vulnerability to him that she suspected had always been there, he just so rarely let show. 'Because I am yours. I always have been. I always will be. And I'll never let you be alone again.'

She pushed herself up to kiss him.

'Yes, sir,' she said, then sat back again with a grin.

He chuckled. 'We'll take things slow. Work it out as we go. Or else you'll be diving into the deep end like the clown of a Captain over there, before you're anywhere near ready.'

She didn't want to dive into anything right now. She just wanted to curl up with him and enjoy feeling safe for the first time in her entire life. Except for a few stolen moments out in a forest with a boy from the army she had accidentally run into and formed a love bond with. One strong enough to withstand betrayal and heartbreak and floggings and demons and revolution and everything else.

'I think I'd like to spend time working on my magic,' she said. 'My healing magic. Something that helps others and can't hurt anyone. Maybe that's something I can think about doing next.'

'That would be something I'd very much support,' he said. 'Something that's yours and which brings good to you, as well as the world.'

'And you, General? You had all kinds of plans for after you'd defeated the demon, I do recall.'

He sighed. 'I did. I still do. I just...' He paused. Looked down at her. 'First I needed to know you'd be alright. None of it mattered if you couldn't be there too.'

She smiled softly. And kissed him again. 'Shall we take such things very slow, do you think? As we take on the world and the conquests to come, together?'

He slipped off the step to stand in the pool and pull her in with him.

'Come on, witch. Let's go join the clown and swim. Tomorrow we can plan conquering the world.' He smiled. 'Together.'

'Yes, sir.'

And she followed him out to join Rorks swimming around. The three of them, together.

~

Author's Note

On the cover of this book, I subtitled it "a dark romance". Only I'm not sure that it is.

I mean, sure, there's trauma. Everyone in this book has been traumatised to some degree and the three key lovers at the centre of things have suffered more than any. Their world is not a pretty one, and as a result, they're not always pretty characters. Their trauma has left its mark, they lash out in complicated, unfair ways, often at each other, and make decisions that aren't always so commendable because of it.

They're human. There's moral greyness in each of them, but that's true for all human beings. Callum, in particular, with his early use of the threat of sexual violence as a means of control, his willingness to use slavery as a tool to further his own ends. Having experienced some of the worst of what people can do to other people, he's learned the lessons of that cruelty, and applies them to suit himself.

Does that make it a dark romance? Maybe? Callum is also a good man, whose ruthlessness is as much a defensive mask as Salryanna's obedience. That's his lesson over the course of the story, learned with the help of his two lovers - he is better than that, than those who did such things to him. Using the tools of his oppressors for his own ends only opens them all up to darker consequences, and he must rise above it if he hopes to succeed.

Callum has an ingrained morality that persists, despite his experiences, and which resurfaces, then wins out in the end. Many of the dark romances I've read don't tend to worry about things like that: morality, consequences.

This isn't a criticism of those stories, just an attempt to determine if I've labelled my own correctly.

Salryanna is in a different position to Callum. She uses obedience as a weapon, and a finely honed one at that. A refusal to fight is not the same as capitulation, and her ability to lie and deceive those she loves is born not so much in a distrust of them, as it is in herself. Enslaved for the majority of the novel, she stills holds the critical information throughout, and the real power with it. At every step, she knowingly keeps Callum and Rorks ignorant of the truth, even while handing over the keys to the castle, and herself, into their hands right on page one.

She sees herself as damned. That eventually she does learn the lesson that she is worthy, and worth fighting for, and deserving of care, takes both Callum and Rorks fighting hard to teach it to her. Of all three lovers in this story, it is Salryanna who clings hardest to the darkest parts of herself, not prepared to give up her suffering until it threatens all else she loves.

And then there is Rorks. The sunshine lighting the darkened worlds of both Callum and Salryanna. The bright optimist looking out for each of them, and spreading himself so thin he leaves almost nothing for himself. His is a light drawn to the dark, if sometimes one that needs to hurt in order to feel. Rorks seeks out damage rather than ask for help, burying his own needs in seeking the fulfilment of others.

I'm presuming that, if you're reading this, then you've already read the book. So you know Callum doesn't let him get away with it, nor does Salryanna. And that's what I mean when I ask the question of whether this book truly qualifies as a dark romance—the ending gives them redemption, absolution. Salvation, even. It's a Romance, it was always going to have a happy ending, but I very deliberately wrote a final chapter not just to be happy, but also to be sweet. Full of brightness, and most of all, full of hope.

I figured these characters had been through enough, they'd earned a fluffy, loving final chapter. This story starts in a decidedly dark place, but it ends in a definitively lighter one.

Rorks, I will note, is also a character who was never intended to be part of this book. Sometimes, as an author, you become surprised by where the writing takes you. This book was not planned as a polyamorous queer romance—possibly obvious in the fact the story is told with two point-of-view characters, but there are three lovers. It was originally going to be a classic het-romance, man-woman, one-on-one, love story. But I guess I'm no more in the habit of writing monogamous heterosexuality than I am in living it.

It's no surprise that my characters end up queer and polyamorous, or indeed, deeply kinky. I'm writing to entertain myself first and foremost, to satisfy my own tastes and desires and cares. That's rarely going to be monogamous or straight. And it's never going to be vanilla. Not with me.

So does that qualify it as the 'dark' part of "dark romance"? The fact that this book, as with all my writing under this moniker, is first and foremost a work of BDSM fiction? I know some others, vanilla but kink-safe and open minded, who undoubtedly would tell me it was. They're accepting, but still can't get their heads around some of freakier things that I just happen to find good fun. I love this stuff, so I write this stuff. I don't see it as particularly dark to write unequal power dynamics, or games with consent and control, or characters with an underlying need for pain and punishment, not in the way I'm aware some others do.

When I first sent this manuscript out for beta readers, I struggled with how much to warn them about the content. You've seen the content warning at the start of this novel—there seems a lot there. Sexual assault threatened, referenced, suffered, used as a threat, dubious consent—that's between Sal and the demon—slavery, punishments, self-harm, humiliation, all the trauma. I had to think carefully about what to include, not because I was worried about the content, but rather because I wasn't. I know from experience that I can forget obvious ones because they don't bother me, and that what I'm comfortable with in fiction can sometimes be confronting for others.

Ultimately, that's why I called it a "dark romance". I don't actually think this book is particularly dark or confronting, I feel it's relatively tame and safe, all things considered. But I am never sure where the line is drawn for others. What qualifies as 'dark' is different for each person. Each reader has their own list of what feels problematic, and it's not the same for everyone. What is dark for someone else, is fun and games for me. What I find genuinely dark...well, it's probably not going to end up in a novel by Misty Stewart.

Novels under my other name, however, are full of it.

Fiction is a vehicle for exploring the dark in life, for understanding humanity in all its variation, including the less palatable aspects. But I do that under another name. This pseudonym, Misty Stewart, is purely for fun. Misty is about entertainment and about desire. No matter how dark some desires can get.

In the end, "dark romance" is a marketing category, as all genre categories in the bookselling world are. They're shorthand for how to link different types of books with interested groups of readers. Unlike genre theory in academic analysis, which is the background I originally hail from, where genre is something fluid, a tool for understanding a work within changing socio-political contexts, and interrogating the text for cultural meaning.

Here, in this context, it is simply a box in which to put a certain type of fiction, and for some, this book will fit that label and be sorted neatly into that box.

For others, perhaps not so much. Such as me. Still, if you've come this far, I'm going to suppose you enjoyed reading it, dark or not. I certainly enjoyed the writing of it.

Misty Stewart
January 2025

Also by Misty Stewart

Truth or Dare

Four years ago, Beth, Caleb and Jack played a game which revealed deeply held secrets and seemed to change everything. Now, Beth is back. Older, a little more experienced and supposedly wiser, she still can't help falling into the same old games.

But the fallout from four years ago has yet to be reckoned with and as the game goes on, Beth's most hidden desires start to come out, whether she likes it or not. Submissive needs she's always run from, yearnings for another's dominance of the darkest kind. And the one thing she wasn't counting on when agreeing to this game was that Caleb, now older and more experienced himself, might this time know what to do about them.

～

Crossing Lines

Matty is done with casual, fleeting encounters. He wants something with meaning, something real—real emotion and real power dynamics too. Like what his friends, Dax and Annabelle, have. They're a lifestyle power-exchange couple with years of experience and they've been his mentors, teachers and only family since his first hesitant stumbles into the world of BDSM. But they've never been his lovers, because that's one line he will not cross—he might be a messy switch, but their relationship is too important to him, so he's sworn never to get in the way. Even if that means never admitting to how much he adores them both.

Until the night they drag him out to the club, determined to remind him of who he is and why he should be proud of that. A night in which he's slowly drawn into their scene, step by step, like a slow seduction...which is exactly what this is. For Dax and Annabelle, always so careful about the boundaries and never encroaching on his space themselves, still have one more thing to teach him: there are some lines which need to be crossed.

∿

Coming soon from Misty Stewart...

The Deal

Meg is on the run. Her father is powerful, ruthless, and already has the murder of her mother on his hands. If she can't get away, she could be next.

So she runs to the only place she knows she'll be believed—his enemy, Sebastian Lightner, owner of nightclubs, developer of communication platforms that outwit official surveillance, and the city's most notorious King of Kink. He has a reputation for being dark, dangerous and the city's very own devil. She's prepared to sell her soul to him, if he'll help her.

That's the deal. He helps her escape and she does anything he wants, even if that's become a pawn in his own quest for revenge. Anyway, she knows what this kink thing is all about, she's done her research. Only she's not quite prepared for how deeply she's drawn into his world of fetish and BDSM. Nor just how much it opens her eyes as to her own needs, and true self, and what she might want in her life, and relationships, and future.

She might not have a future yet. As her battle threatens to hurt too many others she's come to care for, she knows she can't hide behind Sebastian forever. She has to finish this. Even if that means disobeying the one man she promised always to obey and betraying the person she's slowly come to love.

The Deal is a kinky love story of dominance, submission and discovering one's place in the world...then fighting like hell for it.

About the Author

Misty Stewart is a writer of erotic romance with a kink. She lives in Melbourne, Australia, with her partner and their two children, writing amorous adventures by night and masquerading as a mild-mannered librarian by day.

You can find out more, including where to purchase her writing, on her website www.mistywriter.com